HEART OF FLAME

THE FIRES OF AILERYAN

· BOOK TWO ·

HEART OF FLAME

KATE SCHUMACHER

For all those who have the courage to believe in themselves

I see you

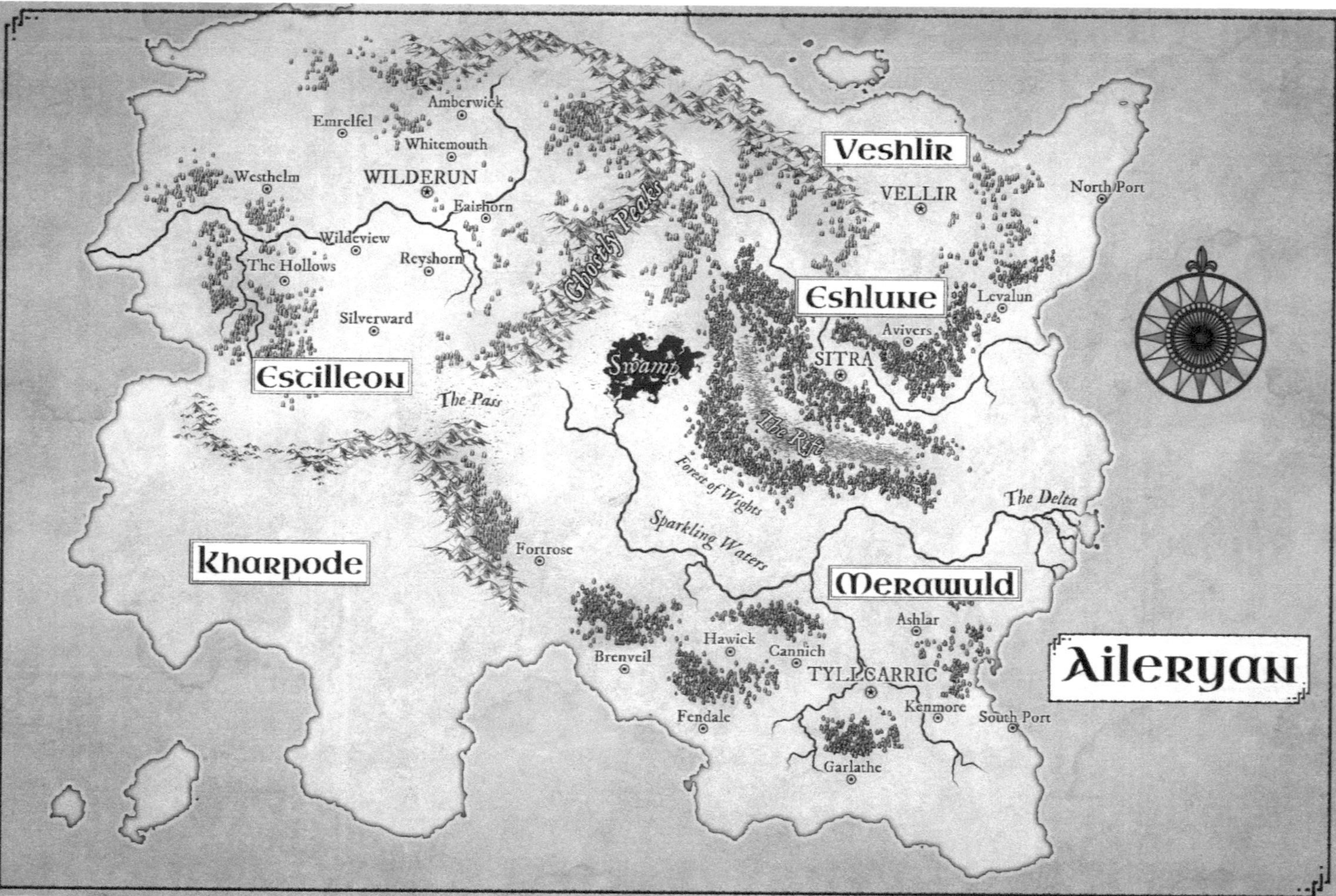

Aileryan
Veshlir
VELLIR
North Port
Eshlune
Levalun
Avivers
SITRA
WILDERUN
Amberwick
Emrelfel
Whitemouth
Eairhorn
Westhelm
Wildeview
Reyshorn
The Hollows
Silverward
Escilleon
Ghostly Peaks
Swamp
The Pass
The Rift
Forest of Wights
Sparkling Waters
The Delta
Kharpode
Fortrose
Merawuld
Ashlar
Hawick
Cannich
Brenveil
TYLLGARRIC
Fendale
Kenmore
South Port
Garlathe

TO THE READER

Thank you for diving back into the world of Aileryan and revisiting with my characters. Like *Shadow of Fire*, *Heart of Flame* is more of an Adult Fantasy, and, as such, some of the events and actions found within this book might not be suitable for anyone under the age of sixteen - it contains adult language, violence, sexual content, death and inferences to sexual assault and child neglect.

Please read at your discretion and thank you once again for returning to my world. I hope you enjoy the story!

CHAPTER ONE

The lingering curfew wasn't damaging Yasper's business. People scrambled into *The Solstice House* to squeeze in a moment of relaxation, drinking and gambling before they were locked inside their homes by the grim-faced Watch. Recalling the presence of those black shirts flexing their muscles on every street corner and outside every business, Ash suspected the Watch were thoroughly enjoying themselves.

As a student at the Academy she had always felt safe in Tyllcarric but, now, she was marked, unable to walk the streets wearing her true face, the magic in her veins a target painted on her back. Even though she'd never seen much of the city while behind the Academy walls, the knowledge that the world was out there for her to eventually step into had kept her grounded and steady when the fire called to her. The promise of a future had given her the strength to keep going.

And now, that security, that surety, had been stripped from her.

Gedeon was looking for her, she had no doubt of that. She couldn't remember the High Mage amongst the chaos and confusion that had wrapped around her mind at Mabon; her memory of her short time in the city's cells was muddled, but when she'd woken lying on that cot with an air mage guarding her, she'd sensed the High Mage's presence like an afterimage – his power, his curiosity, his need for what lay inside her – and it terrified her.

If Jarlath hadn't come for her … Ash swallowed, following Senan into the crowded gaming house. Yasper was behind the bar, blonde hair glowing in the dim light, a smile on his face as he chatted with customers. He twirled a bottle in his hands expertly, before pouring a drink and sliding the glass along the polished bar to a man in a battered grey coat. In the dim light of the bar, people's faces were painted with shadows; Ash cast her eyes about the room as subtly as she could, not knowing what she was looking for. She was no air mage to skim people's thoughts or read their intent in the space around them.

The journey to the city had been filled with panic. As they'd fled Sitra, Ash had half expected the forest to vanish behind them as the safety and protection of that glorious world was ripped from her, her life being torn from beneath her feet again. The Morrigan must be enjoying herself, Ash thought bitterly. She had never been dealt a good hand and now, standing in a room full of gambling and drinking, she wanted to flip every table and burn every card and dice in the place. She clenched her jaw, watching as a man threw his dice into the air, every eye at the table fixed on those cubes, every man praying they'd fall in his favour. These men were living on false hope, as she was, as she had been ever since Jarlath pulled her from that prison cell after Mabon.

Senan touched Ash's arm, nodding towards the back of the room. With his white hair and lined face, he looked like any other elderly man in the city. She slipped her hand under his elbow, a dutiful granddaughter accompanying her grandfather out for a quick drink. He flashed her a quick, approving look.

No one looked in their direction and Ash allowed some of the tension to leave her muscles. Her hair was black, her freckles faded away under Senan's magic. Unlike Biel's glamour, where she could feel the wrongness to her face, Senan's was smooth and deep, the magic tucked in close beneath her skin.

She'd startled when she caught sight of herself in a broken mirror in the abandoned building they'd spent the night in. Tucked out of sight, the place covered in various enchantments and protective spells Senan had mumbled before they curled onto the ground and slept. Though Ash jolted awake with every noise.

When she dreamt, it was to see Jarlath's face, or Mahelivar's, and to feel again that all-encompassing swirl of power as her magic was released into the world that day in the forest. She saw the look on the Prince's face – that awe and fear of what she was.

Ash was scared of herself, too. It was someone like her who had torn the Earth apart.

She followed Senan to a deeply shadowed table in the corner, tucking her greasy hair behind her ear as they sat. She was filthy, in desperate need of a bath and a change of clothes, a decent meal, and a bed with a pillow and a mattress. Senan lifted his hand, calling for drinks as Ash thought about her room in the palace in Sitra, with its opulent bed and cushions, the soft rug on the floor that she liked to curl her toes in, and the view of the sweeping lawns from her window, the forest swaying gently beyond the grass.

She'd told Mahelivar she felt she belonged in Sitra and it wasn't a lie. Useless tears pricked her eyes as a serving girl placed two mugs on the table. Senan drank deeply, while Ash twirled her mug around, staring at the pale, brown liquid within.

She absolutely hated ale. The walls of the gaming house were closing in on her, her heart thudding painfully, anxiety digging deep in her stomach with sharp claws. Any appetite she had before stepping inside this building, with its low roof and noise, vanished and her magic stirred. Alarmed, she shoved her tingling palms in her lap.

'Control it,' Senan said softly and she glared at him, then took a deep breath and grasped her mug, the coolness of the liquid inside instantly warming at the touch of her hand.

Around them, people drank and talked; laughter cut through the air as dice were thrown and a man groaned. Good, Ash thought venomously. She hated gambling as well.

Their mugs were collected by Biel, who scooped them onto a beaten metal tray; Ash reached out to grasp his slender wrist before he could turn away. The halfkin boy looked at her in fright as she let her magic out a fraction, enough to warm her fingers and the skin on Biel's wrist. Sparks danced through her eyes before fading away.

'Ash?' the halfkin whispered, his grip on the tray tightening.

She kept her voice low. 'We need help.'

Biel glanced back towards the bar and nodded once, moving to the next table and collecting mugs, slowly making his way back to the bar. Yasper was engaged in conversation with a young, blond man in a dark shirt. Ash's stomach twisted. The man turned his head and surveyed the room, before swinging back to say something to Yasper, who nodded grimly. The Watchman got up and left without a backwards glance, the front door snapping closed behind him.

Yasper banged on a metal container with a spoon and called in the tabs. People groaned.

'Curfew is still on,' Yasper shouted. 'Pay up and get on home.'

'Come on, Yas,' a man called. 'For the road?'

Yasper shook his head. 'Sorry mate, not tonight. The Watch has shut me down.'

Grumbling, the man and his friends slouched out the doors, a bundle of coins left on the table. Other patrons followed; the coins were quickly picked up by a halfkin girl with blonde hair and a relaxed expression. As the crowd moved for the exit, Ash and Senan lingered at the back. When the last group left, Biel locked the doors.

'The fire caster and the Anomaly. To what do I owe this pleasure?' Yasper said, blue eyes twinkling. He introduced Senan and Biel, the halfkin flashing a tight smile.

Senan removed their glamour – Ash gasped as the magic slithered from her skin.

'Where's your main man?' Yasper asked.

At the mention of Jarlath, the tears threatened to fall again. She'd done a lot of crying lately; her eyes were raw and burning, but she couldn't stop them filling with tears at a moment's notice.

'What about the Watch?' she asked instead, pushing Jarlath from her mind.

'They won't be back,' Yasper said with certainty. 'Not tonight, anyway. They've been in every gaming and beer house in the city lately – and the cathouses – as well as on the streets as usual, flexing their muscles and bullying people. Enjoying themselves too much,' he added with a frown. He turned to Senan. 'By the way, your girl – Fox. Gedeon sent her to Estilleon with one of the last lot of slaves to leave.'

'Estilleon,' Senan breathed, sinking onto a stool. 'She's alive?'

'They'd have no reason to kill her,' Biel said quietly. 'All she had to do was keep quiet and do what she was told.'

Senan laughed, a twisted watery laugh. He put his head in his hands, muttering under his breath about Fox's terrible manners and even worse temper.

Yasper slid him a drink. 'Listen,' he said. 'She's tough, she'll work it out. Anyway, why are you two here? Get sick of the wonders of the fae?'

'Sitra has been invaded,' Ash replied softly, her voice thick. She wished she knew what was happening there. 'The King's sister, Kiarda of Veshlir. We got out before she arrived. We just need a place to hide, until we can work out what to do. Jarlath … he's in Estilleon, a prisoner of war.'

'Shit,' Yasper breathed. 'The idiot went back to the army, then. The whole country knows what happened at the Pass. It's total madness, but the army has not been called home. Instead, they're calling for fresh recruits. Had a lot of that in here as well – word is, if they don't get enough fools signing up on their own, they'll conscript them, mages and healers from the Academy as well.'

'I need to get word to Jarlath,' Ash said, reaching across the bar to lay her hand on Yasper's arm. 'I need to tell him what's happened in Sitra. He'll have no idea.'

Yasper shook his head, his expression filled with compassion, and understanding. 'He's a prisoner, sweetheart. I don't think the Chieftain lets them write to their nearest and dearest.'

'We've a friend in the castle. She can get it to him,' Ash said in a rush. She wasn't giving up on Jarlath, despite what had happened between them. She couldn't, no matter how hard she'd tried. His face was the one she saw behind her eyes. 'One letter can't hurt. Please, Yasper.'

With a sigh, Yasper nodded.

Ash allowed herself a small smile. Something was going right. They would have a bed for the night, if Yasper agreed to it, something to eat, and she'd be able to write her letter. The smile fell as she frowned. 'I'll have to send it to Thalion, I suppose,' she said to Senan.

'Thalion? Thalion Liulfur? The Chieftain's son?' Yasper let out a whistle. 'The stakes in this little game keep on rising, don't they? Someone is going to have to pay up soon.'

'Yasper, can we stay here?' Ash pleaded, not caring how desperate her voice was. Once she got word to Jarlath, she planned to leave the city with Senan, head into the forest to his home, and hide there until … she didn't know.

They stayed the night in Yasper's back room and, in the morning, Ash wrote to Thalion. It was strange, writing to a man she didn't know. She had no idea if she could trust him, but she trusted Laeli, and she didn't have any other option. At Yasper's instruction, she didn't mention his name, or *The Solstice House*, and Biel left with her note tucked into his pocket as, outside, a city under watch came to life.

CHAPTER TWO

There weren't many things happening in this city that Gedeon wasn't aware of. With the Queen confined to her room, healers working their magic – the thought of it made him laugh – around the clock, the Watch reported directly to Gedeon. And the Watch were everywhere.

Gedeon smiled, crossing the room to peer out the window as the sun inched higher, coating Tyllcarric in golden light. From his window, he could see the main square, the effigy of the Corn Mother still standing vigil over the empty market ground. Often, it was only from the highest ground, after the hardest climb, that one could truly see. In his mind, he could see that plume of fire on Mabon night, that beautiful, deadly power released from its shackles by that scrap of a girl. A girl who had managed to evade him for months, another who got away.

Though he trusted it wouldn't be long before he had her in his possession once again. She couldn't stay hidden forever. One way or another, he would get his hands on her. He glanced at his desk where, inside a plain box with a simple lock, the Bloodstones waited. He could hear their gentle hum, feel their power, their emptiness waiting to be filled.

A light knock at the door pulled Gedeon from the window. He waved his hand and the door swung open. Taavi, one of the council elders, stood there. 'What is it?' Gedeon barked. He was in no mood for Taavi's blithering. If he was that concerned for the Queen's health, he could make the visit to the palace himself.

Taavi drew himself up, dark eyes flashing with annoyance, and brushed his hands over his clothes, smoothing invisible wrinkles fastidiously. 'The Watch have brought a man in for questioning.' He had also made no secret of his disapproval of Gedeon's use of the Watch and the extended curfew.

Gedeon sighed internally. He would have to relax the curfew – maybe something small, like an extended hour at night. That should be enough to keep everyone happy.

The other option was to get rid of Taavi. He was sure he could come up with something inventive enough to be believed. A sick relative maybe.

Gedeon dismissed the mage and headed for the narrow set of stairs that would lead him to the rooms the prisoners were kept in. He didn't like the term dungeon – too barbaric, too … Estilleon. These rooms were for special prisoners, ones deemed too dangerous or too important to spend time in the city's stinking cells, fit best for pickpockets, unsolicited whores, and useless halfkin.

He passed the official meeting room of the Mage Council, frowning to notice several mages gathered inside, whispering to themselves behind long-fingered hands the same way they whispered in corridors. Yet another thing he would have to address. He was beginning to resent these people creating more work for him with their sly eyes and mealy mouths. They had been asking too many questions about the Queen, and too many questions in general.

In the last room down a narrow hallway coated in constant shadows, a Watchman was waiting, the blonde of his hair glowing. He was a handsome man, Mal, and a vicious one, his tongue as sharp as his backhand. Gedeon was quite fond of him and gave the young man an approving nod. Darian was already present, the Spirit Rake leaning against the wall outside, long arms folded across his chest, his face as impassive as always.

'A halfkin,' Darian said.

Gedeon was disappointed. 'Why'd they bring him here?'

'Considering where he came from – and what he was carrying – I was certain you'd like to speak with him,' Darian responded in his flat voice. 'He's glamoured. His own work, I'm sure. Good, but not good enough to hide what he is.'

Curious now, Gedeon stepped into the room.

The halfkin was bound to the simple wooden chair by his wrists and ankles. Gedeon could see through the glamour at once. He waved his hand and the magic slid away, revealing the true face of the boy who sat before him. He was a skinny, nervous looking creature, as they all were, with long limbs and messy hair, slightly pointed ears, and unusual purple eyes. His magic, Gedeon realised. Interesting.

He addressed Mal. 'Where did you pick him up?'

'Outside *The Solstice House*, High Mage. Run by the convict, Yasper,' Mal answered.

'Yasper,' Gedeon murmured. 'Why have I heard that name before?'

'Rumour has it that he and some whore from one of the cathouses downtown have been poking their noses into things they shouldn't,' Mal replied. 'I'd bet this one here is involved as well. We've had a man on Yasper's place for a month, but he's done nothing except follow the rules, so we haven't been able to grab him for anything.'

Gedeon tapped his chin with a long finger. He pulled a seat over to sit directly in front of the halfkin, who was beginning to look panicky. 'What's your name?'

The boy clamped his lips shut and Gedeon sighed. He did hate it when they wouldn't cooperate.

'You can make this easy, or hard. Your choice, young man.'

Still the boy said nothing. Gedeon released his air magic, his power skimming the outside of the boy's mind, hoping he'd find a seed of left-over thought, something lingering around that would be enough to give him away. He frowned. There was a shield around the boy's mind, a thick well-positioned shield that was like rubbing against stone. Gedeon could break through it easy enough, but he wasn't in the mood to get his hands dirty.

'Darian,' he called. The Spirit Rake stepped into the room and the boy's eyes widened in fear. Good. He knew who Darian was, which meant he knew exactly what he was capable of. 'Now,' Gedeon said, addressing the halfkin again. 'The easy way, or the hard way.'

'I'm not telling you a thing,' the boy hissed.

Gedeon admired his bravado. The boy knew what was coming, yet he still wouldn't talk, which told Gedeon all he needed to know. He motioned to Mal. 'What was he carrying?'

'A letter, High Mage.' The young Watchman passed over a folded piece of paper. With his eyes on the halfkin, Gedeon unfolded the note. A girl's hand. Neat, flowery script. Educated. He read the letter as the halfkin squirmed on his chair. Names he knew oozed from the page, and Gedeon smiled.

'It would seem,' he said quietly, 'that the fire caster has decided to pay our quaint city a visit.' What was more intriguing was the letter being addressed to Hadrian's son. What games were being played over the mountains that he didn't know about? He decided to store that piece of information for later use.

A mind slammed into his own and his eyes widened curiously. The halfkin had some powerful magic hidden in that scrawny body. What else did he have hidden in there? Gedeon wondered. He folded the note and slipped it into his pocket. At least he knew where the fire caster's soldier friend had ended up. It would have been better for the boy to die at the Pass, Gedeon thought, than spend his days in Hadrian's miserable dungeons. He caressed the letter gently. The words were nervous ones, clouded in uncertainty. The fire caster didn't know if she could trust the Chieftain's son, but she did trust someone else … Gedeon's eyes widened.

Rhodiri's girl had exchanged trees for snow. What would Kiarda be willing to give him for that piece of knowledge? He would sit on it for now. It would be another bargaining chip for later; if he needed it.

Gedeon smiled, pulling his magic from the letter, focusing on the halfkin before him. The boy stared at him defiantly.

'I could crush your mind, little one,' Gedeon said smoothly. 'You know this. Oh, you would fight me, and it would be interesting for a while, but I think you and my friend here need to get to know each other.'

He stood, brushing the front of his shirt free of halfkin stink. 'You should have chosen the easy way,' he told the boy, stepping aside to let Darian pass. Gedeon glanced at the halfkin before he left the room. The boy met his gaze and Gedeon saw an acceptance, an acknowledgement, of the end in those purple eyes.

Leaving Darian to do his job, Gedeon returned to his office. The council room was empty when he passed and he wondered where those little birds had flittered off to, what whisperings and seeds of information and assumption they were passing between each other. He waited for Darian by the window, the fire caster's letter in his palm, her thoughts saturating him: her fear, her desperation, and her longing for the boy who'd left her alone in Eshlune.

When Darian entered, the Spirit Rake had deep shadows painted under his eyes, always worse when he'd used his phenomenal power. He was an Anomaly in itself, but one that suited Gedeon's needs. He nodded and Darian sat, his long, cat-like body folding itself gracefully into a chair. Gedeon had first met Darian after becoming High Mage and had long suspected the Spirit Rake was more faery than human. That sort of extraordinary power in the hands of his enemies would be very damaging indeed.

'Well?'

'His name was Biel. He worked for Yasper, tended his bar, that sort of thing. He had a strong mind – underneath that shield were layers of thoughts, the truth hidden deep, wrapped up in other unimportant thoughts. It took a while to find anything that might be of interest.'

Gedeon had noticed the use of past tense. Pity. He didn't like dead bodies.

'And what might be of interest?'

'The fire caster and the Anomaly are currently with Yasper at his establishment. Yasper and Biel have been working with a whore named Gem to undermine your slave deals with Estilleon.' Darian explained Biel's manipulation of Jonis' thoughts. Gedeon caught both the admiration for the halfkin's abilities and Darian's opinions on Jonis' stupidity. The Spirit Rake watched Gedeon's face. 'Should I order the Watch to pick them all up?'

'Let's use the whore,' Gedeon said slowly. 'I don't want to risk Senan getting away again, and I don't want the fire caster to be able to unleash that power of hers. They need to be brought back here, alive. You will need to keep your wits about you when dealing with Senan. I will need you to bind him, Darian, at least until I can come up with another idea. Keep his magic pinned down.'

Darian nodded, a slight frown between his eyes. 'And the girl?'

'Oh, I think she'll be more willing to cooperate.'

As the Spirit Rake swept from the room, Gedeon took a seat behind his desk, folding one leg over the other, tapping his knee with a long finger. The Anomaly, within his grasp once more. It wasn't that he hated Senan for what he was – quite the opposite, and he wished things had been different all those years ago. The truth was, Senan's power would have rivalled Gedeon's own, so the easiest thing to do was have the man hung. Gedeon's plans had been years in the making. Unable to proceed while Rowena's parents lived, he had bided his time, knowing that, eventually, the girl would take the throne. The plague, which devastated the population of the city, had carried off her parents – he thanked the Morrigan for it occasionally, though fate was not a thing Gedeon put too much faith in.

He was the master of his destiny, not some ageless goddess.

Now, with the Queen not far from departing the world and his allies making good on their promises, there was the fire caster and his old friend to deal with. The girl would break, he could feel it, and Senan … Gedeon's thoughts shifted to the halfkin whore, his rogue assassin, now hunkering down in the wild cold of Estilleon. Would he ever see her again? He didn't think so. He missed her, as strange as it was. He missed their chats, her snarky tone and sharp wit.

Hadrian's son troubled him, however. It appeared that while the father was away, the son was striking out on his own. All speculation, of course, but Gedeon had a sense for it, the things that festered away in people's heads. It was that sense that made it so easy to manipulate the Chieftain in the first place. Hadrian was not overly skilled at keeping his thoughts hidden; they'd leeched through the pages of his letters to the Queen as surely as if the man was standing in the room and shouting his wishes. It was a shame that Hadrian's desires were so base – land and food for his people, simple things that could be achieved with some charisma, but the gruff Chieftain was sorely lacking in charm.

Gedeon believed men should aspire to more than making others happy.

Kiarda on the other hand … Gedeon could still taste the bitterness of her revenge in the back of his throat. He chuckled. It was too easy. Letting the fae kill each other. He was in no doubt that Kiarda wanted more than her brother's realm. Her need for vengeance ran beyond blood, but he was certain he could convince her, when the time came, to allow him to exert his will over Merawuld and its people.

If there was one thing Gedeon couldn't abide, it was weakness. This land had grown weak on his watch – all part of the plan, of course. The Queen had been his puppet for fifteen years and the Mage Council was filled with pathetic men who squabbled amongst themselves and called it leadership. The mayors of each village were sycophants who'd kiss his boots more than they already did when they realised what he was truly capable of.

An autocracy, after all, needed only one ruler.

Gedeon leant forward and trailed his finger along the box containing the Bloodstones.

If Kiarda didn't agree to his terms, he would simply have to show her how far he was willing to go for control.

CHAPTER THREE

As the days drew nearer to the heart of winter, the Bone Mother unleashed on Estilleon. Snow lay thickly around the castle and spread itself across the land without mercy, the wind shrieking and screaming, the bitter cold relentless. When the weather was like this, it was easy to believe in Hadrian's certainty that Bridghe had indeed abandoned them, that light and warmth would never come and they would be drowning in darkness forever.

Thalion was used to these slow days stuck inside, the hours spent watching the flames dance, but Laeli was going stir-crazy, her temper short, her tongue as icy as the weather. She'd read everything in their library, so he'd taught her to play raffle, then hazard. She beat him at chess, and he was certain she cheated at cross and pile, but he wasn't going to tell her that.

A messenger arrived during dinner, stumbling into the Hall, shivering with the cold. Snow dusted his shoulders, his shock of red hair as bright as a flame in the shifting shadows of the room. Hadrian held out his hand; the trembling boy placed a folded and sealed piece of paper in his outstretched palm. Waving his other hand in dismissal, Hadrian turned to the letter with a frown. He held it up in the air, his elbow on the table, raising his eyes to Laeli's face – *Eira's* face.

Thalion forgot sometimes. If he looked closely, he didn't see blood and death and deception. He saw Laeli's true face beneath her skin – the almond shape to her eyes, the pert nose, sharp jaw, and plump lips. She was absolutely flawless and, if he managed to wake earlier than she did, he always took a minute to simply look at her, her face soft in sleep, the mass of her hair spread over the pillows.

It was dangerous – he had to remind himself constantly to play the game, not allow himself to be caught unawares and let the wrong name slip from his lips. If his father had noticed anything was amiss, he didn't say. Sometimes, Hadrian's eyes lingered a little too long on Laeli's face, those eyes often tracking her as she moved around a room, and, every time, Thalion's nerves curled in on themselves and it took everything he had not to rest his hand on the hilt of the sword at his hip. He carried the sword everywhere now, the constant need to be alert wearing him down.

If the Chieftain thought something was wrong with his son, he didn't mention it either. Perhaps he hadn't noticed Thalion's tension; perhaps he didn't care.

Hadrian waved the letter around, those shrewd eyes crawling over Laeli's face. 'From your mother.'

Laeli rose stiffly, approaching Hadrian slowly, closing her fingers around the edge of the letter dangling from his hand. He held it tight – a challenge.

'No secrets in this castle.'

She wrinkled her nose. 'It's for my mother to decide what you know,' she said coldly.

He released his grip on the paper, his eyes trailing her as she returned to her seat to push her food around her plate. Hadrian's eyes narrowed.

'Our food not good enough for you, girl?'

Laeli's glare was as dark and cold as the night outside the window.

'There's people going without in the villages,' Hadrian stated.

'Then give it to them.' She pushed her plate away, reaching for her mead, lifting the mug to her lips, and taking a long sip. Thalion touched her leg under the table, his eyes on his father, his insides burning. Part of him wanted to rip the tongue from Hadrian's head, but the other knew he had to sit there and let his father continue to insult them both, let Hadrian think his son was still comfortably under his iron claws.

With deliberate slowness, Laeli set her mug down, broke the wax seal and unfolded Kiarda's letter. She took her time reading it, aware Hadrian was watching her with burning eyes. She took another sip of her drink, folding the letter back up and tucking it away.

'Well?' The Chieftain barked, thumping his hand on the table.

'She sends her regards,' Laeli answered defiantly.

Hadrian shot his son a glare, as if to say, "get your wife under control, boy, or I'll do it for you". Thalion removed his hand from Laeli's leg, reaching swiftly beneath her stole and retrieving the letter. She hissed, her hand snaking out to snatch it back. He caught her slender wrist, holding it firm enough for her to snarl at him, firm enough that the pretence was maintained. He released her and opened the letter, sweeping his eyes over it while she made a good show of rubbing at her skin, mumbling under her breath, and scowling.

He'd make it up to her later, kiss any part of her she wanted, starting with the tender skin of her wrist. He nudged Laeli's knee with his own under the table as his father gave him an approving nod; she responded by stomping on his toes, making him bite his lip to hide his wince.

'Sitra is holding,' Thalion announced simply. He got up, crossing the room to toss the paper into the fire, where it was quickly devoured by the hungry flames. When he returned to the table, Laeli was still glaring at him. He finished his meal, leaning back to stretch the tension from his neck, one arm reaching around Laeli's shoulders. She shoved him off. He laughed, grabbing her face, and kissing her, feeling her smile against his mouth.

Hadrian tossed his bones on the floor for the dogs as the remains of their meal were cleared away and the Hall settled into silence. The flames of the candles on the table shifted with the slight breeze that slipped through the closed shutters. Thalion emptied his mead and poured himself another, wanting nothing more than to get rolling drunk so he could give his brain a rest.

'What do you plan to do with that runt who killed Rand?' Hadrian asked.

'What would you have me do?' Thalion answered evenly.

'We should put him back in.'

'There isn't a Stadium scheduled for weeks.'

Hadrian rubbed at his chin. 'I've been thinking about that. With winter here, the people need something to cheer them up.' He gave his son a measured look; the sound of crunching bone echoed around the room. 'It's been a while since you were in the Stadium.'

Thalion knew where his father's thoughts lay. 'I won't fight him.'

'Why not?' Hadrian demanded.

'It would hardly be a fair fight,' Thalion argued. 'We're not evenly matched. There is no honour in defeating someone weaker, is there, Father?' He held Hadrian's eyes, hoping that using his own argument against him would be enough. Eventually, Hadrian grunted his agreement.

'Well then,' Hadrian said smoothly, taking a long gulp of his drink, 'we'll have to find someone else for you to beat. Someone more, what did you say, evenly matched, huh, boy?'

Thalion remained silent; a shiver walked his spine as, outside, the wind howled.

'What, you're not up for it?' Hadrian jeered. He waved a hand in Laeli's direction. 'I'm sure she'd like to see what you're made of somewhere other than the bedroom – unless that's enough for you, Eira of Veshlir?'

Laeli maintained her sullen expression perfectly. 'If he performs in the Stadium the way he performs in the bedroom, his opponent doesn't stand a chance.'

Thalion choked on his laugh.

Hadrian narrowed his eyes. Thalion could guess what his father was thinking – this marriage was one of convenience and politics. It wasn't supposed to be enjoyable. Maybe they'd have to try harder to appear less content with one another; which was incredibly difficult when she was so close to him.

There were dark shadows beneath Laeli's eyes; eyes that were slowly shifting from blue to green. Thalion leaned in to whisper in her ear, resisting the urge to close his teeth over that soft lobe. 'Your eyes.'

She laughed coquettishly, bunching her fingers in the front of his shirt, letting him kiss her neck. She shot his father one last abhorring look, then got up from the table without a word, stalking from the room. Thalion watched her go, concerned at how tired she appeared, how draining this was on her. She'd been maintaining this pretence every day for several weeks and if he was tired by it, she must have been exhausted.

Hadrian was watching him. 'You like this woman?'

Play the game. 'She's tolerable.'

'Three days,' Hadrian declared. 'The Stadium. Don't worry, boy. I'll find you someone worth fighting. In the meantime, I want you to organise fresh troops. Though we obliterated them last time, the young Queen's Army has not retreated. The main camp is still stationed outside Fortrose, but a smaller contingent remains close to the border. Not too close, mind you – they're not entirely stupid. Get messages out to the Chiefs in the morning. I want reinforcements there by next week.'

Thalion hid his smile. It would be easier now to get his own messages out, concealed within his father's request. He'd been sneaking around engaging in shadowed conversations for weeks now, constantly looking over his shoulder. There were only so many excuses he could conjure to explain why he had to visit Fairhorn, or Reyshorn, and why his wife had to accompany him. Frode had begun talks with the most trusted members of his community, as had Niall, Ulfe, and Runa. Progress was being made, but it was slow; there wasn't anything Thalion or his allies could really do until Kiarda called Hadrian to Eshlune.

Outside, the wind battered the castle with snow and ice. The dogs snored beneath Thalion's feet as he whittled a bone with his knife.

Hadrian waved him away. 'Don't keep her waiting, for the Allfather's sake.'

Thalion was at the door when his father's voice stopped him.

'Thalion, don't ever let a woman come between you and your duty. Do you understand me? Regardless of what you think you might feel, don't let your cock rule your head.'

Thalion didn't turn around. Upstairs, Laeli was sitting on the bed, in her own face, frowning. Her swords were in her lap, and she was running a cloth over them gently, but she set them aside and jumped up when he came in, her body unfolding with that unnatural grace that made his blood sing. The way she could use that body ...

'My father ...'

'I know,' he said softly. 'What do you want to do?'

Laeli took a deep breath, giving him a pained look. 'I can't leave you here, or Jarlath. At least they knew she was coming, thanks to you. Hopefully, Solen was able to devise a plan worth having but I can't help but think Mahelivar was right – our people are not ready for this. The fae guard, yes, but not the general population. She won't want to kill them because who will she rule over if she does? I have to hope that my father and brother can either escape her, or fight her, but Father ...' She turned from him and began to pace, crossing the floor so quickly she was a blur. She was muttering to herself under her breath, her face tight. He caught her arm as she passed him, pulling her against him.

'You help me here, you'll be helping them,' Thalion said. 'I know it might not feel like it, but your father was right – if we can take control of what's happening in Estilleon it will give them one less thing to worry about. If I can call that darn war off at the Pass, there may be a chance of the Queen's Army coming to Sitra's aid.'

She looked at him, clear-eyed. 'You think they would?'

'It will depend on their commanders and whether Gedeon has any influence over them. We can only hope but we shouldn't hold onto that hope too tightly.'

Laeli nodded, dragging her hand through the length of her hair as he kissed her forehead and sank into one of the chairs by the fire. She slid into his lap, her arms around his neck, her heartbeat echoing in his ear as he rested his head against her chest.

Alone, this was the only time they could be themselves and he held on to it, this light in the dark. They sat together for a while, the fire crackling, flickering shadows dancing around the room. He wanted to bundle her up and take her to bed, kiss his way down her body until he was buried between the firm muscle of her thighs, those strong fingers of hers tangled in his hair as she melted under his tongue and teeth. He lifted her wrist to his lips and licked the hurt away – an apology and a promise – smiling when she trembled.

'Why is he putting you in the Stadium?'

'He either wants to teach me a lesson,' Thalion said with a sigh, 'or he's trying to prove a point. What that point is, I'm not sure. That he controls me, maybe, that he controls everything.'

'I've never seen you fight, except for that night in the forest,' Laeli said quietly.

'I was trying not to kill you,' he mumbled. 'You, however, were trying to kill me.'

She climbed off his lap to stand close to the fire, her eyes on the shifting flame. She held up her hand, and a small ball of fire appeared there. 'If it wasn't raining that night, I would have killed you, Thalion,' she said quietly. The ball of flame vanished, a frown lingering between her eyes.

'But then you would have missed out on my performance in the bedroom,' he quipped.

She didn't smile.

Thalion sat forward, resting his elbows on his knees. 'Don't worry about me, Laeli. I've been in the Stadium many times.'

'Yes,' she said tightly, 'I've counted your scars.'

'And how many did you find?'

'Too many.'

He kicked his boots off, then stood and removed his shirt, followed by his pants, until he was standing naked before her. 'Want to count them again?'

She kept her eyes on his face for as long as she could.

Thalion rose early, the darkness thick and suffocating. The closer the wheel turned towards the heart of winter, the less light crept over the Peaks, leaving Estilleon bathed in shadows. Laeli had been restless most of the night, clinging to him and trembling, until she'd begged him to fuck her again. Ironically, that worried him, because Laeli never begged for anything, and now he had a kink in his back and a few hours' sleep. He left her in bed, that glorious fae body that he now knew as well as his own sprawled under the blankets.

It didn't seem real that someone so beautiful, so powerful, intelligent, and courageous, was in his bed, let alone his life, even if that life was, for the moment, one of pretence. Thalion wondered what would happen to them when this was all over. The thought of her going home, back to the forest, made his gut churn and his palms clammy, so he tried not to think of it.

He sat in his father's official room and wrote messages to the Chiefs, requesting more men for the border. He wrote his own messages and folded them inside his father's, sealing them with wax. Four lads in their early teens met him on the steps, their faces whipped by the cold. After they rode off, Thalion paid Jarlath a visit.

The boy was shivering violently, the skin around his lips tinged with blue, his eyes wild with the cold. After the Samhain Stadium, Thalion had had a fierce argument with his father about the Merawuld soldier – surely the boy deserved some dignity after his win? – and Jarlath was released into the dungeon. He hardly had the comforts of home but at least he was no longer caged like a wild beast.

The dungeons were freezing. Thalion knew from experience, but he hadn't been locked down here in the belly of winter. The water that usually oozed from the ground and slid down the walls was frozen, arrested in its ancient path. The stones were cold enough to burn the skin and the air was so bitter it was like swallowing mouthfuls of snow, one after the other, no respite from the burning frigidity that inched down the throat.

Jarlath was bound to the wall by a long length of chain. Thalion frowned, wondering how long the boy would have to stay down here, wondering how long it took to go mad from such hard solitude. Hadrian had said nothing about releasing him, or sending him back to his army or his home, but Thalion didn't expect him to.

'How do you people live here?' Jarlath moaned, his arms folded tight around his slim body, teeth rattling in his head; he'd lost weight as well. 'I'm so cold I can't think properly.'

'My father will put you back in the Stadium,' Thalion told him.

Jarlath's face lost some more colour. 'When?'

'The day after tomorrow.'

'Who do I have to fight this time? You?'

'It's what my father wanted,' Thalion admitted. 'But I changed his mind. You'll be matched with one of the younger men. It'll be a fair fight. You won't have to kill him,' he added reassuringly. 'I promise.'

Jarlath only looked at him, as if reminding him his promises meant nothing.

'How's Laeli?' Jarlath asked instead.

Thalion eased his body to the floor, sitting with his back against the wall, his legs stretched out in front of him. The cold from the stones sank through his clothes and burrowed under his skin. The words were out of his mouth before he could think about cramming them behind his teeth. 'Sick of this place, I think.'

'I don't blame her,' Jarlath muttered contemptuously.

'I can't help you any more than I am.' Thalion tried to keep his tone light and level, but he could hear the hint of guilt, of powerlessness, that crept into his voice. 'Laeli would have me free you tomorrow, but I can't. If I was caught, I'd be sharing this space with you.'

'Your father would lock you in the dungeon?' Jarlath asked in disbelief.

Thalion shrugged. 'I've been here many times.'

Jarlath blinked at him. 'You know that's not normal, right? Most people's fathers don't lock them in dungeons.'

'Most people don't have dungeons,' Thalion said with a wry smile. He rubbed at his face, sighing. 'Letting you go would jeopardise everything I'm working towards, and I won't do that, not even for Laeli.'

Jarlath eyed him suspiciously. 'And what are you working towards?'

'Change,' Thalion answered softly.

Jarlath was still watching him, those brown eyes reading the lines of his face, searching for the words Thalion hadn't spoken. 'You love her,' he declared.

'I suppose I do.' There was no suppose about it – Thalion loved her fiercely, so fiercely he sometimes forgot himself, content to give her everything that made up who he was. He hadn't expected to fall in love with her in the middle of all this, and it had taken him completely by surprise.

'Why?'

'You have met her, haven't you?'

'That isn't what I meant,' Jarlath said with a shake of his head. He sat opposite, waiting for an explanation to what Thalion knew he thought was impossible.

'I'd started to question my role in this life before I met her, but she helped me view the world differently. She didn't intend it – she was very keen on insulting me – but the things she said … made me look deeper.' He paused, rubbed at his chin. 'This situation we find ourselves in doesn't reflect the world as I want it to be. Surely, we, people I mean, are more than violent beings succumbing to our selfish desires? We should aspire to more than power over others, or, if we do have power, we need to use it in different ways. It doesn't always need to be a tool of oppression.'

Jarlath weighed up his words, his face thoughtful as Thalion climbed to his feet, realising he hadn't answered the question. 'As to why I love her, how can I not? Sometimes, I feel that everything I've ever done in my life led me to that night in the forest. Maybe it's fate, the Morrigan at work, I don't know. All I know is …' he stopped, frustrated with his explanation. 'She's the bravest person I know; she's the best person I know, and I'd be an absolute fool to ever forget that. She makes me want to be a better person.'

CHAPTER FOUR

She was in his arms, her hands sliding with painful tenderness along his spine, his shoulders, the back of his neck. Leaves fell from the sky like rain, the colours of autumn floating gently towards the soft earth beneath their feet.

This was right. This was what should be.

He could taste sunshine on her lips, its glow in her mouth, feel the blazing heat of her skin, as comforting as a hearth fire in the depths of winter.

The leaves continued to fall; they brushed his skin as he wondered how the trees could hold so many leaves at once. One of them caught in her hair. She laughed as he pulled it free, holding it between strong fingers as he examined the veins and bones and the rich red colour of it.

Jarlath paused, his brows pulling together. He could smell smoke, a tickle of it on the breeze. His skin puckered into gooseflesh, drawn to life by the suddenly chilly air and his belly tightened, adrenalin pooling in his mouth.

The leaf in his fingers combusted, a brilliant display of fire and sparks and heat. He dropped it with a yelp. Confused, he looked at her - smoke coiled from her hair, there were sparks in her eyes and as he watched, a thin layer of flame stroked its way over her skin.

'What's wrong?' she asked, head cocked to the side, delicate brows folded together in confusion.

'I …'

'Aren't you going to kiss me again? I thought this was what you wanted. Isn't that why you saved me?' As she spoke, tongues of fire slipped from her mouth, stretching towards him. 'Jarlath?'

He backed away.

She glanced over his shoulder and folded her arms. 'The army is on the move.'

He swallowed and rubbed at his face; his fingers came away wet and smeared with blood. Horrified, he touched his face, his neck, examined the skin on his arms, lower. A gash decorated one thigh; puncture wounds marked the other. He frowned. Why didn't any of it hurt?

'Be safe, Jarlath.'

He looked up to watch her face collapse, then explode into flames.

He fell back, shielding his face, the skin on his forearms blistering as the leaves continued to fall, burning where they touched him. An arrow thudded into the tree near his head. The hair along the back of his neck crawled upright.

Jarlath lifted his head, looking around wildly as the trees vanished beneath a shroud of thick grey smoke.

Shouts and screaming.

Arrows and flames and death.

His hands felt heavy, the sword he held slick with blood while around him, the grass blazed and the sky bled snow. The air was thick and smelled of murder.

Jarlath ran, stumbling over his feet, falling to kiss the black earth. Spitting ash and dirt, he clamoured upright and kept running, the sword heavy in his hands, so heavy the tip dragged along the ground, cutting a deep groove that oozed warm, sticky blood.

Someone spoke his name.

He saw a man with no head holding an armful of fire.

Then it was Orin, his chest open so deep Jarlath could see his heart lodged between the white cage of his ribs.

Then Connor, his eyes blank and staring at the sky as a raven swooped for his face.

Then Ash, burning and blazing and standing beside a pile of human skulls, bleached and picked clean. 'Be safe, Jarlath,' she whispered.

As darkness closed over his head, all he could smell was smoke and all he could taste was the putrid stench of his own fear in the burning cold.

The world tilted. When he opened his eyes it was to the roar of a faceless, nameless crowd, bloodied snow spread beneath his boots, a body sprawled face-down not far from him, burnt beyond all recognition.

'Kill it!' Someone shouted.

Jarlath jerked his head around to find Ash, her face broken and bloodied, her arms trembling as she tried to lift a sword as long as her body.

'Help me!' she screamed at him as from the darkness at the edge of his vision, a black wolf took shape.

'I'm coming, Ash, I'm coming,' Jarlath cried, urging his legs to move. The sound of a chain snapping taut ripped through the air and he looked down to find his ankles shackled, the chain pinned into a block of stone taller than he was.

Leaning against the stone was a woman with a face that was not her face. Her hair shimmered - ice to earth to ice. She turned away from him and disappeared into the swirling smoke, flames trailing her.

Jarlath strained against the bite of the chain into his skin but he wasn't strong enough, couldn't break free as around them the crowd screamed and shouted and all he could taste was the bitterness of his weakness.

'Jarlath!' Ash screamed again.

A voice, deep and tinged with regret and whispering shadows, touched his ear. 'I can't help you any more than I am.'

Jarlath could do nothing but watch helplessly as the wolf, teeth bared and dripping with snow, advanced on Ash and the drums of war pounded incessantly, the sound vibrating through the air around him, sinking into his bones, into the marrow of him, bending and shaping and breaking and breaking and breaking. All that he was and all that he should be.

The wolf opened its mouth and howled a plume of fire into the world.

Heart hammering, Jarlath jerked awake, mouth dry as ash, forehead slick with sweat. He blinked, dream and reality blurring around the edges, fracturing and pulling itself back together before splitting into a thousand pieces coated with snow and fire and ash and blood.

He blinked again, sucked the frigid air into his lungs, his heartbeat echoing the screams in his ears as slowly, the world shifted into focus.

Darkness and stone.

Jarlath sat up, the chain at his ankle jingling its familiar morbid melody as he looked around. Light cut into the gloom from the slit of a window above his head.

A dungeon. He was in a dungeon.

Jarlath dropped his head into his hands.

Be safe, Jarlath.

Teeth chattering and limbs trembling, he closed his eyes and sank back into the blazing darkness.

CHAPTER FIVE

The day of the Stadium, weak sunlight reflected from the blanket of snow that lay across the plain, the light piercing in a world of darkness. There were ten men stepping into the arena to fight, including Thalion and Jarlath, who was shackled and standing to the side, his face tight, lips still blue.

Laeli was in the box, with Hadrian and the Chiefs who had made the journey from the closest villages, the weather abating long enough to allow for travel. She'd been frowning since she climbed out of bed that morning, stalking around their room with a thundercloud of annoyance following her, muttering under her breath about barbarism and male pride.

'I've got a bad feeling,' she'd said in response to his assertion that he'd be fine.

His father had kept his word. Thalion's opponent was Wade, one of Brenna's men. He'd known Wade since they were children; he gave Thalion a nod in acknowledgement of what was to come. They'd fought many times before and were, as he'd requested, evenly matched in strength and skill.

As the fighting began, the noise of the crowd above his head sunk inside his blood and Thalion allowed part of himself – that part that was forgiving and tender, the part that loved – to slip away as he stripped off his shirt, baring his flesh to the chilly kiss of the air. Calling on his warrior's heart, he willed that familiar fire and strength to the surface.

The first fight ended quickly; one of the boys, a lanky kid from Reyshorn with a strong sword arm, had earned himself a scar, his shoulder dripping with blood as he was brought back into the waiting area beneath the stands. He was slapped on the back by his friends, who then stepped into the arena to encouraging cries from the spectators.

The men laughed and joked about what was to come. As always, wagers were made – Thalion wondered who had bet on him, or if anyone did at all. He gave Jarlath a nod as he was led into the Stadium. Unable to see the fight, Thalion waited, muscles tense, a sigh of relief escaping his lips when Jarlath was returned with nothing more than a scratch across his chest.

Thalion's fight was the last one of the day – an honour given to the Chieftain's son.

He didn't look for Laeli when he stepped out; seeing her face would distract him. He didn't listen to the roar of the crowd. He focused instead on the sword in his hands, its weight and deadly power. If he was going to win this match, he needed to keep his head, keep light on his feet, and be quick and precise with his movements. Wade favoured brute strength – he would go in hard and fast. Adrenalin flowed through Thalion's blood as he and Wade approached the box. Brenna was sitting with Hadrian, Laeli on his father's other side.

Thalion kept his eyes on his father, his Chieftain.

He rolled his shoulders back, flexing the muscles there, feeling them stretch and bend, loosening up despite the cold, as they were called to the centre of the arena. The snow beneath their feet was scattered, mud and blood bleeding through the crisp white. Thalion shuffled his feet, finding his centre, letting his weight settle in his thighs. Wade did the same, his gaze voracious and wolfish in the wane light. Thalion adjusted his grip. Wade's eyes flashed, and he struck – a high blow that vibrated through Thalion's body as he brought his sword up to block him.

They parried back and forth, dancing around one another. The crowd cheered, enjoying the skill, the mastery of the sword. Thalion smiled. He had missed this. Despite Laeli's protests, the Stadium was a place of challenge and honour, a place for the men to test themselves, to learn their strengths and their weaknesses. The Chief's Seconds usually oversaw the training of the men and boys and watched each battle. Thalion, as Hadrian's son, was his father's Second, and he used these moments to observe himself from outside his body, to pick apart his performance and then work at filling the gaps. Hadrian, of course, always dissected his son's fighting with a critical eye.

Mere minutes into the fight, something changed.

Wade's strikes became more precise, his movements designed to harm, his sword crashing against Thalion's with more force than was necessary. Thalion stood his ground, matching him blow for blow, the snow around their feet churned into soup, the ground becoming slippery with each step. They broke apart for a moment, their breathing sharp.

'What in the Gods are you doing?' Thalion hissed. The other man ignored him and attacked again. Laeli's ill feelings became clear as Wade attempted to drive his sword straight through Thalion's chest. He stepped aside quickly, using his elbow to deliver a blow to the side of Wade's head. It was a dirty tactic, but he didn't care. The other man growled, shaking the blow off, and took his stance again, his sword held at the ready.

The crowd held their breath, as if they too had realised something else was unfolding in front of them. Wade paused, then lunged, sword swinging. Thalion wasn't fast enough; the blade reared up at him from below.

It opened his flesh easily; warm blood coursed down his side, and he could smell the red rawness of the wound. He gripped his ribs, fingers coming away painted with crimson. He would worry about the pain of it later, pushing the sting deep inside, like he'd been taught to do. He wiped his hand on the leg of his pants and grit his teeth, shifting his weight, adjusting his grip once more. His heartbeat slowed, his breathing steadying as he focused every ounce of himself on the man who stood before him.

'Come on,' Wade said in a low voice. 'Attack me.'

The sword was part of him and, as Thalion moved, he let it sing, let it swing wide, bringing it up sharply at a cross-angle, the weapon sliding beneath Wade's arms. Thalion's sword bit into the other man's chest, slicing through him like he was made of snow, flesh and sinew shredding around the glinting blade. Wade stumbled, eyes wide, then attacked with renewed strength.

It was his first and only mistake. His anger made him reckless and Thalion ducked beneath his raised arms and drove his sword straight through Wade's gut. They were face-to-face; Wade's eyes widened in disbelief and a bubble of blood burst from his lips, droplets spraying across Thalion's face and neck. Skin and blood frayed along the blade as Thalion pulled his sword free, ruined flesh squelching like the wet earth under their boots, the sound echoing around the Stadium and into the ears of every person watching. Wade fell, his body hitting the ground with a thud.

Thalion lifted his eyes to his father as around him, the crowd was silent.

CHAPTER SIX

Laeli was shaking as Thalion stormed out of the arena. The dead man lay on the snow, blood spreading from the body like a creeping mist; she could smell it from where she sat, the steaming heat of it, and her stomach turned over.

Hadrian's face was cold, composed, but Brenna got up with a snarl and stomped from the box. All around them, people were muttering, some shaking their heads at what had occurred. The buzz of talk was almost as loud as the roaring of Laeli's blood in her ears.

The Chieftain turned to her. His blue eyes, so like his son's, combed Laeli's face. She quickly remembered who she was supposed to be and schooled her expression into one of contented boredom, but she couldn't keep the anger from her eyes as she met his gaze. Good, she thought, let him see.

'Did you enjoy today?' Hadrian asked mildly.

'It's very masculine, isn't it?' Laeli waved a hand at the arena, at the body and the crowd, slowly drifting away; two men rushed out and collected the body, lifting the dead man gently, respectfully, between them. She watched until they had disappeared from her sight.

The Chieftain's eyes were still on her face. 'What do you mean?'

She made herself look at him again. 'You don't let your women compete in this training?'

Hadrian laughed delightedly. 'Women! What woman would stand a chance out there?'

You'd be amazed, Laeli seethed. Her fingers twitched but she made sure she kept her face and voice steady. 'Where I'm from, Hadrian, women are warriors.'

'By all means, Eira, take your husband's place at the next Stadium,' Hadrian replied.

'You have female Chiefs, do you not?' Laeli asked coolly.

He nodded. 'I do, that's true, but though they are rather exceptional women with strong heads for politics, they do not step onto the battlefield at all.'

Laeli folded her arms. 'Why?'

'Things are obviously different here. You need to get used to it.' His voice was firm.

Her eyes fell on the blood that painted the snow. 'I could be wrong, Hadrian, being only a woman, but that man was trying to kill my husband.'

'They got carried away, that's all. It happens occasionally,' the Chieftain said, waving the whole episode away like it was nothing. Laeli could smell his lies and thought about her swords, lying beneath the bed, hidden from the world, from this miserable, cold part of the world where the only light she could see was almost extinguished before her eyes. She thought of the magic hidden inside her, the fire that would roar into life at her command. In her mind, Hadrian died screaming as the flesh dripped from his burning body.

He was still looking at her. 'You care about Thalion?'

The question took her by surprise, but she kept her voice steady, and her chin lifted proudly. 'I care about the alliance, nothing more.'

Hadrian nodded and stood, holding out his arm for her. She ignored him, climbing to her feet, and leading the way from the box and to the carriage waiting for her outside that place of death and blood. She could feel Hadrian's eyes burning a hole between her shoulder blades and resisted the urge to shudder. She opened the door to the carriage herself and settled inside, staring straight ahead at the snow that carpeted the landscape around them.

Laeli reached for the door handle, but Hadrian stood in her way. They stared at one another for a long moment before his lips curled into a smile that did not reach his eyes.

'Don't worry about Thalion,' he said. 'He's harder to kill than a mongrel dog.' He stepped back, and she slammed the door closed as Brenna of Whitemouth approached. Brenna was a ghastly creature, all rage and spite and false bravado. Laeli couldn't stand him, couldn't stand to be in the same room as him. Something about him made her stomach turn.

Hadrian steered his Chief away from her; Brenna's lips were moving frantically, his face contorted. Laeli took a deep breath and opened her ears, letting her fae senses reach across the snow to the Chieftain and his most loyal Chief.

'I've lost a man today, Hadrian,' Brenna said fiercely. 'One of my best.'

'Your man was only supposed to scare him,' Hadrian hissed. 'Don't be acting without my consent.' He glanced around sharply, catching Laeli's eye. He held her gaze a moment before he turned his face away. 'He's still my son and what happens to him is my choice, not yours, understand?'

Brenna stalked away as a fresh fall of snow whirled across the plain.

Back at the castle, Laeli paced their room until a furious Thalion came in, his eyes hard, lips a thin line. Healy was with him, a bowl of water in her long-fingered hands, so Laeli let her glamour fall and helped Thalion out of his shirt. The wound was as bad as it looked – long and deep, running from the apex of his ribs halfway to his hip, a big sister wound to the one he'd received in the forest near the Rift. The leg of his pants was drenched with blood. Laeli's scowl deepened as she directed him to sit on the end of the bed.

Healy offered up the bowl. 'I'm sorry, I didn't have time to heat it.'

Laeli dipped her fingers into the water; in moments, it was bubbling, steam rising into the chill that always lingered beneath the heat from the fire. Thalion's eyes were on her face as she dipped a cloth in the water, kneeling before him to gently wipe the blood from his skin.

'You'll have another scar,' she said bitterly, pulling back with a sigh to rinse the cloth out; the water quickly turned red. 'This was deliberate. He tried to kill you, Thalion!'

'I know,' he snapped, then sent her an apologetic look.

The muscles on his abdomen shifted and tensed beneath his skin as he kept his breathing shallow. Laeli held the cloth to his wound. The Stadium was barbaric, and utterly stupid. She shook her head, putting the cloth to the side as Healy slid thread through the eye of a needle with deft fingers. Laeli gave Thalion a quick, worried look. She flicked her fingers – fire eased from their tips.

'I could always …'

'Stitch it,' he commanded.

Laeli had never stitched anyone before. She stepped back and let Healy take her place, the halfkin holding the wound closed with one hand, stitching with the other, pushing the needle through Thalion's skin, Laeli wincing with every movement of Healy's hand. Thalion barely flinched, not even when Healy pulled the thread tight, though it had to hurt; his face was tight and pale, fingers dug into the fur that dressed the bed.

'You're allowed to feel it, Thalion. We won't tell anyone,' Laeli muttered.

Healy snickered. When she was done, she tied the stitches off neatly, dumping the needle and remaining thread in the bowl with the bloodied cloth, scooping them up and leaving the room.

Laeli eyed the scar on Thalion's chest, below his collarbone; there was one on his shoulder, a perfectly raised line, and several others scattered across his back. She ran the tip of her finger lightly over the scar on his shoulder. 'Who stitched this one?'

'My mother. That was my first. I was thirteen, maybe fourteen.' He smiled wistfully. 'She wasn't happy with my father at all. She thought I was too young to be in the Stadium, but I'd been begging him for months and he finally relented. I remember that day because he was proud of me.'

'And the others?'

'Healy did most of them.'

Laeli relayed the conversation she'd spied on between Hadrian and Brenna.

'He must suspect something,' Thalion told her.

She shook her head. 'I don't think so. You will have to be careful, Thalion, because who knows how many others think the way Brenna does? I can imagine what sort of power a man like Brenna might be set to inherit with you gone,' she said; Thalion frowned. 'You need to decide how you will deal with things here when, or if, your father leaves to join Kiarda.'

Thalion's face was darker than she had ever seen it. 'One day soon, I will deal with Brenna. That bastard has been at me my whole life.'

'And your father?'

He hesitated a moment too long.

'Thalion …'

'He's my father, Laeli. I know what he is – I can't deny that – but …'

'If you can't do it …'

His face hardened. 'Could you kill your father?'

Laeli sat beside him, taking his hands. 'Remember what you said? That ruling through fear and hatred wasn't what you wanted? That it wasn't right? It isn't right, Thalion, and we have a chance to change it. I can't make you do it, but if you don't, then I will. I won't let Kiarda or anyone allied with her attempt to destroy the world again.'

He was quiet but she watched his face move as he thought about what she'd said. He didn't give her an answer, didn't respond to her words at all, but she hadn't expected him to. The fire crackled, sparks shooting into the chimney and away into the frost-bitten air outside. He took a deep breath, then winced.

'The Stadium – will you let it continue when you're Chieftain?'

'It's part of who we are. It's a tradition,' he said tightly.

'Traditions are made to be broken,' she retorted. 'If I followed tradition, I wouldn't be here. I'd never have met you, in fact, because – instead of being out there at the Rift – I'd have been swanning around the palace in a silk gown, smiling at people I was pretending to like. Things don't always have to stay the same, Thalion.'

'You're pricklier than usual,' he murmured, letting her help him into clean clothes.

'Watching you almost get killed today and not being able to do anything about it was hard. I wanted to …' She moved away from him, pacing, picking things up and putting them down again in their right place – his boots, a shirt (his), a belt (also his) – giving him a dirty look. She'd spent her life with servants running after her, but she at least cleaned up her own messes. Laeli put her hands on her hips as Thalion stood. 'Sit down, you'll bust those stitches,' she snapped.

He ignored her, shifting stiffly to the table, and pouring himself a drink, his eyes flickering to her face and away again. His shoulders were tense, the line of his body rigid. 'You don't like being here?'

'I'm tired, that's all,' Laeli answered, keeping her voice soft, controlled. He nodded, not acknowledging she ignored his question. In a neutral tone, he told her she should rest and suddenly, that was all she wanted to do, curl up on the bed with its rumpled sheets and soft furs and sleep for days, tucked in this room until it was all over, cocooned in the smell of him that lingered where he lay each night.

The pretending, the lies, and the game, this dangerous game they were playing, was starting to wear her down. She missed her family and her home, the green life of the forest and the tinkle of water over rocks, the sunshine that poured through the trees like a river, but she wouldn't leave him here, not while his father breathed.

'Rest,' he told her again. The moment her head hit the pillow she was gone.

CHAPTER SEVEN

It was after curfew on their third night in the city, and Ash was cleaning the bar in *The Solstice House*. Yasper had been unusually quiet since they'd closed, a frown taking up permanent residence between his brows as he counted his takings for the night. Hours earlier, Ash had tied an apron around her waist and started collecting empty glasses when Biel didn't show up for his shift. She'd enjoyed it, for the simple fact she was doing something other than sitting around worrying about things she couldn't control and didn't have answers to.

'Well,' she said with a smile, 'do I pass as a barmaid?'

Yasper's frown was deep, his face distracted even as his fingers continued sorting coins with practised efficiency. 'Yeah, you'll do, Red.'

'What is it?' she asked quietly.

He glanced at the main door. 'Biel. I haven't seen him since he left to send your letter.'

Ash's heart stopped for a beat, then surged so quickly it hurt. She grasped the cloth tightly, her breathing turned ragged as beneath her skin, her magic surged. Yasper reached over and unwound her fingers from the sodden rag, setting it aside, his eyes on her face.

'He knows how to take care of himself,' he said calmly, but the frown was still there. 'But Gem was supposed to arrive before curfew, and she hasn't shown up. It's not like her to skip out on me either.'

41

'Yasper—'

He shook his head. 'Don't worry about it, Ash. You should get some sleep.'

Tomorrow, Ash and Senan would leave for the forest. She would be glad to see the back of the city. There were too many eyes here, peering from around corners. She thought briefly of the Academy, and Nerida. Had they graduated? Where was her friend now? She was concerned about Yasper's mention of conscription. It wasn't usual for mages to travel with the army. There was always a group of healers who followed the Queen's Army around; if Nerida had been given her White Woman's robes, it could mean she would be sent out of the city. Nerida was a skilled healer, and the army could use her talents.

Senan came in from the back room, where he had been organising their supplies for the journey. He ran a hand through his messy hair and had just sat himself at the bar when his familiar appeared in a burst of shadow. Oden barked loudly, pawing at the Mage-Witch with a dark foot. 'What is it?' Senan asked the dog. Oden's bark grew frantic. He bounded past his master, his long body pointed towards the front door as he growled deep in his throat, the hair rising to attention along the flowing ridge of his back, the smoky shadows that surrounded him thickening.

'Senan,' Ash whispered, 'something's wrong.'

From outside the front door came the sounds of a scuffle and a woman's voice raised in protest, followed by the distinctive sharp sound of a slap. Ash looked at Yasper in alarm, the magic in her veins rushing to the surface; smoke curled from her skin. She pushed it away, held it there, waiting as Yasper reached beneath the bar for his pistols, his eyes never leaving the front door.

Oden growled again, baring his teeth, as something heavy slammed against the door; the lock gave in with the crunching of metal. A body was shoved inside – Gem. She fell to her knees with a gasp, then scrambled to her feet and tore across the room, Yasper meeting her on the other side of the bar. She fell into his arms as a dozen heavily armed men in black poured inside and, behind them, sweeping in on a cloud of fear and power, was the Spirit Rake. Ash could feel him the moment he entered the room, that power of his already threading itself through the air. Searching.

For her.

Oden howled as Darian's eyes swept the room, coming to rest first on Senan, then Ash. Those bloodless lips curled into a smile as he lifted his hands, fingers grabbing at the air. Senan leapt from his stool and pushed Ash behind him, his hands moving quickly. From beneath their feet, the earth rumbled and then a vine shot through one of the windows, wrapping itself around the nearest black-clothed man. Ash watched in horror as that vine strangled him.

Yasper, Gem behind him, her face tear-streaked and her nose smudged with blood, drew his pistol. With one hand, he pushed Gem back towards the bar. 'Now gentlemen, what seems to be the problem?'

Six pistols were drawn and pointed at Yasper.

'Ash, run,' Senan hissed. She nodded, backing up, her feet carrying her towards the rear of the building. Before she could move any further, Darian's magic was inside her head. She gasped, then she was free, and Darian was on his knees, Senan's hand extended towards him. The other held a man in place, a rope of wind tight around his neck, his hands clawing at it, eyes frantic. In moments, he slumped to the floor, dead.

'He wants the fire caster and the Anomaly alive,' one of the men shouted, but the Watchmen hesitated, their eyes flickering from Senan to Darian, who slowly climbed to his feet, his face bloodless and glowing in the dim light of the room.

They're afraid, Ash realised. Of Senan. Of her. Of what they could do.

She felt her magic stir again and clenched her fists, pushing the fire down. It was too volatile. She was terrified of what would happen if she let it out. That day with Mahelivar in the forest behind the palace was branded on her mind; that terrible power, its strength and potency, the way it had felt flowing through her and into the world.

The back door was close. All she had to do was run for it.

Still, the Watch hesitated. A deathly silence dropped into the room as Ash edged closer to the back door, one foot after the other, never taking her eyes from Darian's face. The big man who'd led the way inside turned to her, a triumphant smile crawling across his lips.

'What are you waiting for?' he demanded of the men. 'It's just one girl and—'

Yasper's first shot hit the big man in the chest. Gem launched herself at another, armed with nothing but her fingernails. The Watchman swatted her aside like a fly; she hit the ground hard and didn't get up as the others raised their weapons and moved further into the room.

Darian's magic brushed Ash's mind again and she clamped down on it, calling on her own power. Darian recoiled as the fire inside her slammed into his mind. The Spirit Rake grit his teeth, shaking his head.

Yasper's pistol exploded, the sound tearing through the room. As Ash watched, one of the men took aim and returned fire, the bullet finding a home in Yasper's shoulder. He fell back against the bar with a curse.

Darian lifted his arms, sweeping them out and away from his body. Tables and chairs were launched into the air, smashing against the walls. Fear burnt in Ash's mouth, her stomach churning as the Spirit Rake came closer. Senan knelt and placed both hands on the floor; plant life exploded through the stones, growing with unnatural speed, thick vines and roots writhing and twisting through the air. One reared back like a snake then shot forward, embedding itself through the chest of one man, then another, blood bursting from their lips as those vines tightened around their bodies.

The Spirit Rake faltered as Senan turned his magic on him. Wind ripped through the room, a cage of it wrapping around Darian, driving him back towards the main door, his feet skidding along the ground, Oden's teeth dripping and his eyes glowing red.

'Get out of here, Ash,' Senan shouted, not looking at her. She saw him shake his head, saw Darian's hands push through that wind, reaching in

Senan's direction. She saw Yasper on the ground, blood running from his shoulder, crouched by Gem's still form. She saw the dead men and took a deep breath.

She was not going to run away again.

Ash flexed her fingers. Her magic roared; flames coated her skin. In her mind, the fire reached across the room and closed around the men of the Watch. She pulled her fire to the edge of her mind, ready to unleash it, catching Darian's eye, taking note of the fear and fascination on his face as flames licked at her fingers.

Someone rushed at her from the side. She caught a glimpse of a face covered in a thick beard. Something slammed into the side of her head as bodies converged on each other and Senan fell to the ground.

CHAPTER EIGHT

When Ash woke, it was dark, and she was lying on a cot in a narrow room with a low ceiling. There were no windows, and the walls were smooth stone, the door heavy oak reinforced with bars of iron. The wall behind her was slick with moisture, a dank, mouldy smell rising from the floor to claw its way into her nostrils and make her stomach roll. She could hear nothing except the rushing of blood in her ears, nothing to give her any clues as to where she was.

She could guess. She pushed her heaving stomach down, trying to take deep, steadying breaths, but her head pounded ruthlessly. Wincing, Ash touched trembling fingers to her face, feeling the misshapen lump of a bruise on her temple. What had he hit her with? Groaning, she eased herself upright. She was desperately thirsty and had never been more terrified in her life. She had no idea where the others were, or if they were alive.

It was Senan she thought of, her insides twisting at the memory of the magic he'd let free to protect them, the men he had killed. It hadn't been enough, and one man had ducked beneath the writhing plant life to sink a knife into the Mage-Witch's side as Ash's head exploded and she spiralled away into the dark.

Alone, she put her head in her hands and wept. They should never have come here.

Ash curled onto the musty cot and slept, nothing but the deafening silence for company.

When she woke the second time, it was to find Darian watching her. There were deep shadows under his eyes and the door behind him was wide open. Swallowing, Ash sat up, pressing herself into the wall, ignoring the cold wet that seeped through her shirt.

He cocked his head to the side, those dark grey eyes appraising her as she conjured flames and held them in hands that quivered with fear. Her stomach trembled and her head spun; concussion.

'I wouldn't do that,' the Spirit Rake said, his voice like dry paper, devoid of colour and feeling.

Ash bolted for the door, falling straight into the arms of a young man dressed in the depthless black of the Watch, his badge gleaming against his shirt. She pressed burning palms to his chest; he screamed and let her go, slapping at his shirt front hastily. Panting, she ran, not making it three steps before her arms were pulled behind her and Darian's mind was tunnelling into her own. She lashed out with both her magic and her feet, struggling furiously, but she was pushed roughly back into the cell. Darian smashed his way inside her head; her temples pounded as a ferocious headache assaulted her and she gasped and stumbled, falling back onto the stinking cot.

'She's a pretty thing,' someone cooed. Leaning in the doorway was a handsome man in a black shirt, his arms folded, his eyes combing her body. 'Feisty as well. I like that.'

Darian regarded the man with distaste. 'The High Mage hasn't given you leave to have your way with the prisoner.'

The man shrugged.

Ash choked back a sob as Darian's power wrapped around her mind.

'You're to come with me,' the Spirit Rake commanded.

The Watchman hauled her roughly to her feet and dragged her from the room. He did what he was told, never touching her any more than her arms as he marched her through a series of long, dark hallways, the walls lined with doors. Ash tried not to think about who might be behind those doors.

Her legs trembled so much she could barely walk and the man had to practically carry her up a flight of roughly hewn steps. They entered another hall, this one flooded with light from windows positioned above head height along the smooth walls. Lanterns glowed in their casings; the flames flared as Ash passed and a tingle ran through her, despite Darian's magic still folded sharply around her mind.

The man leading her felt the tingle as well. He shook her, putting his face close to hers in warning. Involuntarily, Ash's fingers twitched, and he pulled back his hand and slapped her hard.

She cried out, her face burning, neck aching from the force of the blow.

No one had ever hit her before and now she'd been hit twice.

The Spirit Rake had drawn ahead but he would have heard the slap. He didn't turn around; didn't give any indication he knew what had happened. Eyes brimming with tears, Ash kept her gaze on her feet as she was yanked forward, his fingers digging into her upper arm painfully.

Darian stopped outside the last door along the hall. His grey eyes combed Ash's face before he swung the door open and stepped inside, Ash hurled along after him, tripping over her feet.

The room was long and dark, with a scrubbed wooden table in the centre. There were no other furnishings except for a smaller table and a chair, and the room had one window; shafts of buttery light poured through it, waves of dust dancing and twirling furiously, captured in that light, as caged and confined as Ash was.

'Lay her on the table.'

The voice rose from the shadows lining the walls, and Ash began shaking with fear as an older man with grey-blonde hair stepped into view. The power seeping from his body was undeniable; her knees weakened.

When he spoke, his voice was warm, gentle. 'Do you know who I am?'

She nodded, throat constricted.

Between them, the Spirit Rake and the man of the Watch, who enjoyed putting his hands on her body again, stretched Ash out on the table, her wrists and ankles strapped down with thick leather cuffs.

Ash struggled violently, her back arching, fear coating her mouth as the High Mage approached the table. The leather bit into her skin.

'I don't want to hurt you any more than you've already been hurt, Ash,' Gedeon said in that low, soothing voice. 'You don't need to be afraid of me.'

'Liar,' Ash managed to spit. He knew her name! He probably knew everything about her, including where she had been. She thought of Mahelivar and his father. Were they in more danger because of her?

Gedeon smiled, reaching a pale hand to stroke her hair, the side of her face, tracing the bruise, the skin on his fingers soft, the pressure he put on her damaged skin anything but gentle. 'Release your magic when I ask, and you won't be hurt.'

She mustered up her defiance, the sort that often saw her in trouble in the village. 'And if I don't?'

The High Mage turned away. 'Darian can be rather convincing, or, if you'd prefer, I can see if Mal could tempt you into letting that fire of yours free.'

Mal. The Watchman. Ash shuddered as he smiled at her, revealing perfect, bone-white teeth, and forced herself to look at Gedeon again.

'What do you want?' she rasped, her throat screaming in protest.

Gedeon didn't answer. He picked up a metal box from the smaller table and carried it over to her. From inside the box, he lifted out a large red stone, the colour of blood. 'Do you know what these are?'

Ash shook her head.

'They're Bloodstones, my dear. An unusual substance, capable of capturing and storing magic. Bloodstones are rarely found, but a large deposit was found near the prison camps in Garlathe.' He paused; his eyes flashed as he looked at her. 'Some might call that fate. You will fill them with your magic for me.'

She shook her head again.

'No? Then perhaps you need some motivation. It is my understanding you are untrained, and untrained magic can be coaxed into being.' He stepped away again.

Ash's heart thundered as Mal came closer, that handsome face shining, a wicked gleam in his eyes. 'Please,' she whispered, but he slapped her again, then again, on the other cheek. Panting, her face burning, she was unable to stop the tears from slipping free. Her fire thrashed and shrieked but she bit down on it.

Mal reached for her face but he didn't strike her again. Instead, he stroked her cheek, wiped the tears away, his touch gentle. Gedeon, meanwhile, moved around the table, positioning the Bloodstones around her body.

The magic under her skin tingled in response to them and Ash thought she could hear them, the strange song they sang, the way they called her. Gedeon's eyes widened, and his smile deepened. He nodded at Mal.

Ash gasped as his fingers closed around her throat. With one hand, he choked her, the other threaded through her hair – he yanked the red strands hard, and her scalp screamed as her vision swam with blackness.

She could feel the Bloodstones, feel their pull, and swept her magic aside defiantly.

'She's fighting them,' Darian said, his mind poking around the edges of hers again and she grit her teeth, clamping down, drawing on the full force of her magic. Darian recoiled as that fiery shield slammed into his power.

Still, she resisted the melody of the Bloodstones.

'Perhaps she needs stronger motivation,' Gedeon murmured. Nodding, Mal left the room, returning minutes later with a bleeding and semi-conscious Senan.

CHAPTER NINE

There was darkness.

Claws of steel wrapped around his mind.

Claws of steel probing and diving, scrambling for the core of his magic.

He heard a voice he knew, a silken caress that hid the sharp barbs on that tongue, a ribbon wrapped around arrogance and a burning hunger for power.

'He's fainted.' A second voice that rustled like dead leaves. Darian.

Senan hadn't fainted. He'd retreated into the pit of his brain, curling himself protectively around the centre of his mind, the part of him from which his dual powers spread themselves through his body. His fingers twitched. Something wet touched his hand – Oden.

'Awaken,' that first voice purred.

Fingers stroked his face as that voice stroked his ears. Gedeon's magic was inside his head, sliding beside Darian's. Gedeon gripped his mind and pulled it to the surface.

Senan was strapped to a chair, his knees spread, feet tied at each ankle, wrists bound behind his back. The rope was tight enough to cause a needle-like sensation to dance over his fingers. With his eyes still closed, there was a scraping sound and a tattoo of heavy steps on the stones.

Slowly, he opened his eyes. He saw a pair of polished black boots between the legs of his chair. He lifted his gaze to see a head of pale blonde hair, a wide mouth split into a caressing smile and sparkling eyes. He was a handsome boy, this Watchman, but he was just a boy, hardly any older than twenty. Yet, beneath the sparkle in his eyes was murder and pain and an enjoyment of both.

The boy waved a knife in Senan's face.

'Easy, Mal,' a voice called. Gedeon.

Mal stepped away, and Senan took in the room – Ash was lying on a long table, her red hair falling towards the ground. He could see the rise and fall of her chest and relief speared through him. She was alive but positioned around her body were Bloodstones, singing their dreadful song. Senan's magic stirred.

He looked at Gedeon in alarm.

Gedeon chuckled. 'A stroke of genius on my behalf, don't you think, old friend?'

'You're not my friend.'

'No, you're correct,' Gedeon said simply. 'But I could be, Senan. If you cooperate.'

He shook his head, the blood rushing in his ears, gasping at the stabbing pain in his side. Senan glanced down to see his shirt stained with blood. His temples were pounding. Darian was still in his head, clinging tight to the thing that made him who he was. He threw a hateful glare at the Spirit Rake standing against the far wall. Darian just smiled at him, a smug curling of his bloodless lips.

'You're wounded and weak.' Gedeon continued in a soft voice. 'You won't be able to fight the both of us and you know it. Despite your powers, you don't have it in you, Senan.'

Senan grit his teeth; he reached inside for his power. It rose at his call, snaking towards the surface, encountering the coercive net Darian had wound around it. Senan paused, his power black with his anger, then let it out – arrows of his magic shredded through Darian's net, pushing their way inside the Spirit Rake's mind. The grey-eyed man screamed and clutched his head. A trickle of blood ran from his nose as he collapsed against the wall, sliding to the floor, his face blank with shock.

'Interesting,' Gedeon mused, watching Darian wipe at his nose.

Senan turned his magic on the High Mage, but Gedeon's shield was well-fortified, a wall of black stone, as slippery as ice and coated in shrieking wind.

The High Mage chuckled. 'It serves me to keep my mind well protected. I've spent twenty years building that shield, Senan, while you've been hiding in the wild. You won't get through it,' he added, still smiling.

Mal approached and pulled back his fist.

Senan's eyes watered and his nose ran as that fist connected with his face. His head snapped back, hitting the wall behind him and stars whirled through his vision briefly. On the table, Ash struggled. He was hit again, in the stomach this time, then the ribs. He couldn't hold his scream as that fist smashed into his wound, the pain red-hot, racing through him. His magic stirred again as Ash's sobs filled the air.

~

The pain of it.

Pain carved its way through her like a hot knife.

Her power rose, drawn to the Bloodstones, to their raw pull, their siren song.

She clenched her teeth. Even as the tears flowed, she fought to keep this part of her, this part that for so long she pretended did not exist, that she despised for the way it marked her.

Forbidden.

Dangerous.

She despised it for what it had cost her, and yet … she did not want to let it go.

The Bloodstones called, their song echoing through Ash's blood and bone; the magic within her sang back and began to move. Against her will, it moved.

Gasping, she tried desperately to hold it steady, to not allow Gedeon access to that part of her the Mother had seen fit to gift.

She clung to the fiery strands of her magic as it twisted and shuddered beneath her skin. As it began to stream from her body and flow into the Bloodstones.

No!

The Stones were a cage, a prison.

Please, Ash begged the magic inside. Don't leave me. Don't leave me!

Everything paused; she heard a voice, whispering and burning and carving a path through her.

What will you give, daughter of fire?

An image flashed behind her eyes – an old woman with frost-bitten hair, her face hidden by a veil that fluttered and danced on a swirling wind. She stood beneath a tree stripped bare of leaves, the world around her shining with snow.

In the vision, a wolf howled.

What will you give?

Me, Ash shouted, choking on a sob. *I'll give you me.*

The Crone smiled, and the fire screamed into the world.

~

Senan could only watch helplessly as fire flowed from Ash's body, arching into the air. It spiralled and twisted like vines, shaping itself into thin streams. Her magic poured itself into the Bloodstones, drawn towards them by their own mysterious power.

Gedeon rubbed his hands together with glee, his eyes shining.

He's mad, Senan thought, watching Ash's power, the core of who she was, was sucked from her body. He's mad if he thinks he can control her magic.

Something shifted in the room.

The air became charged and dry; the hair on his arms lifted and he saw the black-shirted young man's eyes widen. Darian sucked in a breath, pushing himself to his feet, face tight with fear.

Gedeon did not take his eyes from Ash. 'Good girl,' he murmured.

Her fire increased its power.

The Bloodstones surrounding her body cracked and fizzled, the sound echoing through the small room. Gedeon's smile fell – he darted forward, then back, his hands held out in front of him, his air magic attempting to get inside her head. Her skin was blazing, the heat from the flames reaching across the room to brand their faces.

The bonds that held her wrists and ankles fell away, blackened scraps that floated to the ground. She sat up, her eyes filled with sparks, the air around her crackling.

'Ash,' Senan rasped. She looked at him blankly, swinging her legs from the table and standing, her feet not quite touching the floor, her body buoyed by flames. She examined her hands, then turned towards the window. The sunlight caught on the fiery mass of her body, and she threw out her arms and sucked the heat and light from the sun into herself as the room grew strangely cold and dark.

'Impossible,' Gedeon spluttered.

The Bloodstones were glowing, the trapped magic bouncing around inside, calling for its freedom, calling for its master.

Darian fled, his face drained of colour. Mal hesitated a moment before racing after the Spirit Rake, leaving Gedeon and Senan to face the flames.

Ash turned to Gedeon. The High Mage backed up until he was pressed against the stone wall, trapped, the wall of flame reaching for him, curling itself into hands. As Senan watched, Gedeon's hair began to sizzle and, slowly, the skin began to peel from his face as those fingers of flame stroked him lovingly.

He screamed, the sound ricocheting around the room, bouncing from the stones to settle inside Senan's chest.

'Ash,' he called again, louder this time, his air magic flying out to embrace her, but she lifted a fiery arm and the magic rebounded, forcing itself painfully back inside him. Gasping, he struggled with the ropes, the skin around his wrists and ankles raw, his wounded side pulsing. 'Don't lose yourself,' he shouted desperately as she approached Gedeon again. The High Mage was cowering on the floor, his body shuddering with painful sobs, his hands over his head, skin bubbling and peeling. The room stank of charred flesh.

The fire that was Ash turned to Senan, staring at him with that terrifyingly blank expression. His heart stopped for a moment, then roared back into life as adrenalin poured through him. He pulled on the ropes that bound his wrists, stretching them enough that he could slip a hand free.

He held that hand towards Ash. 'Remember who you are,' he said, flicking his wrist. His air magic slammed through that fiery shield, reaching through the flame to the core of her, where he found a face. Senan grabbed hold of that face and pulled, drawing it to the surface with him, placing it in the centre of the fire she had become.

She faltered, staggering, her body trembling. The flames shimmered and pulled back a fraction. He waited, his breathing ragged as, slowly, her eyes focused on his face.

'Senan?'

He nodded. 'Ash, come back. Pull it back.'

'I don't want to,' she said, the voice of a child being denied what she desired, and he realised that it was the fire speaking, not her. That magic which had been dampened and hidden for so long was now alive and it wanted to stay in the world.

He tried again, throwing Jarlath's face in front of her eyes. 'You have to.'

'But ...' she shook her head, that crown of hair shifting with the breath of the fire that bound her. She looked around the room again: the blackened floor, the scorched timber of the table, the winking

Bloodstones. On the floor, the High Mage sobbed. Ash turned to him, her head cocked to the side. She raised her hand.

'Ash!' Senan shouted.

'He hurt me. He hurt you, but I …' The childlike voice paused, then, the fire went out, leaving Ash's skin sizzling. She fell to her knees, her head in her hands, moaning in pain.

'Ash, look at me,' Senan commanded. He freed his other wrist, then his ankles, ignoring the pain of the ripped skin. His face was dry, sucked of moisture, like everything else in the room. The air was charged with sparks, as crisp and starched as paper. He scrambled from the chair and touched the kneeling girl gently on the shoulder; tears streaked her face, and her skin was bloodless, all the fire and rage sucked back inside.

'Come on,' he said, helping her up and leading her to the door, desperate to get out of there.

Before they left, he looked down on Gedeon, on his former tutor and friend. The High Mage was shuddering in agony, his skin a horrible, ruined mess. 'I'm sorry,' Senan said, letting a trace of his air magic free, sliding that invisible hand inside Gedeon's mind, his shield shattered like the rest of him. Senan's magic stroked and soothed, a lullaby, until the High Mage's eyes fell closed. Senan took Ash's hand and led her from the Keep.

They saw no one, except two black-shirted men, who Senan slammed against the wall with his magic. There was no sign of the Spirit Rake, but Senan kept a slither of his magic at the ready, waiting for that now familiar feeling of Darian's mind brushing his. Where Ash's feet fell soot and sparks were left behind and where he walked the earth responded, shoots of green slipping through the stones and spreading to carpet the city streets.

Ash walked ahead of him, trailing sparks that floated off in the darkening sky, her skin still shimmering with her magic. The few people in the streets scattered, tucking themselves into corners and against walls as Ash passed, Senan trailing her, his fingers curling, the green carpet stretching before them now, grass and flowers and vines climbing the walls and looping flexible fingers over lanterns and railings.

At the prison, the guard paled at the sight of Ash, her red hair still sizzling, her skin awash with her magic. He lifted his pistol, but found it too hot to handle, letting the weapon fall to the ground. With wide eyes, he raced from behind the desk and fled the building. Ash glanced at Senan, and they stepped into the hall with cells lining the walls, a place Senan hadn't seen for twenty years. The darkness engulfed them, and he swallowed away the memory of his time in this prison. Ash glowed in the dim light, waves of red and gold running beneath her skin.

Yasper jumped up, then stepped back quickly when he noticed Ash. 'She okay?' he asked as Senan approached his cell, Ash lingering in the background.

'She will be.' Senan unlocked the cell with his mind, and Yasper stepped out, giving him and Ash a bow of thanks. Dried blood coated his shoulder and the flesh beneath the torn shirt was red and puckered and angry. Gem was in the cell opposite and Senan released her quickly, the woman crying tears of relief. A dark bruise littered her cheek. The other cells were full of halfkin and, at Yasper's request, Senan unlocked their doors. In the street outside, they could hear the sounds of a gathering crowd and, beyond that, the men of the Watch, demanding people go home.

Gem looked alarmed. 'They can't catch us again. Yas?'

'I'm all out of hidey holes I'm afraid,' he said. 'But let's get out of here for now and we'll work it out as we go, yeah?'

Senan took Ash's hands, looking into her face. She was dazed, her eyes unfocused. She needed to rest after the magic she had wrought – and after what Gedeon had stolen from her. He thought of the Bloodstones with a pang; he should have taken them, but he'd been so worried for Ash and terrified of what she'd done to Gedeon that he wanted to get her out of there and somewhere safe.

'Ash, you need to put the fire out now,' he told her. 'Back inside yourself, for now, alright? I promise it won't be forever.' He was speaking to the fire now and sensed it listening. Eventually, Ash nodded and closed her eyes. In moments, her hair and skin had returned to normal. Only in her eyes could he see any trace of what was inside her – the whites of her eyes were filled with dancing sparks. It would have to do.

She sunk to her knees again, her face grey, deep shadows under her eyes. Without a word, Yasper picked her up, ignoring his own injury, cradling her against his chest. She looked so small and vulnerable, so unassuming, that if he hadn't seen with his own eyes what she had done, Senan would never have believed it.

They stepped out into the street, coming face-to-face with armed Watchmen.

'Go,' Yasper ordered the halfkin and they scattered, slipping into the shadows, and vanishing. The Watch didn't bother looking at them. The big man at the head of the cluster lifted his pistol.

'You're to come—'

Senan's air magic smashed into him. He was lifted off his feet and hurled through the air, landing with a sickening thud on the stones. The other men looked at each other, fear and uncertainty running through their eyes. Senan's magic was at its end. He needed to rest, sleep, recharge and heal. With the last of his air magic, he forced his way into the minds of the Watch. He'd never coerced so many people at once and could feel his magic straining but, after a moment, they lay their weapons on the ground and turned, walking from the prison without a backwards glance. Senan's knees trembled. Gem rushed forward and collected the fallen pistols, slipping one into each of Yasper's pockets. She pressed one into Senan's hand and concealed the rest beneath her skirts.

The sun sank, plunging the city dramatically into darkness. The only building still lit with the fading light was the tower at the Academy. Senan looked around; there were still people in the streets, watching them with interest, with fear and suspicion and what he thought might be wonder.

He glanced up again as the light slipped from the tower and he knew where they had to go.

CHAPTER TEN

Mahelivar's head was pounding. He clenched his teeth and tried again, his magic pushing on the net woven around the room. Feeling with his mind like he would his fingers, he poked and prodded, searching for a weak spot. Finding none, he withdrew his magic and slumped back with a sigh.

Failed. Again.

His father was sleeping. They were locked in the Royal Suite, although he'd stopped counting the days, watching the cycle of light and dark cross the world outside the window instead. Watching as the world he knew was changed before his eyes, and he was powerless to stop it from happening.

Would this be it, then? How he ended? If death was to be dealt, it wasn't how he imagined it would arrive.

Kiarda had the staff and hammer of the Cailleach. Mahelivar could only speculate how she got her hands on such powerful magic. He couldn't imagine the Goddess would hand them over easily, but how else did Kiarda get them? What had she offered the Mother of All?

The answer came easily: Eshlune. His home. The one place where the snow and ice of winter barely touched. Mahelivar glanced out the wide window again; not long after Kiarda's arrival, the trees had shaken off their leaves with a great shiver, the forest becoming a graveyard of bare bones and snow in an instant. The Cailleach's blanket had never been spread so far.

What bothered him more was what he had seen spring from his aunt's hands - blue flames. He had seen the look on his father's face at that moment as they came to the same conclusion: Kiarda had changed her magic. Mahelivar knew his aunt didn't possess fire magic any stronger than his, but those blue flames had caused a shiver to skid down his spine, a shiver that hadn't faded. He had no idea how she had done it, or that it could even be done.

They hadn't spoken about it out loud, but Mahelivar knew, as surely as his father did, that Kiarda wanted the magic of the Rift. If she had been able to manipulate her own magic, that which flowed through her and was part of her, what else would she be able to do? She'd had over one hundred years to plan this.

Mahelivar swallowed the taste of fear away. He got to his feet and moved to the door, pressing his ear against it. He could hear the guards outside, their murmured conversation about nothing important. He wondered who they were, what they thought they would gain from this, what his aunt had promised them. With the net of magic woven so tightly around the Royal Suite, he couldn't even tell if they were human or fae.

When Kiarda had marched into the throne room with the snows of winter at her heels like an obedient hound, Mahelivar's instinct had been to fight but, with the solstice approaching, he focused his energy on his father instead, on protection not destruction, and father and son had been led from the room without a single drop of blood being spilt.

His face burned with shame – he should have fought. Laeli would have fought.

And be dead for it, a voice whispered in the back of his mind.

They were alive, and unharmed. All Kiarda had to do was wait until Rhodiri's return to the earth. Mahelivar swallowed. He'd told Laeli to be back by the solstice, and now he wanted to scream across the mountains that separated them to stay where she was.

Mahelivar wished he could reach her. There was nothing she could do right now and part of him didn't want to talk to her, worried she'd get it into her mind to come charging in here and try and rescue them. He wanted to hear her voice, to see with his own eyes she was alright, like she'd assured him she would be. She was playing a dangerous game, but she was smart, if reckless, and he had no choice but to trust her. Mahelivar grinned. He pitied those humans in Estilleon. He'd been dealing with his sister and her foul temper for over one hundred years. If Thalion came out of this alive and still smiling … Mahelivar recalled the look on the human's face the morning he and Laeli rode from Eshlune. Thalion was gazing at her like she was a precious jewel he'd uncovered, his thoughts a muddled mess, everything in his head clouded with her face.

The last thing Mahelivar advised his sister was to keep her wits.

'You think I won't?' she said quietly as her horse was led out, the animal pawing at the ground, as impatient and ill-tempered as its mistress.

'I think you might be distracted,' Mahelivar murmured.

She laughed lightly, her eyes finding Thalion across the lawns. He was already on his horse, his posture more relaxed than Mahelivar had seen it in the time he'd been with them. Thalion met Laeli's gaze, her laughter dying, replaced with a slow smile. Mahelivar could hear the furious beating of her heart, could hear the blood as it shifted through her veins in response.

He nudged her. 'Alright, I admit. He's got a pretty face.'

Laeli mumbled something he didn't hear but caught the meaning of.

'There are some things even I don't want to know, Laeli.' His sister and the human had spent the better part of the last three days locked away; apparently Laeli was learning about Estilleon's history and political structure. Mahelivar was certain she was learning which part of Thalion's body she liked the most.

'And here I was thinking you lived for court gossip, Mahelivar.' Laeli turned a cheeky smile on him. 'Make sure those arseholes do nothing but talk about me for at least a few days, alright? And tell them I know they're dreadfully jealous.'

He laughed as she swung herself onto her horse. Thalion joined them, managing to tear his eyes from Laeli's face long enough to acknowledge Mahelivar with a curt nod. Laeli moved off, beckoned by Solen, who had been scowling for a week.

Left alone with Thalion, Mahelivar rubbed at his face. 'If she …'

'She won't,' the human said firmly.

'If anything happens to her, know I'll strip the skin from your body while you're still awake,' Mahelivar said simply. His magic tingled in objection at such a threat. Acts of violence were not things he usually engaged in. He kept his eyes on Thalion's face, his expression stern. 'I'll make sure I take my time and I'll make sure you feel every moment of it.'

Thalion's unnerving blue eyes were dazzling in the muted light beneath the trees, and his smile was as relaxed as the rest of him. 'Noted.' His face became serious. 'I'll keep her safe, I promise.'

Mahelivar sighed and shook his head. 'You might find that more challenging than you think. Laeli has a habit of not thinking about her own safety. So, while she's keeping an eye on you, keep an eye on her.'

Thalion glanced at Laeli, clearly having a hushed argument with Solen; her arms were folded, a deep scowl on her face as Solen gestured wildly at the air around them. 'That won't be difficult.' Thalion had the balls to give Mahelivar a wink, turning his horse around and joining a frustrated Laeli, whose fists were now clenched as Solen stalked away from her. Smoke coiled from the length of her hair.

Mahelivar bit back his sigh. The captain of the fae guard was going to be impossible. Maybe he needed to take a field trip to Avivers for a while, to help them prepare for Kiarda's impending arrival. Maybe he shouldn't have been such an arse forty years ago. Laeli had impressed their father with the severity of the grudge she'd been holding all that time.

The last Mahelivar saw of his sister, she was sitting proudly in the saddle, her swords nestled in their scabbards, the braided length of her hair disappearing over her shoulder. As she slipped beneath the trees, she didn't look back.

Outside, snow was falling lightly, the lawns peppered with white, and Mahelivar's thoughts drifted to Solen and the fae guard. He knew the captain had escaped after fierce fighting with Kiarda's soldiers and was now hiding out in the forest with some members of the guard and Witches. Kiarda had come in here ranting and demanding Mahelivar tell her where they were, but he had nothing to say, and she'd snarled at him before slamming the door.

'You're worried for your sister,' Rhodiri said. Mahelivar turned from the window. His father was sitting up, face pale and pinched as his magic slowly slipped away.

'I'm more worried for us.'

'Kiarda won't kill us.'

'How can you be so sure?'

'She'd have no one to gloat to if she did,' Rhodiri said, a ghost of a smile crossing his face. It faded just as quickly as it appeared. 'You were still young when I sent her away so you wouldn't remember her that clearly. She wasn't always like this – so cold and remote, so brutal. She was caring and sweet as a child.'

'What happened?'

'I happened. When the Cailleach chose me to rule, something broke inside her.' Rhodiri looked at his son. 'I don't want that to happen to you and Laeli.'

'Laeli's made it very clear she doesn't want the crown, Father.'

'I know what she says, but she may change her mind,' Rhodiri replied gently. 'Just be prepared for that, is all I mean. Power is an intoxicating thing, Mahelivar, and the power the Earth bestows on you once the Cailleach gives her blessing is another thing entirely.'

'What is it like?'

'Like light, and the richness of the most fertile earth. Heat and trickling water. The sweetest air.' Rhodiri smiled. 'Maybe you will find out soon.'

Mahelivar knew that, on his father's death, either he or Laeli would receive the blessing of the Earth. He also knew that they might not keep that power. When the Cailleach came, before the wheel turned the final notch that would end the hours of the winter solstice, she would look into their hearts and if they were not pure of thought and intent, if she was not pleased with what she saw, she would not bless either of them with the right to rule. He swallowed.

His father regarded him with a critical eye. 'It's time you start thinking like a king, Mahelivar.'

'She might choose Kiarda,' Mahelivar said.

Rhodiri shook his head. 'She won't. Kiarda is too proud and bitter to understand that. She has not changed in over one hundred years.'

'She has the Cailleach's tools. Surely that means something?' Mahelivar pulled his hand through his hair. 'Kiarda's magic …'

Rhodiri's face folded into a frown. 'What she has done goes against the very rules of nature, of the Mother, and I cannot see the Goddess rewarding such a thing, can you?'

Mahelivar shook his head, but in truth, he didn't know what to believe.

The following morning, Kiarda paid them a visit. The locks on the suite doors clicked and hissed, and the floor to ceiling double doors were flung open dramatically as Kiarda breezed in, flanked by two Air Witches and two guards, armed with long spears and daggers.

'Such a party,' Rhodiri commented. He was standing by the window, watching the snow flutter to the earth. 'Anyone would think you were worried about something, Kiarda.'

Kiarda ignored his jibe. 'Where is your daughter?'

Rhodiri said nothing.

Mahelivar watched his aunt's face closely. She smiled, a slow, cat-like smile that made his skin crawl. He could feel the power radiating from her – her own water and air magic, a touch of fire, as well as the power she had gained from holding the Cailleach's tools. The hammer was dangling from her belt, the weight of it not bothering her, and the staff was clutched between the fingers of one pale hand. She tapped it on the ground and any warmth that was left in the room was sucked into the staff.

Kiarda crossed the room to perch on the edge of the grand bed. She ran her fingers over the bedspread lovingly, tracing the patterns woven through the thread in gold and green, glancing almost fondly at her brother. 'Do you remember when these rooms were our father's?'

'I remember,' Rhodiri said tightly, turning from the window.

'He thought I would rule.'

'He was wrong.'

She fixed the King in a deathly glare. 'You stole that power from me.'

'I stole nothing,' Rhodiri growled. 'The Cailleach looked into my heart and decided it should be me. Are you implying I tricked the Goddess, the Mother of us All?'

'She made a mistake,' Kiarda purred, stroking the staff reverently. 'She knows that.'

'Does she?' Rhodiri murmured. Kiarda narrowed her eyes, then turned her icy gaze on Mahelivar. She pushed her magic inside his head, and he slammed a block of tightly woven branches over his mind. Kiarda laughed.

'I could break through you know,' she said. 'But I don't want to hurt you. Not yet.'

'What have they promised you, Kiarda?' Rhodiri asked. 'Are you so eager for revenge on me that you would let two human men manipulate you?'

'You don't understand, brother,' Kiarda said, her voice drenched in soft death. 'It is I who am manipulating them. What neither of them have been able to grasp, these humans who so willingly allied themselves to my cause, is that I am not prepared to bow to them, not for a second. So, after Eshlune is mine by right, I will first take Estilleon, then Merawuld, and things shall be as they once were – the humans will again bow to the fae, and they will never forget that I spared their miserable lives.'

Rhodiri shook his head. 'Things are not as they were a hundred years ago, Kiarda. They care for the land now more than they once did. They look after it and manage it carefully. They walk softly and hear her music. They dig the earth but tend the soil.'

'And the halfkin? Those poor wretches neither you nor the humans want?'

Mahelivar started, and his aunt saw. 'Touched a nerve, did I? I don't need to get inside your head to see that this is an important matter to you, Mahelivar. I would bet my crown that your father hasn't done a thing to help them, unlike myself.'

'Unlike you,' Mahelivar retorted, 'I don't wish to help them for my own gains. I don't need to get inside your head to see that.'

Kiarda pulled back her lips in a snarl and turned for the door.

'Kiarda, the Rift,' Rhodiri said quickly. 'It can't be left unguarded. If the Lasair escape, everything you want to save will be gone and this will all be for nothing.'

She was silent, her back to him, spine stiff, but she was listening.

'Let my Fire Witches do their job,' Rhodiri implored. 'It's been too long already.'

'Fine. But if the guard comes near my soldiers, they'll be killed.'

'You'll tell them that first, won't you?' Rhodiri asked tightly.

'Of course.' Kiarda's tone softened. She glanced at her brother over her shoulder, and Mahelivar saw for the first time how similar they looked, how the shape of their eyes was the same. He saw the same eyes when he looked into the mirror, or when he looked at his sister's face. 'They're my people too, Rhodiri. I don't want to kill them.' Kiarda swept from the room, the door locking behind her.

With a sigh, Mahelivar curled into one of the plush armchairs, tucking his long legs beneath him.

'Will she do as she says?' he asked eventually.

His father nodded. They could hear murmured voices outside the door.

'You used to always sit like that when you were a child,' Rhodiri said affectionately. 'Your mother and I called it your deep-thinking pose.' He sat in the other chair, his expression tight. 'You can't let her push your buttons.'

'I know.'

'I'm sorry I never wanted to talk about the halfkin, Mahelivar.'

'Why didn't you? What have they done that is so terrible?'

Rhodiri sighed. 'It isn't that simple. There are hundreds of years of history there. What happened when our people walked in the human world so freely isn't easily forgotten. How we were treated – as different. At first, a mutual trust existed but, as time passed, the humans shifted that trust into jealousy and their eyes, once turned to us in friendship, became narrowed at our power, at the things that marked us as different to them.'

Mahelivar considered this, then uncurled his legs and sat forward, leaning towards his father. 'We can't change what lies in the past, but what if the halfkin were shown the right way? I know the council's concern has been the halfkin's unscrupulous morals, but they have been doing what they needed to survive. If someone were to help them, give them the guidance they need, give them the opportunity to thrive, what's to say they won't be a benefit to us, or to the humans?'

His father smiled. 'You sound like your mother. Ever was she one to care for those left behind, whether it be a bird that fell from its nest, or something greater.' He sat back and closed his eyes. 'When you are King, you can change things. Shape the world as you want to see it, Mahelivar – be brave enough to shape the world as it should be.'

CHAPTER ELEVEN

Light cut through the darkness as Ash opened her eyes and a pale stone ceiling swam into focus.

She knew that ceiling.

Her head throbbed. Her mouth was as dry as old paper and her stomach heaved uncomfortably. She grabbed at her belly as a cool hand touched her forehead and her eyes closed again. She was so tired!

'It's okay, just relax.'

She knew that voice. The hand stroked her forehead, lifting away for the space of a breath, returning with a damp cloth that smelt of lavender and peppermint. 'Nerida, is that you?'

Nerida was silent. Ash prised her eyes open again. Sunlight poured through the window by the bed, bleeding into eyes that were tender and gritty. Her friend was sitting on a stool by her bedside, a bowl of water balanced on her knees, blonde hair half spilling from beneath her white cap. There were shadows under her eyes, as if she hadn't slept. Ignoring the pain in her head and her rolling stomach, Ash sat up, reaching for Nerida's hands, grasping them tight.

'You're at the Academy,' Nerida said, her expression one of deep concern.

Ash swallowed her burning throat. 'How ...'

'Oh, some tall handsome blond man carried you through the front doors,' Nerida said casually. She dunked the cloth in the bowl, wringing it out and lifting it to Ash's forehead again.

'Yasper! Is he okay?'

'Gunshot wound to the shoulder but, yes, he's perfectly *fine*.' Nerida grinned, eyes twinkling. Ash burst out laughing, the sound so foreign to her ears she stopped abruptly, fidgeting with the woollen blanket draped over her. She felt drained, completely hollow inside and she knew, instinctively, it was because of the magic she'd wielded. She shut the doors of her memory firmly, not wanting to walk down that particular path right now. Later. She would venture along that road later.

Nerida's smile fell. 'I thought you were dead, Ash. I had no idea what happened after they took you on Mabon. I heard the rumour that you'd escaped the prison – we all did. It was all anyone was talking about for weeks. The Watch turned the city upside down looking for you. They came here and asked me a whole heap of questions. The High Mage himself came and asked after you.' She paused, head cocked to one side, as if seeing Ash for the first time. 'They said you expended some incredible power – more than I've ever seen from you, if what the Anomaly says is true.'

Ash's fingers stilled on the blanket, relief sweeping over her. Yasper and Senan were safe. 'I'll tell you everything, but first. Did a woman come here with us? A …'

'Whore? Yes. She's okay as well. A black eye, nothing more.' Nerida said quickly, her face screwed up.

Ash managed a smile. 'Gem's a friend, Nerida.'

'You have interesting friends these days, Ash. Whores and convicts, the Anomaly,' she said. 'He's not what I thought he would be. I imagined someone … I don't know … much more frightening.'

Ash let go of Nerida's hands, swinging her legs over the edge of the bed. Her knees wobbled. She didn't think she could stand if she wanted to, but still she tried.

'Where do you think you're going?'

'I need to see Senan.'

Nerida shook her head, gently pushing Ash back onto the narrow bed. 'He's been with Radella since he got here. He's come to check on you several times though. Did you know he's known Radella for years? Since they were students here. How strange is that? Radella – our cranky and sometimes boring White Woman, friends with the Anomaly?'

Ash's face fell. 'I've discovered a lot of things I thought I knew about people recently.' She licked her dry lips and attempted to swallow. Nerida fetched her a mug of water and Ash drank greedily, wiping her mouth with the back of her hand. Nerida was watching her closely, her bright eyes scanning Ash's face for signs of fever or sickness. Ash sat with her back to the wall, closing her eyes. Outside, the city was deathly quiet, as if it, too, was waiting to hear what she had to say.

By the time she'd told Nerida everything that had happened to her since Mabon, Ash was tired and thirsty again. She drank more water and ate some of the vegetable broth someone had brought, but couldn't stomach the bread.

Nerida chewed on her fingernails, her face twitching with concern. 'So, your soldier is in Estilleon, which is about to end up in civil war, and your Prince is stuck in Sitra, which has probably been invaded by now, and the High Mage ...'

'Tortured me,' Ash whispered.

'You don't need to worry about him anymore,' Nerida said fiercely.

Ash didn't share her friends' assurances about Gedeon. She could feel her fire beneath her skin, its power damp and weak. She lifted her hands to her eyes, examining them, wondering what they had done. There was a bitter taste in her mouth. Ash swallowed the bile that rose in her throat.

Nerida sat back. 'What will you do now?'

'I don't know. I need to see Senan, Nerida.'

'Rest.' Nerida's voice was firm. She placed her hand on Ash's forehead; Ash was so tired she couldn't resist. She lay back down and slipped away into a dreamless sleep as Nerida pulled the blankets up and tucked them around her chest.

When she woke, the room was shrouded in darkness; through the slit of a window, Ash could see the moon, stars sprinkled across the sky. She knew that view; she was in her old room. Outside, the city was still and quiet – not a sound eased over the Academy walls or through her window. In her mind, Ash saw the Watch on each street corner, their hands on their weapons, eyes trained on a city under lockdown.

She sat up quickly, heart hammering, the feeling of Mal's hands on her body, her throat, so real she wanted to vomit. She scrambled for a bucket, anything, in which to empty her stomach. Someone thrust a bowl in her lap, and she vomited until her eyes streamed with tears and she was sobbing.

'Steady, Ash,' a voice mumbled. 'Breathe. You're safe.'

Senan had taken Nerida's place. The darkness could not hide the shadows on his face, or the unhealthy pallor to his skin. Ash wiped her mouth on the cloth he handed her, setting the bowl down carefully. He'd expended much magic himself.

A memory forced its way through the doors in Ash's muddled mind.

The High Mage, huddled on the floor, surrounded by fire, the skin melted from his face.

'Did I kill him?' she asked in a small, terrified voice.

'No.'

'What happened?'

'He tricked you into releasing your magic. Do you remember the Bloodstones?' Senan asked.

She nodded. 'The red stones.'

'Yes.'

'What will he do with them?' She didn't want to know, didn't want to think about her magic in the High Mage's hands. Her hands twitched, as if she could call her stolen magic back to where it belonged.

Senan rubbed at his face wearily. 'I don't know. It will depend if he knows how to use them.' He paused and looked at her, his gaze deeply worried. 'Let's hope he doesn't.'

'Darian ...'

'He's dangerous. Very dangerous. And Gedeon ... I worry about what he has planned, what he will do with your magic.' Senan's face darkened.

'We need to get out of the city,' Ash whispered. 'He can't catch me again. Or you,' she paused, eyes wide. Those doors swung wide, and the truth of everything rushed in, making her gasp and tremble. 'Oh Senan. I remember! I remember everything!'

The Mage-Witch managed a smile. 'I'm alright, Ash. I dread to think what would have happened had you not released your magic. You saved us both, I think.'

She looked at her hands, clasped firmly in her lap. 'I said I wouldn't use my magic to harm anyone and look what I did.'

Senan leant forward on the chair. 'Ash, look at me.'

She swallowed and raised her head.

'It wasn't you.'

'I could feel it, the fire. It was like it had a mind of its own. I'm terrified that if I let it out again, I won't be able to control it and I'll hurt someone I care about.' She couldn't stop her hands from shaking, recalling the promise she had made the fire inside her. When she spoke, it was a whisper. 'It talked to me, and I saw ...' she paused, unable to be sure if what she had seen was real. 'I saw an old woman. She was wearing a veil and there was snow all around her.'

Senan's eyes sparkled, and he squeezed Ash's hand gently.

'You saw the Cailleach, Ash.'

'What?'

The Mage-Witch nodded. 'What did she ask of you?'

Ash frowned. 'How did you know she asked something of me?'

'Because she is a goddess; *the* Goddess. She would not show herself to you, especially at that moment, if she didn't want something in return.'

Senan was watching her closely. 'The Mother does not make demands lightly, Ash.'

What will you give, daughter of fire?

Ash made herself hold his eyes. 'She didn't ask me for anything.'

Senan just looked at her, and she knew that he didn't believe her. She fidgeted with the blanket, but he didn't press her. 'Are we safe here?'

'Yes, for now. Sleep. Everything will be here when you wake.'

Ash shook her head, but suddenly, she was tired, more tired than she had ever been. She cast a quick glance at Senan before she lay back down and closed her eyes.

When she woke again, it was morning. Ash scurried out of bed, dressing in the clothes someone had left on the back of the chair – her old clothes, her students' uniform of simple, pale linen and sturdy shoes. She tucked her hair under her cap, stepped out into the hall and froze.

The Cailleach had spoken to her, called her 'daughter of fire.' Ash frowned, her magic tingling at the memory of that voice, of the power in it as she begged her fire not to leave.

What will you give?

Ash shuddered and shook her head. Later. She would think about it later. For now, they needed a plan. She took a deep breath and headed down the hall. She passed a few people who gave her curious looks and, one girl, a wide berth. Ash hurried past the dining room. She couldn't blame them. This whole thing – the curfew, the rations, the state the city was in – was her fault.

Ash found Senan with Radella in the White Woman's office. She knocked lightly, and a voice called her inside. Radella rose from behind her desk, surprising Ash by crossing the floor to fling her strong arms around her, holding her tight. Ash breathed deep the scent of herbs with ink, wax, and baked bread.

'Thank the Mother you're alright, Ash.' Radella pulled back to stare into Ash's face. 'You hid it all this time?'

'I'm sorry,' Ash whispered, not understanding why she was apologising.

Radella sighed. 'It isn't your fault you were chosen to bring this magic back into the world.' She let Ash go and rubbed at her face. 'Whatever you need, whatever help I can give, you will have it, both of you,' she added, glancing at Senan.

'We need to leave,' Ash said as firmly as she could. 'If we're gone, surely Gedeon will remove the curfew? Surely life here can go back to normal? No one else will get hurt.'

Radella huffed. 'I'm not so certain. That man is enjoying his power too much since Her Majesty fell ill.' She frowned, returning to her seat. Bright light flooded the room from the window behind Radella's head, illuminating the rows of books stacked on shelves and the polished surface of the desk. 'She isn't responding to treatment. If the Queen dies, it will be without an heir.'

Ash glanced out the window, to the city beyond the walls, where life had always continued on without her. 'The throne,' she mumbled, suddenly remembering her lessons in politics and history. She pulled her arms around herself, looking from Radella to Senan. 'If Gedeon takes the throne, he will have complete control of everything, won't he? No one will be able to stop him.'

'Ash, you can't give up because, if you let him break you, then you've let him win,' the Mage-Witch said firmly.

She turned on him, her magic stirring beneath her skin, still slow and wounded, but rising with her temper and despair. 'How am I supposed to stop him from … I don't know what he wants!'

'The most common way people give up their power, Ash, is by believing they didn't have any in the first place,' Radella said gently.

What will you give?

When Ash left the room, her thoughts were churning.

CHAPTER TWELVE

Hadrian's eyes were gleaming. Mealtimes were the only times Thalion saw the Chieftain these days; Hadrian was often locked in his official room, doing what – Thalion didn't know. His father had recently returned from Whitemouth after an extended visit with Brenna. He could imagine the two men scheming long into the night. While Hadrian had kept his business secret from his son, Thalion got the feeling Brenna knew everything, including whatever it was that had his father grinning like a feral cat.

Laeli sat on Thalion's right side, Eira's features planted firmly on her face.

'I'll be leaving in a few days,' Hadrian announced, that grin growing broader until Thalion thought it would swallow his father's face. 'Kiarda has requested my presence in Eshlune.' He drank deeply then set his cup down; the thud echoed around the room while, outside, the wind pulled at the castle with claws of ice. 'That blasted fae guard has been giving her trouble. Nothing Kiarda's soldiers can't handle, but still. She's asked me to oversee the capture of the Guard, and if they won't be caught, she is more than happy for me to kill the lot of them. Apparently, there are Fire Witches still running around that cursed Rift doing whatever it is they do. I have to leave them alone but, if they get in the way, I can't guarantee there won't be accidents.'

Laeli stiffened. Thalion touched her foot with his reassuringly – it was all he could do in that moment.

Hadrian's eyes crawled over her face. 'Your mother is quite the woman, isn't she?'

'Of course,' Laeli replied with a haughty toss of her head. 'Were you expecting her to fail?'

'No,' Hadrian said. 'But I didn't think it would be so easy.'

Laeli sipped at her drink; her hands shook slightly enough that it could be passed off as excitement. 'What of the King?'

'Still locked up, him and his boy. They haven't been able to find the daughter. They're searching the forest for her but she's proving tricky to catch.' He shifted his gaze to Thalion, not seeing the tiny, smug grin that passed across Laeli's face as she turned her eyes on her plate. 'They'll find her soon enough. There's a contingent of the Queen's Army camped on the other side of the Rift. It might be fun for the men to do some hunting in the forest.' He laughed gleefully.

'What is the plan after that?' Thalion asked, keeping his tone even.

'That will depend on Gedeon. He assures me he will have control of the city soon. Once that happens, we will send our men right through the guts of the Queen's useless army and, from there, to Tyllcarric to see what Gedeon has to offer us,' Hadrian answered. 'To see if the High Mage's promises ring true.'

'And if they don't?'

Hadrian's smile became savage, his eyes dark. 'Then we take what was promised by force. If it is war the High Mage wants, it will be war he gets and the blood of his people will water their fields for decades.' The Chieftain sat back, that smile still planted on his face. 'If Gedeon is as smart as he thinks he is, he won't double-cross me. I've put up with his platitudes for long enough.'

Thalion toyed with his knife, running the tip of his finger along the blade; Laeli's meal was barely touched. 'Am I coming with you to Eshlune?' He prayed his father would say no. He didn't think he could walk into that forest, into Laeli's home, and swing a sword at anyone, not now.

Hadrian gave him a long look before he spoke again. 'No. I need you here. Can I leave Estilleon to you while I'm gone? Can I trust you not to fuck it up?'

'You can.'

Hadrian grunted his uncertainty. 'I'm leaving Cuyler behind, to help you deal with any … issues and help you keep an eye on things.'

Keep an eye on me, more like, Thalion thought, but he nodded.

'Runa, Freda, Arne and Frode will stay here, and the rest will come with me, along with men from each village. Two hundred all up,' Hadrian continued. 'I'll be taking some of the fighting men from the castle as well. You won't need them. The rest, send down to the Pass.'

'So many men,' Laeli cut in, her voice clipped.

Hadrian's eyes narrowed. 'What's your point?'

'I wonder why you feel the need to take such a force with you. Surely a smaller contingent of your warriors can deal with the fae guard,' Laeli pointed out. She sipped at her drink, her eyes on Hadrian over the rim of her goblet.

Colour rose in Hadrian's cheeks but before he could speak, Thalion put his hand on Laeli's arm. 'You don't have the right to question the Chieftain, Eira, regardless of the alliance with your mother. You need to remember that.'

Laeli put on a good show of pouting and looking unimpressed, but Hadrian's eyes were on his son. Slowly, he smiled, an approving smile, one that Thalion rarely saw. Laeli excused herself, running her hand over Thalion's shoulders – he could feel her anguish through her fingers.

When Hadrian finally granted his leave, Thalion took the stairs two at a time. Laeli was tucked up under the blankets, her hair spread out over both pillows like an ink curtain. He paced in front of the fire, chewing his lip. He couldn't begin to imagine what was churning through her head. She rolled over with a deep sigh.

He kicked his boots off and peeled his clothes away, sliding into bed. Laeli curled against him, burying her face in his chest. Her breathing was ragged, muscles tight. He kissed the top of her head, slid his hand down her arm until he found her fingers, and squeezed.

She burst into tears, clinging to him while she sobbed. He didn't know what to say, didn't know what to promise her, so he held her as she cried.

'I want to go home,' she whimpered.

His heart pinched. 'I know.'

She sat up, her face streaked with tears, her eyes desperate. 'It would take me less than a minute, Thalion. He can't add his forces to hers if he's dead.'

Thalion rubbed at his face, his heart thundering. 'The Chiefs, not to mention Kiarda and Gedeon, would expect me to take his place, Laeli, and I can't do that. I won't march two hundred men into your home. I won't order them to kill your people.'

'You were happy enough to kill my people before.' Her face was tight.

'You know I would turn the wheel back and change what I did if I could.'

She wiped her face with the edge of the sheet. 'I know. I'm sorry. I didn't mean …' She sniffed and lay down again. 'I'm going to kill her. For each life she has taken, I'm going to cut off a limb and when I run out of limbs, I'll carve out her organs one by one and feed them to the wolves,' Laeli whispered venomously, before exploding into tears again.

Thalion stroked her skin until she cried herself to sleep.

Over the next few days, Thalion walked cat-soft and light, allowing his father to crow as much as he needed. On the day of Hadrian's departure, man and horse shared breath in the frosty air of a morning that dawned with clear skies and aching cold, the land brushed with fresh snow.

Elan led the Chieftain's horse from the stables, the great black beast pawing at the ground, churning the snow beneath his hooves into mush and eyeballing everyone around him with distaste. Thalion hated that horse, the way it watched him, the way it went for whatever piece of flesh it could close its teeth around. He had always thought his father and that beast were perfectly matched.

The rest of the men were already mounted and ready to go. Thalion caught Ulfe's eye, then Niall's. He wished his father had chosen to take Cuyler instead. The Chief of Silverward was standing at the bottom of the steps, arms folded as he surveyed the men before him.

Hadrian came charging from the castle, longsword buckled to his hip. His smile was wide, as happy as Thalion had ever seen him. He paused when he reached his son; Thalion noted the dark hair shot through with grey and the lines of his father's face, deeper than he had realised. Hadrian clapped Thalion on the back and continued down the steps. The wind picked up, whipping their hair about wildly, blasting their faces with a cold so intense it burnt.

'Keep the home fires burning, boy,' Hadrian said, swinging on to his horse. 'We will have a great feast when I return.' His eyes lingered on his son's face long enough to make Thalion's stomach tighten, then he kicked his horse in the ribs and rode at a gallop from the yard, the men following him one after the other, a stream of horseflesh and fur, the snow flying behind them, the wind licking at their bodies.

From where he stood, Thalion could see over the castle walls, out over the landscape and the river, winding like a dark serpent across the earth, snow piled high along its banks. In the distant north, the mountains began their march onto the land, their peaks coated in ice, dark green fir trees clustered at their base. The Bone Mother's grip was tight, and he wondered again if his father was right, if the Goddess Bridghe had indeed forsaken them; for it seemed the warmth of summer would never come.

A black bird soared low to the ground, its shadow a crisp outline on the Bone Mother's blanket. The bird followed Hadrian's party a while, before veering back towards the castle.

'The Morrigan,' Laeli whispered, nodding at the bird. Thalion watched the bird come closer, before it swooped upwards on powerful wings and disappeared over the castle. He wasn't sure he shared Laeli's belief about the Goddess of Fate. Laeli let her head rest on his upper arm.

'Now, we can begin,' he said in a low voice.

She nodded, and when he looked, her eyes flashed green, making him smile.

It was time to peel back his shadow and unveil what was hiding within. He wanted to be able to step away and see what lay at the heart of him. He didn't know what he'd find, not truly. He knew what he wanted to see – all the things that could have been and what he would have done had he been able to act without fear of the consequences. His father thought he was weak and indecisive, and maybe he was.

Thalion was about to take the biggest risk of his life and he had no idea whether it was going to pay off.

Cuyler turned to glance up at them. His expression remained neutral, but the way his eyes slid over Thalion's face caused his heart to race. Laeli gave the Chief a baleful stare. He gave her a curt nod in return, marching up the stairs, not looking at either of them.

Like Brenna, Cuyler had been in Hadrian's pocket for as long as Thalion could remember. He'd been Chief of Silverward since Thalion was twenty and was not only respected by his people, but by many of the other Chiefs as well, including Frode. Cuyler's allegiance could prove key. If Thalion could convince him, he might have a chance with some of the other Chiefs, like Freda in Emrelfel, another staunch supporter of Hadrian's rule.

Then there was Whitemouth, both the biggest key and the largest threat to what Thalion wanted to accomplish. Brenna was buried so deep in his father's pockets Thalion knew he'd never reach him, but with

Brenna gone to Eshlune, he was hopeful Caden might listen, but it wasn't a hope he clung to – Whitemouth was a hard place, its rulers even harder. Breaking through those walls would be challenging.

That night, they dined with Cuyler, who had made himself at home in the castle. Healy served them roasted meat, carrots, turnips, and loaves of bread. She placed jugs of mead on the table, not looking at anyone. Cuyler grabbed her as she passed him, pulling her into his lap. Her eyes were desperate and wild as he closed his arms around her.

'Let her go, you piece of human shit.'

The table fell silent. Laeli held Cuyler's gaze, her face daring him to speak. Cuyler laughed and let Healy up with a slap to her backside. Thalion's grip tightened on his mug as the half-breed scurried from the room.

'Just having some fun,' Cuyler laughed again, then indicated Laeli. 'You going to let her talk to me like that?' he demanded of Thalion.

Thalion sipped his drink, setting his mug down with deliberate slowness. He said nothing. Muttering, Cuyler turned back to his food, glaring at Laeli with undisguised anger. Without a word, she got up and left, slamming the door on her way out, her temper as hot and quick as the fire that simmered in her veins.

'She might be easy on the eye, Thalion, and no doubt easy to fuck, but you might want to think about smacking some sense into that mouth of hers or someone else might do it for you,' Cuyler said, not bothering to veil his threat.

'You lay one hand on her, and I'll slit your throat myself,' Thalion shot back. He forced a smile onto his face, showing it was all one big joke. Cuyler narrowed his eyes then laughed, taking a long sip of his drink. Thalion sat back in his seat, as relaxed as he could be, toying with the remains of his dinner.

'Why didn't you go with the Chieftain? I thought you would have been the first to put your hand up for some adventure.'

Cuyler set his mug down, the thud echoing through the room. 'Your father wanted someone to stay behind and give you some guidance, Thalion.'

'He doesn't think I can do this by myself?'

Cuyler held his eyes. 'He's not sure you're ready.'

'What do you think?'

'I think,' Cuyler said, leaning forward, 'that you're young and idealistic, and the country doesn't need ideas, not right now. We need to get through this winter and then, maybe, once this is all over, your father might be more willing to listen to anything you have to say.'

'What do you know about my ideas?'

'Nothing,' the other man said. 'I only know what your father has said.'

'And that is?'

For a moment, Thalion didn't think the Chief would answer him, but then Cuyler said, his voice low, 'That's a conversation for you and your father to have.'

CHAPTER THIRTEEN

When Fox woke, it was silent. The last time she'd experienced a silence this deep was waking in a tiny hut in the forest with a hole in her side. The time before that, it was to find herself alone in a dilapidated building in the back streets of Tyllcarric. Her brother had been taken, ripped from her in the night.

Elan. She could hardly believe he was here, in this miserable country. It had been a shock to see him, standing there with Caden's horse, his face turned towards the earth, as still and compliant as he had always been. She had been the wild one, the one that caused their mother to groan and the other halfkin they knocked about with as kids to want to leave her behind whenever they entered the market square with twitching fingers.

Fox rolled over, ignoring the ache in her belly and her side. She would get out of here, and she would go get her brother. They would run away together, and they would finally be free.

The silence of the morning made her suspicious. Normally she could hear someone downstairs, whether it be Caden or one of the others. The Chief, Brenna, had gone with the Chieftain. Fox hadn't been told but she'd heard it, her fae senses flying through this house, as they had been since the moment she arrived. Although she had no love for the fae, she hoped the Chief and his men would be cut to ribbons by the guard. She hoped they left their bodies in the forest to become food for animals.

If it was up to Fox, she'd string them up by their ankles and let the Morrigan's ravens take them apart. She'd remove their eyes and then drop them into the belly of the Rift. She'd peel their flesh from their bones an inch at a time, or dump them into the middle of the Forest of Wights.

But it wasn't up to Fox. She had no say in anything, not anymore.

She was exhausted, not used to being on such high alert all the time. She was not used to looking over her shoulder. She was not used to her skin crawling from her body or jumping at the slightest sound.

Any power she might have had in her old life vanished the moment she was thrown into that stinking carriage.

She had been brought here to serve Brenna, whose home, a large and lavishly furnished place close to one of the taverns, was to be her new prison. Fortunately for her, the Chief didn't like her much. His big fist had shattered her ribs when she spat at him and clawed at his face. Unfortunately for her, Caden didn't mind a fight and had happily thrown her on the back of his horse and taken her with him, not caring that she hissed and moaned with the pain of her broken bones.

Fox eased her aching body from the pitiful bed with its lumpy mattress and threadbare blankets. It never crossed Caden's mind to give the girls nicer beds – it wasn't like he slept in any of them. There were two other halfkin girls in the house, one heavily pregnant, shuffling her grotesquely swollen stomach around the place as she managed to sweep the floors and clean the benches in the kitchen.

Fox poured some water from the ceramic jug into the wash basin and splashed her face, before going to peer out the window.

Whitemouth was more of a town than a village, and Fox had learnt it was one of the largest settlements in Estilleon. From the back of Caden's horse, she had seen two taverns and an inn, although Fox couldn't imagine who would choose to stay here. That day, she'd counted and taken note of everything she saw: two blacksmiths, the forges and bellows pumping in the chilly air; a butcher and slaughterhouse; apothecary; trading post; two bakeries, the smell of fresh bread tickling her nose; a clothing store; and a shop that sold tools – sickles and scythes, hammers and horseshoes; and an armoury. She'd made careful note on where that was located as they'd continued into the belly of the town.

The people she'd seen that day were dressed in layers of clothes to ward off the cold, while she shivered like a wretched thing on the back of Caden's horse. She hadn't wanted to touch him, but if she hadn't grasped his sturdy middle, she'd have fallen several times on their journey from the castle.

The streets of Whitemouth reminded her of the city – arranged in a collection of paths and alleys running in all directions from the town square, which featured a well. Caden led her on a convoluted trek through the village, no doubt designed to confuse her sense of direction, but she'd be able to find her way out of there blindfolded and in the dark.

Outside the window, the streets were coated in a layer of snow that would have covered her ankles, had she been allowed out to see it. A wicked wind snuck through the window and Fox shivered. She untangled the bundle of clothes from the foot of her bed and dressed as warmly as she could before tying her hair beneath a ragged scarf. The front door of the house opened and closed, and rough voices floated up the stairs. Fox took a deep breath and headed down before they came looking for her.

She still hadn't learnt to curb her mouth or keep her face clear of her hatred. Every time Caden caught her glaring at him, he slapped her and, at night, when he was drunk … Fox didn't like to think about it. It meant he left Cora and Faren alone, most of the time.

The first time Caden had forced her onto her back, she kneed him in the groin and had been slapped so hard for it her ear rang for a week. The second time, she bit him, and he hit her hard enough she thought he'd broken her jaw. The third time, she tried to claw his eyes out; so he bound her wrists. By the fourth time, Fox just shut her eyes and pretended she was somewhere else, in a hut in the forest surrounded by trees and leaves and a soft breeze that smelt of earth.

Light-headedness and nausea were her constant companions. Bursts of searing pain raced through her when she moved, and she was certain her ribs were still broken. The pain that two nights ago was sharp and blinding was now dull and distant, but still there – a throbbing reminder of where she was and what she was now.

A plaything. A toy. A husk of who she once was.

Her goal was to survive this prison, to be free, but she knew freedom wasn't given – it had to be won, and the secret to freedom was courage. It was difficult to have courage when, for the first time in her life, she wanted to give in to the darkness. She kept telling herself the same thing: *you are allowed to scream, to cry, to rage, but you are not allowed to give up, Fox.* It became a mantra, filling her head each morning when she pulled herself from her nightmares to face the grey sky and the suffocating insides of this house.

Downstairs, Caden and two others were seated at the table. She didn't know the names of the other men and didn't wish to know. She could feel their eyes on her as she crossed the room, entering the kitchen. Faren was nowhere to be seen and Cora was likely doing the washing at the boiler at the rear of the house. Fox scowled. The wind was so cold in this place it could cut a person in half, yet a pregnant woman was expected to wash the laundry or get on her knees and scrub the floor.

Fox fetched vegetables from the storeroom. A slab of meat had been left for her, which meant someone had been out to the butcher to get it. She wasn't allowed out yet. She dragged a large cooking pot from the cupboard and fed some more wood into the fire, checking the hook above it was attached properly. The last time it hadn't been and dinner had ended up in the coals – and Fox had ended up with a black eye.

She set about cutting the meat, imagining that each slice through that dead flesh was a slice through Caden's body. She risked a glance at him.

She'd start at his face – carve off those fat cheeks, then the muscle of his upper arms and the layer of fat around his belly.

Caught in her daydream, she didn't realise she was still looking at him.

'What are you looking at?' he barked at her.

She dropped her eyes; her hand tightened on the handle of the knife. 'Nothing.'

Caden laughed. 'Look your fill, girl,' he said smoothly. 'Later.'

She said nothing. His chair scraped against the floor and, moments later, he was standing in the kitchen with her, his body filling the space, his breath filling the air. Fox kept her eyes on the table, on the meat, the blood oozing from it, as he ran the tip of his finger down her cheek. She closed her eyes, begging herself not to flinch, although her skin was screaming, and she thought she'd be sick. Caden's finger trailed down her face, over her jaw, down the column of her throat, over the bruised collarbone, until he reached the curve of her breast.

'See?' he whispered, lowering his face close to hers. 'I can be gentle.'

Fox could kill him with one flick of her wrist. The knife was like lead in her hand, her body hollow, eaten from the inside out. Her hand stayed where it was. She kept her eyes closed as he continued touching her, the men in the kitchen watching them. She could smell their excitement, Caden's lust, and her own fear.

'You're a pretty thing, for a half-breed,' Caden murmured. 'I was glad when the Chief decided he didn't want you.'

Still, she said nothing.

His strong fingers threaded through her hair, and he pulled, hard enough to force her eyes open. 'You should be more grateful.' He let her go, swaggering his way back to the table.

Trembling, Fox prepared the stew, listening to the men talk with half an ear, begging Faren or Cora to come back so she didn't have to be alone.

In her dreams, she wasn't alone.

She was in the forest with the sun on her face, a pair of gentle arms cradling her body.

CHAPTER FOURTEEN

'I want to avoid any fighting within our borders but I'm aware that might not be possible. I'll start with Cuyler. I hope he's willing to listen to me.' Hadrian had been gone for two days and Thalion had arranged to meet Cuyler in the Hall to discuss the next strike at the Pass. He knelt to look into Laeli's face as she slipped her boots on.

'I was a child when Kiarda ripped my world apart,' she told him quietly. 'I remember it as clearly as if it were yesterday. I remember the screaming and the terror – I was so scared, Thalion. After it was over and I learnt what had happened to Faleria, I made two vows – to guard the Rift, because it was all that was left of her, and that I would never be like Kiarda.'

'You're not like her.'

'Aren't I?'

He traced circles on her knee, his touch burning through the cloth of her pants. 'You don't have to be involved in this if you don't want to be, Laeli.'

'I do, though, that's the thing. My father has ruled for two centuries, and he has done it without bloodshed, without fear and hatred. Power doesn't have to be like that. Power can be kind and gentle and compassionate. It doesn't have to mean fear and terror.'

When Thalion was gone, she took several deep, steadying breaths. She could still recall the day, one hundred and thirty years ago, when her father sat her and Mahelivar down, their mother lingering in the background, her beautiful face sad. That day, they learnt they had lost their aunts, one to a fiery death and the other to the ice of Veshlir. It was a lot for them to take in and, as she grew, Laeli's fascination with the Rift, her remaining connection to Faleria, grew as well – as did her abhorrence of her aunt Kiarda and what she had done.

She had to trust in her brother to keep their father as safe as he could while she did her job here. Laeli was determined there would be minimal life lost, even if some of these people made her blood boil. She glanced at the door – she cared for Thalion, and she cared what happened here.

That surprised her.

She hadn't expected to care so much. She could be herself with Thalion; she was at ease with him, her guard down, as relaxed and comfortable as she'd been in a long time – perhaps ever. He didn't expect anything from her.

Laeli swallowed, not wanting to think about what that truly meant, not now, not when there was still so much to be done.

Standing, she stretched the muscles in her back and arms, feeling her magic flow through her in anticipation. She made sure her glamour was in place, then walked calmly down the stairs and turned towards the Great Hall.

There were four armed men waiting outside the door. They nodded at her, hands on their weapons, their eyes taking in her clothes and the swords they couldn't help but notice and she wondered what Thalion had told them. She didn't know their names, and vowed to change that, after this morning was over with.

Laeli hoped Cuyler would listen. Her senses told her he was smart, and smart men were often dangerous and skilled at playing games; but they could also be shrewd and canny, and able to see what others did not.

The Chief of Silverward was sitting in Hadrian's seat at one end of the long table like he owned the place. Thalion was sitting at the other end, his expression neutral, the length of that table a buffer between them – between the old and the new. The castle was still, as if it, too, was waiting for what was to come.

Laeli took a steady breath and stepped into the room, closing the door behind her. Cuyler's eyes narrowed in confusion as he took in her clothes, the form-fitting dark green and the weapons at her hip and back. She headed straight for Thalion, throwing off her glamour as she went. Cuyler's eyes widened, and he pushed his chair back in fright, climbing to his feet as she positioned herself beside Thalion, one hand on the back of his chair.

'What is this? What the fuck is going on?'

'Sit down,' Thalion said calmly. 'We need to talk.'

The Chief was shaking his head, his hand gripping the hilt of his sword, but he did not draw his weapon.

'You're being given a chance to listen to him,' Laeli said, nodding at Thalion. Cuyler's eyes combed her face. 'All you have to do is listen.'

'Who are you? Where's Kiarda's girl?'

'Dead,' Thalion said.

'My name is Laeli Enthelme,' Laeli said quietly.

Comprehension dawned on Cuyler's rugged face. 'What have you done, Thalion?'

'Put your weapon down and sit, please,' Thalion said, gesturing to the seat Cuyler had vacated. He held out his hand, waiting, his expression carefully schooled – patient, and calm.

The other man shook his head. 'You've got to be joking.'

Laeli did not have Thalion's cool manner. 'Sit down,' she commanded. Cuyler did, unable to refuse the power in her voice, in her stance. Smoke swirled from her skin. No one spoke for a long moment, until Cuyler laughed hollowly.

'This is a coup?'

'If you want to name it such,' Thalion replied. 'Last night, you called me an idealist. There are things I want to share with you. My father won't listen. I'm hoping you will, because you're a smart man, Cuyler, and I need smart men with me now.'

Cuyler's gaze fell on Laeli's face. He did nothing to hide his scepticism or his suspicion of her and she didn't blame him. He wouldn't be smart if he didn't mistrust her. Still, he said nothing, his grip tightening on the hilt of his sword.

Thalion leant forward to rest his elbows on the table. 'Is this what you want? To be planning a war with Merawuld in the middle of winter? Surely, you must have questioned how much the Chieftain has been willing to sacrifice for his vendetta?'

'Your point?' Cuyler folded his arms.

'My point is, things don't have to be this way,' Thalion said. 'Between us, we can call this war off, bring the men home and get through this winter with food in our bellies and warm fires.'

'And when your father finds out?'

Thalion didn't reply.

Cuyler sighed. 'You've gone mad. She,' he pointed at Laeli, 'has fucked with your head, haven't you, Witch?' He glared at her a moment, before addressing Thalion again. 'Send her home and let Kiarda deal with her, and we can forget this lapse in your judgement. Your father doesn't have to know about any of this.'

'I can't do that, and I think you know it.'

Cuyler stared at him, as if seeing him for the first time and, for a wild moment, Laeli thought he was going to agree, but he stood and shook his head. 'Then we've nothing to talk about.'

Thalion's calm slipped. Laeli knew he could feel this going wrong, could feel himself losing before he began and she wanted to tell him to take a breath, take a moment, but they didn't have a moment. His voice was urgent when he spoke. 'Cuyler, do you care about the people in your village?'

'You know I do,' the Chief of Silverward said in a soft voice.

'Did you receive what you asked for at the gathering?'

'Not entirely,' Cuyler muttered. He sighed and shook his head again, the action slow, regretful even. 'Your father is my Chieftain, and I won't stand against him, Thalion.'

Thalion turned to Laeli and gave her a nod. She hesitated, seeing the unhappiness on his face, but when he nodded again, she hurried across the room, flinging the door open and sticking her head out, gesturing to the men waiting there. They came in, hands on their weapons, faces steely, and Cuyler put his head in his hands, then sighed deeply. Without being asked, he stood.

He regarded Thalion gloomily. 'You have no idea what you're doing, do you?'

'Then help me,' Thalion urged.

Shaking his head, Cuyler left his sword on the table, along with the dagger from his hip, and let the men lead him out.

'Is this the best way to deal with him?' Laeli asked quietly. She knew that the Chief was being escorted upstairs to the room Hadrian had given him, where he would remain under guard until he either agreed to talk, or Thalion came up with some other solution for him.

'I can't risk him contacting my father or any of the other Chiefs. Tomorrow, we ride for Westhelm. We'll take Jorah and Tomlin with us, and hope Arne is more willing to talk than Cuyler was.'

Laeli nodded, leaving him sitting there, a deep frown on his face. Now that Cuyler was out of the way for the moment, she headed straight for the dungeon, doing what she'd wanted to do ever since she saw Jarlath in that cage before Samhain. In the castle, Healy organised a simple room and a warm bath, her face a picture of deep sympathy.

Jarlath sat on the bed with his head in his hands, his shoulders shaking. He was thin and damaged, his eyes haunted. From the window, they could see the Peaks, their caps coated in white, and on the other side of that mountain range was Sitra, where Kiarda had turned the world upside down.

'I know you want to run off to find Ash, but you can't, not yet.' Laeli forced some softness into her voice. She was desperate to run off as well, torn between her loyalty and worry for her people and her family, and the promise she'd made to Thalion. 'I think things are about to get messy here, Jarlath.'

Jarlath peeked at her through trembling fingers. 'What do you mean?'

Laeli ran her hand over her face. 'Thalion wants to avoid civil war and, if we move fast enough, we might be able to, but it isn't safe for you to go back to Eshlune right now. Hadrian has joined Kiarda in Sitra and—'

'Then I must go now, Laeli! If Ash is in danger—'

'She isn't. You need to trust me.'

'You've said that a lot lately,' he mumbled.

She didn't have time for his petulance. She opened her mouth then stopped, pulling her anger inside her. He loved the girl and wanted her to be safe. She wanted to tell him he shouldn't have left her in the first place, but she was certain he'd chastised himself enough over that. 'I promise I will give you the whole story soon, but for now, you need to rest, bathe and eat, Jarlath. You're thin and weak and in no condition to go anywhere in this weather.'

'Why are you doing this? Is it for him?'

'Yes, and no.'

Jarlath regarded her almost warily, as if he couldn't believe what he was hearing, couldn't believe what he was about to ask. 'Do you love him? Is that why?'

Laeli held his eyes as she dipped her fingers in the bath, withdrawing them when steam curled from the surface of the water to caress her face. 'Get some rest, Jarlath.'

Two of the men from downstairs were guarding Cuyler's door. Laeli stopped and asked their names – Ari and Eric – and they hesitated before letting her in.

'I'll be fine,' she assured them, but their faces didn't relax. She put her hands on her hips in disbelief. 'Seriously? I don't need Thalion's permission. Open the door.' Still, they didn't move. 'Do I have to go back down there and get him?'

The men exchanged a look before Ari, tall and lanky, with red hair, and the younger of the two, shook his head quickly, and pushed open the door.

Cuyler's room was almost as large as Thalion's, with a generous bed, chairs, and a small table and a fireplace. Two windows were positioned either side of the bedhead, offering views over the landscape. In the far distance, Laeli could see Whitemouth rising from the snow. The Chief was standing at one of the windows, his arms by his side.

Laeli shut the door quietly, watching him, taking note of the line of his body, the broad shoulders, his muscles thick from swinging a sword. His stance was fluid, a soldier's stance. She cleared her throat and Cuyler jumped when he noticed her standing by the hearth. The fire had simmered to nothing, and the room was like ice. She bent and fed wood into the flames and waved a hand, the fire roaring into life.

'Neat trick,' Cuyler mumbled. 'You his bodyguard, Witch? Or his whore?'

Laeli ignored his crude remark. 'Is it so difficult to listen to what he has to say?'

Cuyler's face twisted. 'I don't know what he's told you, or what you're doing here, but he's more like his father than he'd have you believe. Remember that, Witch. I've known him since he was born. When you want to know what's going on in his head, you come back and talk to me.'

'What do you mean?'

He gave her a secretive smile and turned away from her.

She left him to enjoy the view.

CHAPTER FIFTEEN

Ash stared at the slice of moonlight on the floor. The silver-blue light was like liquid, spreading to fill the gaps between the stones. It reminded her of how the moonlight would splash over the floor of her bedroom as a child, where she'd stare out the window and wish she were somewhere else when she should be sleeping. Now, what she wouldn't give to be at home in her old room, nothing more than another young woman of the village, mapping out her future, perhaps dreaming of the Beltane festival where some young man might take a fancy to her.

The Academy was silent, everyone sleeping, caught in the dreams that normal people had, people who weren't plagued by a magic that shouldn't be.

At home in Brenveil, Ash experienced a persistent feeling she was out of place. She loved her parents, but something had always tugged at her, drawing her gaze north, to the Rift, the magic that lay within a beacon, tugging at the core of her. Sometimes she felt other people must know it, must somehow see that invisible chord that linked her to something more than the farms and the harvest that made her different to them.

She'd always known the truth about herself, though knowing it and admitting it were two vastly different things. She'd never been able to truly face the fact she was different, that, for some reason, fate had decided to give her something it had given no human for generations. Long ago, Ash had let it break part of her, let it be a catalyst for loss, for the things that went wrong in her life, for the choices she hadn't yet had the opportunity to make.

If it wasn't wrong to be a fire caster, would she still have hated that part of herself? Would Jarlath? Would he have feared her? Or would both of them have been able to simply accept it and let it be part of their lives?

She would never know.

It was time to face the truth – she had to start making decisions. Ash had always had this belief that the world was a place of transcendence, of oaths and loyalties and honour, duty, and love. Instead, the world was an open-ended game of cards where there were no rules and no one wins, except the dealer, who happily takes your coin and slides it into their deep pockets.

But Ash had never had any of her own cards on the table.

≈

Jarlath's voice was at her window. 'Come on, Ash. Wake up.'

Rubbing her eyes, she crawled out of bed and padded to the window. 'What are you doing here?'

His fifteen-year-old face appeared. He'd broken his nose recently, playing rough with the other boys, and now it was crooked across the bridge, the faint smudges of bruising still visible beneath his eyes. He hadn't cared, wearing his injury like a badge, his admittance to some club she wasn't ever going to be part of.

Jarlath's eyes glittered, his mouth a slash of white teeth in the darkness. 'Let's go climb that tree of yours.'

She broke into a smile. Her father would have kittens if he knew they did this. Jarlath ducked out of sight; Ash threw a coat over her nightdress and crammed her feet into her boots. She pulled herself onto the window ledge, sliding out into the moon-soaked night, his arms closing around her before she hit the ground. His touch made her shiver, but now wasn't the time to acknowledge it. Jarlath grabbed her hand and they hurried through the quiet streets, the village around them sleeping, both feeling wicked and free. Ash loved the world at night – it was the one time when no one was looking at her.

The tree near the creek was her favourite. Tall, with broad branches that stretched protectively over the landscape, she loved the view from halfway up the trunk, where the branches created the perfect place to rest her body. It had been large with age when she first climbed it and now she had grown, while the tree stayed unchanged, branches dipping and dripping with leaves in the warm months, and with frost in the cold.

Out in the fields, the world was still, but the sounds of life burrowed into the night as they crept through the undergrowth. Ash listened: an owl, small rodents scurrying through the grass, the water in the creek tinkling as it meandered along its bed.

'Up you go.' Jarlath gave her a boost, not that she needed it, and she climbed, muscle-memory her guide in the dark. How many times had they shimmied up these branches? The bark was smooth under Ash's palms as she found her favourite spot and sat back, resting against the strong trunk. Jarlath joined her, stopping on the branch below, and, together, they watched the sky, the stars wheeling overhead, the branches forming a leaf-lined box to view the moon's path across the sky. A gentle breeze tickled Ash's face – summer was coming to an end.

'I'm going to join the army,' Jarlath announced.

Ash tore her eyes from the stars. 'What?'

His excitement was evident. 'I'm going to sign up. When I'm old enough, that is.'

'But … it's dangerous!' Ash argued softly. 'Why do you want to go and get sliced up?'

'Because what else am I supposed to do? Stay here?'

Yes, she thought.

'What's wrong with staying here?'

'I don't want to be a farmer,' he whined. 'How boring!'

The stars and the wonder of the night took on a dull hue as she listened to him talk about all the amazing things he would do and see; the whole time he chattered, one thought screamed through her head:

What about me?

~

As the flames danced, so did she. It was Beltane night, and the village was alive with the revival of summer. A pregnant moon hung in the star-coated sky. Laughter floated through the air, blending with the darkness and the flames that tickled Ash's blood.

For once, no one seemed to care she was out amongst them – Ash was able to just *be* without the stares and the whispers that had always followed her.

The bonfire cackled and she giggled, pausing mid-swirl in the line of dancers that wove around the fire. Jarlath was standing off to the side, his gaze flitting across faces grown oddly devilish in the distorted shadows and rebounding fire light. Ash willed him to look at her; when he did, she beckoned, and he shook his head with a bemused smile. She rolled her eyes and left the dance, going to stand by him, close enough that she could smell the warm, familiar scent of him – apples and sunshine.

'You're boring tonight,' she stated.

'You know I hate dancing.'

She laughed. 'You didn't hate it on Ostara, Jarlath. You looked ridiculous by the way.'

'I was drunk!'

Ash smiled, reaching up to remove the garland someone had placed on her head hours ago. The flowers were wilted but their perfume still held strong. 'Traditionally, you're supposed to crown me with these, but I guess it wouldn't hurt to break tradition for one night.' Before Jarlath could protest, she placed the garland on his head and burst out laughing.

He growled but left the flowers where they were as the bonfire leapt higher, sparks shooting into the sky. Ash swallowed; the tingling was in her palms again and she forced herself not to think about it, to focus on Jarlath's face, on the lopsided smile and the flames reflected in his eyes. She ignored the singing in her blood and bones as the heart of her pulsed with her hidden magic. She pushed it away, tucked it down deep.

Without warning, Jarlath slipped his arm around her middle. He was seventeen, a man, his chest grown thick, his arms tight with wiry muscle. A shadow dusted his chin and jaw – she wanted to touch it, feel the sharp hairs under her fingertips.

'Does it ever make you wonder,' he began, eyes glinting in the firelight, 'why so many babies are born nine months after Beltane?'

Ash's blood burnt. 'Other people's intimate lives are not something I think about, Jarlath, but hey, whatever you're into …'

He laughed; she could see stars in his eyes now.

'So,' he asked casually, his laughter fading; his fingers on her waist tightened. 'Will you be collecting any May flowers in the morning, Ash Griffyn?'

She blushed, glad of the dark. Around them, the crowd had thinned. It was nearing midnight, the turning of the tides, Beltane over for another year. Usually, Ash had a headache on these nights, not trusting that hidden part of her to stay hidden with so much flame around, but tonight she wanted to be out here.

She wanted this moment.

All she had to do was lean forward a fraction, and she'd be able to catch his mouth with hers. All she had to do was step closer and she'd be pressed against him, like she had been so many times before. But not on Beltane night, not in the fiery dark, and not when he was asking what she thought he was asking of her. She swallowed, her belly tightening.

To disappear into the darkness with him, to spend the night in his arms, to lie together as if they were … she could barely breathe.

He was looking at her; slowly, he removed the garland of flowers from his hair, and placed them back on her head. 'Ash, the May Queen.' His voice was low, softer than she'd ever heard it. Sparks shot the length of her spine.

She managed a smile, earning one in return. It lit up his face but, before he could kiss her, or her him, his brother came wandering over, demanding Jarlath take him home, even though Finn knew the way in the dark.

∼

'You're leaving.' Ash didn't try to keep the plaintive tone from her voice.

Jarlath nodded, reaching for her hands, but she pulled them away and hid them in her lap. They were crouched behind the grain silos on the edge of the field, where she'd been hiding for a whole twenty minutes before he found her. Earlier that day, their lives had been torn in two different directions – Jarlath to the army, and Ash to the city to begin her education at the Academy. So caught up in her own excitement that the path of her life was finally unfolding, she hadn't considered what it truly meant until he knocked on the door to her family's cottage and shared news of his own.

'It won't be forever,' he said.

'You're leaving *me*,' she said fiercely.

Jarlath's face shifted. 'Ash …'

It came, the tingle, the roar under her blood, stronger than it ever had been before. She shook her head, trying desperately to push it away. Jarlath reached out both hands and cupped her face, holding her steady so he could look into her eyes. His thumbs stroked her cheeks, the skin on his hands rough from working in the fields, his face soft, eyes half-closed.

'Ash …' he murmured. Something kicked deep in her belly, an ignition, a spark within, begging to be let out. She pulled away with a gasp. Jarlath reached for her again, but she shook her head, holding up her hands.

His eyes widened as fire licked at her fingertips, then her palms, spreading quickly down her arms. The hair began to lift from her scalp and as the fire rushed to swallow her body, Jarlath stumbled back.

She'd spent years telling herself it wasn't so, but there was no denying it now. She took a deep breath, trying to pull a layer of calm over her, but it wouldn't come. All she could think about was she'd never see him again.

'Run,' she whispered, and he shook his head, bewildered and scared, as confused as she was. 'Please. Just run.' She was crying now, unable to stop as the fire inside burst into the world, reaching out with hungry fingers to rip through the fields and lick at the silo behind them. It was free, finally free, and it sang and danced with a glorious surge of guilty power.

Through the flames and the smoke, Ash saw Jarlath's face. He was unharmed, unburnt, protected somehow. The fire spread around them, encircling them in blazing gold and red. Jarlath's eyes streamed.

'You're …' he began, shaking his head and coughing as the smoke swirled around them.

'A fire caster,' she finished, as the silo behind them gave in to the flame.

~

Sitting on her bed at the Academy, Ash closed her eyes. In her mind, she saw Jarlath's face as she had last seen it – the agony and confusion, the love – and the fear – in his eyes. The fear of what she was. Of what that meant, not only for him, but for her as well; she could see that now.

Where was he at this moment?

'He's alive,' she whispered. She had to hold on to that.

Her eyes were drawn to the night sky outside her window, the moon so clear and pure a thing, hanging above this world that was quickly turning on its head. In the distance, the spires of the palace rose, lit by silver light, and, below them, bathed in shadows like a great hulking beast, was the Keep.

Ash closed her eyes and, when she opened them again, it was to see a single star winking at her and she knew that without the obscurity of the dark, the stars couldn't shine.

She would be a star, from this moment on. She owed it to everyone – she owed it to *herself*. She would burn and blaze with light. The darkness that was steadily encroaching would not win.

CHAPTER SIXTEEN

It was a two-day journey to Westhelm, the weather bitter, the wind shrieking and clawing at them all the way, throwing snow in their faces. The depth of winter was getting closer; the wheel was turning. Thalion could feel Laeli's impatience – with him, with this whole situation. Not for the first time did he wonder if she regretted her decision to come here. She pushed her horse ahead of them, waiting until he drew level with her, Jorah and Tomlin behind him, barely veiled frustration in every line of her face.

The men hadn't said anything, holding their reservations behind their teeth, but Thalion knew they were trusting Laeli only because they trusted him. And he knew she knew it, and he knew it bothered her, but he didn't have the words for her, not today, not when Westhelm loomed on the horizon like a beast.

He'd felt Laeli's eyes on him for most of the journey here; she'd been watching him a lot lately, those sharp green eyes flickering over his face, reading him, the lines of his body, and the way he held himself.

Now, he was sitting stiffly in the saddle, the muscles in his legs and arms bunched up as they drew nearer to the village. Laeli watched him as he rested his hand on the hilt of his sword; an anxious gesture, one that he recognised but had never thought too much about, until now.

He wasn't sure he could do this. His father's voice was in his head, reminding him of all the ways this was going to fail before it even began. Thalion scowled into the wind and pushed the voice to the back of his brain, where its sting lingered like a thorn he couldn't dig out.

Westhelm was a sprawling village, the main streets lined with shops and trade guilds. There was a large tavern set off the village square, the shutters pulled tight against the wind and snow. Despite the weather, there were people milling about the streets, mostly women with baskets over their arms and children clutching at their mothers' skirts. Many stopped what they were doing as Thalion's party rode past. His belly flopped and his fingers dropped to caress the hilt of his sword again.

They found the Chief at his home, one that Thalion hadn't set foot in for years, always finding a way to avoid the place, to avoid Westhelm and its Chief altogether. They were led down a short, dark hallway and into a richly decorated main room with a long, wooden table. Tapestries hung from the walls and a fire blazed in the hearth; the room was stifling and dark, the air thick, a thin stream of light cutting through the gloom from the window behind the Chief's head.

Arne sat at the end of the table, his men flanking him, one standing either side, both heavily armed. He kept his expression smooth; nothing shifted in his dark eyes, and no muscle twitched in his strong jaw. His hair was long and dark, pulled back from his face in a series of tightly woven braids and decorated with beads of silver and bone. Heavy brows, a prominent nose, and wide mouth completed the picture.

The Chief sat back in his chair, eyes moving over them, his disinterest obvious. Thalion ground his teeth. Arne's conviction in himself was also obvious and Thalion felt Laeli's eyes touch his face briefly.

Arne gestured to the seat at the other end of the table, but Thalion did not sit. Arne held his eyes and Thalion knew the other man would see the stiffness in his spine – his weakness – but he could not make himself relax, no matter how many steady breaths he pulled into his lungs, no matter how hard he schooled his expression into one of calm.

The tension that had held him tight for weeks, months, *years*, had dug in deep.

Laeli took it on herself to pull out the chair for him, to place her hand on his shoulder and ease him into the seat, Arne watching her closely. With her hand bearing down on him, all her strength behind it, Thalion couldn't not sit, and did so with frustration he kept hidden but knew she'd feel. It annoyed him for a moment, how he couldn't hide a gods-darned thing from her, but this wasn't the time to think about it.

Arne rested a large hand on the tabletop. There was an ornate ring decorating his finger, like the one Thalion sometimes wore, the one he was wearing today. The symbol of Arne's family, of his village, was a hawk. It was engraved on the main door to his home, a motif repeated on the tapestries and wall hangings, the furniture, the silver mugs on the table, much like the wolf in the castle at Wilderun. Thalion glanced down at the ring on his finger, at the wolf that stared back at him.

Arne's lips curled. 'I understand your father has made you interim Chieftain while he is gone, but you didn't travel two days in this weather for a friendly chat, Thalion.' A pause. 'What do you want?'

Laeli removed her glamour, letting her true face be seen, but Arne and his men barely blinked, although the Chief's eyes lingered on hers with interest when she revealed who she truly was. Thalion's hand stroked the hilt of his sword again as Arne looked at him.

'So,' the Chief began, 'you've shown your claws at last, wolf pup.'

Thalion ground his teeth; the tightness in his jaw was painful and anger simmered beneath his skin, his father's voice echoing in his ears once more. Laeli touched his arm. He should have told her what to expect, but it hadn't crossed his mind, his head so tangled in memories.

He and Arne had never been friends; a strange sort of rivalry had existed between them since they were young; one that, when it first reared its head, Thalion didn't understand. They'd faced each other in the Stadium as younger men, their fights vicious. As Thalion had gotten older and Arne became Chief, Arne's animosity, his ambition and his desires, became clear.

It was power the Chief of Westhelm was after, and it was Hadrian's seat he truly wanted. Thalion's father couldn't see it, or, if he could, he didn't consider Arne any sort of threat to his rule. To Thalion it was obvious and, now, that desire hung in the air between them, so thick and heavy he could almost see it, and he knew Laeli would be able to sense it. From the corner of his eye, he watched her face fold into a frown, before her expression became smooth again.

Arne's eyes shifted between Laeli and Thalion, and when he spoke, his deep voice dripped with boredom. 'Make your offer, then. What can you promise me that your father, my Chieftain, can't?'

Thalion's answer was swift and sharp, his hands tight balls where they rested on his thighs. 'Autonomy.'

He felt Laeli look at him in surprise, but he held his expression, kept it composed. Arne's dark eyes were pinned to Thalion's face. 'Bullshit,' he stated.

'Why is it so hard to believe?' Laeli asked in a low voice.

The Chief didn't even look in her direction. 'The answer is no,' he told Thalion firmly. 'You can take your ideas of rebellion – or whatever you want to call it – go back to your castle and pretend to be man enough to wear your father's furs, Thalion. You may as well enjoy it while it lasts.'

Rather than grow angry, Thalion laughed. Here it was, as out in the open as Arne would ever let it be, and part of him relished this moment, this opportunity to say what he'd wanted to say for years. Through all the meetings, the gatherings, the moments where he could have said something, and didn't. Where he took the insults, outwardly letting them roll over him, while inwardly, a storm churned in his belly and his father did nothing.

'You'll never sit in my father's seat, Arne, no matter how much you might wish it – and I know you wish it. I know that, since you became Chief, you've practically begged my father's favour. You may as well have crawled from Westhelm to Hadrian's Hall on your knees, but he still would have turned you away. My father doesn't praise those who lick his boots.'

Arne's face finally shifted; his eyes flashed a warning, but Thalion went on.

'He knows what you want. I know it. The whole damn country knows it.' He paused and leant forward in his seat. His voice pitched low when he spoke next, and it was Hadrian's words, his tone, his threat, that left Thalion's mouth. 'You need to get Brenna out of the way, but there is truly only one path to my father, Arne.'

Beside him, Laeli stiffened. They had not discussed this and it wasn't something he'd even considered until now, until the moment presented itself. His fingers curled around the hilt of his sword in anticipation and his blood roared, thundering through his ears, drowning out all other sound. He kept his eyes on Arne, and smiled.

'Thalion,' Laeli cautioned under her breath, but the Chief of Westhelm had already taken the bait. He snarled, and the room erupted. Thalion sprang from his seat, drawing his sword and meeting Arne halfway down the table, unable to stop the feeling of relief that raced through him – he could let it out, all the self-doubt, the fear, the worry. He could let it out through his sword, through the one thing that he had true confidence in.

He could show his father, show everyone, that he could do this.

Thalion was half-aware of the others fighting, the sound of clanging swords passing through his ears, but he didn't take his eyes off Arne.

The Chief was skilled, but Thalion was better and, as another of Arne's men fell to the ground, he slammed his elbow into Arne's face, slipping behind him as the Chief clutched his broken and bloody nose. The blood pounded in his ears, raging through him, urging him on. Thalion fisted his fingers in Arne's hair, forcing his head back.

Pressing the glimmering blade of a dagger to the Chief's throat, Thalion blinked, not knowing how, or when, he had swapped weapons.

Silence, as thick and heavy as soup, spilled into the room. He didn't have to look to know Arne's men were dead.

'Thalion,' Laeli said firmly, but he ignored her, his attention on Arne, on the life he held between his hands. The vicious power of it swept through Thalion's belly.

'Do it,' the Chief whispered, the words a challenge. 'But no matter what you do, wolf pup, you'll always be that little boy who wished he was more like his daddy.'

'If I were my father, I would have done this years ago.' It was a whisper, the words for none but Arne. Thalion pushed Arne's head over the blade, and cut his throat. There was a roaring in Thalion's ears, a buzzing in his blood, as Arne's blood coated his fingers and dribbled down the front of his shirt. He let the Chief fall to the ground, his open throat gaping like a second mouth.

Thalion looked up and met Laeli's gaze.

He saw the horror painted across her flawless face. She held his eyes, then turned and left the room, not looking back. Thalion sucked in a breath, wiping his bloody hands on his legs. Jorah and Tomlin were watching him, but he found he couldn't look at either of them.

'Clean this up,' was all he said, before stalking from the room, his heartbeat still dangerously fast, adrenalin pouring through him, his father's voice still in his ears, reminding him about power, about what it meant to rule, what it meant to hold the fate of a country in his hands.

In the hall outside Arne's main room, Thalion leant against the wall, forcing his breathing to steady, forcing the anger in his blood to cool. He licked his lips, stood up straight, and rolled his shoulders, sliding his sword back into its sheath, and strode from the house.

Laeli didn't look at him when he came out, busying herself with her horse, checking the girth strap and bridle that didn't need checking. His stomach tightened but he didn't approach her, waiting until Jorah and Tomlin came out.

'I need you to stay here and talk to Will when he returns,' Thalion instructed them. Arne's Second was currently in Wildeview. Jorah nodded; neither man said anything about what had happened. Laeli was on her horse, her face composed, but Thalion could almost hear her mind ticking over. He wiped his hands on his pants again, knowing she would see the tremor he couldn't stop from dancing through his fingers.

'Get things in order here,' Thalion told Jorah as he swung onto his horse. 'Send a messenger with any supplies you might need. When Will wants to talk, tell him I'll listen.'

Laeli frowned at him but he ignored it.

He turned his horse from the village, Laeli following him, her eyes burning a hole between his shoulder blades.

That night, they camped off the main road with the sky dumping snow on them. It was the two of them and a guard, who stood outside the tent shivering in the cold.

'Is that necessary?' Laeli asked, motioning to the guard. 'It's freezing out there.'

'He'll be fine.' Thalion sat so he could take his boots off. He beckoned, patting the bed roll beside him. Laeli stared at his hand, at the fingers curled towards her. Blazing anger flashed across her face.

'Wash your hands first,' she snapped.

'What's wrong with you?' Thalion shot back, even as his stomach tightened.

'You didn't tell me you were going to kill him.'

'I wasn't.'

'Yet you did.'

He frowned. 'What did you think was going to happen, Laeli?'

'I don't know, but I didn't think I'd be watching you murder a man, Thalion. There are better ways to do things. Why couldn't you have locked him up, like Cuyler?' Laeli fumed. She glared at him as she paced the short space between the tent flap and the far wall. Smoke curled from her hair. His eyes tracked her movement, took note of the tension in her body, and suddenly he was angry, too, all the rage and fear he'd been feeling racing to the surface of him on a pair of great wings. He yanked his boot off and threw it across the tent.

Laeli stopped her pacing and folded her arms and the words were out of his mouth before he could check himself.

'If I'm not mistaken, you killed in that house as well, Princess.'

'That was different,' she hissed, fists clenched at his use of her title, at the way he spat the word. 'That was self-defence. What you did ...' She shook her head, disgust coating her features, and spoke through her teeth. 'What happened back there? Why did you let him goad you like that?'

He didn't know how to start explaining it to her, so he turned away instead, taking the coward's choice and not wanting to see the look on her face any longer. He was surprised when she didn't storm from the tent, climb on her horse, and vanish into the night.

He'd fucked up, he knew it, could feel it all crashing down around him, but it was too late to take it back, and that only made him angrier. Laeli refused to speak to him, to even look at him, and they spent an uncomfortable night lying next to each other, the space between them as cold as any sheet of ice. She still wouldn't speak to him in the morning, and Thalion hadn't slept, unable to stop his head from turning over and over and over.

By the time they rode into the outer bailey of Wilderun, Elan was waiting, his face tense, scruffy hair ruffled by the wind. 'There's been a messenger, from Emrelfel, and another from Whitemouth. They rode through the night to get here. The Chief of Westhelm is dead?'

'Good news travels fast,' Thalion mumbled and passed the reins over. Elan was watching him closely.

'My sister.' The halfkin was unable to hide the fear in his voice and Thalion realised the boy knew – that his sharp ears and sharper eyes had seen what was happening, had perhaps sensed it, the tension in the air surrounding the castle.

'I'll think of something,' Thalion assured him. It was just another thing to add to the growing list of things he had to deal with. He rubbed at his face, then headed inside, Laeli trailing him, the power of her glare almost nailing him to the wall in the Great Hall where he sat with a sigh and unfolded the note that had arrived. He read it quickly then left it on the table, pushing his chair back to cross the room and hold his hands out to the fire, his head still spinning. Laeli picked up the note as Thalion swallowed his stomach, pushed it back down before he dropped to his knees and vomited.

In Emrelfel, Freda had locked up the village and it was under heavy guard, and Caden had barricaded himself inside his house in Whitemouth and no one was allowed in or out of the town. Hadrian's traitor son would have his head removed from his body if he came near the place, and a special fate awaited the fae bitch who stood by his side.

'Oh this is just wonderful,' Laeli said darkly. 'Well done, Thalion.'

'Laeli —' he began.

'Don't,' she growled. The flames in the hearth crackled violently.

Thalion did not turn from the fire as Laeli strode from the room.

CHAPTER SEVENTEEN

Mahelivar's heart twisted painfully at the sight of so much snow stretched across the landscape. The great lawns of Sitra were coated with white, the vibrant green life buried beneath snow that didn't stop falling. If he were to go outside, it would cover his ankles. He wondered about the creatures of the forest; where had they gone when the snow began to fall? Winter did come to Sitra, but it was gentle and brief, over in a snatch of time, never lasting long enough to brown the grass or send life scurrying away.

Beneath his skin, his earth magic was sluggish. Where his blood would usually sing with life, it was now dampened by the cold and ice. He was tired, his body as soft as feathers, his energy depleted without that green life to fuel him. Mahelivar ran a hand through his hair, reaching inside for his magic, for the power of the earth. It came at a crawling pace. He turned his hands over before his eyes, watching the veins on the back of them flutter with a hint of green. He couldn't draw it any closer to the surface. He didn't bother with his air magic. Kiarda's net was still tight above them and his fire magic ... well, he could usually only manage a spark at best.

He remembered when his earth magic showed itself, one hundred and forty years ago. He was seven, close to eight, and woke one morning to find his room shrouded in plant life, the vines still twitching as they continued to grow. He'd been dreaming of plants, of the different hues and shapes of them. He'd seen his father's magic and had wanted his own with a hunger that burnt deep inside. His air magic arrived not long after, followed by the insignificant flutter of fire.

Laeli, on the other hand, was all fire, all the time. She burnt things, and she appeared to enjoy doing it, her eyes bright and her smile fierce. Once her water magic appeared she was tempered, but not enough so that she stopped trying to set her brother on fire. No one knew Laeli possessed any earth magic until she managed to dangle herself upside down from a tree while trying to reach a bird's nest. She'd spat fire and sparks at everyone who tried to help her, leaving herself hanging for hours, their mother waiting patiently until she managed to work out how to get down.

Mahelivar sighed. He missed his sister. He missed their mother. Fifty years she'd been gone, but it still felt like she'd walk through the door, kiss his father, and set to scolding her children for whatever they'd done that they shouldn't have. Mahelivar smiled. The number of times he'd taken the fall for something Laeli did …

She would repay every debt she'd ever accumulated by staying alive.

Rhodiri was sleeping, as he did most of his days, his lifeforce slowly slipping away like the last warm breath of summer. Mahelivar cast a glance at his father. He appeared older than he'd ever been, his face drawn, skin lacklustre, and, when he opened his eyes, Mahelivar saw the weight of his two hundred and thirty years there.

Was it his fault? He wondered. His father had been urging him for years – decades even – to start thinking like a king, to throw off the child and become a man. Had all that time wandering in the human lands chasing halfkin, trying to find where it was he fit, somehow to blame for the situation they found themselves in?

Because surely this alliance between Kiarda, the High Mage, and the Chieftain of Estilleon was not something that sprang up overnight. But even Thalion, seated at his father's right hand for much of his adult life, didn't have much to share, no more than they'd already worked out for themselves. The warning hadn't come too late, but Mahelivar's actions certainly had.

Instead of focusing on helping a young Witch find her magic, he should have been helping his people, his land, prepare for war.

No one, not even his father, had imagined Kiarda's bitterness and her need for revenge would lead to such bloodshed and pain.

Mahelivar had no idea how many were dead. How many had died fighting for their freedom.

Like he should have.

With a sigh, he turned back to the window. His path was less clear now than it had ever been. His hesitation, his doubt in himself – this was what had led them to this. Kiarda had waited until the moment when Rhodiri would be weakest, when his power had waned enough that Eshlune was left without the defensive magic of the King of the Forest.

Instead of questioning himself, Mahelivar knew he should have been more alert. More watchful. More prepared.

Like his sister was. Laeli's natural suspicion of everything was what he needed. Her shrewd gaze and her capacity to make decisions, to push people into doing what she knew was right. Her ability to spring into action – in the past, he'd criticised her rashness, that fire that drove her, but now he would give anything for the smallest bit of what his sister had.

Her knowledge of who she was.

If it came to it, and the Cailleach deemed his sister should be Queen of the Forest, he would be the first to fall to his knees. Laeli would have protected Eshlune with her life. He wanted to believe he'd have done the same, if given a chance. He wanted to believe he would have fought.

But he knew he wouldn't. He wasn't like his sister. The fire in his veins was small, smothered in the richness of the earth. His father would say Laeli was a hot head, whereas Mahelivar was steadfast, strong, and grounded. Patient.

But it wasn't patience that was needed now. It was fire, and courage. And he didn't have enough of either.

Outside, across the lawns, the snow shimmered and flexed, and then it was gone, and Mahelivar was looking once more on the gentle sweep of green. He stumbled back, then forward, pressing his face close to the glass. There was no sign of Kiarda's Air Witches, no sign of any human or fae life in the forest beyond the lawn. The trees once again wore their dress of leaves, and the sun was warm – he could feel it through the glass.

He reached out his hand, touching the smooth glass, withdrawing it quickly. It was as cold as it had been since his aunt arrived, with the snow and ice trailing her like a cape. Outside, a raven called, its harsh screech echoing across the world.

Something flickered at the tree line, an amalgamation of shadow and feathers. A shape quickly took form until a tall woman dressed in a black gown, a cloak of feathers trailing along the ground, stood at the edge of the forest. Her hair, as black as the wing of the raven, shifted in the summer breeze tickling the leaves on the trees. She stepped free of the shadow of branches and leaves and began to cross the lawn, heading straight for him, her sharp gaze piercing the glass of the window. A sword appeared at her hip; her fingers touched the hilt and her lips curled into a smile.

The Morrigan.

Mahelivar swallowed as she drew nearer. The Goddess of Fate had never shown herself to him. Without breaking stride, she stepped through the glass to stand beside him, gazing out over the rolling lawn that was once again painted white with snow.

'The King who shall be,' she said, her voice low and musical, like the wind through the bare branches.

He shook his head. From beneath her cloak, the Goddess withdrew a card, holding it between pale fingers flecked with feathers. She released it and it hung in the air, spinning slowly, Mahelivar's face changing before his eyes. On one side, he saw his face as he was now and, on the other, the face of the King of the Fae, a pair of antlers rising from the crown of his hair.

'Choose,' the Goddess said.

'It isn't my choice,' Mahelivar argued.

The Morrigan cocked an eyebrow. 'Isn't it?'

It was all he had ever wanted, to be King, but why? Was it a true reflection of his desire, or was it the dreams of a boy who wanted to be like his father? He frowned, unsure of where to start, where to begin looking for those things that were most important. The answer should be there, in his heart, but he was scrambled, his thoughts and his desires a jumbled mess.

He forced his mind to still, forcing the swirling chaos that was his thoughts to rest.

The human world flashed into his mind, the world he found on the other side of the Sparkling Waters. Rather than tyrants and purveyors of environmental destruction, humans were warm-hearted and affectionate. They were hard-working – he had watched the men in the fields, their muscles straining, brows gleaming with sweat – as happy as they were when the fruits of their labours were rewarded. Humans were kind – he had watched a barefooted village girl scoop a baby bird from the ground, wipe it free of dirt and shell, and shimmy up a tree to place it gently back in its nest. He had watched a boy feed sugared water to an injured squirrel, and he saw the tenderness and love of human mothers for their children. Humans, he learnt, were capable of sacrifice, great love, and loyalty. They lived in each season as it passed, resigned to the influence and power of the Earth. Even if one in ten of them stopped to smell a flower, or run their hands over the trunk of a tree and feel the texture of its bark.

He fell in love with them – even with their flaws. Their arrogance and conceit, their bitter words and selfish natures, fascinated him; here was a race that only experienced life in a mere moment. Their emotions were short, sharp, powerful, and he began to see these weren't the flaws of humanity but the flaws of all – weren't his own people not capable of causing grief and harm to each other?

Laeli called him a fool; his father called him a stubborn romantic. They couldn't see what he saw – beauty and grace, potential for greatness – in humanity.

So Mahelivar went in search of the halfkin, hoping to find that bridge between the worlds, hoping to find knowledge and an understanding of humanity, but what he found roused an anger so bitter he tasted it for decades. It was in the halfkin that he truly saw the effect of the worst humanity had to offer, and the worst of his people as well.

Why, he'd asked his father, did the fae reject them? Why did the humans?

There was no answer that satisfied Mahelivar, and his time on the other side of the Sparkling Waters grew. He met the Mage-Witch and brought him home to dine at his father's table. He met a halfkin assassin who tried to kill him first, then snarled at him second, then asked him why he bothered. Why hunt for knowledge that no one wants to give?

He had no answer. His sister thought him mad. 'Let it go,' Laeli had said. 'They made their choices.'

But they hadn't, and Mahelivar knew that. The halfkin had the power of choice taken away from them through the oppressive power of rejection. He vowed to change it, but his arguments fell on deaf ears, his words turning in circles until he had confused himself.

And he thought of his own people, who dwelt within their forest realm, shut off from the rest of the world, content in their long-lives and in the ever-turning of the wheel. He thought of the fae guard, who trained and patrolled their borders, their presence a reminder to the world beyond to stay out. No one was welcome. No one could possibly offer the fae anything they, in their intellect and their superior abilities, could not offer themselves.

But now, as the world Mahelivar knew fell apart around him, he still didn't know where his truth lay. He still didn't know if he was worthy of the choice the Morrigan was presenting him with.

'How do I know what is right?' he asked the Goddess.

She fixed him in her steely, black gaze. 'You don't. You are free to choose your choices, but you cannot choose the consequence that accompanies them. You must be willing to accept the responsibilities of your choices, young King,' the Morrigan answered. 'But'—the card stopped spinning and Mahelivar was face-to-face with the image of himself as King—'make sure your choices reflect your hopes, not your fears, because the choices you make will determine the future.'

'Isn't the future already decided?'

'No one's future is decided, until it is decided. There are two possible paths for you, son of the forest. Choose the one that best reflects the you that you wish to become.'

Mahelivar gazed out the window again, at the layer of snow. In his mind, he could see shoots of green life pushing through the cold earth. He could feel them beneath the snow, straining for a sun that could not warm them. 'When the Cailleach looks into my heart ...'

'She will see those choices and she will see the consequences.' The Morrigan's voice was soft. 'Know that the Mother, like the Fates, sees the consequences of your choices, good or bad. What she will see will depend on what she looks for.'

The Goddess snapped her fingers. The card vanished and she turned to face him, taking his chin between strong fingers. Her eyes raked his face, tore right through to the inside of him, and he knew she could see everything – every doubt and every moment where he wished he had acted differently.

'You must decide what *you* wish to see, what you wish this world to be like,' she said softly, kindly.

The answer came swiftly, swooping in with such precision it took his breath away.

Peace.

Unity.

The Morrigan nodded and released his chin, a small smile playing on her lips. As she stepped through the glass, she became a black bird, the darkness of her shadow imprinted on the carpet of snow outside the window. A black feather lay on the white stone near the window. Mahelivar bent to collect it, tucking it into his pocket, where it hummed with a power of its own. As he watched the snow continue to fall, he made his first clear decision.

The choices he would make from this moment would reflect the man he was to be.

He thought of Kiarda, of Gedeon and Hadrian, and their desires for control, but the Earth did not need to be controlled – it was control itself. The gentle authority of nature's assurance – how dawn would always follow night, and spring would always follow winter – was all he would need to guide him. He would look deep into the Earth and find the answers within.

Mahelivar would give himself to the Mother and love the richness of her body like he loved his family and his people – *all* people.

CHAPTER EIGHTEEN

Laeli didn't sleep for two nights and, on the second, her eyes gritty with lack of rest, she crawled from bed and threw on her thick, woollen dress and cloak, padding down the stairs in the dark. When she closed her eyes, she saw only death and blood, and her own hands as she plunged her sword into a man's gut. Was she any better than Thalion? She glanced at her hands, and it was his she saw, slick with blood.

She knew Thalion was capable of such violence – all humans were – and it wasn't the act itself that shook her, but the way it had happened, so calmly and with such measure. She closed her eyes, forcing steady breaths into her lungs, but all she could see was Thalion's hand and that weeping blade.

To the fae, all life was sacred, part of the balance of nature, an integral cog in the wheel that turned the year. Taking life should only be in protection of your own, or the lives of those you cared about, and only as a last resort. She'd killed a man in Westhelm, sliding her sword through his gut, the blade cutting into his flesh with ease, not thinking until after the act was done.

Kiarda's face flashed into Laeli's mind. How many lives had she taken already? What had led her aunt to hate so deeply that she was happy to kill? To go against everything they believed in?

The stones were bitterly cold under her bare feet as she paced the halls, muttering to herself. Her thoughts were caving in on themselves and her anger was simmering below her skin, burning with a fire of its own. Laeli ran her hand through her hair, pulling her bottom lip between her teeth and chewing on it.

Thalion had offered no explanation for his behaviour and they'd still barely spoken. Laeli couldn't. She couldn't look at him without seeing the darkness in his eyes when he killed Arne. The darkness in his face when he killed Bran.

She thought she knew him. She'd been watching him for weeks, assessing and learning who he was. She'd learnt the way his face shifted when something worried him, the way his eyes would darken when he didn't agree with her opinions, and the way his mouth twitched when he was desperately trying not to smile or laugh. She could read his body language, recognising the tension in his shoulders as a sign of anticipation but not stress, and the way his gait would shift from casual, long strides to quick, sharp steps when he was agitated. He, like her, was prone to pacing. He wrung his hands and rubbed at his face when he was thinking. He ground his teeth some nights or didn't sleep much at all, and he mumbled to himself when he thought no one was around.

But she didn't truly know him, she understood that now, and it made her want to put her fist through the wall. She wanted to scream into the bitter darkness that shrouded the castle, or run out into the shrieking wind and not look back; but she'd made a promise to her father, and she was determined to keep it, no matter how difficult.

Her eyes were drawn to the ceiling above her head. Upstairs, Thalion lay snoring. Even in his sleep, a frown rested on his brow and his face was tight. She'd half considered punching him awake, but crawled from bed before she did something she would regret.

Pushing a breath through clenched teeth, Laeli forced herself to be calm. She went back upstairs, walking straight past Thalion's room. She needed some answers and, if he wasn't going to give them, there was someone else who might.

The guard on Cuyler's door had fallen asleep; Laeli slipped the keys from his pocket with deft fingers.

The room was bathed in thick shadows, light flickering over the walls from the blazing fire in the hearth. Cuyler was asleep. Laeli bit her lip, then approached the bed and shoved the man around until he woke. Seeing her standing over him, his eyes widened, and he sat up swiftly as she scooted away to stand with her back against the wall. The shock on his face dissolved and his expression shifted into something closer to a leer.

'Well, well.'

Laeli narrowed her eyes as Cuyler laughed and climbed from the bed. She kept her eyes on his face, not on the flesh he had on display. He took a step towards her, and she held up her hand in warning; flames danced on her fingers, just enough to remind him who and what she was.

He laughed again. 'You're absolutely glorious. Much better to look at than the other one, I'll give Thalion points for his choice.' Cuyler's eyes combed her body; there was a sheen to his skin that made hers want to crawl from her body. 'I bet he thinks he's died and gone to some paradise every time he gets to fuck you.'

Laeli's flame grew, until she was holding a ball of it in her palm. 'You do realise I could snap your neck? And I might, if you don't stop looking at me like that.'

The smile didn't fall from Cuyler's face. 'You won't – you have questions. I take it things aren't going to plan?'

'Put some clothes on,' she snapped.

He smirked at her. 'Am I making you uncomfortable?'

Her ball of flame floated from her hand and moved close to Cuyler's head. He hissed and quickly got dressed.

'There. Happy now?'

She ignored him. 'How well do you know him?'

Cuyler rubbed at his face. 'He has no idea you're here, does he?' When she didn't answer, he nodded, as if her being in his room in the middle of the night with questions on her tongue was to be expected; he waved at the chair near the smouldering fire. 'Sit, make yourself comfortable, Witch. What do you want to know about the man whose bed you're sharing?'

Laeli didn't sit, and neither did the Chief. 'Can he do this?'

'Betray his father? He already has,' Cuyler answered, gesturing towards her. 'If you mean his little coup … it depends.'

'On?'

Cuyler's eyes flashed. 'If he can keep his cool. He's got his father's temper, but you already knew that. You want to know if he's got his father's cruelty, don't you? Whatever has happened since you two locked me in here has scared you. He's scared you.'

'I'm not scared of him,' Laeli said hotly. 'I'm worried that he's not—' She stopped abruptly, her cheeks warming. Cuyler was watching her with a knowing expression. She glared back, the ball of flame floating above their heads, throwing warm light and deepening the shadows in his temporary prison.

'If you want to know what a man is truly like, give him a taste of power,' Cuyler mused. 'Thalion is a dreamer, and there is no place for dreamers here. He doesn't think things through. Why do you think his father has never listened to him? Hadrian has been waiting for the boy to grow up. Yes, I know, he's a man, all that bullshit, but he doesn't know shit about what it means to lead a country. I don't know what things are like in your world, but here, it takes strength and balls to make decisions that affect thousands.' He paused. 'You don't know anything about this place. This isn't your pretty forest and your fancy palace. You have no power here, Princess. If you want to help him, convince him to give this charade up.'

Laeli waved her hand and the ball of fire vanished. 'Perhaps, if you were willing to dream yourself, you wouldn't be locked in here.' She turned for the door, her stomach churning, mind spinning.

'Come again if you need to know more. Next time, I'd prefer it if you were naked as well. I've never had the pleasure of fae flesh.'

She was being baited, but she didn't care. She was across the room with Cuyler's head between her hands before he could blink, forcing the man to his knees, a foot jammed between his shoulder blades. He sucked in a breath as she tightened her grip on the bones of his skull.

'Fae enough for you? You can't outrun me, or better me with a sword, and I'm stronger than you'll ever be, so go on, continue to insult me, continue to show me what sort of man you are, and I'll snap these fragile human bones.' Laeli squeezed his head tighter, her foot pressing against him; he gasped, his heart racing furiously, sweat pouring from his skin. She licked her lips, tasting the fear that saturated the air. 'One twist and that will be the end of your miserable life, and Thalion would never know. I'd have you buried under five feet of snow for the wolves to dig up and be back in his bed before dawn.'

Even as the words, the threat, left her lips, her stomach turned over.

Cuyler swallowed. 'If you want me to listen to him …'

Laeli didn't release him. 'And will you? Of your own free will?'

'Free will?' He managed a disbelieving laugh.

'This is a different matter, Cuyler,' she hissed. 'I'd advise you not to look at me like you just did ever again, or I'll remove your eyes and feed them to you. You will keep your hands to yourself while you're here as well. You will show respect, understand?'

Slowly, he nodded. She released him and stepped away, keeping her eyes on him as she backed towards the door. His face was pale, sweat sliding down his neck. He licked his lips nervously and nodded again.

Laeli locked the door behind her, returning the keys and heading back down the stairs. She sat by the fire in the Hall, watching the flames leap and dance until dawn was teasing the horizon. Her magic stirred in response to the fire, and she conjured a ball of flame, juggling it between her hands, frowning as the orange tongues stroked her skin, her conversation with Cuyler skimming through her mind on an endless, repeating loop. She shouldn't have lost her temper, but she was wound so tight she thought she'd snap. She sat until Thalion came in, rubbing his face and yawning.

He took a seat beside her, running his hand through his messy hair, his face creased from sleep. He reached a hand towards her then withdrew it, tucking it in his lap. She could feel his tension; he rubbed at the back of his neck and sighed.

When she could stand the silence no longer, she forced her voice to be steady. 'What happened in that village, Thalion?'

He sat back, keeping his eyes on the flames, and mumbled, 'You won't understand.'

'Try me.' Laeli continued to juggle balls of fire between her palms.

He flashed her a look, then turned away, and refused to speak.

She might not have any air magic, but Laeli had over one hundred years of reading men, of watching and taking note of the things that drove them, that caused them to act irrationally, to let their tempers get the better of them. Fae or human, it seemed there was no difference.

Her disappointment in him made her cruel, her tone sharp and bitter. 'You think your father would have preferred someone like Arne as his son? Someone cold and unfeeling, someone with obvious ambition?'

Thalion stiffened, and she knew she'd hit on the truth. Instead of sympathy, her anger roared into life. 'He'd be proud of you now though, wouldn't he? His son, a cold-blooded killer. Do you feel better about that? About what you did? Is that how you're going to be approaching this? With death and blood?' When he didn't answer, she flicked a hand at the fire in the hearth – flames roared up the chimney as her frustration surged. She closed her fist, and the fire went out, plunging the room into darkness. 'You're making a mistake, Thalion. A horrible, horrible mistake.'

He said nothing for a long moment, before he stood abruptly and snapped at her, his tone so perfectly matched to his father's a shiver of fear skimmed her spine. 'You don't know what you're talking about. You don't know how things are here. If you're not willing to support what I'm doing—'

She stood also as Cuyler's words spun through her head. 'I support your objectives, not your method. How does killing people solve anything? You told me you didn't want to rule through fear like your father, but that's exactly where this is leading if you don't stop. Can't you see that? You've got one man locked up and you've murdered another,' she exclaimed, taking in the angry lines on his face.

Thalion took a step towards her, his jaw clenched. 'What do you want from me?'

'I want to see the man who came to me for help,' she shot back. 'The man who spoke about doing what was right for his people, but all you're about to do is hang another yoke around their necks!' She poked him in the chest, hard; he stumbled back a step. 'I want you to put your stupid, stubborn pride aside and be that man. If you can't do that, then I will leave but don't ever come asking for my help again, because you won't get it.'

Shaking her head in disgust, Laeli pushed past him, making it as far as the door before he caught her, his fingers closing on her upper arm, his touch burning, her blood roaring under her skin. He pulled her into his body, his other arm snaking around her waist. She shoved him away, her face hot, muscles pulled tight, ready to fight. He took another step towards her; flames coated her palms as she moved back.

Thalion stopped abruptly, his features freezing at the reminder of what she was, what she was capable of. His eyes lingered on her hands.

'How does any of what you've done so far make you a better man than your father? How does it make you the better choice to lead this country?' she asked him bluntly, and the eyes he turned on her were hard.

They stared at each other, his glare ripping a hole through her, tunnelling into her fear and her worries that he couldn't do this, that his human need for power and control would see him fail before he started.

She wanted to see him smiling; the flames on her fingers flickered. 'Thalion …'

His face collapsed suddenly and she saw the regret, the fear, the realisation of the line he was walking already. He needed her help, not her anger.

He needed her to believe in him, so he could believe in himself. She took a deep breath and let the fire go out. He'd listen to her, she knew it, but she needed to be gentle.

Thalion sighed deeply. 'Am I so like him that you'd leave?'

'I don't know.'

'And I don't know what I'd do without you, Laeli.'

She let him step closer, the hesitancy in his movement breaking her heart.

Thalion swallowed. 'Are you afraid of me?'

He'd asked her that once before, and like before, she shook her head.

'I'm afraid of what this whole situation could do to you, what it *is* doing to you. I'm afraid you're confusing strength with brutality. A strong man understands that words are powerful; passionate words, not threats or intimidation. You can't force people to think the way you do. You need to show them who you are, let them share your dreams. You need to talk to them, like you talked to me in Sitra, because what you said that day changed my mind about you. It made me see that you did want the world to be a better place. Others need to see that as well,' Laeli replied, forcing her tone to be soft.

She touched his cheek; his eyes closed, and he turned his face to brush his lips against her palm. She stroked his skin with her thumb, ran the tips of her fingers over his jaw, his lips. 'Offer them something different, not more of the same. No one can continue to wear two faces without finding the line between them blurred. Show them your true face and I will happily stand by your side through this.'

'And after?' His voice was small, filled with longing and uncertainty.

She couldn't answer him. Jarlath's question screamed through her with all the force of a winter storm as she buried her face in Thalion's neck, her body sighing with relief as his arms closed around her.

Do you love him?

Outside, the wind stroked at the castle walls, whispering *here is what is right, here is where you belong.* She'd be haunted forever if she didn't stay and keep him safe, if she continued to deny that which sang through her blood, urging her to love him as he so desperately needed to be loved.

As she needed to be loved, for who she was.

CHAPTER NINETEEN

What will you give, daughter of fire?

In her dreams, Ash was burning.

Gedeon's face loomed at her from the darkness, his lips curled into a smile, and the light of the world winked out.

The Bloodstones sang and twinkled while she screamed and burnt; the world became fire, consuming and devouring and suffocating her.

And that voice … a voice dripping with power, scorching the inside of her with the weight of its question, with the weight of that which she could not, would not, be able to control.

In her dreams, Ash became a smudge of soot on the floor of Gedeon's office. She became sparks and embers and all things burning. She became nothing but fire as that primal power that lived inside called out to her.

It pleaded.

And raged.

And demanded its freedom.

Demanded release.

And, all the while, she screamed and screamed and screamed, her body a tapestry woven with threads of flame, her bone liquid glass, transparent and bleeding an inferno into the world.

What will you give, daughter of fire?

CHAPTER TWENTY

'This is a stupid idea,' Jarlath said as Laeli dragged him down the hall.

'You've been sitting in that room for too long,' she snapped.

No tender mercies here, then, he thought.

'You need to get outside—'

'It's snowing, Laeli, in case you hadn't noticed,' he grumbled. She growled in response and pulled on the front of his shirt. He couldn't fight her otherworldly strength as she flung him out the doors of the castle and sent him stumbling down the steps. His leg pulsed; the bite wound from the wolf in the Stadium had healed, but it ached terribly and Jarlath saw those teeth sinking into his flesh whenever he closed his eyes.

It had been weeks since he'd been released from the dark chill of the dungeon and, though he had a warm bed and plenty of food in his belly, all he saw were shadows and blood. When he opened his eyes some mornings, he was smiling, his brain caught in the lingering snatches of a dream, but, when he realised where he was and what he'd gone through to get there, the smile fell away. He'd barely spoken to anyone. The halfkin, Healy, had come every day, bringing food when he wouldn't come down the stairs; or it was Laeli, standing frustrated in the doorway as he lay on the bed and wouldn't face her while the snow continued to fall outside and the wind screamed his name, or Ash's, or the man he'd murdered in the Stadium.

Sometimes, it was a howling black wolf he heard.

Trapped in the darkness, Jarlath couldn't shake the idea that no matter what he did in this life, it was always going to be wrong – others could find their path, but the way forward was lost to him. He was terrified of making decisions that would end up costing him something, so he'd vowed not to make them anymore, to hand himself over to fate and live with whatever he was given.

It was a coward's choice, he knew that, but he didn't care.

He slept but, some days, Jarlath was so tired sleep wouldn't come, no matter how long he lay and stared at the flickering shadows cast from the fire in his room. He knew he looked dreadful – he felt it. He had decided that it was better to be alone because, if he was alone, no one could hurt him, and he couldn't hurt anyone else. He couldn't explain his feelings, couldn't explain what was going on inside his head. It was easier to keep it to himself, to hide what was churning through him day and night.

Sighing, Jarlath rubbed at the phantom pain in his thigh, blinking at the sharp clarity of the day that lay before him. Snow stretched as far as his tired eyes could see. Snow, and more snow. An entire miserable world of it.

Sometimes, Jarlath wished he'd died in the Stadium, that it had been his blood spreading across the ground like a stain that could never be washed away.

Laeli nudged him, turning his attention to where she gestured.

At the bottom of the steps were two horses, both saddled and waiting. Laeli strode past him to snatch up the reins of the first horse, a large, grey mare that flicked her tail impatiently. Laeli's beautiful face was set in hard lines and, through the mountains of fabric and furs wrapped around her, Jarlath could sense the tightness to her body.

'Get on the horse, Jarlath,' she ordered. Snow fluttered down around them as he mustered up a shred of defiance and folded his arms. The fae sucked a breath between clenched teeth. 'Please.'

'That must have cost you,' he muttered, but did what he was told. She'd throw him on the animal's back if he refused, judging by the look on her face.

'You'll need these.' She shoved a pair of soft leather gloves into his hands. Grumbling, he slid his feet into the stirrups as someone swung themselves onto the second horse. Jarlath turned his glower on his companion, then gulped, his stomach twitching uncomfortably.

This was the first time he had seen Thalion without the bars of a cage, the terror of the Stadium, or the chains of the dungeon separating them. Thalion's expression was carefully composed, but those sharp blue eyes stripped the flesh from Jarlath's body, ripping right into the guts of him. What could the man see in him, Jarlath wondered? His weakness? His pathetic misery? He swallowed and turned his face away, wondering what sort of torture he was in for, then cringed and hung his head, pushing the thoughts away.

Laeli was trying to help him. He could see it in the flicker of worry behind the forest green of her eyes and the hard mask of her face.

He tried to give her a smile as she moved away from him, but it felt wrong.

She rested her hand on Thalion's thigh. The warmth of the smile he gave her transformed his whole face. He bent to give her a lingering kiss on the mouth, his gaze sliding back to Jarlath's face when he straightened. It was the first time Jarlath had seen them together like this and he still couldn't believe it. He averted his eyes, focusing instead on Laeli's hand – she wore no gloves, and the silver wedding band on her pale finger glinted in the sharp morning light.

She gestured in Jarlath's direction. 'He's all yours,' she told Thalion, before stalking back up the stairs. Instead of going inside, she waited on the top step, her hands on her hips.

Jarlath focused his attention on the saddle. It was comfortable, the cantles padded, the leather soft. The high pommel was imprinted with images of wolves, their jaws open wide. Wherever Jarlath looked in this place, that animal was staring at him – the wolf motif could be found in the silver clasps holding back Laeli's hair or the stoles she sometimes wore, in the carved-bone medallion that dangled from Thalion's neck today, and the thick silver ring on his finger. The wolf was engraved on the stems of the ornate goblets, the pottery, the tapestries, the hilt of Thalion's sword, the scabbard at his hip … Jarlath was being watched wherever he went.

A wicked wind ripped across the dreary courtyard and Jarlath shivered. Thalion didn't notice – it ruffled through his hair and pulled teasing fingers through the fur on his cloak.

The words were out of Jarlath's mouth before he could stop them. 'Don't you people feel the cold?'

'Don't you ever stop whinging?'

Jarlath looked at his horse's ears as Thalion clicked his tongue and moved off, riding with his knees as he pulled his gloves on. Without turning around, he called over his shoulder, 'Come on then.'

'Where are we going?'

No response. Jarlath cast a final look at Laeli, still standing on the top step. He didn't have much choice in the matter, with the two of them ganging up on him. With a little sigh, he nudged his horse forward. On impulse, he turned and lifted his hand in a wave. Laeli's face relaxed and she smiled, giving him a quick wave in return and it made him feel better, if only for a moment.

Jarlath slipped his gloves on and followed Thalion through the castle grounds, crossing the bridge over the moat, the water below them black with the cold. Snow caught on their hair and clothes. Since his release from the dungeon, Jarlath had heard whisperings of the rebellion Laeli had warned him about, stories of murder and imprisonment, of blood and death. He didn't know what to think, what was true and what was not, and he hadn't asked, not wanting to get caught up in whatever was going on in this country.

He just wanted to go home.

Once free of the castle, Thalion urged his horse into a canter. Jarlath hesitated, wondering how far he would get if he turned his horse in the other direction, if he pushed the animal east instead of west. He swallowed, knowing already it wouldn't be far. He had no food or water, no weapons … he kicked his horse in the ribs and followed Thalion, taking the coward's choice once again.

They rode north-west, over the flat expanse of land, the outlines of two of the villages visible in the distance, one either side of them. Jarlath didn't know their names. He knew nothing about this country, he realised, tearing his gaze from the Stadium, rising proudly from the landscape.

Thalion twisted in the saddle – there was no mistaking the challenge in his eyes. He grinned and bent low over his horse; they sped up, hooves flicking snow and dirt into the air. Jarlath took a deep breath and let his horse have its head.

The wind ripped across his cheeks, sucking the moisture from his skin and making his eyes water. His fingers were stiff, his muscles bunched uncomfortably, legs burning as he lifted himself from the saddle and held his body steady.

It had been forever since he'd ridden like this and, as they left the castle and that horrible dungeon far behind them, Jarlath relaxed. The wind and the snow began to brush his face rather than tear it apart, and the horse's hooves were thunder beneath him, a pounding rhythm against the earth. It sank into his blood and the further they went, the snow stretched around them, a glorious blanket of brilliant white thrown over the landscape. Instead of stunted, the few trees he saw stood proud and strong, clinging to life in a world that gave them little warmth and tenderness.

The horse was enjoying the wild gallop, the animal connected to the earth through the steady rhythm of her hooves, and the rhythm of the blood that pounded through her veins. Jarlath pulled his hand free of his glove and reached down to pat the mare's neck, to feel the warmth pulsing through her strong body, feel the muscle twitch and shift beneath his fingers. The horse was at home out here in this place of reckless beauty, where the caramel of the landscape sliced through the never-ending crystalline white of the snow. The sky above them pierced Jarlath's eyes with its unapologetic brightness.

The land began to climb gently and, up ahead, a rocky outcrop rose from the ground. Thalion didn't slow until they were upon it and he pulled hard on the reins; the tor was surrounded by masses of rocks and boulders scattered around the ground. It wasn't as large as the smallest rises of the Peaks that arched from the earth and separated Estilleon from the rest of the land, but it was imposing enough to be impressive.

'What is this place?' Jarlath asked. Wind whistled over the rocks, moaning through cracks and crevasses, shaping itself into fingers that grabbed and flexed around granite boulders flecked with mica and quartz, the clear crystals glinting with captured snatches of sunlight. Clouds gathered beyond the mountains, their undersides blue-grey, and the land was smooth and flat around them.

Thalion dismounted, tying his horse to the only tree for miles, its branches bare of leaves. He glanced up at the wind-whipped tor. 'We call it the Wolf's Head. This is where the Bone Mother and her wolf lie in wait when the season turns. The rocks are shaped like a wolf's head, see?'

Jarlath nodded – he could see the elongated snout hiding rows of sharp teeth and wicked intent. He swallowed. 'What's on the other side?'

'Flat land then ice floes and water.'

'And beyond that?'

'More water. The sea. Whales, seals, bears. The best time to go there is when the ice is firm, because when the melts start it's too dangerous. The ice thins and can shatter beneath your feet without warning. If you fall in that water, you'll be praying you freeze to death because hypothermia,' he paused, giving Jarlath a serious look, 'isn't pleasant.'

Walking back to the castle in this weather wouldn't be pleasant either. Jarlath dismounted, tying the horse's reins tight to the tree.

Steam billowed from her velvet nostrils and he stroked her neck, trying to gather his thoughts – Ash's face, the wolf, the Stadium, a bloodied sword, all tumbled through his mind on constant repeat. He could feel Thalion watching him, so he gave the mare a final pat. 'What are we doing here?'

Thalion pointed at the Wolf's Head. 'We're climbing that.'

Jarlath gaped. The rocks stretched into the sky, cutting through the canvas of blue dotted with white as the clouds inched closer. An immediate fear seized his bones. 'You have got to be joking.'

'Have you never climbed before, Jarlath?'

'There aren't many things to climb where I come from, except trees.'

Thalion's lips curled. 'I won't let you fall to your death.'

'That makes all the difference then,' Jarlath mumbled as Thalion drew ahead of him.

'I didn't take you for a quitter,' he called over his shoulder.

Jarlath's face warmed. Once, he wouldn't have considered quitting. He would have been the first one in there, his blood burning with anticipation of the exhilaration such a climb would bring. He would have been the first one to the top and he would have crowed his success for all to hear. But now, as he looked at his hands, he saw the blood that coated them, and he saw again the fear in the wolf's eyes. The teeth marks on his leg throbbed.

Thalion was at home here, amongst the cold, the wind, the snows, and the ice, his temperament shaped by this hard landscape. The Wolf's Head loomed above them. Thalion disappeared behind a boulder. Heart hammering, Jarlath scrambled after him as the wind pulled at his clothes; it died to a teasing breeze as he stepped between towers of rocks that reminded him of stacks of cushions. The further in they went, the rocks took on a life of their own – shaped and scoured by thousands of years of wind and cold, they folded over one another as if trying to keep warm. Holes and sweeping dips cut through their sides, veins of quartz running across the stone faces like lines on a map.

Thalion was waiting at the base of a giant tower of rock. 'Ready?'

'No.'

'Put your hands and feet where I do.' Thalion stripped his gloves and furs off and began to climb; Jarlath watched as he pulled himself up that stretch of rock with strong hands and shoulders, his movements sure, steady, confident – so confident that Jarlath hated him for a moment. He took a deep breath and approached the rock, considering refusing to do it. Looking up, he could see the natural handholds that Thalion was using. It didn't look so bad, Jarlath thought. He peeled the gloves off and flexed his fingers, reaching for the first handhold, pulling himself in tight to the body of the rock.

He climbed. The earth fell away beneath his feet, adrenalin launching into life inside him, urging him to do what he thought he could not. Hand over foot, up and up, higher, his heart in his throat, the wind blasting him, the shock of blue sky weighing down on him. Jarlath licked his lips; the muscles in his hands were straining. He glanced up. Thalion was gone, over the ledge at the top, so nimble and quick. Body burning, Jarlath pushed off again, reaching for the next handhold.

Each inch higher he left something behind; it slid from his body to tumble to the hard earth below. That invisible force that had held him down for weeks couldn't compete. He'd been so tired, a thin, grey veil clouding his senses, an unbearable burden crushing him day and night, filled with failure and longing and the bitterness of defeat. With each inch further up the rock face, something of himself returned. Smiling, he reached up.

His foot slipped.

Mouth flooded with terror, Jarlath clung to the cold, grey face of the rocks. All those parts he had shed like skin – failure, rejection, defeat, fear, pain – surged back and engulfed him, digging their claws in once more as the white flakes of snow whirled around him in a vortex of anger and self-hatred: the darkness, the wolf, the blood and fire, the weight of that sword in his hands. The look on Ash's face as she turned from him under those glorious trees of Sitra.

'Fuck!' Jarlath screamed. His voice echoed back to him, drenched with anguish.

'You're alright, you're almost there, Jarlath. The next hold is to the right, then –'

Jarlath shook his head as much as he dared. Useless tears pricked his eyes, but he would not cry, would not give either Thalion or the darkness inside him the satisfaction. 'This is stupid!'

'No, it isn't,' Thalion countered from above him. 'You're pissed off. I get it, believe me, I get it, but you can't keep it inside forever. Let it go.'

'I can't.'

'Yes, you can.' Thalion said firmly. 'Listen to me. You survived the Pass. You survived the Stadium, and you survived the dungeon. You survived, Jarlath, but Laeli is worried about you. If you can't do this for yourself, then do it for her. You want to get back to your girl? Then get up these rocks.'

Jarlath shook his head again.

'From what I understand, you made a dumb decision and you're still sulking about it. We all make dumb decisions but, now, it's up to you to start making the right decisions.' Thalion tried and failed to keep the frustration from leaking into his tone.

'You are so full of shit!' Jarlath exploded. 'Swanning around like you're King of the fucking world, acting like you've never made a mistake in your miserable life. Don't pretend you know what I'm going through!' Without thinking any further, he hefted himself higher up the rocks, fingers digging in deep, the muscles in his shoulders and calves pulsing. 'I'm sick of this place. I'm sick of this cold and snow and the fucking cold! I want to go ...'

'Where? Where do you want to go?'

'I want to find Ash!' Jarlath shouted.

'And how are you going to do that when you can't defeat a pile of rocks?'

'Stop talking to me like I'm a child!'

'Then stop acting like one,' Thalion growled. 'Climb the fucking rocks, Jarlath.'

'When I get up there, I'm going to knock your teeth in,' Jarlath snapped furiously.

Thalion crouched to hang his face over the ledge. 'Come on then.'

Jarlath glared at him.

Cursing and sweating, his blood burning and his muscles liquid, Jarlath pulled himself up, higher, until the rock face was gone, and he was sucking gulps of chilly air into his lungs, sprawled on his back, blinking at the fierce blue sky.

The weight had vanished, and his body shuddered in relief. Thalion's face appeared above him. He held out his hand and Jarlath took it, letting himself be lifted to his feet. He brushed his hands on his thighs then looked around, his heart freezing in his chest.

The view from the top of the Wolf's Head took his breath away.

In the frozen north, the ice stretched forever, blue and shining, great waves of water arrested mid-break, curling upwards. To the west, Jarlath could see the shimmering sea, sheets of ice floating across the surface, sunlight ricocheting from the endless white expanse. The world sparkled, a gem of ice and snow radiant in the winter sun. The clouds that hung over the edge of the world weren't grey – they were silver and black and blue, shot through with yellow, green, and white.

To the south, the river stretched across the land, dark and frozen with the cold. Jarlath turned to face the east. He could see the spine of the world in the far distance, the castle, the villages, the strand of boreal forest that formed a broken circle around the country, the deep green of that conical life offering shelter and refuge from a land that breathed with the cold, that thrived in it – that survived.

'We need to come face-to-face with our weakness before we can comprehend our strength,' Thalion said quietly.

Everyone has a weakness.

Jarlath licked his lips. 'What's your weakness?'

He wasn't sure Thalion would answer, but the other man sighed and pulled his hand through his hair. 'I've spent so long hiding who I am that, when it was time to let that person out, I was afraid to do so. I made a dreadful mistake because I didn't know how to be myself, and now a man is dead. Someone recently reminded me that if I want people to believe in me, I must believe in myself. I have to let my armour soften and fall away.'

Jarlath knew what that felt like.

'What will you do now?' Thalion asked him.

Jarlath turned his gaze on the landscape again. 'I don't know. I don't know where to start,' he admitted.

'Just start. Throw off the dark of what's been and let it go.'

'I don't know if I can.' Jarlath was ashamed to admit it, staring firmly on the horizon, where he wished some answer would make itself clear. 'I've felt more animal than human recently, if I'm being completely honest. I'm not sure who I'm meant to be anymore.'

'Then be the animal. Let him out. Be fierce and be steered by your instinct. Be enraged. Fight. You've been gutted, your insides thrown to the wind, but if you let your pain devour you, you can't let it fuel you,' Thalion said. 'Take the wolf, for example,' he added and Jarlath tensed.

'People see wolves as vicious predators, killers by nature – and they are – but the wolf is also resilient and adaptable. They are strong, brave, and wise. They lean on their pack for support. They are instinct and survival,' Thalion said. He didn't look at Jarlath when he spoke; his eyes were on the windswept beauty of the landscape. 'Be the wolf, Jarlath. Don't fear it.'

A black bird wheeled across the sky, the clouds rolling in after it.

'Is that what you're doing?' Jarlath asked. 'Being the wolf?'

'I'm trying to be.'

They headed back down, the descent much easier, and, as they were mounting up, Thalion gave him a serious look.

'Until you work out what you want to do, you're welcome to stay here.'

'Is that you speaking, or Laeli?'

'As I'm rather prone to doing what she says, it's both of us speaking. I can't make you any grand promises, but I can tell you that it's never too late to be who and what you want to be.' Thalion glanced towards Wilderun, towards that which called him home. 'Sometimes, you need the right person to give you a good kick up the arse and point you in the right direction.'

The sun was long gone, their shadows swallowed by the night and the chilled air when they returned to the castle. Jarlath's stomach was empty and rumbling. He couldn't remember the last time he enjoyed what he ate.

Laeli was standing exactly where they had left her. They handed their horses over as she dusted the snow off her shoulders and bounded lightly down the steps to meet them. Her expression was cautiously optimistic, her cheeks pink with the cold and her shoulders were still tight. She stared first at Jarlath, then Thalion, and they seemed to have some wordless exchange before he cupped her face and kissed her tenderly. All her tension melted away as her body flowed towards him, her arms winding around his middle.

'Have you been waiting here all day?' Thalion asked, his forehead resting against hers.

'Of course not.'

'You have. Did you miss me?' His voice was smug.

'Whatever you need to tell yourself, Thalion.'

Jarlath laughed; they both looked at him in surprise, and he was still laughing when he went inside and sat down to dinner in the Hall. The part that doubted and questioned and wondered if he had done the right thing was still lurking inside him and always would be, but the part that resented and detested the decisions he'd made was mostly sitting on top of the Wolf's Head being smashed by the wind.

He ate, tasting his food for the first time in weeks, savouring every mouthful while he listened to Thalion and Laeli bicker and snipe over nothing half-heartedly. Thalion couldn't stop looking at her, and some part of him was always touching her. Jarlath watched Thalion closely when Laeli touched his cheek and swiped her thumb over his skin – his eyes closed, the line of his jaw softened, and he leant into her palm. Laeli was the most relaxed Jarlath had ever seen her, all her toughness stripped away, candlelight reflected in her eyes and coating the sharp angles of her face.

Their affection for one another made Jarlath think of Ash but, instead of regret, he thought about her with promise. If these two could make it work, if he could defeat a wolf, *become* a wolf, he could afford to have hope.

CHAPTER TWENTY-ONE

Sitting beneath her favourite tree in the Academy grounds, Ash rubbed at her face with a wobbly sigh. She was exhausted by the senseless violence she had witnessed – against her, against the world. The images that raced through her battered mind on an endless loop had forced her to re-evaluate what she thought the world to be.

She'd been nothing short of naïve, she knew that now, and had become aware of the smallness of her view of the world, the smallness of her experiences with what life had to offer.

The world was not populated with heroes, like the ones in the stories her mother used to read her. It was not populated with big-hearted people. It was populated with nightmares, with men like Gedeon and Darian, who would break the world and reshape it to suit themselves.

But, Ash thought, glancing up at the slice of blue sky that speared through the branches of the tree she sat under, there were people like Senan and Yasper, Radella, Nerida and Jarlath. There were people like Laeli – fierce, determined to stop the world from becoming a place of terror.

Laeli had left her home on the brink of something dreadful. Ash couldn't imagine what that felt like, to make the decision to turn away and put your energy into something else, something that would undoubtedly benefit everyone in the land. That sort of sacrifice … she couldn't comprehend it. If Laeli succeeded, then there would be no war between Estilleon and Merawuld, no more loss of life in a needless cycle of blood on the border between the two countries. Ash didn't know much about the Chieftain, only that he was Kiarda and Gedeon's ally. She thought of what she did know, gleaned from conversations overheard in Sitra. She believed Hadrian's aims were admirable, just that he was going about it the wrong way. She thought of Thalion, and what he had chosen to do – betray his father and ask the fae for help while warning them about Kiarda's plans, not for himself, but for the people he hoped to rule over.

Ash had never had to make decisions that affected more than herself, or more than a quick moment in time. She didn't have the future of a country and its people riding on her shoulders. Thalion could have walked away – he could have let his father continue with his plans and not interfered. Yet he, like Laeli, chose to focus his attention outside of himself and act for the greater good.

As did Jarlath. Ash knew that now; after meticulously going over every conversation, every moment, every glance they had shared since he pulled her out of that prison cell, she knew. She understood he didn't leave her in Sitra because he was running away from her – he left to be involved in something bigger than himself. He left to do the only thing he thought he could do to help.

The end of the world was bigger than any one individual, Ash realised with a sudden burst of clarity. It was more than Gedeon's desires or Kiarda's revenge. It was more than a Chieftain's bitterness. It was more than her fear.

Yet, she was still terribly afraid.

The dreams plagued her, left her as wrung out and limp as an old dish rag, as if she'd been using her magic for real. When she woke, she could feel it tingling beneath her skin and every morning, she pushed it aside, like she used to do. Only now, the fire had had a taste of freedom, and it wanted more, demanded more of her.

But she didn't think she could give it what it craved.

She wasn't sure she should.

Ash stood, dusting her backside free of leaves, and went back inside, walking the halls until she found Senan. The Mage-Witch was sitting in an empty classroom, a pot of dirt in front of him. There were pots all over the tables. Senan waved his hand and a shoot of green unfurled from the soil to reach into the air, waving around, growth in infinite speed. She leant in the doorway and watched until he looked up.

He beckoned her closer. 'I've been put to work. Are you feeling better?'

Ash nodded. 'I've been thinking,' she began. She dragged over a stool and sat opposite him. The life he had coaxed from the soil was still growing; a white flower burst into being. 'A bean,' she commented.

'My mother loved having me in the garden,' Senan said with a sad smile.

Ash couldn't imagine the Mage-Witch as a boy, but she knew he had been, once, no doubt filled with the hopes and dreams of any young boy. Like her, Senan's life, his future, had been ripped from him by what lived inside him — his dual power, like her forbidden one, marking him as different, as something to be feared. She studied his face, noting the tenderness in his eyes as he worked his magic. Senan was kind and gentle, but she'd watched him have to become something he was not, to protect her.

She was tired of other people having to sacrifice themselves for her. The strength she needed to continue this path was not something another person could give her. Ash watched the bean seedling dance, tendrils grasping at the air, searching for something to cling to. She'd spent her life clinging to something: the certainty of life in her village, Jarlath, then the Academy and the routine it gave her.

It was all a ruse to avoid admitting the truth about herself.

Ash wanted to be the support that others clung to.

Senan waved his hand again and the plant sucked itself back into the soil, that delicate green life coiling back inside the seed until the moment when it would unfurl and seek the sun once more. He glanced up and caught her eye, his face coated with unsaid things.

'I want to help but I'm still afraid,' Ash admitted in a small voice. 'Part of me wants to stay here and hide until all this is over.'

'Running away won't help your fear – the only way you can conquer your fear is to confront it. You have to run towards the thing that frightens you,' Senan said quietly.

'You've spent your whole life running away,' Ash retorted.

'I know. And that's for me to deal with.' He gave her a serious look, his brown eyes, so like the colour of the earth, combing her face. 'And the other part of you?'

She was quiet for a long moment. 'The other part of me knows I have to face this.' She took a deep breath. 'If I'm going to fight, I need to resume my studies. I need to practise and learn how to control my magic. I need to not be afraid of it – not be afraid of *me* anymore. But I'm scared to let it out, scared to give it what it seems to want.'

Senan was watching her carefully. 'And what is that?'

Ash swallowed. 'It wants to be free. I feel … I feel like … this will sound silly.'

'Go on.'

'It has something to do. It has a purpose, but I don't know what that purpose is and I have no idea how to work it out,' Ash answered softly. 'When I was a student here, I didn't study magic. I studied herbs and healing. I wish …'

'You wish?' Senan prompted.

Ash sighed and rubbed at her face. 'I wish I'd had more time with Laeli, more time in Sitra, to learn about what's inside me.'

'When you use your magic, what do you think about?'

She frowned. 'I don't know. I don't think I do think – it just happens.'

'So much of our magic is instinctive, Ash,' the Mage-Witch explained gently. 'It comes from you, it's a part of you and, while more time to learn would have been good, I think you'll find you *do* know how to use it.'

Ash watched the bean seedling push its way through the soil again, watched Senan's hands move, conductors of this symphony of life. 'So I should trust my instinct?'

'Yes.'

She swallowed. 'What if I don't?'

'You have to. You have to make peace with what happened to Gedeon, Ash. You have to trust in what you have been given. Even if you don't think you know what to do, the magic inside of you does.'

'I need to hand myself over to it? Give up control?' Ash wasn't sure she could do that, when she'd spent her whole life hiding it, fighting to control what was inside her.

Senan smiled. 'In a way. At its core, your magic reflects what you want. If you are clear in your intent, in what you want to happen, the magic will respond to that.'

Ash was still frowning; Senan took her hands in his dirt-smeared ones. 'Listen to me. You are strong enough to do this. I know you don't believe it, but I do. You kept this phenomenal power hidden inside you for years, Ash. That takes strength and courage. You just have to believe in yourself.'

Ash took a deep breath, and slowly, she nodded.

The moment with Gedeon was her moment in the dark, the marker for the diversion into her strange new existence. It was time to move forward and accept the cards that had been drawn for her, but she knew it wouldn't be that simple, but Senan was right. She had to let the fire be her guide. To trust it, and trust herself. She shivered, not knowing what handing control over to that raw magic that lived inside her would do to her, how it would change her.

What will you give, daughter of fire?

Ash had trained enough with Laeli to know what she needed to do. She asked Radella for some space, a room, where she could let her fire free and work on controlling it. Over the next week, she made shapes of fire and, as she grew stronger, she made coils and ropes of it, letting it swirl around her, directing the flame to where she wanted it to go.

She made balls, small ones, then larger, until she could hold several in the air at once. She learnt how far she could push before she grew tired. She learnt the different colours of her flame – a glorious spectrum that ranged from dark red on initial combustion, to a dull red, then a bright red the colour of cherries, to orange, bright yellow, and white. Finally, at the centre of the hottest fire she made, was a mysterious, dark space that sang to her, called to her.

She read texts on elemental magic, and she was a more dutiful student than she had ever been. She read until she thought her eyes would fall from her head. She didn't want to stop for anything; Nerida made sure she ate and slept, and Ash would crawl from her bed the next morning and return to her study room, picking up where she left off the night before. She thought of those Fire Witches who came before her, those who had their magic bound and had been burnt at the stake for what they were. Were they like her, or was she different somehow? She didn't know and there was no one to ask. None of them had lived long enough with their magic to be able to delve into it, to train to use it and move beyond being a conduit for something greater and more powerful than themselves.

Ash finally began to understand the role of magic – that it was part of nature, each element fulfilling an age-old role. Energy was the foundation of magic, and the energy that lived in the body was what mages drew on, transferring that energy into the magic they wrought. It was the four elements that allowed life to flourish and prosper – earth was the foundation of all life, air was light and fuel for living things, water represented the flow of life, and fire … fire was the source of creation and destruction.

Fire did not exist in a natural state, unlike the other elements. Ash watched the flames shimmer over her skin – would she be a creator, or a destroyer? She chewed her lip. Fire took form only when it consumed, so she would become a consumer. She learnt the colours of the materials she burnt – wood gave off an orange glow, metals were green. She studied the flame – the part of the fire closest to the wood or candle wick was white, and the further away, the flames became orange with red tips. She put her hand in that fire and learnt the different temperatures and she replicated the muted blues that danced along the surface of the timber, learning it was hotter than the white part of the flame.

It was the black space that Ash returned to. To her hand, that black fire was as cool as water, but when she directed that flame to a piece of wood, it disintegrated in seconds, leaving a small pile of ash. It melted metal. It turned glass into liquid. When she let that black fire consume her body, her feet left the floor and she hovered over the ground in the empty room. When the walls darkened with soot, she pulled the black fire back inside and vowed only to let it out when all other options were lost to her.

The black fire, Ash decided, was death.

CHAPTER TWENTY-TWO

A crowd had gathered in the Great Hall. Notably absent were Freda and Nara, and anyone from Amberwick. Tomlin and Jorah had been unable to come from Westhelm, the village still unsettled. Instead, they'd sent a messenger with a long list of demands – cloth and food, timber, weapons – all things that could be easily accommodated.

Also absent was Caden from Whitemouth. Thalion's message had been answered with a simple 'fuck you,' the words scrawled across the page so harshly the paper was torn.

The days had shortened. They were in the heart of winter now, although the solstice was a way off. Laeli had been tracking the steady decline of the days; the sunlight snagged on the sharp tips of the Peaks in the East as the wheel turned, and the nights were thick with snow and cold. The fire in the Hall simmered, the room managing to maintain its warmth despite the open shutters and the chilled stone beneath the large, woollen rugs spread over them.

Thalion sat at the head of the long table, Laeli beside him, wearing Eira's face, Eira's white dress and furs. Many of the people in the Hall didn't know who she truly was, and Thalion and Laeli had agreed that if he was going to show his true face, then so was she. It would make it harder for people to listen to him with Kiarda's daughter, Hadrian's ally, clearly visible at the table.

Now, as people were taking their places, Laeli was filled with nerves, her throat tight, mouth dry. This could all go horribly wrong - this was Thalion's moment, his one opportunity, to persuade Estilleon's Chiefs to turn from his father and follow his rule. He may not wear a crown, like her father, but Laeli was certain that if he did, he'd be feeling its weight today.

Frode sat on Laeli's other side, the big Chief whispering a running commentary in his rumbling voice. Frode's Second, Colm, was at the Pass, and a dark-haired man sat next to him instead, his serious gaze sweeping the room, muscular arms folded over his chest. Owen was quick with his laughter. Laeli liked him and found him to be sharp-witted and practical and he hadn't batted an eyelid when he discovered who she was. Next to Owen was Gage, from Wildeview. Gage's blue eyes darted around the room, over the faces of those present. A nervous energy radiated from him but beneath it she could sense a sincere kindness. The Chief of Reyshorn, Runa, was present, with a thick-set older man, his white hair tied at the base of his neck. Her husband, Aeron, a metalworker.

'Reyshorn produces most of the country's weapons in their forges,' Frode whispered as Runa and Aeron took their place; Laeli noted Aeron let his wife sit first, pulling out the chair for her. 'Aeron is a master craftsman. He made my sword, and Thalion's, I believe. Take a good look at the workmanship on the hilt when you can, and you'll see why Aeron is so sought after.'

Laeli kept her surprise hidden. Artisans and craftsmen, respected here? She smiled to herself. Her brother was always telling her not to make assumptions about the human world and she had been trying, for Thalion's sake. This meeting would see Estilleon and Eshlune as allies, regardless of what Thalion's official line was, and Laeli was mindful of that. Ending the war before it truly began was the priority from this moment on.

Voices paused mid-sentence as a tall man with almond-coloured skin and a generous chest strode into the room, one hand resting purposefully on his weapon. He moved like an animal, graceful, stalking, limbs long and supple. All eyes tracked him as he found a seat, sitting back leisurely, expression composed.

'Bredon, from Silverward, Cuyler's Second,' Frode said quietly. 'Owns the silver mines, something he doesn't let people forget. All the jewellery is made from those mines.' He glanced at her. 'Including those pins in your hair and the ring on your finger. He's done quite well for himself – his great-grandfather was Kharpodean, indentured to the Chief of Silverward at the time.'

Laeli knew that once, Estilleon and the desert-country of Kharpode had been firm trading partners. For centuries, people from each country crossed the low mountain range that served as the border, and many settled in the lands they found themselves in. She recalled what her father had told Thalion – that he had fought alongside Thalion's great-grandfather when trading between Estilleon and Kharpode turned to war. Those of Kharpode heritage still living in snow-covered Estilleon found their status in society quickly diminished. Healy had told her some Kharpodeans had found themselves like her – slaves – but, unlike her, they were allowed to work off their indenture and become free people.

And, in Bredon's case, a powerful man.

Ari and Eric escorted Cuyler into the Hall. The big man looked around the room, his eyes settling on Bredon. His lips curled into a sneer he did nothing to hide, his eyes burning with anger. He'd been given his weapons back and wore them proudly.

'Bad blood between those two,' Frode muttered, watching as Cuyler crossed the room. 'I told Thalion he should have left Cuyler where he was.'

Laeli shook her head. 'He needs to be here.'

Cuyler glanced along the table; spotting Laeli, he gave her a knowing smile. She showed him her teeth. He laughed and took his seat.

Several nights ago, Thalion wrote a message to Bredon, Laeli leaning over his shoulder, watching his neat letters strike their way across the page. They hadn't thought he'd bother coming. Bredon had crafty brown eyes and close-cropped black hair and was wrapped in more furs and jewellery than was necessary: a status symbol, Laeli had come to understand.

'Well,' Bredon said. He leant his elbows on the table, giving Cuyler a smug smile. 'Been enjoying your visit?'

Before Cuyler could respond, a woman hurried into the room, a gust of wind trailing her, blowing her thick black skirts around her ankles. She turned and shut the door firmly, reaching a slender hand to push her hair from her face. Rose coloured lips pulled into a gentle but nervous smile as she faced them; her hands brushed the front of her dress, and she adjusted the fur-trimmed cloak around her shoulders before approaching the table.

The room was silent, and for good reason. This woman, whoever she was, was beyond beautiful in the human sense. Her black hair framed an olive-skinned face, a pert nose and sharp cheekbones dusted in an artful splattering of deep-brown freckles. A ring of decorative silver, like the one Runa wore, was displayed on her slender neck, and bands of thick silver braceleted her wrists. She cleared her throat; those at the table relaxed, assuming more natural poses.

'Who is she?' Laeli whispered to Frode.

'Galina, Niall's daughter. Caused quite an uproar when he announced her as his Second, but she is whip smart. The Hollows control access to the forests west of the village, and therefore the timber, which is highly sought after. Galina is a staunch advocate for proper management of the forests. You'd like her,' he added with a smile. Frode fingered his chin as Laeli watched the Galina take a seat at the table, next to Gage, who looked at her with undisguised interest.

'Hadrian wanted Thalion to marry her, before the world went to shit,' Frode murmured under his breath. 'For no reason other than control of the forests and the timber.'

'Really?' Even to her own ears, Laeli's voice sounded small.

'Thalion would have had no say in it; I'm not even sure he knows,' Frode said with a shrug. He shot Laeli a quick look, before clearing his throat and looking away. Laeli glanced sideways at Thalion. His posture hadn't changed; he acknowledged Galina with a nod, as he had everyone else, but the smile she bestowed on him had Laeli wondering.

You don't own him, she told herself ruthlessly, but it was too late – a barb of jealousy burrowed deep, leaving a bitter taste in her mouth.

Healy and the servants entered, bearing plates of bread and hard cheese, trays of pork and venison, roasted vegetables, and jugs of mead and water. Laeli kept her eyes on Cuyler; his gaze tracked Healy as she moved around the room. Realising Laeli was watching him, he relaxed back in his chair, expression smug, and she wished he had been left in his room. The food was placed on the table, along with plates and serving utensils, and soon, people were eating and talking.

Laeli's stomach was tight, so she ate little, gazing towards the window and the snow that cloaked this world she'd found herself so immersed in, her ears tuning in to the scraps of conversation that floated around her: the weather (always in this place), the men at the Pass, what was happening in each village (someone had gotten married and someone had borne a child, a hard labour) and beneath it all, anticipation about this meeting. They all knew Thalion had been left in charge, but no one except Frode and Owen, and now Cuyler, knew what was planned.

In her mind, Laeli saw Eshlune covered in layers of white. Her heart twisted.

As the plates were taken away by the servants and the jugs refilled, Thalion banged his mug on the table; conversations dried up instantly, and all eyes, except Cuyler's, swung to him.

'Now that our bellies are full—'

The door was flung open, and a hard-faced woman marched in, followed by a dark-haired, heavily armed man. They paused in the middle of the floor.

'I missed the feast,' the woman stated. Dark curly hair, tossed wild by the wind, fell like a curtain over her shoulders. She smiled, stripping off her snow-coated furs and handing them to the man. She had a striking face, with heavy brows, deep-set eyes and a sharp jaw. She wore a curling silver band on each upper arm, and her dress of dark wool, pinned in place by two ornate silver brooches, highlighted her severe beauty. 'You all know my brother, Kellan.' She indicated the man, whose expression didn't alter.

'Nara.' Thalion gestured to the table politely.

She swept through the room to find a seat near Bredon, an obvious alliance. Kellan did not sit, remaining standing not far from her, his fingers curled around the hilt of his sword.

Thalion was frowning. 'Freda didn't mention she'd be sending anyone.'

Nara waved him away. 'It was a last-minute decision.'

Laeli raised her eyebrows. Emrelfel was a two-day ride with the wind at your back.

Nara took her time glancing around the table, her eyes combing each face diligently. 'No one from Whitemouth or Amberwick?'

There was no response. Nara took a deep breath and sighed dramatically. 'We know what happened to Arne, and Caden is locked in his village -'

'As is Freda,' Runa pointed out, her face set in hard lines. It was obvious there was bad blood between Reyshorn and Emrelfel as well, and Laeli repressed a sigh. If Thalion could get people to listen to him, there would still be other issues to sort out between the villages and their Chiefs. These people were powerful, and they would cling to it.

Nara smoothed her hands over the tabletop. 'For now. I'm here to listen, and then Freda will decide where her allegiance lies.'

'I will deal with Caden,' Thalion answered; Bredon snorted into his drink and Laeli's fists curled.

'Will you?' Nara asked, examining her fingernails; behind her, Kellan practically flexed his muscles as he rested his hand on his sword. Her gaze swept over Laeli before it shifted to Cuyler, where it remained.

Frode spoke, his rumbling voice flowing over the table, his anger undeniable. 'If you think your bodyguard is going to be enough to stop me from throwing you out of this meeting, continue to insult your Chieftain, Nara.'

Nara's head whipped around and her eyebrows rose. 'Chieftain?'

Silence, then, a bark of disbelieving laughter from Bredon. 'The rumours are true. Your father will skin you alive, Thalion.'

Thalion sat forward. 'Not if you all help me.'

Nara was shaking her head. 'Freda will not support this.'

'It's my understanding Freda requested supplies that she did not get,' Thalion pressed. 'If those supplies are still needed, all you have to do is ask.' He addressed the table. 'That invitation is extended to you all. If I can help you, I will.'

Laeli watched everyone's faces carefully. The power of words was what would bring these people close, not the power of Thalion's sword arm. What the people of this country needed was his strength, the persistence of his will, to lift them from the darkness of their lives and this horrible situation. With people like Frode and Owen on his side, Thalion's commitment to creating a more just world would become a reality.

Frode pulled a piece of paper and a stick of willow bark from beneath his furs. He lay them on the table in front of him. 'This isn't the gathering, but if there is something you need urgently, add it to this list. When we're able, we will be finding out exactly what is stored at Whitemouth.'

Being Hadrian's most trusted accomplice, Brenna's giant storehouses in Whitemouth held more than the goods needed or produced by his village. Hadrian hadn't left much of a paper trail and Thalion was desperate to get a look inside those storehouses. He had told Laeli he'd seen the amount of food harvested last season and she'd been amazed to learn each village in Estilleon paid a tithe – food, weapons, other produce – to Hadrian, as payment for simply being their Chieftain.

She thought it absurd. Her father asked nothing of his people.

Bredon and Nara exchanged a glance as Runa asked for the paper. She listed her items, then passed it along the table. Even Cuyler, who was still scowling at everyone, wrote something there. When the list reached Nara, she picked it up and took her time examining it, letting the paper flutter to the table with a sigh.

'You might have Frode twisted around your little finger and your wife,' she waved a long-fingered hand in Laeli's direction. 'I don't know what game she's playing – gods, I'm not even sure what game you're playing. What would her mother think, or does Kiarda support this?'

Laeli took a steady breath and let her glamour fall.

Several people jumped to their feet. Kellan had drawn his weapon and Nara's mouth dropped open. Cuyler kept his arms folded, muttering under his breath. Bredon had pushed his chair back and had half-drawn his sword. Galina had her hand held over her heart, her beautiful eyes confused, and Gage was staring at Laeli in wonder. Owen was struggling to contain his laughter.

'Eira is dead,' Thalion said bluntly. 'This is Laeli Enthelme, Rhodiri's daughter. When I left here, before Samhain, it was to travel to Eshlune, to the fae, to warn them about my father and Kiarda, and to ask for their help.'

A murmur spread down the table like wildfire.

'That's … treason,' Bredon bit out. Several others nodded in agreement.

'Perhaps,' Thalion said. 'But I had my reasons.'

Nara snorted. 'I'm sure you did,' she mumbled, peering at Laeli from beneath her dark lashes. 'What were you thinking, Thalion?'

'That I've had enough of watching people suffer,' Thalion answered evenly.

Galina frowned. 'Aren't they your father's motives as well?'

'Yes, but he entered into this alliance with Kiarda, and with Gedeon, without consultation with any of the Chiefs, save perhaps Brenna, committing all of us to his foolishness – a war on two fronts, one that we cannot possibly sustain over winter. We now have the power to change the direction he steered us in.' Thalion lent his elbows on the table. 'Things can be different if you're all willing to take a chance. If we want things to change, we have to be the artisans of that change.'

The spirit of a dreamer, of an idealist, was awake and Thalion was finally willing to let himself be seen. Behind Nara's fierce stare was uncertainty; Laeli could smell it in the other woman's sweat, in the rapid blink of her eyes and the nervous flutter of the vein in her temple. She was afraid, Laeli realised, of how far Freda was willing to take the allegiance she had given Hadrian so many years ago. Laeli kept her eyes on Nara as she fidgeted, the movement of her hands gone unseen by everyone else.

Bredon shifted in his seat, giving Laeli a speculative glance. 'But that is the question though isn't it, girl? What are you here for?' he said carelessly, his tone dismissive, as if he didn't have the time to be bothered with her, with any of them. Laeli narrowed her eyes, opening her senses. Bredon's boredom with this whole meeting saturated the air around him. The silver and iron mines would continue to be needed regardless of what the outcome of today was – he knew he was valuable.

'Girl?' Laeli echoed. 'I've seen one hundred and forty years on this earth and will see one hundred and forty more long after your life is over.' Laeli let her senses shift over them all, reading them, searching for the barb's humans were good at hiding from one another, those hidden motives and desires they thought no one else could see. She reminded herself of her own advice – words were powerful. They didn't need to see her anger. They didn't need to see her disgust in their behaviour and their blatant self-interest.

'Hadrian and Kiarda have invaded my home. I'm here to ensure that the suffering of my people doesn't become the suffering of all people, because neither of them will stop at Eshlune. Kiarda will want Estilleon next, I am certain of it.' There was a murmur around the table. Thalion touched her leg, the familiar heat of him washing over her. She allowed it to calm her, to soothe the twitching under her skin. 'I'm here to help Thalion change things. There is no alliance between Estilleon and my people. We need you to understand that. I am here for my father and, although I am acting alone, it is with his blessing.'

Nara laughed delightfully. 'And there's nothing else in it for you? We all know how the fae enjoy playing games with humans.' She turned to Thalion, a knowing smile tugging at her lips. 'But I bet *you're* enjoying yourself, aren't you?'

The insinuation of her words wasn't lost on the others.

'What Thalion does in his own bed is no one's business but his,' Galina cut in coolly.

'I'm surprised you'd defend him, Galina,' Nara said, the lightness of her tone betraying her spite. 'Considering how I heard you wouldn't leave your house after he married that other one.'

Galina lifted her chin and Laeli felt a stirring of respect for her as she refused to look away from Nara's glinting eyes. 'None of that matters anymore. Thalion is our Chieftain now – you and Freda would do well to remember that.'

'He's not my Chieftain,' Nara growled. 'Freda—'

'Has made her position clear by closing up Emrelfel and by refusing to attend this meeting, regardless of sending you here today.' Thalion's voice cut through the room, the firmness of his tone unable to be ignored. He linked his hands behind his head, leaning back and closing his eyes; outside the wind moaned and the snow continued to fall. The fire crackled gently in the hearth, and Laeli could hear the heartbeats of each person in the room, could feel all eyes watching Thalion, watching her, assessing, wondering.

Thalion's hand came to rest on the back of Laeli's neck. It was a declaration, an obvious and public one. Her breath caught in her throat.

'But if anyone truly has any issues with who shares my bed, perhaps you need to reassess the reasons why you're here, and perhaps reassess your position, because I can't have Chiefs who are happy to bicker and gossip but not willing to act. Fighting amongst ourselves isn't going to solve any of the problems we face.' Thalion's expression remained calm but steady as he looked at each of them in turn. Nara sighed and gave him a curt nod.

Laeli's gaze fell on Galina. The other woman held her eyes.

'Now,' Thalion said, his fingers stroking Laeli's skin, 'how do you all feel about autonomy? The right to rule your people as you see fit. You are, after all, the ones who know what they need.'

Cuyler's face became interested. 'With no interference from you?'

'That's right, but within reason, Cuyler. There would need to be laws, mandates that everyone agrees to,' Thalion said.

'The tithe?' Nara asked quietly, her face thoughtful.

'Ten percent. And a more equal distribution of produce across the country, giving people what they need and when. There will be no more poverty, no more exploitation. We can ultimately change the state of people's lives.'

A subdued excitement rose around the room at this, but it was excitement nonetheless, and a small victory, the first steps towards change. Thalion had played this card perfectly, correctly judging that, regardless of where their allegiance lay, the Chief's genuinely cared for their people and did not like to see them suffer.

Bredon shifted in his seat. 'What's in it for you, Thalion? Because if this is about having a dig at your father ...'

Thalion shook his head. 'If we can present a unified country who is willing to negotiate and not make demands, then, ultimately, I would open up communication with Merawuld and Kharpode regarding trade. Wouldn't it be nice to sell your silver over the mountains?'

'Your father was never able to get Merawuld to trade with us,' Bredon pointed out.

'My father, as you all know, is not overly conciliatory,' Thalion replied quietly, and someone laughed.

'What else?' Galina asked softly.

Thalion looked at her when he spoke. 'An end to slavery. No one will be permitted to engage with slave dealers and, if they do, there will be harsh penalties.'

A few faces pulled into frowns at this.

'It's not right to keep people where they don't want to be,' Thalion argued gently. 'We can't change what has happened to them in the past, but we can offer them a better future. I am willing to bet that, provided they have been well-treated, your half-breeds will choose to stay here, with the rights afforded to everyone else in the country. Remember, they aren't wanted anywhere else,' he added, and Laeli felt a stab of shame.

'I don't think I've ever heard you talk so much, Thalion. You've got quite the silver-tongue when you need it, don't you?' Gage muttered, but he was smiling. 'You would know that Ulfe has already agreed to support you.'

'As has my father,' Galina put in.

'And Fairhorn.' Frode's eyes were bright under his heavy brows.

'Reyshorn as well,' Runa added.

Thalion nodded. 'And I thank you for it.' He glanced at Cuyler, Bredon and Nara in turn. 'I'm not asking for your allegiance today. I want you to consider what the future could look like, if we're brave enough to shape it ourselves. In several days, I will be travelling to the Pass to endeavour to forge a treaty with Merawuld.'

'A treaty?' Bredon barked, not bothering to hide his amusement.

'We cannot remain engaged in warfare, not with the darkest days of winter yet to come,' Thalion said simply. 'I want those men back where they belong, as I'm sure you all do.'

'And if we don't agree with this treaty of yours?' Nara asked, her voice quieter, more reserved than before, some of her spite extinguished.

Bredon shook his head. 'Isn't that obvious? The same fate that Arne met awaits us, or have you all forgotten what happened in Westhelm already?' He looked at Thalion. 'Has the irony of your actions been lost on you?'

'I made a mistake,' Thalion answered gravely. 'One that I won't make again. You don't have to support this, Bredon, but it will cost you. All communication entering or leaving your village, and your home, if need be, will be watched, because I cannot risk you contacting my father, or sending any of your men out of the country.'

Bredon leapt to his feet and made to draw his sword, but his hand seized on the hilt of his weapon. He cursed, his glare swinging to Laeli's face and her outstretched hand. 'Release me, Witch,' he snapped.

She shook her head. 'No.'

'I could crush you with one hand,' he spat.

Laeli held his eyes, letting her magic swirl around her body – sparks and smoke floated from her skin and the liquid in the goblets lifted into the air and hung there; every person at the table sucked in a breath.

'Bredon,' Cuyler said wearily, 'sit down.'

Bredon glared at him mutinously.

'If you want to try and fight that —' Cuyler gestured to where Laeli sat bathed in smoke, 'then be my guest, but you are not in charge of Silverward, however much you might like to be.'

Thalion still had his hand resting on the back of Laeli's neck, completely unafraid of her or the swirling storm of magic that surrounded her. Her body tingled and she pulled her magic back inside herself, the mead dropping back into the goblets with hardly a splash.

Cuyler sat back in his chair. 'Keep talking, Thalion. I'm listening. But it might not be as easy as you think to convince the general population of your dreams. Things have been the same in this country for a long time. People don't like change.'

'Surely, the promise of peace and their independence will be enough?' Gage argued.

'Perhaps,' Thalion mused. 'But look at it this way: challenges aren't sent to destroy us – they're sent to empower us. What we do with those challenges is up to us.'

CHAPTER TWENTY-THREE

The crown sat heavy on her head.

Kiarda didn't want to admit it, especially not to herself, not when this had been all she had wanted since she was a child. And she would not admit it to her brother, he whose head she had removed that circlet of glimmering gold from. It wasn't an ornate crown, like the one worn by the human Queen, an object designed to awe, to remind people who held power.

The crown that decorated Kiarda's pale hair didn't need to be lavish, for the crown of the fae carried with it more weight than any material man could plunder from the earth. It was more valuable than any gemstone, for it contained within it the power of the Mother, and their connection to the earth and the wheel of existence.

It was the past, present, and future that Kiarda now carried on her head.

Rhodiri had not fought her. He had not tried to stop her from taking, not only the crown, but the city – indeed, all of Eshlune. Her brother's eyes had flashed golden as he'd lowered himself to one knee, for her. And they'd flashed again, as she'd lifted that unassuming crown of gold from the nest of his hair.

When Kiarda had set that crown on her head with her own hands, she had felt its power.

And she had felt its weight.

The look Rhodiri had given her – he knew. He knew she felt it, as he had felt it for nearly two hundred years. Their father's crown, and his father's, and so on, back through millennia and all that time contained, from the moment the first stars swirled and the fae were called into being by the Mother, created to guard her physical body, to protect and love and sacrifice for She who was All.

Kiarda had made many sacrifices, but this, this power that thrummed through her, that swam at the corners of her vision, flecked with gold and green and whirling flakes of snow, *this* was what she had dreamed of. What she had yearned for with everything she had.

This was what had been stolen from her all those years ago.

Eshlune and her people were Kiarda's now, as they should have been all along. It should have been her hand guiding them, her will and her might leading them. She would never have given up their power to the humans, would never have let them lay their boots on her throat, would never have stood by while they ripped up the soil and dug their filthy hands into the body of the Mother.

But still, the crown was heavy on her head.

As if it, too, knew how much work there was to do to correct the mistakes of the past.

And the throne … it was like a homecoming, only there was no celebration for her. No parties, no dancing, no council loyal to her, bowing to her. Instead, the throne room had been empty of all that should have been.

Kiarda did not mind. Soon, after all this was over, after the Cailleach had come and the wheel had turned, she would have her coronation. She wondered who would place the crown on her head in that moment, the act proclaiming her chosen by the Goddess.

Eira's face flashed into her mind. It should be her. Eira should be here with her now, standing at her side, not trapped on the other side of the mountains in a world that was not hers. She would perhaps be sitting in one of the smaller thrones, the ones belonging to the cousins she had never met.

Another thing Rhodiri had stolen from Kiarda – family.

Her daughter, whom the Cailleach had now stolen.

Her daughter, whom she did not even desire until she held the tiny body in her arms while, outside, the wind tore at the towers of Vellir. Eira, who had been born in the middle of a fierce storm, a true child of Veshlir, of the cold and the barren land that surrounded them.

Rhodiri had banished her and her supporters over one hundred years ago. Less than fifty people had left the green cathedral of trees that surrounded Eshlune for the cold bitterness of Veshlir. How her brother had expected them to scratch life from that frozen wasteland was beyond her but, maybe, that was the point. Maybe they weren't meant to survive. For that, Kiarda had decided all those years ago, they would. The people who looked to her had not only survived, but thrived. Vellir had become a sanctuary for those like her – those with dreams and ideas not listened to, those whom the Morrigan had forsaken, tossing them aside like game pieces she no longer enjoyed playing with.

Kiarda stroked the staff in her lap, running her fingers gently over the gnarled knot of hawthorn wood. Within that knot were symbols – stars and the sun, the mountains and the rivers, the great trees of the forest that were now stripped of their leaves and cloaked in thick white snow. Eyes closed, Kiarda continued to explore the staff. A wheel. A stag, the antlers reaching around the top of the staff, all things contained within it; her fingers trembled as she withdrew them.

She bristled with anger, fresh and remembered, as she recalled the look on her brother's face when those antlers of his first grew, springing from his hair as the Goddess blessed him.

Had the Mother not looked closely enough? Kiarda wondered, her gaze drifting out the window, over the lawns she remembered running over as a child, Rhodiri and Faleria with her. Had the Cailleach not seen what truly lay in Kiarda's heart? Had her vision not been enough? She let a flicker of blue flame dance along her knuckles. Was she being punished?

It had been the Cailleach who deemed her not fit to rule. But Kiarda had earned it. She had spent her life working towards being Queen, sitting at her father's side and studying until she mastered the subtleties of politics, the smooth order of military tactics, and the vileness of a court full of sycophants? She had simpered and smiled and showed her teeth when necessary, and kept her barbed grins to herself and cringed in private.

She had earned the right to the crown. Her brother had proven that he was no more than a man, a coveter of power, who had shown his true character. His betrayal, his choice to exile her, was evidence of his cruelty. Rhodiri had always thought too deeply and feared to act. He was not strong enough to stand up to the human world, to demand sacrifice in blood and death for the pain they had caused. He was not strong enough to wear the crown that now sat on Kiarda's head.

True strength, Kiarda had learnt, was holding yourself together when the world expected you to fall apart, for the world could break everyone, if they let it.

She had not let it break her.

She thought of the Rift, of that great wound in the earth that had been her sister's legacy. Kiarda recalled the night the Rift came into being, the night Faleria betrayed her and tried to trap her in a desperate attempt to end what Kiarda had begun. When the ground at her sister's feet tore and the earth opened up, Kiarda had run, not away from it, but towards it, pulling her brother to safety.

Her reward? Banishment.

In the cold dark of Veshlir, Kiarda had devoted herself to the Cailleach and the bitter shroud of winter she threw over the world. Her people held the cold in reverence; they came to love it like they had loved the trees they had been forced to abandon, and they learnt to live in darkness. They grew strong with the cold in their veins. They sculpted a frozen world into a home and the city of Vellir became a beacon of promise, a light in the dark, and the pulsing, throbbing heart of who she was meant to be.

A leader. A Queen.

Kiarda's fingers returned to move over those carvings on the Cailleach's staff. She traced the antlers of the stag again, then again.

The wheel would turn and once Rhodiri was truly gone ... Kiarda swallowed. She loved her brother, she did. But this wasn't about love. This was about power. It was about taking what was rightfully hers. Her thoughts settled on Faleria, on their younger sister, the girl with fire in her veins and in her heart. The one whom Kiarda had poured her soul to, whose shoulder she had cried on in those first few days after their father's return to the earth. The girl who had to ultimately make a choice: her sister, or her brother.

Kiarda shook her head. Faleria chose wrong.

And she thought of her niece and the magic Laeli held in her veins, the fire that had eluded Kiarda, that had eluded the majority of those who dwelt in Vellir with her. Fire magic, the ultimate gift of the Goddess – the power of creation and destruction, of life and death itself.

Kiarda did not require fire to create the world she wanted to see. She did not require it to destroy the world her brother had crafted, but she would harness the power of the Rift and she would utilise it, and would not allow her Fire Witch niece to use the flame against her. Mahelivar she could handle. He was weak, mild-tempered, like his father. There was no spark in him. She had seen it when she strode into the throne room and put her brother on his knees. She had seen it in how he had obeyed Rhodiri's whispered request, as defeated as his father was. She had seen it in the bowed head and the shoulders that curled in on themselves.

A boy, not a man.

Certainly not a King.

Outside, the snow fell harder. Kiarda stroked the staff of the Cailleach and, this time, she ignored the weight of the crown that rested on her head.

CHAPTER TWENTY-FOUR

After the meeting, Thalion had spent hours in his father's room, digging through paperwork, eventually appearing wearing a frown. Hadrian, he'd discovered, had been mismanaging resources for several years. What had been paid by each village as a yearly tithe was not reflected accurately in the inventory and he was desperate to get into Whitemouth, but there was still the issue of Caden. It had been decided if Caden wouldn't come to them, they would go to him.

Laeli and Thalion had been accompanied by Owen and, to Laeli's surprise, Galina. The other woman sat astride a grey mare, her beautiful face tight with the wind. Nara had left looking thoughtful, her eyes flickering over Laeli's face as she marched from the Hall, her brother shadowing her. Bredon had glowered at everyone as he left, and Cuyler... Cuyler had surprised them all, agreeing to pull his men back from the Pass when instructed and offering to help with the organisation of supplies and resources. Currently, he was in the castle with the list of requested goods from the meeting, going over the records they did have, instructed to prioritise what people wanted with what was truly needed and able to be accommodated at this time. He was under guard though – his turnaround wasn't enough to earn him trust, but it was a start.

Laeli was impressed with him, and she'd told him so before they left. He'd raised his eyebrows but gave her a nod, a tiny smile playing at the corner of his mouth.

Outside Whitemouth, the wind shrieked from the north. With Thalion's body shielding her, Laeli knelt and placed her palm on the cold earth; beneath the frozen ground, she could feel it, the green life, but it was weak and stunted, not enough for her to draw on. She sighed and straightened.

'There's nothing there,' she told Thalion. The main gates to the town were bolted shut, a perimeter of armed men surrounding it. There was nowhere to hide out here on the plain and they had stopped several hundred metres away, out of range of the archers. Laeli had planned to give them cover, let them approach from behind a shield of green. In the distance, she could see the boreal forest, like that on the tundra between Sitra and Veshlir. If she could get over there …

'Fire and water then,' she mumbled.

'Laeli, you don't have to do everything,' Thalion said. His arms were folded, his face tight. Beside him, Galina was watching her curiously; Owen's gaze was on the village in the distance.

'How do you plan on getting in there without me?' Laeli answered.

Thalion glanced across the barren ground that stood between them and Caden.

Galina's voice was gentle. 'You know what he's like when he feels he's been backed into a corner, Thalion. I wouldn't trust him not to use those people in there against you.'

Thalion sighed, his head shooting up as his name was called. Coming across the plain towards them were two men on horseback. Laeli narrowed her eyes.

'It's Caden,' Thalion murmured in astonishment.

'It's a trick,' Laeli hissed. Owen agreed with her; he drew his weapon.

Caden and his companion stopped a fair distance away. Thalion swung onto his horse and kicked the animal in the ribs before anyone could do anything to stop him.

'Wait …' Laeli said urgently.

He didn't, moving towards Caden at a trot. Cursing, Laeli flung herself onto her horse and followed, drawing ahead of him, swinging the animal around to block his path. The horse pranced and pawed at the ground in opposition to the tightened rein.

'The whole point of me being here is to keep you alive, which I can't do if you're doing stupid things like this! You got everyone else to agree to your plans and now you're going to get yourself killed?'

Thalion frowned at her. 'I don't need you questioning me, not now. Trust me, please.'

She stared at him, then let him pass as Owen drew level with her, Galina stopping a way back from them. Laeli chewed her lip. What was wrong with her lately? She scowled as an icy wind flecked with snow smacked her in the face. That was what, she thought. This blasted cold and never-ending miserable wind. She looked at Thalion's back. *She* didn't have to trust Caden.

As they came closer to Caden and his companion, she thought of the Rift and conjured a ball of flame, letting it rest in her palm. The wind tugged at the edges of the flame; it gutted then flared back to life. Laeli frowned. That wasn't normal.

Caden pulled his horse up, his eyes appraising them.

'So, this is the crazy bitch who's got you by the balls, Thalion?' he sneered in greeting.

'At least someone's got a hold of my balls,' Thalion replied.

Laeli eyed Caden's companion suspiciously. Their face was shadowed, hidden by a thick hood pulled low over their eyes. They shifted their weight, their horse snorting and dancing beneath them and she tensed, narrowing her eyes as a mind gently brushed hers.

'Who's your friend?' she asked.

'Not your business, Witch,' Caden smiled smugly.

'They're fae,' she told Thalion. 'One of Kiarda's.'

Caden's smile fell. The fae reached up to remove their hood; deep blue eyes were offset by a pale face with sweeping cheekbones and hair the colour of ash. His thin lips curled as he leant towards Caden.

'She's Rhodiri's daughter, the missing Princess.'

Bloody Air Witches. She hadn't felt him inside her head that time.

Caden laughed. 'Oh Thalion, what games you're playing?'

Laeli's ball of fire swelled and grew, her gaze on Caden, her warning clear. His fae companion flicked his wrist lazily and the fire went soaring towards his outstretched hand, where he bounced it around effortlessly.

A Fire and Air Witch. Fear skidded along her spine.

'Thalion,' she hissed urgently. 'We need to go!'

'Better listen to her, Thalion,' Caden called haughtily. Laeli kept the fae in her sights. He smiled at her and flicked his fingers – three more balls of fire joined hers. They shot into the air, circling his head. They hovered there, waiting. He waved his hand and the glowing, writhing balls of flame rushed across the space between them. Laeli kicked her horse forward, putting herself between Thalion and the fire, drawing her hands together in front of her chest. The air shimmered before her as her shield of fire sprang to life. The fireballs crashed into it; Laeli grit her teeth as the shield buckled. Sweat beaded on her forehead as the fireballs pushed against her shield, trying to force their way through. She held them, her magic straining as the wall of flame slowly absorbed the balls of glimmering fae fire.

Caden's echoing laugh carried on the wind as he and his fae retreated. Laeli's magic slipped – the shield dissolved into dust and ash. She shuddered, a wave of tiredness flowing over her; her hands trembled, and the sweat dried quickly on her skin as the wind rippled over her.

'Laeli…' Thalion began.

'Let's go,' she whispered, turning her horse around, unable to look at either Owen or Galina. She could feel the other woman's eyes on her back as the horse plodded along obediently, Laeli struggling to keep the tears from her eyes or the fear from digging in deep.

At the castle, she handed her horse over and stumbled her way inside, falling into a chair in front of the fire in the Hall. She was exhausted. Moments later, Thalion's footsteps crossed the floor, followed by Owen's heavy stride and Galina's lighter one. Laeli kept her eyes on the flames in the hearth. She thought of darkness, of cold, and they went out; she thought of heat and the Rift, and they surged back to life. Her head was spinning.

'What happened out there?' Thalion asked her. There was no reproach in his voice, only concern, as he sat beside her.

'I can't defeat him,' she said with a shake of her head. 'Caden's pet fae. He's a Fire Witch, like me, but he's an Air Witch as well, and fire and air are a lethal combination.' She glanced at him. 'My aunt, Faleria, had the same combination of elemental magic and look what she did – she made the bloody Rift by accident. An Air Witch can get inside your head, and a good one can take control of not only your thoughts, but your magic as well. That's what happened today – he took that fire right out of my hands, and I couldn't stop him. My brother used to do that to me when we were kids, before I learnt how to keep him out of my head. This fae, whoever he is, he's much more powerful than I am,' she said quietly.

'What about the other elements you can control?' Thalion asked her.

She shook her head. 'I can control each element on its own, and I can use them side by side, but not together. My father is the same, whereas Mahelivar can manipulate his air and earth magic, so they combine, if that makes sense. What he can do is much more impressive, but what I do takes more control, because I have to think about each element individually.' She sighed. 'Something else went wrong today, Thalion. Holding that shield was harder than it should have been.'

He frowned. 'What does that mean?'

Laeli conjured fire in one hand, and water in the other, both twisting until they formed two small balls. She could sense Galina and Owen watching with interest. She drew her hands together; steam rose into the air before their eyes. 'Without being able to use my earth magic I'm out of balance. Everything green here is covered in ice and, while I can still feel the earth, it's dormant, as if it's asleep, and while it sleeps, so does that part of me. Do you understand what I mean?'

'You need trees?' Galina cut in gently. 'I have trees. It won't be the same as the forest in Eshlune, but the forests behind The Hollows are alive with life. The trees are there if you need them, if they will help.'

Laeli nodded, her throat thick. That Galina would offer her this … Thalion was smiling.

'Go with Galina to see her forest and do whatever it is you need to do there. If you need to rest, do it. If you need … I don't know … tell me what you need, and I'll make it happen.'

All she could do was nod, and let him lead her upstairs to their room, leaving the others staring after her. She let Healy draw a bath for her and sank into the warmth of the water gratefully but was unable to relax. Her magic had never not responded in the way she wanted it to. She wished she could speak to her father for a moment, or Mahelivar. Tears pricked her eyes, but she blinked them away furiously, not giving herself leave to think about them, not when she'd failed today.

Laeli rose early the next morning – it was still dark, the air chilly. She dressed and made her way to the Hall, leaving Thalion asleep. Her insides were in knots. She fed the fire and gave it a little push and soon, it was roaring, and the room grew warmer. Outside, snow swirled across the world, the wind grabbing at the castle with claws of ice.

As dawn broke and weak light inched into the room through the open window, Thalion came in, his face scrunched from sleep, his hair everywhere, his slobbery dogs on his heels. They were ugly brutes, Laeli thought, with long legs and shaggy tails, heads too large for the rest of their body, but he loved them, so she put up with their dripping mouths and hot breath on her legs. They spread themselves before the fire as breakfast was brought in.

The table was covered in stacks of paper and maps, lists of names of each person in each village, lists of supplies and rations, weaponry and fighting men.

Laeli spread the lists across the table. The border was still an issue; the Queen's Army were camped in huge numbers outside Fortrose, their losses before Samhain holding them back far enough to not engage, but the threat was there. She chewed her lip, an idea forming in her mind. Jarlath had been more himself after returning from climbing the Wolf's Head with Thalion, but Laeli suspected he was feeling useless, like he was in Sitra when she was training Ash, and she'd just worked out what he could do to help.

Thalion needed to hold the country. The best thing he could do for everyone right now was end this war.

Caden's face floated into Laeli's thoughts. He was desperate and desperate men were dangerous. He was also arrogant. Elan had come to them again several days ago, his face paler than usual, his thin body trembling. Before Thalion could stop her, Laeli promised the boy she'd get Fox out of there. Thalion had been angrier than she'd ever seen him, raising his voice at her after Elan had gone, stalking the length of the room furiously, telling her to forget it. The presence of the fae complicated things and she'd have to be smarter than ever before, reaching deep into the bag of tricks she'd crafted over time. She had to hope his arrogance would be his undoing – he knew he was more powerful, and would underestimate her, which she could use to her advantage.

Laeli rolled her shoulders. She would get into that village and get the girl out. She shoved the lists aside and picked up a map of Whitemouth, scanning it for an easy entry point. Thalion's plate of food was untouched, his arms folded, and he watched her with a worried expression.

'You're still going to rescue the half-breed?'

'Yes.'

'If anything happens to you …' He scooted his chair closer, leaning over so that his breath tickled her neck. He slid the map out of her reach, ignoring her protest. 'Marry me, Laeli,' he whispered, lifting her hair out of the way so he could kiss the spot below her ear.

'Nothing will happen to me, so stop fretting.'

He didn't respond and when she turned to look at him, at those eyes, like the clearest summer sky, her smile fell. First his unspoken declaration at the meeting, and now this?

'Thalion ... I don't know if I can watch you grow old and die.'

'Then let's hope I die by the sword. That way, you get to remember me like this,' he said, taking her face between his hands and kissing her gently. 'Marry me.'

Her heart skipped a beat. That she should be so happy in this moment, when her family and her home were being torn apart ... it wasn't right, yet she couldn't help it. This man, who she met by chance in the rain, who'd let her peel back his layers and see who he truly was, flaws and all, had become everything to her. It shouldn't be, yet it was. She had tried to decipher it, had put it down to that fascinating magnetic pull of his human self, but in her heart, she knew that wasn't true, not anymore, and hadn't been for a long time.

Perhaps this was the Morrigan at work and, if so, she needed to listen.

Thalion would die, while she carried on. He would age and alter before her eyes, and it was completely out of her control. That thought ripped through her heart constantly, whenever she caught him looking at her, his eyes smouldering. Whenever he made love to her, making her blood sing, the thought was always there, a voice whispering in the back of her mind. She understood why the fae retreated to the forest all those years ago. She understood the painful choices they'd had to make.

But she also knew running and hiding away from the world wasn't the solution to heartache. And he was offering her something no one ever had – a life of her choosing. He would never force her to do anything she didn't want to do. He'd let her make her choices and stand by them with her.

Until she met him, she'd never realised how exhausting and unfulfilling it was going through the motions, the same thing year after year: protect the Rift, argue with her father, annoy her brother, practise her sword skills and her magic. Lie around in the sunshine nibbling on grapes while the wheel of the year continued to turn in its never-ending cycle.

Humans, Laeli had come to learn, felt the brevity of their lives. They didn't wait or deliberate for long. They acted, mostly ruled by their emotions, and above all, they *lived*. They lived their short lives with a ferocity she never knew they could possess. They were passionate and courageous and completely captivating, and she could finally see what it was about them that held her brother in thrall.

Her father would tell her to be happy, to live, especially now. He would tell her to walk the path she had chosen, and she'd chosen this icy wilderness on the other side of the mountains. She'd chosen Thalion with the knowledge that he would be taken from her one day. Time would change him, but it wouldn't change how she felt about him.

'Alright,' she whispered. 'I'll marry you.'

Thalion flashed her a radiant smile and lifted her hand to his lips, the one wearing the ring she hadn't taken off. 'What does a marriage ceremony look like for your people?'

'We don't get married.'

'You don't?'

She shook her head. 'Not in the way humans marry. It's more like an agreement, to be with that person until you've had enough of one another, or you want someone else for a while. When you live for so long …'

'I could spend a hundred years with you, and it wouldn't be enough,' he said fiercely. Her heart pinched. 'Who knows how much time we have left? What if this is our chance? What if this is our moment, Laeli?'

She took a deep breath. Lost time could never be replaced, and the only thing more precious than time itself was the person chosen to spend it on. This was what Laeli had wanted – the freedom to choose what she did with her life, what she did with the time she had.

'You're right.'

Thalion raised his eyebrows. 'I am?'

Laeli laughed. 'It has been known to happen. Find whatever and whoever we need, and I'll marry you any way you want.'

Galina entered, stopping abruptly when she noticed them sitting close at the long table. She fidgeted, squeezing her hands together; Laeli heard her knuckles crack. Thalion sat back. He still had hold of her hand, his finger absently stroking the ring.

'I'll be leaving now,' Galina told them. She nodded at Laeli. 'Will you be joining me?'

'Not yet,' Laeli replied. 'But soon. In a few days maybe.'

Thalion motioned to the table. 'Will you eat first, Galina?'

'Alright.' She sat down, reaching for the platter, scooping some cheese and bread into her palm. Laeli didn't know what to say. Thalion, if he'd noticed anything, didn't show it. He sat back and talked about The Hollows, about Niall and people he and Galina both knew. After she'd eaten, Galina stood as Owen stuck his head inside the Hall and announced he was leaving, and Thalion rose to walk them both out.

When she was alone, Laeli let her smile slip. She had never pledged herself to one person for the rest of their lives. Her relationship with Solen had lasted twenty years. It wasn't that he didn't love her, and it wasn't even that he had used her to get what he wanted – favour with her father, his position as captain of the guard: it was that he didn't believe in her. He didn't believe she could be more than what she'd been born as and, at the time, neither did she. She accepted the love she was given because she thought that was all that she deserved.

It was only later, after raging and crying, that she understood she deserved more than that, so she hardened herself, hid herself in anger and spite once again, as she had done when she was young, and the world had been ripped apart.

Laeli wanted to be met where she was, to find that person equal to her, that person who would fight for her, as she would fight for them. She didn't want to have to beg for someone's love. For too long she held onto the wrong thing, not understanding, not knowing that the right thing would look nothing like she imagined.

Thalion returned, reaching for the map of Whitemouth with a little sigh of resolution.

'Since I can't talk you out of it, I may as well help.'

'Really?'

His eyes were shadowed. 'But if you don't come home, I'm coming to get you, screw the Gods-darned consequences. If Caden lays one finger on you it will be the last thing he ever does.'

Laeli's heart latched onto one word. *Home.*

She swallowed. 'I'll come home. I promise.'

CHAPTER TWENTY-FIVE

The Academy was still; most had found their beds hours ago, but Ash had only just returned to hers. She was exhausted. She'd pushed herself hard the past few days, expending more and more of herself, giving more to her magic, which devoured everything she fed it with a greed that continued to frighten her, no matter how much she told herself she was doing the right thing.

She had to be ready, but for what, she didn't know.

All she was certain of was she would not stand by and do nothing, not again. Senan's wound had healed, but there were shadows in his eyes that were not there before they left Sitra. The lives he had taken weighed on him. Ash didn't need to be an air mage to know it.

Earlier that day she had come across Yasper and Gem, sitting beneath the tree in the courtyard, Gem wearing the plain clothes of an Academy student. The simple linen shift and lack of face paint could not hide Gem's beauty. Seeing them together, Yasper's arm draped around her shoulders and the small smile that played on her lips as she looked at him, had Ash thinking of Jarlath and wishing again she could talk to him. Just knowing he was alright would be enough at the moment.

Ash had never considered that anyone would find her desirable. She'd never once looked in a mirror and thought there was anything extraordinary about the face looking back at her. She was just herself, the same girl she had always been, with the same messy red hair and eyes that always seemed too old for her face, the same scrawny limbs and skin that turned red in the sun.

Yet, the way Jarlath had looked at her in Eshlune, with the trees all around them and a sword dangling uselessly from her hands … she had no words to describe it, only that no one had ever looked at her like that. As if she was important; special. Precious. Something that needed to be guarded and protected.

She hadn't had time in that moment to think about it, because once he closed his arms around her, the world had shrunk, everything fading to nothing – Eshlune, the Rift, all she had left behind and all that had been taken from her – it was all nothing.

Only her magic remained, her magic and the way Jarlath's lips had felt pressed against hers. The way it had felt so right to be so close to him, to feel the curve of the muscle on his arms and the heat of his skin, made her burn with a different sort of fire, one that started in her belly and spread like a storm through her blood and bones until she thought she would melt into the earth.

And in the moment when he had kissed her, even her magic had stilled, lulled into softness by the gentle firmness of his hands and the welcoming touch of his body as he pressed himself against her.

With a sad sigh, Ash stripped off her clothes, turning to the washstand. The water left for her was like ice, so, with a smug little smile, she dipped her fingers into the water, like she had seen Laeli do. She was so tired she could only manage a small amount of magic, but it was enough to leave the water in the basin steaming. She washed quickly and pulled on clean clothes, reaching for the food that someone, Nerida most likely, had sat on the small table near the wall. Sitting on her bed, Ash balanced the plate of bread and cheese on her knees, her eyes moving automatically to the window, as they had always done, night after night, year after year.

Her whole life was once contained within this room and behind the walls of the Academy.

Night covered the city once more, the sun completely swallowed by the darkness, and the world was silent. There was no moon, and the night was oppressive, the air thick with cold.

With waiting.

Ash could almost taste the anticipation that seemed to linger in the space around her. It burrowed beneath her skin, mingling with her exhausted magic. Part of her wanted nothing to change, for the wheel to stand still long enough for her to work out how to move forward. Long enough for her to plan what she would do next.

Another part of her was sick of waiting. She just wanted Gedeon to do whatever he was going to do, to get on with it and play his hand. That impatient part of her bristled at being kept at the High Mage's leisure. If he was coming for her, she wished he'd hurry up.

At the same time, she wished he'd just forget about her. He had the Bloodstones, so what more could he need her for? She remembered what Mahelivar had said about Kiarda, that she would want Ash's power, and that Ash wouldn't be able to fight her. She hadn't asked what it meant but now, she understood. She had nothing in which to protect herself against the powers of a fae Witch, or even an air mage – Mahelivar had told her once her mind was wide open, and, as with most things that had happened to her since Mabon, she hadn't asked what that meant, how she was supposed to change that, but she wished she had.

She was vulnerable, more vulnerable now than she ever had been.

Ash put the food aside, any appetite she had vanishing. All her life, she had felt there were two distinct parts of her: the dutiful daughter, the village girl who followed the rules and did what she was told, and the part of her that writhed beneath her skin, that urged her to scream at people when they ignored her, or encouraged her to clench her fists in defiance of the world around her.

She knew, now, that that part of her was her magic, the fire that lived inside her finding its way out. The short, sharp bursts of temper that had left people shocked – her magic. The boldness she felt in brief snatches, moments that felt she'd stolen them from someone else – her magic.

In understanding her fire, Ash had hoped she would understand herself better, but she didn't. She just knew she was tired, of being afraid, of worrying, of hiding what she was.

But she still didn't know how to protect herself, how to shield herself against those who wanted to use her magic for their own desires.

Her thoughts drifted to Jarlath again. If he were here, he'd no doubt tell her not to worry, that he would protect her, because that was what he did – played the hero, even if it cost him. But he wasn't here.

Ash held his face in her head as she climbed beneath the covers, rolling onto her side and imagining what it would be like to fall to sleep tucked close to him, to feel as safe and secure as he'd once made her feel.

CHAPTER TWENTY-SIX

Gedeon would wear his scars like a badge. He would wear them proudly into this new world he was ready to create. With the fire caster's power at his disposal, there would be nothing in this pit of a city to stand in his way. Not her and not Senan. Reports had come to him while he was lying in the darkness that the two of them had escaped again and were hiding somewhere within the city, the convict Yasper and his cathouse whore with them. The Watch had shaken down several halfkin picked off the streets but none of them were talking.

More bodies. Gedeon sighed, resisting the urge to rub at his face.

A week trapped in his bed, his face bandaged, his eyes crying with the harsh light that slammed through the window. He'd made his servant move the bed so he was tucked in the shadows against the far wall where the claws of light could not reach him.

He examined himself in the mirror again. He'd taken to this ritual once he was able to rise from bed. Dress, drink, and then the examination, the scrutiny. On one side of his face, the skin was tight, shiny in places, and it felt like he was wearing a mask of white leather. His neck was covered in raised welts that itched terribly. All the cool compresses, aloe vera, and honey in Aileryan wasn't going to restore his skin but it had, at the least, saved him from any infection.

Gedeon was terribly thirsty. The fire caster's flame had sucked all the moisture from his body – he felt paper-thin, easily torn, but he was alive. He dressed warmly, though it wasn't any colder than usual in the Keep. Another side effect, he decided. He was always cold now.

He cast another look in the mirror before heading out. No eyebrows or eyelashes remaining; his hair was singed and brittle and his left eye … he leant closer to the mirror, fascinated by the milky colour. He couldn't see from it anymore, and part of his recovery had been adjusting to his limited vision. He had come to rely on his air magic more than he ever had, a piece of it always held at the ready. It became his other eye, helping him see around corners, his magic creeping like fingers to feel about rooms and hallways.

Darian met him in the hall, the Spirit Rake averting his eyes from Gedeon's ruined face.

'Look your fill, my friend,' the High Mage said calmly. 'It's a small price to pay for the power I have gained.'

No man had ever received power to dominate and control others without reaching out and taking it for themselves, and Gedeon had given himself the right to do just that. Once he had Hadrian's soldiers in the land, he would use them to help strengthen his hold over the villages. His plans stretched beyond the city. In his vision, all small farms would amalgamate, leading to larger ones that would be controlled by a select group of people. When the villagers resisted – and they would resist, at first – he would have them arrested, and if a few sharp beatings weren't enough to dampen any ambitions of rebellion or resistance, a period of exile to the frozen waste of Veshlir would do perfectly well. Gedeon hated the idea of expanding the prison camps – all that fertile agricultural land had better uses – but Estilleon and Veshlir were the ideal solutions to such a problem. He would make as much use of his allies' land as he did his own. He hated things going to waste.

Managers would need to be arranged for the mass-scale farms. Other industries would soon become collectivised as well. The way Gedeon saw it, why have a blacksmith in every village when one large-scale workshop could be utilised? He could picture it now, the giant buildings that would house forges so large and hot they would require three men to work the bellows. He imagined the plume of dark smoke rising above the forest. He imagined the land stripped bare of trees, the oxen dragging the plough over row after row of earth, ready for planting. There would be no need to wait for the seasons to turn – with earth mages on hand, food could be grown all year, regardless of the weather. The populace would be well-fed and well-fed people were happy people. They would thank him for it, in the end.

The Mage Council would, of course, object to his plans, but they were backward thinking peasants. The sooner he got rid of them the better. Gedeon had his eyes on a few key members of the Watch. Made up of thugs and bullies, most Watchmen were pliable and used to following orders, but he knew that in some of them lurked higher ambitions.

He couldn't let ambitions go to waste, either.

The army could do with a lift as well; although, with Hadrian as a trusted ally, who would they fight? Gedeon's thoughts turned to the deserts of Kharpode. Nothing there held his interest. Perhaps he needed to think bigger still. Across the eastern sea were the lands his ancestors once inhabited. Maybe it was time to build ships again and spread their wings, flying home like birds to see what fruit was ripe for the picking.

The problem with most people, Gedeon thought as he made his way to his office, Darian his loyal shadow, was that they didn't think big enough. It was their failing, he realised, the lack of ambition. That would change. Men, he'd come to understand, sometimes needed a push to realise they could aspire to more than they were. Power was an aphrodisiac. Look at Hadrian – always happy to complain but the man never thought big enough until Gedeon had poured some suggestions into his ears. He hadn't had to use any of his magic to bend the Chieftain to his will.

In his office with the familiar sights and smells, Gedeon reached onto the highest shelf and removed a wooden box. Contained within were his plans – blueprints for workshops; not blacksmiths, but weapons. There were maps of the known lands, all written over and carved up, new boundaries and new borders marked sharply, the parchment torn in places in his overexcited charcoal strokes. There were ink splatters on one map – the map of Eshlune, the great wound of the Rift standing out like the eyesore it was.

He traced his finger around its outline, imagining the magic, the raw power, that was used to create it, then followed the path to Sitra, to that grand city of white marble nestled in the trees. He'd never been, he realised. Had never received an invitation, after all these years as Rhodiri's faithful friend.

Gedeon sat, steepling his fingers beneath his chin, his eyes fixed on Sitra, the sudden urge to visit the forest growing stronger. He dismissed the Spirit Rake, wanting to be alone with his thoughts. He pulled a fresh sheet of parchment from the drawer. His plans were itching at his skin, as real and ferocious as the burns on his face.

He wrote two letters. One he stamped with the royal seal to send to the Pass.

The other would make its way to Eshlune. He paused, quill hovering over the page. Should he tell the Chieftain about his son, or let it be a nice surprise, a homecoming Hadrian would not have ever dreamt of? Gedeon smiled. Such matters were between Hadrian and his son, and Gedeon would drive that wedge deeper when he needed to. For now, as long as the war at the Pass went ahead as planned, he would let Thalion Liulfur continue to play whatever game the boy was playing. Gedeon knew nothing of the Chieftain's son, but – if he was cut from the same piece of brooding cloth as his father – he would be just as easy to manipulate.

The fae Princess was another matter entirely, but he was still reluctant to hand that piece of information over to Kiarda, so he chose to wait, and play that card when the fae Queen decided to turn on him, as he suspected she would. Gedeon chuckled, not overly concerned. She wouldn't be worth his time if she wasn't planning on double-crossing him. It made him smile, that she thought she could.

Gedeon folded his letter to Kiarda, careful not to let any of the thoughts that swam around his head find their way onto the page. While her game was obvious, he was yet to see just how powerful she was. It was better not to risk it.

The one thing Gedeon didn't have factored into his plans was the fire caster and her deadly power. If he couldn't bring the girl under his control, then he had no need of her, not now he had the Bloodstones.

CHAPTER TWENTY-SEVEN

Frode and Owen arrived as the light vanished and the castle was bathed in shadows. Laeli heard their voices from upstairs, their presence bringing the reality of what she was about to do crashing through her mind.

Nerves were not something she was familiar with; everything she usually did, she did with confidence, with assurance in her skill with the sword, or her skill with her magic, but this was different. *This* required a different sort of courage, one she didn't know if she possessed.

Laeli rubbed at her belly, at the ache that had dug its way in there earlier and not let go. She hadn't eaten all day and she hadn't seen Thalion since that morning – he'd got up, kissed her cheek while she grumbled at being woken so early, and vanished. Another strange human tradition. Laeli had been stuck in their room for most of the day, pacing around between the window and the fire, her thoughts a muddled mess.

She'd been told that the ceremony would be conducted by Frode. Laeli tried to imagine the gruff Chief of Fairhorn, with his wild beard and giant shoulders, marrying her and Thalion and couldn't, overtaken by a fit of uncharacteristic giggles.

Healy had found a dress suitable for a wedding, but hadn't let Laeli see it, marching into the room and ordering her into the bathtub. Even after having servants her whole life, Laeli still wasn't fond of anyone fussing over her. Mostly, the women who served her sat and gossiped amongst themselves while she polished her swords and scowled, wishing they'd go away.

Laeli knew she wasn't anyone's idea of a Princess, and, for most of the time, that didn't bother her. She didn't like clothes or jewellery or pretty trinkets, although she did miss her favourite gown, as green as the first flush of leaves in the forest, the material so light it was like wearing air.

She sighed, swishing the water around her body, the firelight painting the skin on her arms golden while the fist of her stomach clenched tighter.

'I've known Thalion since he was a boy, still clinging to his mother's skirts,' Healy said fondly, her fingers on Laeli's scalp. The scent of apple blossoms filled the room.

Laeli twisted to look at the halfkin in surprise. 'He never said.'

'When I first came here, Thalion's mother saw how terrified I was and let me stay in the castle. I've watched him grow from that boy to a young man who mourned his mother and followed his father around, hoping Hadrian would throw him a scrap of affection. Thalion's like his mother, gentle and kind, but also like his father.'

Laeli's blood froze.

Healy squeezed the water from Laeli's hair. 'He shares Hadrian's determination, his drive, but none of his cruelty.'

'He can be cruel,' Laeli whispered. In her mind, she saw Bran die again, and felt the iron's poison leech through her. She saw Thalion slide the blade of that dagger across Arne's throat, his face dark.

'Can't everyone, when they need?' Healy responded softly. Laeli kept her eyes on the water, watching the way the light danced across the mirrored face of the bath. Her shoulders were tight, muscles bunching and tugging. She pushed a sharp breath between her teeth and tried to relax.

'Are you nervous?' Healy asked.

'No,' Laeli replied; butterflies pummelled her stomach in objection to the lie. 'Well, maybe a little. It's such a serious thing, marriage – for a human, that is.'

Healy's hands stilled on Laeli's hair. 'Don't you love him?'

'I don't know,' Laeli admitted. 'I'm afraid to love him, to be honest.'

'You're afraid to watch him die,' Healy corrected.

Laeli stiffened, her chest tightening, her breathing shallow as she fought to get her emotions under control. 'Yes,' she whispered finally. 'I'm terrified.'

'Don't be.'

'How can I not? I've got another hundred years left on this earth and … I don't think I can do it,' Laeli said, keeping her voice even.

Healy's hands were gentle, her voice even more so. 'Then why marry him?'

Laeli couldn't answer.

'He deserves to be happy; you deserve to be happy, so take the time you have together and be happy, Laeli. It's as simple as that, really. Don't complicate it. He knows what's coming, because death comes for everyone; some sooner than others,' Healy said softly.

Laeli swallowed the lump in her throat. She did deserve to be happy, she knew that, but she also knew that if she didn't take this chance, this risk, she might never be. At least with Thalion, she had a chance at something more. She had a chance to choose the path of her life. He would let her do that, and expect nothing but the same in return.

'You're right,' she said, tipping her head back so Healy could pour water over her hair. She climbed from the tub and dried herself by the warmth of the fire as Healy unveiled a dress that conveniently matched the colour of Laeli's husband-to-be's eyes. The dress shimmered with magic.

Laeli's eyebrows lifted. 'You can glamour?'

The halfkin blushed. 'Not people, only things, and only some things. It won't last long.'

'It's perfect,' Laeli whispered. The dress had sleeves all the way to her wrists, with a long skirt that trailed behind her when she moved. She allowed Healy to help her to dress, using her fire magic to dry her hair, leaving it to tumble down her back; then, after another deep breath, she followed the halfkin down the stairs.

The closer Laeli got to the Hall, the harder those butterflies flapped. She thought she'd be sick and was glad of her empty stomach. The castle was quiet and still; she could hear nothing but her own shattered breathing and the blood racing through her veins. Healy prepared to push open the doors to the Hall, but Laeli grabbed her hand and held it tight.

'Can you come in with me?' Though she'd only known the halfkin a few months, Healy was a link, a bridge between the world Laeli had left behind and the world she had stepped into. She needed that now, when she was about to do something she had never thought she could, or would, do.

Healy shook her head, eyes wide. 'I shouldn't. I'm a servant. I'm—'

'My friend,' Laeli whispered. 'Please. Thalion won't mind.'

A smile lit Healy's face and she nodded, pushing the doors open. Laeli took a steady breath and lifted her chin, determined to be strong, to show courage.

The moment she saw Thalion those butterflies stilled, and it was like there was no one else in that room with them.

This was right. This was exactly what was supposed to be happening at exactly the right time. Laeli felt the Morrigan's hand in this, felt the Goddess walking beside her in her black feathered cloak as she crossed the floor to stand at Thalion's side near the blazing fire.

He didn't take his eyes off her, his expression more serious than she had ever seen.

Nobody moved; Laeli shifted her weight, uncertain. Was this part of it, this silence? A quick glance at Frode made her roll her eyes – the

Chief's face was dazed, his hands dangling slack at his sides. Owen was similarly afflicted.

Thalion gave her a broad smile as she scowled. 'You can't blame them. You're the most beautiful thing any of us have ever seen. Although, I'll ask you two to stop looking at the woman I'm about to marry like that.'

Laeli smiled at him and got a cheeky wink in return, making her laugh. She couldn't help it – she stepped forward and gave him a lingering kiss on the mouth.

'You're not supposed to do that yet,' he whispered against her lips.

'I don't care,' she whispered back.

Frode cleared his throat, and they broke apart. 'Let's begin, then. Marriage is not only a connection of two people, but a connection of souls in an acknowledgement of all that is, by the Allfather and the Bone Mother, by the earth and the wind and by that which connects everything that was, is, and shall be.'

From beneath his furs, Frode pulled out a long piece of black cord. Laeli was instructed to take Thalion's hands, left in left, right in right. As Frode wrapped the cord around their joined hands, he spoke again, his voice reverent and soft. 'These are the hands that will love you through the years. These are the hands that will offer comfort when fear fills you, and these are the hands that will help build your future. These are the hands that will hold your children,' he paused, wrapping the cord over again as Laeli felt a stirring deep in her belly. Did Thalion want children? Did she? It wasn't something she'd seriously thought about before.

As Frode continued, something dissolved inside her, pieces of her armour falling to the ground like autumn leaves.

Don't be afraid to love him. The voice came from deep inside her.

'And these are the hands that will give you strength.' The cord was knotted gently, Frode's large hands surprisingly deft and quick. He stepped back a moment, and there was no sound in the room save the breathing of the fire.

Laeli couldn't look away from Thalion's face. 'Can I kiss you now?'

'Gods yes.' He bent his head to catch her mouth, not stepping away until Frode chuckled. Owen unbound their hands with a smile as Frode passed them a goblet of mead and that was it.

They were married.

CHAPTER TWENTY-EIGHT

If anyone had told him at Mabon he'd end up deserting the army, rescuing a girl from prison, going to Eshlune with the Anomaly and a fae prince, running back to the army, then marching to war only to watch his friends die, ending up a prisoner of the enemy, fighting in and surviving Estilleon's legendary Stadium, discovering the Chieftain's son was a traitor to his country (not that Jarlath minded) and the fae Princess was undercover posing as his bride while helping plan a revolution …

Jarlath shook his head.

The whole thing seemed completely unreal, even to himself.

Yet, here he was, in his room in the castle at Wilderun, with a warm fire, food in his belly and a grudging respect for Thalion Liulfur. For the enemy. Sighing, Jarlath pulled a hand through his hair. This country and the people in it were nothing like he had been taught to believe. As a child, he'd heard stories of this place over the mountains – human sacrifice, cannibalism, blood lust, and a people so hard they lived to die in battle. He'd heard of heads taken as trophies, nailed to walls and front doors.

None of it was true (except the heads, and Healy said no one really did that anymore), and that sat uneasy with Jarlath, because if the things he had been told about Estilleon, were false, then what else was?

Ash's face flashed into his mind, followed by the fiery innards of the Rift, pulsing smoke into the air. Even without any magic, Jarlath had been able to feel something from that place, something that tugged at him.

At the time, he hadn't given it any thought, too afraid to wonder what it meant.

But now … maybe it was the girl with fire in her veins who tugged at his insides, and not the magic of the Rift. He didn't know and would probably never know.

Jarlath was restless, his agitation growing by the day. They wouldn't let him leave and, while he knew he was no longer a prisoner, he also believed Thalion when he told him that to go now would be to dance with death. Regardless of the fact he had welcomed Jarlath into his home, Thalion wore his feelings in his eyes – he didn't think Jarlath had it in him to do whatever he was going to do.

And maybe he was right.

Apart from finding Ash and falling to his knees before her and begging her forgiveness, Jarlath had no idea what he was going to do. Currently, Estilleon was coated in snow, storms of whirling white rolling in most afternoons and lasting all through the night. No one was going anywhere in a hurry.

So, he found himself waiting it out, like the rest of them, while the path of his life remained unclear. Once, he had grand plans, although he'd spoken to no one about them. He would rise through the ranks of the Queen's Army, becoming a respected commander. He would ride into whatever village Ash was stationed in as a White Woman, and they'd ride off into the sunset together and live happily ever after.

Jarlath snorted. A fairy-tale, that was what he had imagined, and he'd ended up being the villain in his own story. The mists that plagued his thoughts for weeks may have parted, but he still could not stop himself from seeing the look on Ash's face when he told her he was leaving.

Not once, but twice he had deserted her. And, now, there was a mountain range, a blanket of thick snow, and an army of fae warriors separating them.

After dinner on the third night of continual storms, Laeli rapped on his door, Thalion in tow, the Chieftain seeming too large for the space outside Jarlath's room, so he invited them both in.

Jarlath didn't know what to say to either of them. He'd barely seen them since the day he climbed the Wolf's Head with Thalion, both busy running around doing whatever people did in a rebellion. He'd heard messengers come and go; heard voices he hadn't recognised and the castle dripped with schemes and unsaid things. He was interested, despite himself, by how Thalion had managed to do any of this without getting himself killed.

Jarlath wasn't sure which one of them came up with the idea, but he was certain they were both crazy.

'You want me to … wait, say again?'

Laeli was sitting in one of the chairs by the fire, juggling a ball of flame, her face tight. It was the same expression she'd often worn when training Ash – a mixture of frustration and understanding, of expectation and acceptance that things might not work out as she wanted them to.

Thalion was calm, patient; such a contrast to the Fire Witch currently frowning into the flames as he repeated the request. 'Convince your commanders to stand down their men and agree to meet with me.'

Jarlath couldn't help it. He laughed.

Laeli raised an eyebrow, her ball of flame vanishing.

'You're actually serious,' Jarlath murmured. As Thalion nodded, all that self-doubt and fear came rushing back, threatening to swallow him. He couldn't do this. Gristel and Leod wouldn't listen to him. They wouldn't. 'I can't.'

'Why?' Laeli demanded, still frowning as she took in his face. Her expression shifted. 'Jarlath, we wouldn't ask this of you if we didn't think you could do it.'

Thalion shot her a look and Jarlath suddenly understood. This was Laeli. It was her idea, her faith that was being put in him. He swallowed, forcing himself to stand up a little bit straighter, to lift his chin.

'When do we leave?'

'When the weather clears,' Thalion answered, then strode from the room. Laeli watched him go, and when his footsteps had faded, turned to Jarlath.

'At least we can get out of this castle for a while,' she quipped, her eyes shifting to the window, where the snow continued to fall. 'It's a four-day journey to the Pass.'

'I remember,' Jarlath mumbled.

'I know,' she said softly, then sighed. 'Don't worry about Thalion. He's nervous.'

'Him?'

She smiled. 'Yes. There's a lot on his shoulders, as you can imagine. You have a lot in common, did you realise that? You're both capable of doing much more than you do, but you both let your fears stop you from acting.' She stood and turned back when she reached the door, her head cocked to the side, her eyes glowing in the warm-shadowed darkness. 'You shouldn't let fear stop you from accomplishing anything, Jarlath. If you do, then you will never get what it is you truly want.'

After she was gone, he stood by the window, watching the snow fall.

All his life, all he had wanted was the chance to prove himself, whether it be a small thing, like who could pick the most apples in a day, or who could cut the most wheat. In the prison camp in Garlathe, the need to prove himself had been ever present, from the moment he arrived until the moment he left. There was never a chance to let his guard down because there were too many people willing to take advantage of the weak. Jarlath had seen it many times, that corrupt display of power over others. Then he met Yasper, and his friendship and ability to charm everyone around them provided Jarlath with enough security that he was able to relax, but only enough to allow some of the tension from his shoulders.

Even there, though, in the camp with the threat of death and a flogging hanging over his head, the need to play the hero outweighed his self-preservation. The scars on his back were testament to Jarlath's ability to get himself into situations he couldn't talk himself out of, but he'd save Gem again, just as he'd sacrifice himself for Ash as her fire ripped apart the fields and both their lives.

Jarlath looked at his hands, examining them in the muted light from the fire and the two candles burning on the small table. His knuckles were misshapen, but his fingers were strong. A soldier's hands.

He hadn't picked up a weapon since the Stadium and he wasn't sure he could. His hands were instruments of death. He clenched his fists, shoving them behind his back. He used to be so sure of who he was and what he wanted, so certain of the path his life was going to take, but now?

It seemed nothing was within his control anymore, and he wasn't sure how much of himself he was willing to hand over to fate. Perhaps this new challenge was part of it, a way to help him forge forward. A way to help him work out who he wanted to be.

How Laeli had convinced Thalion of giving him this task, Jarlath had no idea. He wasn't sure how he was going to persuade his commanders to agree to a treaty with the Chieftain of Estilleon, but he had the four-day ride to the border to work it out. Gristel was the sort of man who followed orders and wasn't likely to go against them.

Outside, the wind continued to scream and batter the world with snow and ice.

Jarlath swallowed, staring out into the darkness.

If it meant no one else had to die … he would be the wolf, he supposed, his eyes returning to the door to his room, thinking of the man who had not long walked through it. Jarlath knew he had a hard task ahead of him, and Thalion a harder one.

CHAPTER TWENTY-NINE

It was a two-day ride to The Hollows. Laeli spent one night in Wildeview, arriving when the sun had vanished completely for the day. She rose early and was on the road again before the sun had inched over the Peaks. The nearer she got to the forest, she could feel the earth calling, that green life she had missed singing through her blood. Thalion had hated the idea of her going alone but she'd won in the end. It was allied territory she was passing through and who would be stupid enough to try and stop her?

What worried her more was she'd left Jarlath to Thalion.

'He's still healing, Thalion,' she'd said pointedly. 'Please don't torment him too much.'

Her husband had smiled. 'What do you think I'm going to do to the poor boy?'

'Just … don't.'

The Hollows was a small village, with a grocer, butcher, blacksmith, carpenter, and a fletcher and bowmaker. There were craftsmen and a dressmaker, and the streets were tidy, swept clear of snow, the cottages well-kept and proud. Laeli rode into the main square; a well stood in the middle, a group of women and girls gathered around it with large wooden tubs for washing. The scent of lye and animal fat floated over the village from the soap-makers and Laeli could smell the warm ale and spiced mead from the tavern tucked off to one side, hear the fires crackling in hearths across the village. In the distance, she could also hear axes landing and smell the fresh cut timber.

She was given directions to Galina's house by a stout woman with windblown cheeks, who appeared to know exactly who she was. It appeared people were aware of more than just Thalion's coup, if the whispers behind hands were any indication. One girl went so far as to curtsey, making Laeli blush, and she rode from the square in relief, heading deeper into the village.

Galina's home was as simple and unassuming as the rest of the cottages in The Hollows, with a thatched roof and stone walls. A servant saw Laeli coming and ducked inside; Galina met her at the door, inviting her in for a meal before they headed out to the forest.

Laeli didn't know what to say to the Chief's daughter, who pressed food and drink on her in the simple kitchen, the smell of drying herbs in the air. Galina's smile was warm, her eyes sparkling, the warm colour of her skin adding to her beauty. Galina caught her looking.

'Is something wrong?'

'You're beautiful,' Laeli blurted, cursing herself inwardly. She was hopeless at small talk and more hopeless at talking to a woman like Galina, who was genuine in every way. Laeli was used to ulterior motives and Galina had none.

Galina laughed. 'Next to you … no, I don't think so.'

Laeli lowered her eyes and was relieved when Galina stood, leading her back outside where the servant was standing with her horse, a spritely chestnut mare, the saddle bags bulging, rolls of bedding secured firmly to the rear of the saddle. 'I thought we might stay out there,' Galina said. 'If you like.' She glanced up at the sky. 'It won't snow tonight.'

'Alright,' Laeli agreed, enjoying the thrill – her husband would be annoyed when he found out, though he knew she was perfectly capable of protecting herself. She smiled – husband, it hardly seemed real –

and followed Galina from the village, heading due west, the sunlight throwing their shadows across the ground. The wind was soft and light and, as they approached a dense strand of trees, Laeli's heart began to race. They passed into the shade of the forest and, around them, the earth sang. It wasn't the same as Eshlune; the trees here were dark and heavy, the foliage thin and needle-like. Names Laeli knew rushed into her head – pines, firs, spruces, larches; on the forest floor, moss, liverwort, and lichen clung to life.

Laeli could feel Galina's eyes on her as she dismounted and wandered beneath the branches, her fingers twitching. She rested her hand against the trunk of a large pine, closing her eyes and feeling its life force pulsing beneath her skin. She pulled the forest inside her, feeling that green life fill her veins, slowly at first, sluggish in its winter slumber, and then faster, until it was like lightning. She gasped, then laughed out loud, turning in circles, letting her magic stretch through her until it reached her fingertips. She bent and touched the earth; grass and flowers pushed their way through the hard ground.

Galina sucked in a breath. 'That's incredible,' she whispered, sliding from her horse, approaching the flowers in wonder.

Laeli grinned, giddy, and joyous as the scales inside her tipped, the balance of her powers righting themselves. Now, she could take on Caden's pet fae – she could take on anything. The thought sobered her, and she stood, dusting her clothes. Galina's face was alive with questions.

'How does it work? The magic?'

'I don't know, exactly,' Laeli said. 'It's part of me. Without it, I wouldn't be myself. I wouldn't be able to breathe. That's why this,' she smiled, gesturing at the trees, 'is so important. Thank you,' she added earnestly. Galina blushed, then retrieved the bed rolls from her horse, setting both on the ground beneath the trees. She busied herself with food and drink from the saddlebags, then collected wood and fallen pinecones for the fire. Laeli let Galina light the fire her way, content to sit and let her magic hum beneath her skin. They ate cheese and fruit, bread, and salted meat, sitting in silence, the delicate sounds of life swimming around them — the soft wind teasing the branches of the trees, the light footfall of small animals beneath the shrubs and the occasional call of a bird.

The forest grew dark around them. Galina poked the fire with a stick; sparks shot into the sky, and Laeli's magic danced and spun as she stared into the flames.

'I'm glad he found you,' Galina said quietly, her words startling Laeli out of her meditative state. Her face was closed. 'No doubt Frode told you, if you hadn't worked it out after Nara's nasty words. Nothing was ever confirmed, but I knew my father and Hadrian had talked about it.'

This was a conversation Laeli had not been prepared for but had sensed was coming. 'I'm sorry,' she said eventually. 'That things didn't turn out how you would have liked.'

'I've known him since we were children,' Galina said, then shook her head, giving Laeli a sincere smile. 'Perhaps, when this is all over — war and rebellion — we can be … friends?'

Laeli was taken aback. 'I've never really had friends,' she admitted softly.

'But you're a princess!'

'Perhaps that's why. When your father is a king, everybody wants something from you. I got sick of sending pieces of myself into the world and not getting anything in return. It became easier to keep myself to myself.' Laeli looked up at the wind ruffled trees.

'Someone broke your heart?' Galina asked gently.

'Yes. He loved me, but not for me. For who I was,' Laeli answered.

'It seems men are arseholes no matter if they're human or fae.'

Laeli laughed. 'It appears so.'

'But not Thalion.'

'No. It's one of the reasons why …' she stopped, swallowing the words away. 'He doesn't care about all that. It doesn't matter to him who my father is, so I know that what he feels is genuine. It's real and that's important, especially now, when everything around us is so out of our control.'

'You're talking about what's happening in Eshlune?'

Laeli nodded. 'I don't know what I will find when I go back there. I'm terribly afraid things will have changed beyond recognition, and I'll have been too late to stop it from happening. Sometimes I wish I hadn't come here, but then, if I didn't ...'

They fell into silence again, until Laeli stood and moved into the trees. She turned and beckoned, and Galina followed her, Laeli lighting their way with a ball of flame. Leaving the fire dangling in the air, she bent and touched the earth, drawing tiny pink flowers from the ground. Galina was smiling.

'I love flowers,' she said.

Laeli touched them one by one; they sank back into the earth.

'Oh! Can't they stay?' Galina asked wistfully.

'It isn't their time,' Laeli explained. She paused, watching the other woman's face carefully, an idea growing in her mind. 'Do you want to meet a goddess?'

'What?'

'If I leave these here,' Laeli explained, drawing the flowers back to life, 'she'll come for them.' She caught Galina's eye. 'The Bone Mother.'

'Won't she be cross?'

Laeli smiled. 'I'm hoping she has a sense of humour, but yes, she will be cross with me.'

Galina grinned. 'I'm game if you are. Let's meet a goddess.'

The two women settled under the trees to wait. Around them, the night grew colder, the wind chilled. Soon, they could hear footsteps crunching over dry earth and fallen twigs. The Bone Mother stepped into view, her belt of skulls dangling, the grey wolf stalking at her side. Galina sucked in a breath.

The Goddess lifted her veil, glaring at them with red-rimmed eyes. 'You think you're funny, daughter of the forest. How do you like my snow?'

'It's ... white,' Laeli said, smothering her grin. 'But beautiful.'

The Bone Mother's laugh was wind over the rocks.

Galina held her breath, her heartbeat furious, as the Goddess stomped on the flowers.

The Bone Mother gazed up at the trees. 'These aren't your trees,' she said to Laeli, fixing her in a curious stare. 'Yet you are still here. Why? When your forest, Eshlune, is in danger? You are still here. Do you like my snow so much that you cannot leave?'

Laeli couldn't lie to a goddess. 'No.'

'Ah. It isn't my snow, but a son of the snow that ties you to this place.'

'It is.'

'Is your love for him stronger than your love for your home?'

Laeli bit her lip. 'I can't answer that question, Cailleach.'

'You can, but you won't. You will go back to your forest. You will be there by the solstice, and you will have to make a choice,' the Goddess said. 'Him and the snow, or,' she paused; the air shimmered, and then, the Cailleach was standing directly in front of Laeli. She bent, until they were eye to eye. Head spinning, Laeli sucked in her breath, her body frozen, her blood screaming with the power the Goddess held inside. 'What I can give you.'

'I don't want it.'

The Goddess pulled back. 'You are quick to answer.'

'It isn't who I am,' Laeli argued.

The Cailleach considered this. 'We shall see.'

In the blink of an eye, she was gone, the air swirling with snow and leaves and sparks. Laeli let out a breath and closed her eyes. When she opened them, Galina was looking at her in concern.

'I don't ever want to speak to a goddess again,' Laeli whispered. She was trembling.

'What did she say to you?'

'You didn't hear that?'

Galina shook her head. 'No. I … she talked to me as well. She told me …' Her voice trailed off and Laeli didn't ask any questions. What the

Cailleach said to Galina wasn't for her ears. Galina would do what she thought was right with the information.

They settled down to sleep under the trees, and in the morning, silently packed up their camp and rode back to the village, each mulling over their own thoughts. When the sun had risen fully, Laeli put her face to the bitter north wind and snow and made her way home.

CHAPTER THIRTY

It was just another night, Fox thought, dabbing at the wound on her forehead. The bruise around her eye was slowly fading, as were the ones on her legs. She pressed the cloth firmly against her broken flesh. It would stop bleeding soon; head wounds were always the worst.

On the bed in the corner, Cora slept, her pregnant belly cradled between her scrawny hands. It was freezing in this miserable house within this miserable village in this gods-forsaken corner of the world. What Fox wouldn't give to be back at *The Persian*, in her rumpled red bed with her view over the shitty city, a place that, in comparison to Whitemouth, sparkled like a jewel.

The room the girls were kept in was plain, the window barred with thick iron. Those bars were firm; Fox had spent hours trying to prise them free, only to be beaten with an iron bar as thick as those that framed her window in punishment. The worn timber floor was covered in dark stains Fox didn't want to think about too much, although she could guess what they were.

Cora moaned in her sleep. That baby was due any day now and the girl was terrified of what would happen to her child.

Fox knew what would happen.

She'd found the children downstairs by accident, having been ordered into the kitchen to prepare food for Caden and his friends. Unable to find enough vegetables to make a simple soup with, she'd discovered the door at the rear of the kitchen, bolted shut with a heavy slide lock. Assuming she was about to enter the pantry, Fox opened the door, falling back in shock to find two children, dressed in threadbare clothes, their filthy faces peering out at her. Before she could do anything, Caden cuffed her around the ear and slammed the door shut, warning her viciously to never open that door again.

Fox growled into the darkness. She'd like to open his head.

Faren had made her bed on the floor, Cora's belly too large to share with anymore. The halfkin girl was younger than Fox; she rolled in her sleep, her tiny body curled in on itself the way Fox had seen her curl when Caden drove his boot into her stomach. Fox glanced across the room. The rope that tied Cora to the stinking bed had left a ring of raw flesh around her ankle. What threat a pregnant girl posed, Fox couldn't work out; she assumed Cora had been tied up in some sort of punishment for being pregnant in the first place, as if Caden didn't know how it happened. Fox and Faren were free to wander the room, but not free to wander the house, or the village outside.

She had to get out of here. She glanced over her shoulder again and scowled at herself. She wouldn't leave those two here to suffer any further. There was nothing in the room she could use as a weapon – there were two metal buckets, one for washing, one for relieving themselves, two narrow beds and a pile of musty, moth-eaten blankets. Between them, they had five sets of clothes, no shoes, empty bellies, and no hope.

Downstairs, the men talked and drank. Sooner or later, one of them would stagger up here, unlock the door and decide which girl he was going to fuck, whether they liked it or not.

While the other girls slept, Fox sat vigil on the bed, her eyes on the door, willing it not to open, willing them to be so drunk they couldn't manage to climb those stairs. Outside, the village slept, those people lying peacefully in their beds. Fox liked to think they didn't know what went on inside this house. She knew, though, that some probably had an idea, like the elderly woman she'd glimpsed one day when she was downstairs dragging a broom over the rough stone floor. The woman's eyes had shone with pity and Fox had turned her face away, her belly burning with shame.

She got up and peered through the pathetic little window. Chilled air snuck inside to claw at her face, but she didn't care. She'd been so cold since she arrived in this land, she couldn't remember what it was like to feel the sun on her face. In the street below, Caden's fae friend was standing in the ankle-deep snow that covered the street. Halin, his name was. Fox could see the top of his head. With him were two others. They were laughing and talking, having a great time while she sat up here, a prisoner.

Caden's voice echoed from the room below and she shrunk back from the window, darting across the floor to sit back on the bed, resuming her watch. She'd hear his voice in her nightmares long after she'd killed him. If it took ten years, she'd kill him. What Caden didn't know about Fox was she had incredible patience.

Fox's ears twitched. Something moved by the window; a shadow passed across the weak moonlight and then, a female voice, rich and musical.

'Fox? Are you in there?'

The window was two storeys up, with no real ledge other than a narrow strip of wood on the outside. Fox leapt from the bed, eyes on that window, half afraid of what she might see. Gloved hands appeared, fingers wrapping around the bars. The voice moaned and Fox watched, her heart thundering, as those bars were ripped free and dropped into the darkness. Trembling, Fox backed up cautiously as a body slid into the room, landing on cat-like feet.

'Cursed iron,' the voice spat. She was wearing dark green, the clothes fit close to the curves of her body. A hood covered her face and, as she straightened, Fox glimpsed a rosebud of a nose, a narrow chin, and skin like cream.

A fae.

'Who are you?' Fox whispered.

'Laeli,' the fae said quietly. She reached up and removed the hood. Fox sucked in a breath at the shock of dark hair, bound in a braid, that fell to her waist, the green eyes, sharp cheekbones and hunter's bow mouth that remained steady – there was no hint of emotion in that unearthly face. Rising above her shoulders were the hilts of two swords. With her glowing skin and glimmering eyes, the fae was shockingly beautiful in this dark, desperate place.

'I saw you, with the Chieftain's son. I was in the street, watching through a gap in the barricade,' Fox blurted. She didn't add how badly she'd been beaten for daring to leave the house. 'What are you doing here?'

'Your brother sent me.'

'You know Elan?'

'Yes.' Laeli glanced at the pitiful room. 'Let's go. I can carry you down.'

Fox shook her head, gesturing behind her at the sleeping forms of Cora and Faren. 'Not without them.'

Laeli peered around her, her face creasing. 'Alright.'

'What are you doing here, in Estilleon?' Fox asked bluntly.

'It's a long story, too long for the moment.'

'Are you one of hers? Kiarda's? I've heard them talking about her,' Fox added, waving at the floor and the room below it. 'I've heard many things in this place.' She eyed Laeli with interest. 'Rebellion and traitors. Murder.'

'I'm not one of Kiarda's. Let me get you all out of here first and then I'll tell you what you want to know,' Laeli replied, her voice even and low.

Fox gestured at the swords. 'Give me a weapon and I can get myself out of here.'

From the scabbards at both hips, Laeli withdrew two daggers, handing them to Fox without any hesitation. A shiver went through her as Fox closed her hands around the hilts.

'I could kill you with these,' she said quietly.

'You could try.'

They looked at each other; Fox didn't trust her and didn't do anything to hide it. When had a fae ever done anything to help her? She turned to find Faren was awake, her large grey eyes watching Laeli warily. Fox nodded and Faren scrambled to her feet, gently waking Cora, the pregnant girl sitting up and rubbing at her thin face.

Laeli approached them slowly. 'What did he do to you?'

Fox lifted her chin. 'Things I bet no man has ever done to you.'

'Did he—'

'What do you think?' Fox growled. 'If it wasn't me, it was one of them, even Cora. It doesn't matter that she's pregnant. Caden cares less for the baby in her belly than he does for us, and he hates us.'

Laeli looked like she was going to be sick.

There were heavy footsteps on the stairs and the door was unlocked and flung open. Caden strode in, his face tight, his eyes clouded. Fox wrinkled her nose – she could smell the drink on him from the other side of the room and she tensed. He was always worse when he was drunk and lately he was always drunk, moaning about how he was going to kill those who'd betrayed their Chieftain.

Caden stopped when he noticed Laeli, his hand flying to the sword he, recently, always wore at his hip. 'Well, well. Thalion's whore. Come to join the party?'

Laeli shed her cloak and drew the two swords at her back, her face hard.

Caden slowly pulled his own sword free, his movement unhurried and measured. 'Come on, bitch, show me what you've got.'

Laeli's wrists bent and flexed with speed no human could match as those swords spun and twirled before her; Caden swore and took a hasty step back, narrowing his eyes, before he laughed, full of drunken bravado.

'What else can you do? What other tricks have you shown Hadrian's boy, huh? Or did you just have to open your legs and wrap that pretty mouth around his cock to get him to do what you want?'

'It would suit you to believe that, wouldn't it?' Laeli replied. 'Where's your pet? Have you checked on him lately? If you look outside, you'll see him – parts of him anyway.'

Caden's expression hardened, and Fox's fingers tightened on the hilt of the blades. Caden hadn't paid her a shred of attention, his eyes on the fae and her swords. He didn't think Fox or any of the girls in this horrible suffocating house were a threat to him. He snarled and rushed towards Laeli, his sword swinging, but she ducked beneath it and slid across the floor, one of her swords reaching out and biting into Caden's ankle, cutting easily through the leather of his boot. He stumbled, blood dripping onto the dusty wooden floor as she flipped onto her feet and faced him again. He adjusted his grip, his sword held out before him, and came at her again.

As Fox watched, Laeli darted to the side, her feet leaving the floor as she ran *up* the wall and dropped down behind Caden, who swung around so quickly he lost his balance and stumbled. He couldn't possibly match her, Fox thought, inching to the corner where Cora and Faren were clutching each other in terror.

Laeli was playing with him, like Fox sometimes used to play with her marks before she killed them. Those swords slashed, slicing Caden's chest open. He staggered back, his hand clutching his front, blood oozing between his fingers.

While Caden was distracted, Fox freed Cora, pushing a blade into Faren's hand. She turned back to Caden and Laeli, her body shielding the girls from his eyes.

Caden swung his sword with a grunt, blood seeping from his chest to drip onto the floor. Laeli danced away effortlessly, her eyes gleaming.

'Where is he, anyway? Letting a woman do his dirty work? Perhaps you need to be fucked by a real man,' Caden taunted, his breathing growing ragged. Fox could smell his fear, despite his swagger and his self-assurance.

He was going to die, and he knew it. Her muscles tensed in anticipation.

Laeli moved so quickly Fox found it difficult to track her. One moment she was standing across the room, the next, she was behind Caden, her swords pressed against his neck, one on either side. Fox jumped as flames licked the blades of those swords. Caden screamed horribly as his skin melted and boiled. The fire died as Laeli put her mouth close to his ear, close to that ruined flesh.

'And you're a real man, are you?' she said with deadly calm. The swords tightened; a line of blood dripped down Caden's skin and disappeared beneath his collar as he whimpered. 'Real men don't rape women. They don't keep them bound and tied like an animal.' She paused. Caden's sobs and the furious pounding of his heart were the only sounds in the room. 'I'm going to take your head back to my husband as a wedding present. Or maybe I'll take all of you back and let him feed you to his dogs a piece at a time. No, I've got a better idea.' She looked up and gave Fox a nod.

Fox approached, her stomach tightening, adrenalin pouring through her veins, as potent and sweet as any wine. She let Caden see the blade in her hand, let him watch as she twirled it expertly between her fingers, smiling as he did nothing to hide his fear, his eyes pleading, the skin on the sides of his face scorched and raw. The stench of burnt hair and flesh threaded through the air and Fox breathed it deep, letting it fill her.

She ran the tip of the blade down Caden's ruined cheek with a smile.

'Who are you?' he moaned.

'Before I came here, to this hell, I was the assassin to the High Mage of Merawuld. I never missed a mark, so you know,' Fox added. She moved closer to him, until she was looking directly into the eyes that had haunted her dreams. 'I can be gentle too, Caden. And slow. So very,

very slow, slow enough that you will feel everything I do to you. Would you like that?'

He opened his mouth, but she took hold of his ear and, true to her word, slowly carved it from his head as he howled, blood running down the side of his neck, coating the blade of Laeli's sword. Caden lifted a hand towards her, a mumbled plea escaping his lips. Fox grasped his wrist and leisurely drew the blade along his skin, opening his arm from wrist to elbow. Caden thrashed, truly panicked, but Laeli's swords pressed against his skin.

Fox saw it in his face – his acceptance of it, and she almost felt that he should have fought harder for his life, but then, she knew what it was like to give up, how easy it was, the strange sort of peace that came with it. She looked into his eyes for the last time and got to work.

Laeli never looked away from what unfolded in front of her. By the time Fox had finished, Caden was mincemeat on the floor, his insides spread on the outside, his eyes wide, his tongue ripped out. Fox removed his hands, hacking them off one at a time, then his eyes, plucked from his skull with her bare hands. She left his charred and mangled corpse there and hurried down the stairs before Laeli could stop her, the front of her dress soaked with blood.

In the kitchen she found their other usual tormentors, both drunk and both asleep with their heads on the table. Winding her fingers through their hair, Fox lifted their heads one at a time and sliced their throats open, disappointed they weren't conscious and would never know who it was that killed them. As their blood spread across the table like a cloth, Laeli came down the stairs, Cora and Faren following. Faren spat at the men, her face screwed up with anger and relief.

Cora didn't spare the dead men a glance, hurrying into the kitchen. Laeli watched curiously as she pulled the key down from the peg on the wall and unlocked the door hidden in the corner. The fae's eyes widened as two children, no older than eight, a boy and a girl, slipped into the light, their faces pale and dirty, their eyes watering.

'Who are they?' Laeli whispered.

'Their mothers are dead,' Fox said quietly as Cora held the children to her, shielding them from the table. 'Their father's—' she waved her hand dismissively at the miserable house. She had no idea who their fathers were, but assumed it was one of the now dead men, or possibly the Chief himself.

Laeli swallowed audibly. 'This is …'

'What happens to people like us,' Fox finished. 'People no one cares about, or notices. I thought my life was bad before I came here. At least, as a whore, I had a choice.'

'I'm sorry.'

'No, you're not,' Fox said. 'Did he know?'

Laeli met Fox's doubtful look with a fierce glare. 'You need to understand, even if he did know, there was nothing he could have done about it, not until now, not until his father was gone.'

Fox held her gaze, noticing how green her eyes were, how they shone in the dim light. 'You're Mahelivar's sister, aren't you? You have the same eyes.'

Laeli nodded.

'Well, Princess, lead the way.' Fox strode to the door, flinging it open and stepping into the hard grey light of the dawn. In the street, three bodies lay face-down in the snow, their blood spread like spilled wine. Halin's head was on the ground next to his body, his arm laying a few feet away. Fox glanced at Laeli over her shoulder; the fae was on one knee, peering into the face of one of the children, the girl, talking to her in hushed tones. Fox turned back to the street. She couldn't help but be impressed; she'd heard nothing, hadn't known Laeli was there until she'd appeared at the window and spoke. There was no way she was going to tell her that though. She looked back to see Laeli pick the child up and hold her filthy body against her own. She met Fox's eyes.

'There's two horses. I only brought one extra. I didn't know there would be more of you,' she said quietly. She glanced back at Faren, Cora and the boy. 'They can have mine.'

'And you?'

Laeli shifted the child to her hip; the girl tucked her head against the fae's neck. The Princess' eyes were glittering, but her voice was firm. 'I'll walk.'

Around them, the village was waking up. A door opened down the street and a hard-faced woman stepped out, a basket of laundry on one hip, a thin child on the other. As her gaze fell on the dead men, she shoved the child back inside the house and shut the door, approaching them warily, stopping far enough away to stay out of reach of their weapons. She set the washing down slowly.

She looked at Laeli for a long time. Her stare was untamed, a wildness to her face that spoke of hidden strength and courage that Fox understood. The wind blew around them, sharp and bitter; Fox shivered, her teeth rattling in her head, her thoughts beginning to freeze like the rest of her. Eventually, the woman nodded at Caden's house. 'Is he dead?'

Laeli nodded, clutching the child tighter. Fox's nostrils flared as the wind breezed past them again – she could smell her, the fae Princess, and the child in her arms, but there was something else, something Fox couldn't identify. A scent that shifted with the breeze.

The woman gave a little sigh of what Fox thought was relief. 'Tell Thalion we'll elect our own leader, until Brenna returns. We'll send a messenger when it's done.'

'He needs to see the storehouses,' Laeli said firmly.

The woman nodded. 'Tell him to come, then. No one will challenge him.' She picked up her basket and moved off, not looking back and not looking at the bodies.

With the child held close, Laeli walked down the middle of the street, her feet leaving slight prints in the snow. Fox and the others followed, the boy clinging to Cora's hand as they found the horses and left Whitemouth behind.

CHAPTER THIRTY-ONE

When Thalion woke, the other side of the bed was empty and grey light crept through the room. Sitting up, he rubbed at his face, fingers scratching over the stubble on his chin, the chill of the morning embracing his bare flesh. His wife was dressed; not in the dark, heavy woollen dresses she'd been wearing, but in her fae Witch's uniform, that otherworldly material accentuating every dip and curve of her body. Her hair was pulled back in a tight braid and her face was calm, but there was determination and fire blazing in her eyes.

'Morning,' Thalion said softly, his eyes sweeping over her again; she was also wearing her scabbard and there was a dagger at her hip, one that he'd given her recently. 'Has something happened that I don't know about?'

'I need to train,' Laeli answered curtly.

'It's barely dawn.' Outside, the sun was slowly pushing through the heavy clouds in a feeble attempt at lighting the world. Snow blanketed everything, a layer of white stretching from the castle to the horizon in all directions. 'And it's cold. Come back to bed.'

She ignored him, collecting her swords from their resting place against the wall near the fire. She slipped them into the scabbard firmly. 'In Sitra, I trained most mornings. I'm out of practice.'

'Who did you train with?'

Her eyes slid to him, then away again. 'Solen mostly.'

'Who won?'

'It wasn't a competition, Thalion.' She tossed him an irritated look.

'Sure, but who won?' he pressed.

Laeli's lips curled slightly. 'Me.'

Thalion yawned. 'How much practice does a one hundred and something year old fae warrior need?'

Laeli threw a bundle of clothing at him; he recognised his pants and shirt. Boots followed, landing near his hip, and leaving a scattering of dried mud in the bed. 'You need to train as well.'

'Laeli—'

'There is a war coming,' she reminded him quietly. 'I – *we* – need to be ready.'

He swallowed. 'I know,' he said solemnly.

Unspoken was the truth that hung between them – that in the end, her loyalty was to her family, to her people. She would return to Eshlune. He just didn't know when.

Laeli's eyes cut to him again. 'I'll meet you in the training yard.'

The training yard, where he'd seen her lingering while still wearing Eira's face, her expression one of interested boredom, as was Eira's way. What Thalion had seen that others didn't was the stiffness in Laeli's spine, and the way her fists curled in the fur of her cloak, as if her fingers itched to hold a blade.

She left him to dress; by the time he was approaching the training yard in the castle grounds, his belly empty and his head still fluffy from sleep, Laeli was standing in the middle of that snow-covered circle, face hard and frustration leaking from every part of her.

Facing his wife, leaning casually against the wooden railing, were five young men, all wielding swords and, he quickly noted, amused expressions.

In Estilleon, women didn't step into the fighting circle or the Stadium. They didn't hold swords or daggers or axes. They didn't ride to battle or spill blood on the earth. They kept hearths burning and food on the table. They managed the household and the children, occasionally a village, but they were not warriors.

Despite what had happened in Whitemouth, despite the rumours that had spread, Thalion's men still wouldn't let Laeli train with them. His stomach turned, and anger rushed through him, not at these young men, but at what she had uncovered in that village.

She'd told him everything, in enough detail that he didn't have to imagine a thing. She'd been so quiet and still after she returned that he debated finding a healer to tend to her, but Laeli had woken one morning and insisted she was fine. Though there was a hardness to her face that wasn't there before and he'd not seen her truly smile since.

Thalion shifted his weight from one foot to another, knowing where this morning was going to lead them. He let his fingers caress the hilt of his sword and shook the last grasp of sleep from his head as Laeli turned her gaze on him. He could read her thoughts, the absolute dismay and anger she couldn't hide from him, her exasperation at the traditions of his world.

Taking a deep breath of the frigid morning air, Thalion stepped into the training yard. Seeing him, the men straightened and dipped their heads in the same way he had seen countless others dip their heads to his father. Something in his chest tightened, but he swallowed it away. There were some red faces amongst the men, and much muttering. If Thalion was his father, he'd punish them for humiliating his wife.

Laeli wouldn't condone it, so he remained silent.

She didn't need to prove herself to him, but he had a feeling she needed to prove herself to herself. Although she'd returned from Whitemouth without a scratch, her eyes had remained haunted, her face shadowed and she walked stiffly, muscles bunched, fists clenched.

So, he would give her what she needed.

No one spoke as Thalion removed his furs and rolled his shoulders, letting his muscles warm and stretch. No one spoke as he slid his sword free, the steel hissing welcome in the chilled air.

And no one spoke as he strode to the middle of the yard and faced his wife.

Laeli's lips shifted into a barely-there smile. Her eyes glimmered as she freed her blades. With the tip of one sword, she swiftly drew a wide circle in the snow around herself, then raised her eyes to his again. Thalion nodded to show he understood. If he could push her out of that circle, if he could step over that line, she'd concede defeat.

One of the men snickered; Laeli ignored it, so he did as well.

As he readied his hands and found his centre, Thalion knew what the men were thinking. It wasn't a fair fight. He was bigger, he appeared stronger, the bulk of his body almost twice that of the woman who stood before him, eyes shining and expression lethal. They'd all heard of fae fighting prowess, and some had witnessed it, but the men knew Laeli as a Princess, as a Witch.

They hadn't glimpsed the warrior.

She dropped into a crouch, left foot forward, her weight on the right. She held those swords parallel to the snow-coated earth, and nodded, just once.

Swordplay was like a dance, Thalion thought, and his wife wanted to dance. He smiled, moving quickly into the leading steps, an invitation of sorts, and a streak of green and shining steel answered.

It wasn't long before Thalion realised he'd never seen the warrior either. The night they first met flashed into his mind – she'd taken it easy on him, despite her claims that she was trying to kill him.

Now, after having to hide who she truly was, Laeli was unleashed. He felt it, the moment she let go. He watched her face, watched that mask of deadly calm never shift as, arms a blur and twin swords singing, she attacked over and over again, forcing him back, forcing him to move quicker than he ever had before. To defend like he never had before. No sweat beaded her skin, yet it ran in a river down his back, over his chest and stroked the side of his face.

She moved like the north wind, like the fiercest winter squall; he felt the true strength of her in every blow he blocked, and in every stroke of the longsword she deflected – it was like attacking a pillar of stone, hard and unyielding, ancient, and powerful. Where he swung, she was already gone, already bringing those blades towards him.

Laeli paused and stepped out of his reach. Giving him a moment. A wicked wind tore across the training yard, as Thalion held out his hand for a second sword. One of the men behind him rushed forward. He could hear them murmuring, their awe barely veiled as his fingers curled around the hilt of the borrowed sword. He prepared his grip, feeling his muscles adjust to accommodate the heaviness of two swords.

His wife just raised her eyebrows.

'Thought I'd even things up,' he stated mildly.

She snorted. 'If it makes you feel better to try.'

The addition of his second weapon didn't help. She still slipped beneath his blows, or danced away with ease, light on her feet, her eyes never leaving his. She read every movement before he'd executed it, shifting her stance to counter him, barely leaving a mark in the snow to show where she'd been.

In the end, with her feet still firmly inside her circle, Laeli's swords came to rest on either side of his neck as, behind him, someone gasped.

Thalion only smiled. 'Well,' he murmured, 'that was fun.'

Her eyes flashed with the memory of those same words in a rain-drenched forest when he was a different person. She let her swords drop and laughed, her face alight with the thrill of it, then pushed herself onto her toes to kiss him on the mouth, not caring they had an audience.

He held her against him, both arms crossed over her back, swords still gripped tightly in hands that could suddenly feel the exact weight they carried. 'Why didn't you kill me, really, that night in the forest? You could have. I see that now,' he whispered, his forehead resting against hers.

She pulled back, her smile falling. 'We don't take life unless it cannot be avoided.'

Thalion let her step away from him, let her walk out of the yard, the men parting for her, their whispered awe following her as she headed back to the castle.

He finally understood why his actions in Westhelm had angered her so much. His lack of understanding about her and her people, about how they viewed the world, had almost cost him dearly. She'd been right to challenge him on it, to force him to truly think about the methods he had begun to employ. He was better for it, he knew that, and vowed once again to be the man she deserved.

A small part of him hoped it would be enough to keep her. She'd married him, pledged herself to him, despite the differences between them, but he didn't know how much of her was here, with him, and how much was in the forest, rooted into the trees and wound within the branches of that world.

Thalion watched her glide up the steps, her swords tucked away. Before she stepped inside the gaping mouth of the castle, Laeli turned and caught his eye. She didn't smile; the look on her face told him her thoughts lay with his, twisted together in what had been, what was, and what was yet to come.

She thanked him for the training yard later, when they were lying curled around one another, the fire crackling in the background, throwing warm shadows over the room. He could sense her lingering annoyance. She hadn't said anything, but he could guess what was bothering her.

'They need time to see you differently, sweetheart,' he murmured, feeling her stiffen, then relax, at the endearment he'd been wanting to use for a month.

She shifted so she could see his face, her weight on her elbows, that curtain of hair dangling over her shoulders. Her eyes were glowing. 'Time. You humans talk about time as if you have aeons of it to spare, as if your lives weren't over in the blink of an eye. But,' she said softly, her fingers running over his collar bones, 'you're patient, Thalion, so patient sometimes I can't understand it. I have another hundred years waiting for me and I can't be as you are. I can't be patient. My father has always told me to wait, to slow down, to think, not be rash but … I don't know what to do with all this *time*.'

Time. The one thing Thalion wished, now more than ever, he had more of. He tucked a chunk of hair behind Laeli's ear, fingers lingering over that pointed tip. 'Maybe it's because we have so little time that we want to make sure we use it wisely.'

Laeli considered his words, then sighed. 'This is why my brother will make a much better king than I would a queen. Mahelivar is patient, and calm and steadfast and grounded … all the things I'm not,' she added with a huff, flopping onto her belly, and burying her face in the pillow.

'I didn't think you wanted to be Queen.'

'I don't. I just wish sometimes I could be more like Mahelivar.'

Thalion grazed his fingers down her spine, a smile pulling at his mouth at the uncharacteristic display of vulnerability. He couldn't help the little thrill that danced through his blood when she revealed something deeper, something *more*, about herself. 'You are the way you are supposed to be, Laeli.'

She lifted her head and gave him a puzzled look. 'What do you mean?'

'Well,' he began, indicating she should lie back down. She did, and he resumed stroking her skin, thinking about her magic, about her extraordinary talent. 'Your skill is with fire, so you are like fire, and fire isn't patient. It isn't calm and steadfast. It's a whirlwind of power and strength and it does what it likes. It doesn't ask permission and it makes no excuses for what it is.'

Laeli was very quiet and still, and then, softly, 'You talk like you understand it.'

'Fire is a gift from the Gods,' he explained gently. 'Without it, we couldn't cook our food, or stay warm through the long winter. Without it, we would die here – this land would give us no mercy, no quarter, at all.'

Laeli let a trickle of her magic out – tiny flames skimmed the length of her spine, before dissolving into her skin. Thalion kissed his way down her back, tasting smoke and breathing deep the smell of her. She sighed happily and rolled over, draping herself over him.

He felt her smile against his chest.

'Maybe you're right,' she murmured.

'Of course I am,' he declared smugly.

She snickered, then kissed her way down his body, fingernails following the path of her lips. Thalion clenched his teeth against it, that combination of pleasure and pain as his muscles tightened and his breathing quickened. He dug his fingers into the bedding. Laeli paused, tongue and nails still.

'Have you told them?'

'Told who what?' he managed.

She sank her teeth into his thigh, making him gulp down a sharp breath of air. 'Your men. Have you told them I'm your wife?'

He couldn't answer, not knowing what to say, what the right thing to say was. The truth was he hadn't told anyone – except for those who were in the Hall that night, nobody knew their Chieftain was now married. It had been hard, so hard, to stay quiet about it when he wanted the world to know this woman, this amazing woman, had agreed to marry him.

This woman who he was ridiculously in love with, who he would give everything, if she asked it.

Laeli's lips skimmed his lower belly and his hips lifted, a groan escaping him. She chuckled wickedly but still wouldn't touch him, wouldn't put her remarkable mouth where he wanted. Sometimes, it was like they were discovering each other for the first time, the most minute of touches like lightning slamming through him. The intensity of her gaze set a fire in his flesh, the way her eyes devoured every piece of him and he couldn't breathe, couldn't remember his own name, or the world that existed outside of her hands, her mouth, the blazing heat of her skin.

'Have you told them?' Laeli asked again, her breath tickling his flesh. Close, she was so close and not close enough, her hair falling over his belly, those soft strands almost painful as they brushed his skin.

'No,' he breathed.

She lifted her head, surprise coating her features. 'Why not?'

Thalion swallowed. 'I wasn't sure you'd want me to shout it from the top of the castle.'

Her lips curled. 'You'd do that?'

'If you let me, yes, I would.'

She shifted so she was straddling him, the slight weight of her pressing down on him such exquisite torture, those firm thighs clenching his ribs. She leant forward and kissed him softly, before pulling away, looking at him for a long time, studying him like she had when all this began. His heart thundered beneath her hands; her fingers curled, the sharp points of her nails biting his flesh as she angled her hips and slowly, so slowly, her expression never shifting, took him inside her body.

Thalion's blood exploded but he stayed still, waiting, watching her face, watching the way the colour of her eyes deepened, the way her chest heaved as her breathing became thick and heavy. Still, she didn't move, just looked at him, until he thought his heart would burst.

Unable to bear it any longer, he sat up, folding his arms around her, and kissed her, one hand buried in her hair, the other firm in her lower back as she tucked her legs around him. When he pulled away, her eyes were shining; she rolled her hips, once, twice, then stopped again. He watched her throat shift as she swallowed.

'I wouldn't mind,' Laeli said softly. 'If you told the world.'

The following morning, and the one after, had them back in the training yard and slowly, as word spread of the Chieftain and his unexpected sparring partner, their audience grew as well, until it seemed every man, and some women, within riding distance had come to watch, the girls hanging on the fence, faces alight with wonder – and possibility.

And it took less than a week for the first of those watching men to swallow his pride and step into that training circle to face a fae warrior, who just happened to be a Princess.

Jarlath, despite watching every day, never accepted the offer to pick up a sword. Thalion kept his thoughts to himself, but he recognised the look on the young man's face: fear – and not of the woman with the twin swords and flashing eyes. He wondered again if Laeli was right in insisting the young soldier could help them end a war.

CHAPTER THIRTY-TWO

Jarlath waited at the bottom of the stairs, already on his horse. Elan stood with Thalion and Laeli's horses, the animals nudging him with their soft noses, the halfkin speaking to them in a gentle voice. He glanced up sharply; Jarlath followed his gaze as Thalion, dressed in black and looking particularly sombre, appeared in the doorway, Laeli shadowing him. There were no more gowns and pretty fur stoles for her. The fae was wearing her forest green, those twin swords strapped to her back, her face tight. She slipped past Thalion and was on her horse before the Chieftain had made it halfway down the steps.

Laeli's face was set in hard lines; snow swirled around them, pulling pieces of her hair loose and whipping them across her face. She scowled and pushed them away. Jarlath had seen her face when she had returned from Whitemouth with three halfkin women and two ragged children. He'd never seen anyone look so broken. Whatever she had discovered in that village had shattered her – no one had told him the particulars, but he could guess. Laeli had been in the training yard kicking Thalion's arse almost every morning since then, and he'd watched her face closely in those moments, watched them both, and saw, beneath the smiles and the laughter, the uncertainty at what was to come in two sets of shining eyes.

'Are you alright?' Jarlath asked her.

'Fine,' she said quietly. 'Let's get this done.'

They were joined by a thick-set, older man named Angus, who met them in Reyshorn, offering his home for the night, along with three servants and two pack horses loaded with sacks, tents, and rolls of blankets. They dined with the Chief, Runa, and spent the next night in Silverward. Thalion and the Chief, Cuyler, a big man who looked at Jarlath with interest, stayed awake most of the night talking, leaving a grumbling Laeli to find her own way to bed. On the third night they huddled by the side of the road, the wind held at bay by the heavy oiled tents and the layers of furs.

Despite the swirling snow and the endless cold, the weather was kind and, as the sun was at its peak on the fourth day, they rode into the Estilleon war camp.

Instead of ordered rows of tents, the men of Estilleon organised themselves according to village groups, with the largest and most powerful of the village's tents set up closest to the Chieftain's. Jarlath had learnt that the people of each village pledged their allegiance to their Chief in return for protection and security. The Chiefs in turn offered their allegiance to the Chieftain.

Looking around, Jarlath was amazed by the sheer size and scope of the camp. Going by the number of tents, horses, and wagons spread out before him, there had to be a thousand men there.

And, if what Healy had told him was correct, most of those men were now pledged to Thalion.

The Chieftain rode ahead of the rest of their party, at home in the saddle, the black of his horse's coat shining in the sunlight. Some of the men gathered in the camp had been here since before the battle that had changed Jarlath's life and he swallowed tightly, wondering if any of the faces he saw were the last ones his friends looked on before they died. Most of these men had been outside the swirling loop of politics that engulfed the country, but all of them would have heard the news by now. There was a lot of whispering behind hands as Thalion passed by, and a lot more interested glances at Laeli, who kept her eyes straight ahead, her spine stiff.

'He's nervous,' Laeli had said about Thalion. Looking around, Jarlath could see why.

There appeared to be an equal number of men representing each village, whether their Chiefs supported Thalion or still clung to his father. Their loyalty to their country sat first and foremost in their minds, although Jarlath saw more than one frowning face and mutinous glance at them. He knew there were still some villages who didn't completely agree with the way things were unfolding. This was a test of sorts for the self-appointed Chieftain.

But if Thalion could end this war, he'd have them all.

The weight that bore down on Jarlath's shoulders threatened to send him tumbling from the saddle. He swallowed, and tightened the reins, his horse snorting in objection.

The best warriors from each village made up their front lines, due to their reputation and courage, often best displayed in the Stadium, where more than training went on – minor conflicts between villages over resources or hunting rights were often solved in the arena. After what Jarlath had seen and experienced in the Stadium, the Queen's Army had been woefully unprepared.

As they passed through the camp, Angus rode beside Jarlath and explained that each village had an officer who oversaw it, and all those officers, often the Chief's Seconds or the Chief themselves, reported back to the Chieftain when he was in the camp; otherwise, the army was led by one of the Chiefs, selected to act as the Chieftain's proxy in war. As most of the Chiefs were with Hadrian, the villages were being run by the Seconds, leaving the best warriors from each village in charge of organising the attacks and keeping the camp running.

It seemed chaotic in comparison to the strict organisation of the Queen's Army; when Jarlath murmured so to Angus, the bigger man just raised his eyebrows – a reminder of what had already happened – and may happen again – at the Pass.

Jarlath glanced at Thalion again; the Chieftain swung from his horse, holding his hand out for Laeli. She let him help her down – Jarlath could see her eye roll from where he sat, but the smile she gave Thalion was warm and filled with respect. They disappeared into a large tent set up far from the border and the battle zone.

A thousand men. Twice the number that waited on the other side of the Pass, men who would die if Jarlath failed to do what Thalion asked of him.

Angus turned his horse around, leading Jarlath to the Reyshorn tents.

'You can share this one,' he said, indicating a large tent. Jarlath nodded and dismounted, his body stiff from the long, cold days in the saddle. He untied his saddle bags and bedding and ducked into the tent. He was alone, but was obviously going to be sharing with several others – most of the space was taken up with masses of bedding that appeared well-slept in.

On foot, he followed Angus back across the camp. Men were gathered outside their tents, smiling despite the miserable weather and the fact they were in a war camp. They sat around their fires, talking, and laughing, jostling each other. Jarlath studied their faces as covertly as he could – varying ages, from men younger than he was to older men, like his father, their smiles more restrained, their eyes hardened with experience.

In contrast to the soldiers' tents, Thalion's had a real bed, covered in luxurious furs and blankets. There was a large wooden table and several chairs set on the other side of the cavernous tent, and the floor was decorated in a thick rug. Another small table held a pitcher and a handful of mugs. The canopy was a patchwork of goat leather squares, the whole thing held up by two centre and four corner poles. A fire was burning in a brazier, the air thick and warm already.

Thalion was pacing from one side of the tent to the other, his face tight. He'd left the Chief of Fairhorn at the castle in his place, and the big man whom Jarlath had met a few weeks ago, Owen, stood behind the larger table; he stopped mid-sentence when Jarlath blundered his way inside.

Thalion stopped his pacing and turned his gaze on Jarlath.

Jarlath automatically shifted into a soldier's stance; feet shoulder-width apart, arms behind his back, his spine straight. He didn't know why he did it – maybe it was being in the camp, the battleground not far away, the ghosts of the dead in his head. If Thalion noticed, he didn't say anything.

'How many men do you think are here?' Thalion asked him.

'A thousand?'

'Nine hundred and twenty-six,' Laeli piped up. She was sitting on the middle of the bed, her swords in her lap, face soft, no sign of the scowl she'd been wearing for most of their journey. She continued to polish her weapons, not sparing any of them a glance.

Jarlath swallowed. 'And you're going to send nine hundred and twenty-six men over the border into my country if I can't get Gristel and Leod to agree to meet with you?'

'I don't want to,' Thalion responded, his tone low and measured, 'but I have a responsibility to each of those men and I need to make the right choices for them, but also for my country, even though I want this to be over.'

'What he is trying to say is that it is up to you to convince your commanders to talk or he'll invade, and they'll all be taken prisoner or killed,' Laeli said simply.

Thalion threw her a look.

She climbed off the bed, laying her swords gently on the furs, her eyes shifting from Thalion's face to Jarlath's. 'We're counting on you to make this happen.'

'No pressure then,' Jarlath muttered. Laeli managed a smile, but Thalion's face didn't shift, and he was still frowning when Jarlath left.

The Chieftain didn't think he could do this. It shouldn't bother him, but it did. Jarlath returned to his tent. He ate a terse meal with his tent mates, who spoke little – at least to him – but they knew exactly who he was.

Jarlath was certain Thalion didn't need him, that he could glower at people until they did what he wanted, and he was certain Laeli had batted her eyelashes at, or more likely threatened, Thalion until he agreed to let Jarlath feel useful.

Useful was the last thing Jarlath was feeling right now. He had no power over his commanders – he was a deserter, and they thought him a liar. What Thalion and Laeli wanted him to do … Jarlath shook his head. He was determined to find a way to make Gristel and Leod listen to him.

The following morning, after sleeping terribly, Jarlath woke to find the world blanketed in snow and the tent empty. Outside in the dawn, he could hear the clang of steel on steel as the men threw their weapons around, laughing and joking with one another. Shivering, he dressed as warmly as he could, smiling at the respect he was developing for the people he'd once viewed as savage. They weren't any different to him, he decided, watching a couple of younger men taunt each other outside one of the Reyshorn tents.

Thalion and Laeli came to see him go, Laeli wrapped up against the wind in thick furs, the length of her hair tucked beneath them. They rode as close to the border as was safe, the Merawuld regiment visible in the distance, their banners fluttering, bright blue against the cold winter sky. A rippling sea of tents poked above the barren stretch of land that served as the marker between the two countries. Jarlath was going alone and unarmed.

He glanced at the giant monuments ahead of them, positioned at the end of the mountains on each side of the border. At least ten times the height of a man, they appeared to be growing from the rocks themselves. He'd barely taken the time to look at them the last time he was here, as flames rained down on his head, death soaked the ground, and he couldn't see a foot in front of his face.

Now, he couldn't take his eyes off them. Each statue was a man, with hair that flowed over his shoulders. One eye was covered with a patch, and he held a sword between two large hands, clutched at his breast. His cloak brushed the ground.

'What are they?' he asked.

'The Verndari,' Thalion answered. 'The Allfather's guardians; left to protect us.'

'How old are they?' Jarlath asked quietly.

Thalion shrugged. 'I'm not sure exactly.'

Laeli was looking at the Verndari. 'They were made by my people, when they ruled here, as they did everywhere,' she said softly. 'They were designed to guard Estilleon from its enemies, long before you had any,' she added to Thalion.

'How did they know to build them then?' he asked her.

'Intuition, maybe. Perhaps the Allfather told them to.'

Thalion gazed at the Verndari for a while, then looked to Jarlath. 'Laeli assures me you can be trusted, so I'm trusting you to do this, because I trust her,' he said, his voice snatched by the wind, his expression troubled.

Jarlath nodded and kicked his horse into a trot. He could feel the Chieftain's eyes, and the eyes of the Verndari, on him until he was no more than a speck on the horizon, swallowed by snow.

Two scouts came out to meet him, their suspicious glares shifting to shock as Jarlath told them who he was and where he'd been, reaching into his saddle bag to remove the remains of his army jacket, the insignia charred but still visible. He followed the scouts into the camp, resisting the urge to turn and look for the Chieftain in the distance.

He could stay here, Jarlath realised, and not go back. It wasn't like they'd come to collect him. His gut twisted. He was being trusted to do a job, and he was determined to do it, to be honourable about it. They'd saved his life, and he owed them both. He would see his commanders and ride back across the border. As he was led through the orderly rows of tents, he was shocked by how quiet and still it was.

No one was laughing and joking here. The camp of the Queen's Army was miserable.

Men watched him pass, faces he thought he recognised but quickly realised he didn't know. They muttered amongst themselves, their eyes noting the furs and the Estilleon saddle, the war horse he'd been given, and the scouts escorting him.

Outside the commander's tent, Jarlath dismounted, tying his horse to the hitching post. He took a deep breath, dragging fingers that trembled through his windswept hair, and swallowed his stomach as he was led into the warmth of the commander's tent.

Gristel glanced up quickly, then rose from his seat in shock. 'You're alive!' He hurried across the tent to clasp Jarlath on the shoulders, staring into his face, then pulled back, his eyes moving over Jarlath's clothes – the thick woollen pants and wolf pelt. He raised his eyebrows.

'It gets cold there,' Jarlath said simply, and Gristel laughed.

'You escaped? Clever boy.'

Jarlath shook his head. 'I'm here to make a request of you.'

Gristel's weathered and weary face folded into a frown. 'What are you talking about? Request for what?'

'The new Chieftain—'

'*New* Chieftain?'

'Hadrian's son, Thalion,' Jarlath explained quickly. 'It's a long story, Sir, but he's taken control from his father, who is now in Sitra with most of the Chiefs who supported him and this war, but, from what I understand, the country is his. Thalion wants to meet with you. He wants a treaty.'

'Does he now?' Gristel murmured suspiciously.

Jarlath motioned to the tent flap, still singing his entry. 'He's over the border and—'

Gristel's eyes lit up and his face grew hard, the face of a commander, whose responsibility lay with the lives gathered in his camp. 'Then we need to move out. If there is any chance, I'm going to take it. Their army won't act without their Chieftain – cut off the head of the monster and it will die.'

Jarlath sank into a chair and let his head fall into hands that he didn't realise were still trembling. 'You need to hear him out, Sir, please. Please trust me on this. Look at me. I'm alive. I shouldn't be. They put me in the Stadium but I'm still here because Thalion helped me. And the moment Hadrian and his men moved out for Sitra, I was released. I've been treated with dignity, respect, and kindness. I've had everything I needed, and more.' He looked up at his commander, not wanting to plead but not knowing what else to do. He was a soldier, not a diplomat or a politician, and he'd carried nine hundred and twenty-six men over the border with him.

Gristel's expression didn't shift.

'I don't want to see boys like Orin and Conor ...' Jarlath took a deep breath, forcing away the memory of that blood-soaked battlefield. 'And I know you don't either, but if you don't meet with him, you'll all die.'

Gristel ran a hand over his face with a sigh, his eyes conflicted. Jarlath didn't need to hear him say it – the commander still thought he was a liar, and no doubt a coward as well. 'I need to speak with Leod. Stay here.' He left abruptly; an armed man stepped into the tent, fingers on the hilt of his sword. Jarlath waited, time moving excruciatingly slowly, and when Gristel returned, the big man's face was creased with concern. 'Any wrong move and he's dead. He comes with one man only. This afternoon.'

Jarlath jumped to his feet, heading for the opening of the tent, the brightness of the winter sun easing through the flap, the fresh air and the wind calling him. He'd done his part. The relief that coursed through him was as sweet as a summer breeze.

'Jarlath,' Gristel called. 'I hope you're right.'

CHAPTER THIRTY-THREE

The Goddess of Fate was reclining in Kiarda's throne, one long leg folded over the other. Her cloak of black feathers spilled onto the floor like liquid. Light poured through the long windows that lined the walls and the world outside was coated with a layer of powdery snow.

'What are you doing here?' Kiarda asked coolly, closing the door and walking the length of the red carpet to stop in front of the raven-haired Goddess. The staff of the Cailleach was gripped tight in one hand, as it always was. Kiarda rarely put it down and never let it out of her sight.

The Morrigan raised a dark brow. 'You dare ask questions of a goddess?'

'Of you, yes I do.'

The Goddess's laugh was like the raven's cry, scratchy and bleak. As Kiarda watched, one of the black birds soared right through the white marble wall to perch on the arm of the throne, digging its claws into the carved timber. She shivered as the bird turned its depthless gaze on her face.

'It's the raven's job to carry the souls of the dead to the next life,' the Goddess said, stroking the bird with a pale finger. 'This one knows your face.'

Kiarda eyed the bird warily. 'How?'

The Morrigan's smile was mocking and tight with secrets.

'If you've got nothing useful to tell me, get out,' Kiarda ordered. She lifted the staff of the Cailleach. The Morrigan's smile fell and she narrowed her black eyes; a swirling wind of snow rushed around Kiarda's body, and her hand was frozen, her magic arrested in her blood.

'You dare to attempt to use the Cailleach's staff against me, Witch?' The Goddess rose from the throne and stepped from the dais; her expression was lethal, as hard and deadly as the ice of Veshlir, as treacherous as melting snow. Kiarda wanted to step away but could not move. She could taste her fear, could smell her own sweat, could feel it cooling on her skin, and she sucked in a desperate breath.

The Morrigan came closer, the raven now riding on her shoulder, black wings spread as if preparing for flight, beak open a fraction, those soulless eyes boring into Kiarda's own. The Goddess's hair, like midnight silk, tumbled over her body, shifting in an invisible breeze as her glimmering black gown vanished in a swirl of smoke and feathers, replaced with close fitting black pants and a tunic made of goat hide leather. A sword was strapped to one hip, the scabbard gloriously decorated, the hilt of the weapon glinting silver and covered in wolves.

The Morrigan fingered the hilt of the sword slowly, waving her other hand through the air; black smoke curled from her fingers and shifted into two large wolves with black pelts and glowing eyes. They settled beside the Morrigan, one on either side, and growled low in their throats. Kiarda felt magic slide over her skin, and her knees buckled beneath her, pulling her towards the floor as she was forced to bow her head to the Goddess and her power.

'You think you can give me orders, she who would be Queen?'

That voice echoed through the core of her, banging against her ribcage painfully, burrowing under her skin with claws of ice. Kiarda shook her head. 'No.'

'You dare to assume power over me, who holds your fate in her palm?' The Morrigan closed her fist, opening it swiftly, thrusting her hand under Kiarda's nose – a card wearing Kiarda's face rested there.

Kiarda gulped. 'No. Forgive me.' She was trembling as she was pulled to standing by the Goddess's magic. The Morrigan stared into Kiarda's eyes for a long time, before lifting the card and studying it with great interest. With a snap of her fingers, the card vanished.

'You have played with fate, Kiarda of Veshlir. Fate does not appreciate your interference.' The Goddess's voice was like the winter wind, all around and all powerful, capable of stripping bare the trees and the land, of pulling the flesh from the body to reveal the bare bones beneath. 'You think you have power here but you need to think again. You are not who you think you are. You are not what you think you are.'

Kiarda kept her gaze on her feet. Before she vanished, the Morrigan tossed a card to the ground, face-down. When she was sure she was alone, Kiarda licked her lips, bending to scoop the card from the carpet, her heart freezing as she turned it over in her hand.

Eira.

She had a mere breath to study her daughter's face before the card turned to smoke and disappeared, leaving a solitary black feather resting in her palm. She crushed it in her fist defiantly.

The door to the throne room opened and Hadrian strode inside, his face pulling into a frown as he looked on her standing stupidly in the middle of the carpet. Before he could speak, Kiarda shook back her hair and climbed the stairs of the dais, taking her rightful place on the throne, laying the staff of the Cailleach across her lap, allowing the hum of power to soothe her, shaking the Morrigan's words from her soul.

The Goddess was playing with her, as she was inclined to do.

'What is it?' Kiarda barked at the human man, her ally, who had thrown all he had, including his own son, into the melting pot of her dreams. It was nothing less than she had done, Kiarda thought, nothing less than he should do, for the realisation of dreams always came at a cost.

Hadrian held up a folded piece of paper. 'From Gedeon.'

Kiarda kept her expression neutral. 'What does our ally have to say?'

'It won't be long until the puppet Queen is dead.'

'You believe him?'

'Why wouldn't I?' Hadrian replied simply. He folded the letter and slipped it beneath his furs, approaching the dais but not daring to place his foot on it. 'He has been true in everything else – what would he have to gain by lying to us now?'

Kiarda stroked the staff. 'You must be pleased. Your army is ready to march on Merawuld?'

'They are. Thalion will make sure of it.'

'You trust your son?'

Hadrian's gaze was fierce. 'I trust him to follow my orders.'

'You forgave his indiscretion easily,' Kiarda said. 'Tell me – where was he again?'

'He was under a spell,' Hadrian snapped. 'I could hardly blame him. Thalion has always been soft in the head, easily swayed. It doesn't surprise me that a fae Witch was able to mess with him. He's lucky she didn't kill him.'

'Yes,' Kiarda said softly. 'He didn't tell you who it was that cursed him?'

'He didn't know her name. Why?'

'It must have been powerful magic, to last so long,' Kiarda mused.

'Your point?'

Kiarda trailed her finger along the arm of the throne; ice gathered where her skin touched it. 'They still haven't found my brother's daughter. She's a powerful Witch. A Fire Witch, a guardian of the Rift.'

Hadrian's eyes narrowed. 'What are you getting at?'

'Nothing,' Kiarda said simply. Hadrian might trust his son, but Kiarda had her reservations. Her thoughts shifted to Eira – her daughter was smart, and much more powerful than any human man. 'How long will it take your army to arrive in Tyllcarric?'

'It will be four weeks of steady marching from the Pass to the city,' Hadrian answered. 'I don't expect any resistance from the villages, and by the time my men arrive in Tyllcarric, Gedeon will have smoothed the way for them. They will march straight through the gates, leaving soldiers at each village they pass through.'

'And then what? Gedeon will simply hand over control of the city to you?'

'He will accommodate my men until I arrive to meet with him,' Hadrian answered snappishly. 'And if he doesn't, he dies.'

Kiarda hid her smile. He was too easy to antagonise, this human, so bitter and twisted with his silly vendetta. The sooner he was gone from Eshlune the better, and, if by some reason his plans with Gedeon fell through, Kiarda would kill him herself, as she would anyone who got in her way.

She had not shared her plans for the Rift with anyone, not even Birka. Rhodiri's Fire Witches would earn their place at her table by using their talent to help harness the power of fire, and, once Faleria's magic was under her control, Kiarda would have the greatest weapon Aileryan had ever seen. The humans would get on their knees before her. If they did not ... she would show them just how savage fire could really be. The earth would recover, because from destruction there was always creation.

Hadrian was watching her closely, so she circled back, interested despite herself.

'Tell me, Hadrian,' she began smoothly, 'what sort of man is my son-in-law, really?'

He was taken aback by her question, the manner of its phrasing, as if he'd forgotten for a moment that she had given her daughter in this alliance, as she had in an alliance of a different sort. Kiarda swallowed tightly. The solstice was drawing nearer. She would have to make sure Eira was here before the turning of the wheel. She clutched the staff tighter.

Hadrian took a seat on one of the chairs near the wall, usually reserved for Rhodiri's council. 'What do you want to know? If he's going to treat her right? He will. He has been.' He laughed. 'I think they like one another. Imagine that.'

Kiarda bared her teeth. 'Yes, imagine that.'

'Thalion is a better man than I am,' Hadrian said quietly, his eyes on his hands, clasped tightly in his lap. 'He's more caring, considerate. He'll make a good Chieftain, one day, when he toughens up.' He glanced at Kiarda. 'Me leaving the country in his hands is a test of sorts. If he can prove himself capable …'

'Then you will be more willing to let him take control over future events?'

'Yes. He's not a fool … he's smart, a thinker, like his mother was. But he thinks too much, gets too caught up in his head, and doesn't act. To be Chieftain, you need to be able to act, to make decisions quickly,' Hadrian continued. 'I'm sure he thinks I hate him.'

'Don't all children think that of their parents at some stage?' Kiarda said quietly.

Hadrian gave her a small smile. 'Your girl is a tough one.'

'She is.'

'Has some interesting ideas though.'

'Does she?'

Hadrian laughed. 'Wanted to know why I didn't let women compete in the Stadium. I thought she was going to volunteer herself. I can't imagine her swinging a sword.'

Neither can I, Kiarda thought, the smile freezing on her face. She made the decision to contact her daughter sooner rather than later, seeing again the card the Morrigan tossed away so carelessly.

A raven was perched in the nearest tree, its beady black eyes piercing the glass, coming to rest on Kiarda's face.

CHAPTER THIRTY-FOUR

After delivering his message, Jarlath had been dismissed, Thalion and Owen sitting down to discuss the upcoming meeting, Laeli flitting about in the background, throwing comments and suggestions at them in a sharp tone. With nothing to do, Jarlath wandered the camp, keeping the Chieftain's tent in his sight. No one had asked him to come to the meeting but just in case, he didn't want to be hard to find. Laeli and Thalion were both so tense he thought they'd snap.

Pulling his cloak tighter, he sat on the ground to wait. Someone brought him food – a bowl of stew and a hunk of bread. It was one of the men who shared his tent, a young man with closely cropped dark hair and heavy brows. He nodded to Jarlath and left, head down against the wind. Grateful, Jarlath ate quickly, the stew cooling before it touched his lips. He hurried back to his tent, leaving the bowl outside the flap to deal with later, then rushed back to the Chieftain's tent. Two horses were saddled and waiting.

Thalion's guard shook his head, preventing Jarlath from entering as the sound of bickering came from inside.

'You need to stay here.' Thalion, as frustrated as Jarlath had ever heard him.

'No. It's dangerous and I wouldn't trust them.'

'I'll keep this handy.'

'I don't doubt your capacity to protect yourself, Thalion,' Laeli argued. 'Although your left side is always open, just so you know.'

Thalion sighed and Jarlath could hear the humour in his tone, the sudden switch in his mood. 'Is this the rest of my life then? A woman who won't do what she's told?'

'If I wanted a man to tell me what to do, I'd have stayed in Sitra,' Laeli retorted. Thalion cursed and the tent flap was thrown aside. Jarlath backed up, wringing his hands as Laeli raised her eyebrows at him.

'They said one man …'

'I'm not a man.' She took the reins of her horse and swung herself into the saddle, turning the animal around and moving off through the tents. Thalion stormed out of the tent, a deep frown on his face.

'That woman will be the bloody death of me,' he mumbled.

'Can't you make her stay behind?' Jarlath asked, withering under the glare he received in response. Thalion told him to mount up, and Jarlath nodded eagerly, a thrill shooting along the length of his spine. If this worked, it would change everything.

And if it didn't … his blood ran cold. He would work that bit out later.

They caught Laeli at the edge of the camp, her horse prancing beneath her. She gave them a quick, impatient look but didn't go charging off, waiting until Thalion had drawn level with her. Owen joined them, his dark gaze scanning the horizon. He was Thalion's one man, and was armed to the teeth – a longsword, daggers in his belt and a dangerous spear Jarlath didn't think would be appreciated.

At the border, they were met by the scouts, who eyed the party suspiciously, stopping several metres away. Above them, the sky was heavy, the clouds thick and dirty. Rain clouds, Jarlath noted.

'One man only,' one of the scouts said. He pointed at Jarlath. 'He can come.'

'They all come, or I don't,' Thalion replied.

The men exchanged a glance as Jarlath held his breath. The sky groaned; the first drops fell, splattering against his cheeks. Not rain, sleet.

'Then they stay outside,' the scout said.

'No.'

Jarlath thought his nerves would explode as Thalion and the scouts stared each other down, the sleet and wind slanting around them. Surely this wouldn't be the thing to end the treaty before it began? Laeli was being unusually quiet and that worried Jarlath as well, but he could feel her glaring from under the hood of her fur-lined cloak.

Eventually, the men nodded. One on either side, they rode into the belly of the Queen's Army as the sleet turned to rain. There weren't many men outside in the weather, but there were fires burning and the smell of food floated over them as they made their way to the commander's tent, where men were waiting to take the horses.

When ordered to hand over their weapons, Thalion shook his head. 'You can't seriously expect us to step in there unarmed?' His voice was loud enough that those inside the tent could hear it clearly. The silence became so thick Jarlath thought he would drown in it. After a moment's pause, Gristel's voice called out – the Chieftain and his party could keep their weapons but were being trusted to keep them sheathed.

Thalion waited until one of the guards held open the tent flap for him, and when Jarlath finally stepped inside, his shoulders painfully tight, Gristel and Leod were standing in the middle of the carpeted floor, arms folded. There were no handshakes, no smiles, only deep distrust as Thalion looked from one face to the next, Laeli and Owen flanking him. Behind the commanders stood five men, all heavily armed. A small table was set to one side; rolls of parchment, stacks of paper and maps pinned down with stones decorated the top.

Jarlath had forgotten how tall Thalion was, how broad his shoulders were. Draped in fur, chin lifted proudly, his expression calm but determined, calculating and alert, he was a wolf amongst a pack of dogs.

The commanders shifted their gaze to Laeli, eyeing her with suspicion. Beside Thalion and Owen, she cut a tiny figure, but there was no denying the weapons at her belt or the stiffness of her spine. She radiated power.

'I said one man. Who is this?' Gristel demanded.

'My wife,' Thalion answered.

Jarlath started. When did that happen?

Laeli removed her hood, her unnatural beauty released like a living thing, filling the shadowy corners of the tent with light. Her green eyes flashed.

'A fae!' one of the men hissed, his hands tightening on the hilt of this sword.

'I wouldn't,' Thalion warned simply.

'What's a fae of the forest doing here then?' Leod asked.

'Trying to stop you from doing something stupid,' Laeli answered, her tone clipped. 'If you attack them,' she paused and indicated Thalion and Owen, 'you'll be slaughtered. Again.'

Gristel motioned stiffly to simple wooden chairs, taking a seat on the far side of the tent, keeping as much distance as he could between them. They were offered ale, warmed milk, but refused all. Thalion's attention was on the men sitting opposite him, on their folded arms and faces tight with suspicion, some with wonder as they gazed at Laeli. One man had dropped his sword; the weapon dangled from boneless fingers.

'So let me get this straight,' Leod began, his dark brows drawn together. 'Your father makes an alliance with the Witch of Veshlir and you're in league with Rhodiri Enthelme?'

'That isn't your concern.' Thalion said evenly. 'I might not support what my father started here but I won't let you invade my country. My men will stay where they are until you put your weapons down and move out.'

'And your men? What will they be doing in the middle of all this?' Leod countered.

'What I tell them,' Thalion answered evenly. Gristel and Leod exchanged a glance.

'What about your father?' Gristel asked suspiciously.

'My father made his own choices,' Thalion said lightly, but Jarlath caught the hint of sadness in his tone. 'And the way I see it, you have two choices: stay here and die, or go home and return to your lives.'

Leod gave a bark of astonished laughter. 'You expect us to believe that if we lay down our weapons, you'll just let us go home?'

'Wasn't I clear enough?' Thalion leant back in his chair, his posture relaxed, confident – his mask, Jarlath realised suddenly. There were small things – the way Thalion's fingers flexed constantly where they rested against his thigh, the way he held his shoulders, and how that small shift of his body drew him closer to Laeli – things that the commanders wouldn't even notice.

'You really don't want to be here any longer than necessary. The Bone Mother already walks my land – it won't be long before she's throwing her blanket across yours as well.' Thalion's expression switched to one of concern. 'You'll die out here. Your tents, your men'—he waved a hand at the camp around them—'from what I've seen, you aren't prepared for what the wolves of winter will bring you.' His face changed again. 'And you aren't prepared for what my men will bring you if I order it. You already know this.'

Leod was frowning. Gristel's expression was openly scathing.

Thalion rubbed at his face, a gesture Jarlath had come to understand indicated frustration. 'You need more assurance?' Thalion asked, then went on before anyone could respond. 'Then here it is: I have no interest in your country. I don't want it. I don't want anything from it. There is nothing you have that I need. Estilleon is more than capable of providing for its people.'

'Your father—' Gristel began.

'Is wrong,' Thalion interrupted firmly. The two men looked at each other for a long moment; silence dropped into the tent, so deep and dense Jarlath could hear the blood moving through his veins and could hear the thundering of his heart. He didn't take another breath until Gristel relaxed a fraction.

'Put your weapons down and move out,' Thalion repeated.

'Or,' Laeli interjected; men jumped at the sound of her voice, so musical and rich, compelling. 'You could help us take Sitra back.'

Leod looked at her in shock. 'From the Ice Witch? You've got to be kidding.'

Her eyes were hard. 'I'm completely serious.'

The commanders glanced at each other again, their expressions more nervous than before. 'You'd be aware we have soldiers stationed on this side of the Rift,' Leod began.

'I'm aware,' Laeli said coolly. 'What's your point?'

Leod addressed Thalion. 'Your father's men have engaged them several times. He seems to have stationed his own forces on the southern side, near the base of the Peaks.'

Thalion nodded. 'Yes, that was his intention.'

Gristel kept his eyes on Laeli's face. 'The fae guard has been sighted in the forest but they haven't engaged with our soldiers. There has been heavy fighting on the other side though,' he added.

War was raging in Eshlune. Laeli's lips were a thin line.

Gristel rubbed his forehead. 'We need to think,' he told Thalion.

'We don't have time for thinking. My people need help – my father needs help.' Laeli's tone was fierce, her face like stone. Comprehension dawned as Gristel and Leod realised who and what she was. Thalion lay a hand on her arm, but she shook him off, springing from her chair and darting across the room; Gristel quietly told his men to put their weapons down. He did not back away from Laeli's anger, folding his arms and meeting her glare for glare. Eventually, she growled deep in her throat and stalked out of the tent, the flap swishing behind her. Jarlath heard her bark at some poor soul standing nearby.

Gristel turned back to Thalion. 'What are your terms?'

'We will meet again in two days to discuss the terms of a treaty. That should give you enough time to think about it,' Thalion answered.

'Two days?' Leod spluttered. 'That isn't enough time for us to consult the Queen or the High Mage. We're here on Her Majesty's orders and we can't just—'

'Your Queen has been corrupted by her High Mage,' Thalion said. 'And your High Mage is allied with my father and Kiarda of Veshlir. You can waste time seeking approval from your Queen, or you can act, and stop this. The choice is yours. At this moment, you hold the lives of everyone in this camp in your hands.' He leant forward in his seat, holding Gristel's gaze. 'I want to be able to send my men home to their families, sooner rather than later, as I'm sure you do. If we can't come to an agreement, there will be further death and blood will be on your hands, and mine,' he added softly.

'And Eshlune?' Gristel's eyes shifted to the tent flap.

Thalion frowned. 'If you think Kiarda will be happy with just conquering the forest, well, you might find yourselves sorely mistaken. Gedeon will open your city and your villages to her as easily as he was prepared to open them to my father but, instead of soldiers on the front line, you'll have civilians. I could be wrong, but your people aren't warriors.'

'Two days?' Leod sighed.

'Two days,' Thalion confirmed. 'Send a man when you come to your decision.' With a last look at the commanders and an unreadable glance at Jarlath, he headed out into the storm-choked day, Owen trailing him. Gristel's soldiers hurried out, hands on weapons.

Left alone with his commanders, Jarlath didn't know what to say. An I-told-you-so danced on his tongue but he swallowed it away.

'That wasn't what I expected,' Gristel mused. 'He wasn't what I expected.'

'You don't need to go back there, Jarlath. There is a place for you here,' Leod offered.

'I don't know,' Jarlath said. 'It's pointless, this death and bloodshed. There is no meaning in it. It tears people apart. It breaks them. I can't forget what I saw, what I went through. Shouldn't what we do with our lives matter more than this?'

Sometimes, in his dreams, he was the wolf in that arena, terrified and bleeding. Sometimes, he was Rand and he watched as a sword was driven into his insides. Sometimes, Ash was there, and she turned away from him when he went to hold her, his hands covered in blood. Other times it was her in the Stadium, that long sword dragging her down with its weight while he was forced to watch, caged, as her blood was spilt on the snow.

Before they let him walk back out into the blistering cold and pull himself up onto his horse, Gristel clamped a big hand over Jarlath's shoulder.

'Jarlath, think about it.'

As he was riding towards the border, edging his horse through the rows of tents, he thought he saw a familiar head of chestnut hair. He pulled hard on the reins, heart thundering, light rain falling around him. Shivers raced from his head to his toes, curled tightly in his boots. In the distance Owen waited, his horse stamping the ground impatiently.

Swallowing, Jarlath kicked his horse forward.

'Jarlath!'

He swung around, almost tumbling from the saddle.

'Finn? By the Gods, what are you doing here?'

His younger brother grinned. 'Seeking some fame and glory on the battlefield. You have no idea how boring it is in Brenveil.'

'Finn,' Jarlath hissed, 'this is war! You could die! Get on home.'

'No.' Finn surveyed the border, where Owen was still waiting. The big man gestured for Jarlath, urging him back. Finn eyed him doubtfully. 'What are you doing, Jarlath? I heard you're with the enemy. I heard they caught you and now you're their errand boy.'

Jarlath shook his head, exasperated. 'It's complicated, Finn.'

His brother folded scrawny arms over an equally scrawny chest. In Jarlath's mind, he saw Finn's boyish body shredded, saw his lifeless eyes staring at a sky that bled snow. 'You'd better go. It seems like they're waiting.'

'I'll explain later, I will. It's not as simple as it appears,' Jarlath implored.

Finn nodded again at Owen, who was now headed towards them, Gristel's scouts riding out to meet him.

'Shit,' Jarlath cursed. He turned his horse around, peering back at his brother over his shoulder. 'Stay in one piece, okay? For Mum and Dad?' He didn't wait for Finn's reaction, urging his horse towards the minor conflict that was about to bubble over because of him.

CHAPTER THIRTY-FIVE

He had dreamed of the power that would come to him.

Gedeon examined his face in the polished mirror in his office. His skin had healed well enough, the burns and blisters no longer weeping and oozing vile liquid. He touched his cheek tenderly, feeling the puckered and ruined flesh. He touched his eyelid and ran his finger over the place where his eyebrow used to be. All in all, it wasn't that bad.

It could have been much worse. The pain had been dreadful, even with Senan messing around in his head. Air magic was not enough to ease the agony, and the weeks he'd spent in bed were fuzzy, his thoughts a clouded mass of bandages and crying flesh. He'd refused the opium, choosing instead to let that pain fuel and inflame him.

Darian was sitting on the other side of the desk, waiting while Gedeon smoothed his hair back from his twisted face. He wouldn't hide his disfigurement.

A monstrous face for a monster.

'Bring me the Bloodstones,' Gedeon ordered. Darian collected the metal box from the desk, carrying it over gingerly and holding it out; Gedeon flipped the lid, reaching in and withdrawing a Bloodstone.

It was warm, and it thrummed with power. He let a snippet of his air magic free, shaped into a needle-thin thread. He stroked the stone – the fire inside sighed and purred, rubbing against the edges of its prison.

'Beautiful,' Gedeon cooed. 'Shall we let you out?'

Darian took a step back.

Slowly, Gedeon coaxed the fire free from its cage. It came hesitantly, like it was scared, as timid as its true owner. Only he was its master now; he needed it to be strong, fearless. With his magic encouraging it, the fire rose in a cloud from the stone, hovering in the air in front of his face. His ruined skin tingled with the memory of that fiery kiss. With his mind, he commanded the fire to halt, and it did. He ordered it into shapes, Darian watching from the other side of the room. Gedeon had the fire performing tricks like a well-trained animal, putting it back inside the stone, the flame obedient and compliant.

His.

How he would make them cower.

He slipped the Bloodstone back in the box and beckoned Darian. The Spirit Rake followed wordlessly as they left Gedeon's office and headed from the Keep, crossing the short space to the palace, where the Queen lay like one dead. Gedeon ushered the servants away, approaching the grand bed. For a moment, he considered hiding his disfigured face from the Queen – she would ask questions – but he decided it wouldn't matter soon anyway.

Rowena blinked at him, at the scarred flesh and the unsmiling face. 'Gedeon? What has happened to you?'

'The fire caster happened.'

Her eyes widened and she broke into a violent coughing fit. Darian did his job well.

'Gedeon …'

'I'm truly sorry, my dear, but you see, Merawuld needs strength. It needs a ruler that will lift this country to its glorious potential. It needs someone who will not bow to our enemies, who will act without hesitation,' he said simply. 'As you have no heir, you would be aware that rule of this country passes to the High Mage in the event of your death.'

'I am not dead.'

'The people will mourn you, I'm sure, for a moment at least.'

She frowned, lifting herself into a sitting position, the effort leaving her panting and sweating. Gedeon wrinkled his nose. Rowena eyed the Spirit Rake lingering in the doorway.

'Gedeon, what are you …'

He lifted his hand. As the blood froze in her veins and her lungs gasped, he closed his fist. Rowena fell back on the pillows, her blonde hair forming a fan around her pallid face. Her eyes fell shut, a breath of air escaping her bloodless lips.

'The Queen is dead,' Gedeon whispered, turning to Darian. 'Long live the King.'

Gedeon left the palace and the pathetic body lying there, sweeping back into the Keep, collecting the box of Bloodstones as he passed his office. He headed for the Council room, where he knew he would find them, where they had been gathered every day since his accident, whispering and hissing like the snakes they were.

They looked up in surprise as the door flew open and he strode in, the Bloodstones tucked under his arm. Gedeon paused, taking in their faces, their old, tired faces, grey with lack of ambition and their boring compliance. None of them had any fire in them, any spirit, although he supposed that was his fault.

He set the box down at the head of the table but did not take his usual seat. 'By all means, don't let me interrupt.'

'High Mage,' Taavi began. 'We didn't expect you up and about so soon.'

'Have you been planning which one of you would be my successor? Did you think it would be you, Taavi?' Gedeon laughed; Taavi's face coloured. 'Or you, Marin? Were you hoping for the title? I'm not sure you're right for the position, either.' He paused, running his finger along the back of his chair – droplets of water beaded on the timber, glimmering like jewels. He left them there long enough, waiting, waiting, until finally—

Taavi gasped. 'You're an Anomaly!'

'I'm rather disappointed it's taken you so long to work it out,' Gedeon mused.

Taavi rose from his seat; Gedeon waved him away like the annoying insect he was.

'I'll let my Council be the first to know – the Queen is dead,' he announced, wringing as much fake sadness from his voice and his expression as he could. The Council members gasped and Gedeon did not miss the nervous glances they exchanged with one another.

'Yes, it is rather unfortunate,' he continued. 'And without an heir as well.'

Darian flung his arms out – every mage at the table found themselves pinned in their seat, faces slack with compliance as Darian's magic slammed into their minds. As one, their eyes shifted to Gedeon.

The Spirit Rake was clearly enjoying letting his power loose. Like Gedeon, Darian had spent years holding back, never showing more than a touch of his extraordinary ability. Gedeon was impressed – Darian's power was greater than he could have hoped. The Mage Council were powerful yet, now, they were rendered mute.

Gedeon opened the box containing the Bloodstones.

'No doubt you're all wondering exactly what I did to get this.' He motioned to his face. 'The fire caster possesses powerful magic. Think about it – the first Fire Witch to exist in generations. Naturally, such power should not be left in the hands of a child.' He reached into the box to touch the Bloodstones. They hummed. 'I thought it best to unburden her of that power. Now, you might disagree with me – and that is your choice – but I choose not to burden myself with the weight of others' judgement.'

Gedeon took a moment to stare into each of their eyes, the ten members of the Council, once the most powerful people in the land, before they allowed their weakness to overtake them. 'The people of this city will look to me now. I do not expect a smooth take-over – in fact, I relish the opportunity to show people how out of touch their ideas are. Ideas are powerful things but the people of this city will find out there is no place for their ideas. There will be no space for revolutionaries here. The dreamers and the idealists will find themselves dangling from the gallows until the ravens come for their eyes.'

He paused, smoothing back his hair, touching the rippled flesh of his face. 'You may condemn me with your stares – it matters not, for history will remember this as a moment of great change and me as the one who had the courage to bring about such change. Once the city is under my control, I shall find the fire caster and, with her power and the Bloodstones, I will harness the magic of the Rift. Long have the fae held that over our heads, but no more. Fire magic shall be mine, in time, and by then, there shall be no one left to stand against me.'

It was a pity none of them would be alive to remember his glorious words. Gedeon removed two stones, holding one in each palm. The fire jumped at his call. He cast a final look at the mage council.

'Goodbye, friends.'

He let the fire caster's power free.

Gedeon, wearing his most sombre expression, made his way to the wooden platform constructed specially for this moment. Such an announcement needed an audience. The Queen had been dead two days, her body lying in the royal tomb, ready for burial. He had decided to send her into the next life in the correct manner. He wasn't entirely a monster and the rites of the dead needed to be obeyed.

Darian had seen to it that none of the servants in the palace had any memory of the Queen's untimely passing, and if they did their tongues stopped in their mouths.

Today would be a true test of Darian's powers. Coercing hundreds of people into strict compliance was no easy feat. The Spirit Rake's unusual powers had been stretched recently, but rather than the usual shadows under his eyes, Darian wore a smile. Gedeon, of course, had a contingency plan. He eyed the Watchmen standing at the ready.

The main square was packed tight with bodies. Merchants and gambling house owners, whores and mothers with their children clinging to their skirts, along with soldiers preparing to leave for the Pass. Flyers had been delivered to every house and business and nailed to every wall in the city. The only people not represented were those from the Academy. He stored that away for later. He would need to have a chat with Radella.

A nervous hush rippled through the crowd as Gedeon raised his hands.

'My friends,' he began, 'it is my solemn duty to announce that our dear Queen, Rowena, has passed into the next life after a long and debilitating illness.'

There were cries of dismay – Gedeon resisted the urge to roll his eyes. It wasn't like any of them knew her personally. Thanks to him, Rowena had rarely interacted with her people.

Gedeon fixed his face into a picture of deep grief. 'As the Queen has died without an heir, it now falls to me to mind the people of this country until a new ruler can be appointed.' This wasn't news – the line of succession was widely understood.

The Watch were positioned at the edges of the crowd. Gedeon had overseen the recruitment of the Watch for years, making sure their ranks were filled with those loyal to him. The men of the Watch moved towards the platform, slipping outside of the net of magic about to be woven over the square.

'The Queen has left strict instructions for the citizens of Tyllcarric,' Gedeon said. All faces in the square were turned in his direction, every set of ears open to him. He let his air magic free, let it thread across the square. Beneath it, Darian's magic crawled through the air like a poisonous cloud. The Spirit Rake's power entered mind after mind; faces twisted in confusion, then slowly went blank. When Darian had them all enthralled, Gedeon began speaking again.

'The curfew will continue. No one shall be on the streets after dark. There shall be strict punishment for those who break this rule. Please, friends, I implore you to spread the word and do not be afraid to inform the Watch of the actions of those unwilling to keep our city safe.' He paused. When he next spoke, his voice took on a low, chanting quality. 'We have in our midst two dangerous criminals, threats to our way of life. I am talking of the fire caster and the Anomaly.' Into the minds of each person, Gedeon projected an image first of the girl, then of Senan. 'They must be found and brought to justice. This was our Queen's dying wish. Anyone who harbours these abominations shall suffer terribly.'

The crowd of blank faces shifted as one; eyes that before had been soft became hard as grief transformed into hatred. Gedeon clapped his hands. The crowd turned from him, dispersing quickly, people moving off through the city to spread the word.

Back in his office, Gedeon found a stack of papers waiting. The posters he had commissioned. He picked one up – it showed the faces of the fire caster and the Anomaly, the word 'wanted' plus an incentive to report sightings to the Watch beneath the pictures in bold lettering. He would have the Watch distribute them throughout the city.

Gedeon glanced up; his favourite Watchman was standing in the doorway.

'Reporting for duty, sir,' Mal said.

'You are to go to the Academy. I need ten air mages, the most powerful they have. They are to be assigned to each legion of the Watch.' He touched the box containing the Bloodstones. 'Each legion will be given one of these.'

Mal's eyes sparkled. 'The fire caster's magic?'

'Yes. The air mage will support the Watch in the use of this magic. Once the mages have been assembled, they will report to me for training on how to use the stones. When the dear people of this city do not comply … you are to give them a demonstration. Understood?' Gedeon said.

Mal smiled. 'Understood.'

'Good. You will go far in this new world, Mal.'

The young man turned to leave.

'Oh, and Mal,' Gedeon said. 'It's not a request. Make sure Radella understands that.'

The Watchman nodded, that wonderfully wicked gleam in his eye shining in the sun that poured through the window and flooded the room.

In their box, the Bloodstones winked.

Gedeon smiled.

Chaos was the antecedent for great change, and great change was coming.

CHAPTER THIRTY-SIX

Jarlath ignored the whispered words and the eyes of Thalion's soldiers. He headed for the Chieftain's tent, intent on telling them he was leaving to get his brother. Neither Gristel nor Leod had mentioned Finn. Voices inside made him pause.

Thalion and Laeli were fighting. Again. Jarlath could feel their anger as surely as he could feel the bitter wind at his back and exchanged a look with the man on guard duty. From the expression on his face, he was trying hard not to listen.

'I can't let you go back there alone,' Thalion said furiously; his voice contained all the fury of a storm.

Laeli snarled something Jarlath couldn't hear.

'The Allfather help me, woman, you're my wife!'

'I'm not your property,' she hissed in response. 'You won't tell me what to do!'

'If it stops you from getting yourself killed then yes, I will tell you what to do. Why won't you listen to me? Despite what you appear to think, you're not unbreakable. Letting you go off after Caden was hard enough.' Thalion's voice softened. 'Give me some time, sweetheart, please.'

'They don't have time, Thalion!'

Their voices dropped. Jarlath heard a mumble, followed by Thalion's deep voice, quiet and steady. He swallowed and, ignoring the warning of Thalion's guard, marched into the tent. Laeli had her face buried in Thalion's chest and his hand was stroking her back; the other was cupped gently around the nape of her neck and her arms were tight around her husband's waist. Thalion glanced up, and frowned.

Jarlath shuffled his feet, all his bravado fleeing. 'Umm... sorry, but...'

Thalion's frown deepened. 'You have choices to make as well, Jarlath. You can return to your commanders, who I'm pretty certain aren't going to let you go running off looking for the fire caster, or you can come back with us, and I will let you go after her once it's safe to travel.'

'It's not just Ash. My brother is there, in the camp. I saw him as I left,' Jarlath said quickly. 'I won't leave Finn to die like my friends did. He's a kid. He should be at home on the farms, not here. None of these people should be here.'

'Then we hope they agree to my terms.'

'And if they don't?'

'Then I need to stick to my word.' Thalion's voice was steady, that large hand still stroking Laeli's back, the gentle gesture at odds with his determined expression, his promise of further bloodshed.

'You don't care, do you?' Jarlath said hotly, his fists curling, his temper, borne of desperation and fear, rising before he could stop it. 'You've got what you want, so too bad for the rest of us, right?'

Thalion said nothing, watching him with that infuriatingly composed expression. Slowly, Laeli pulled away from him to sit on the bed. Jarlath caught a glimpse of her tear-streaked face before she rolled over and curled herself into a ball.

'We'll discuss this later,' Thalion told him tersely.

'But ...'

'Later.' Thalion spoke through his teeth, his composure finally rattled as Laeli's huddled form began to smoke and spit sparks into the air.

Jarlath watched incredulously as Thalion sat on the bed next to her, completely unafraid of the magic leaking from her skin. He slipped his arms beneath her, pulling her close while she sobbed and shook and tried to push him away. Smoke danced from the length of Laeli's hair as Thalion murmured to her, his tone soft and gentle. Eventually, she took a deep, unsteady breath, her magic fading as she gave up fighting and flopped in her husband's arms with a sigh.

Jarlath left, his thoughts churning.

Why couldn't he have been like that with Ash? If Laeli asked Thalion to stand in front of an army for her, he would, and if she didn't ask, he'd do it anyway. Did that mean he loved her more than Jarlath loved Ash? Deeper, maybe, or differently? He didn't know. All he was sure of was that he'd left when Ash needed him the most.

Perhaps it was simpler than that – perhaps he was just a coward.

He had no idea where Ash was. No longer in Sitra, he was certain of that. Maybe he wasn't meant to find her. His mother would say to trust the fates, but the Goddess of Fate must have been having a laugh when she decided what she'd lay on the table for Jarlath.

Jarlath fell asleep that night with Ash's face in his head, the taste of her still on his lips, his belly burning with regret.

Jarlath spent the days brushing down his horse and watching the snow fall, his impatience growing as short as the hours. He was invited to spar with some of the younger men, and did so nervously, wondering what they thought of him, what they expected from him. The sword was heavy in his hand - he tried to hold it firmly, to not let them see the way his muscles trembled.

Memories threatened to engulf him, but he pushed them aside, knowing he couldn't hide from it forever. He had to face it, this fear. Not of dying, but of the death he had delivered, even in defence of his life.

Now, more than ever, he had to be the wolf. Fearless, clever; strong, but willing to ask for help, for support.

In the makeshift fighting circle, Jarlath held his own but the Estilleon men made him work for it, leaving him slick with sweat, his arms and shoulders burning. During his second round against an older man with a deeply lined face, Owen came to watch, standing at the edge of the fighting circle with his arms folded. When Jarlath looked again, the Fairhorn Second had vanished.

When he wasn't swinging a sword or scowling at the ground, Jarlath walked to the edge of the camp, stopping at the last line of tents. Finn had been on his mind constantly since he'd seen him. His younger brother had an uncanny ability to find himself in the wrong place at the wrong time, and Jarlath had spent a lot of time bailing Finn out of trouble, whether it be for pocketing some apples from the market, or something more serious, like falling asleep on the job and letting the livestock escape into the fields. He couldn't comprehend what his brother was doing here, or why his parents had let it happen. Finn never took anything seriously.

As dawn was approaching on the morning of the second day, Jarlath was already awake, the cold sneaking under the edge of the blankets to bite at his skin. His tent mates were still sleeping, snoring loudly, so he climbed from his cot and dressed hurriedly, stepping out into the crisp morning air, blinking at the blinding white that stretched over the camp – the Bone Mother's blanket. The snow crunched under his boots, his breath mist, his fingertips quickly freezing even as he shoved them in his pockets and crossed the campgrounds.

A young man was standing several metres from the Chieftain's tent, an earthen jug in one hand, a spear in the other. He looked cold, bored, and half-asleep.

'I'll take that for you,' Jarlath said, snatching the jug from the man's hands.

'Wait—'

Jarlath ignored him, striding across the snow and pushing into the tent, his head filled with his brother, with Ash, and the commanders. Regret and indecision swirled around inside him, making him feel ill and edgy, his brain foggy.

His greeting died on his lips as he was confronted with Laeli's naked back and the sight of her long pale legs poking out of the bedding. Those legs, Jarlath quickly noted, were folded around Thalion's middle and his hands were tangled in her hair. He tugged, making her gasp and tilt her head back, exposing her throat so he could sink his teeth into her. Her gasp became a moan, echoed in the rhythmic rolling of her hips.

Whorls of smoke lifted from her flesh and her spine arched as a watery, broken sound erupted from her throat, sending an arrow of heat through Jarlath's body.

He sucked in a breath; Thalion looked up, his eyes as dark as shadows.

Jarlath froze, then scurried out of the tent.

Thalion's guard tried, and failed, to hold his laughter as Jarlath shoved the jug at him, cheeks scorching, his stomach in knots. They stood in silence as the morning broke, focusing on the sun slowly lighting the camp, on the gentle snorts of the horses nearby, the voices of the men as the camp woke, listening to anything other than what was happening behind them.

Jarlath's belly flopped. What would it be like to hold Ash like that, to have her legs wrapped around him? If he never got out of here, he'd never find out.

A frigid gust of wind blurred with snow edged around them.

'Where are you from?' Jarlath asked the man beside him, wanting to distract them both from this shitty situation and the cutting cold for a moment. They were about the same age; the other man was shorter, but stockier, his dark hair brushing the furs that were wrapped around his shoulders.

'The Hollows,' the man answered. 'About four days that way,' he pointed north-west. 'You're from over the border, aren't you? The one who killed that giant in the Stadium on Samhain. I think the whole country was talking about it.'

Jarlath felt sick, but he nodded. The other man nodded along with him, completely accepting of what had happened.

Time stretched on. Jarlath was getting restless, his legs twitching.

'How long …'

'An hour; two maybe.'

'Two *hours?*'

The young man nodded. 'I wish they'd hurry up because I can't leave until he tells me I can.' His eyes took on a glazed look. 'Although have you *seen* her?' His face changed lightning fast. 'Don't tell him I said that.'

Jarlath smothered his laugh. He'd seen more of Laeli than he'd ever wished.

In the background, Laeli laughed softly, probably able to hear everything they'd said. Moments later, Thalion was standing outside, shirtless, completely mindless of the cold. His hair was ruffled, his skin glowing in the weak light. The man from The Hollows carried the jug into the tent and left.

Trying to look anywhere other than at the Chieftain, Jarlath joined him.

'Two days are up.' Thalion was all business, no pleasantries spared; he'd probably used them all up for the day. Thankfully, he didn't mention Jarlath's indiscretion. When he bent over and rested his hands on his knees, stretching his back, Jarlath saw handprints, lightly seared onto his skin.

'Her magic … doesn't it bother you?' he blurted.

Thalion straightened. 'Why would it?'

Jarlath focused on the ground. 'You're not scared of her?'

'I was, but not anymore. It's part of who she is and, honestly, without it, none of us would be where we are right now. You'd be dead. I'd be dead. Besides, she'd tell me to get lost. Well, maybe. She likes me too much, I think. Parts of me anyway,' he added with a smile, his face soft. From inside the tent, a voice mumbled something Jarlath couldn't decipher, but Thalion's smile deepened. He linked his hands behind his head and stretched again, his back cracking, the fresh scar on his belly still pink. Jarlath traced it with his eyes, noting the others spread over Thalion's skin.

'How do you do it?' he asked quietly. 'Kill a man and walk away?'

Thalion rubbed at his chin. 'You do, Jarlath. You do because, if you don't, if you think for one moment that it should have been you, the next time, it will be. It doesn't mean you forget them, their faces, because you never forget what death looks like. Killing a man in defence of your life or in defence of the things that are important to you doesn't make you a butcher. It doesn't mean you enjoyed it. It's survival, and it means you survived when someone else didn't.'

Jarlath nodded. He focused his gaze east, over the Estilleon camp, imagining travelling over that vast stretch of barren earth where Conor and Orin and hundreds of others lost their lives. In his mind, he marched through the Merawuld camp and into his commander's tent and demanded his brother. 'Gristel will send a messenger today. He won't dishonour his agreement with you.'

'And what will he say?'

'I'm hoping he sees things the way you do,' Jarlath said softly.

'And if he doesn't? What will you do then?'

It was a question that took them beyond this one moment. Jarlath surveyed the cloudless sky; a black bird wheeled through the expanse then darted away until it was nothing but a tiny speck of dust on the horizon. 'I don't know. I thought it was what I wanted, to be a soldier, but now ...'

'All the men here in this camp have other roles, Jarlath. They're farmers, blacksmiths, hunters - they have roles in their villages and in their families. When and if conflict arises, they put down their scythes and hammers and pick up their weapons because their Chieftain asks them to. That's why I want this over. I want to let these men return home where they're needed, where they belong, because none of us belong out here.' He paused. 'I'm sorry your brother is caught up in this. If I could help him, I would.'

Jarlath believed him.

A gust of cold wind rushed through the camp. Thalion stepped inside the tent, motioning for Jarlath to follow him. He did so hesitantly, worried about what he might find. Laeli was still in bed, the blankets pulled high so that the mass of her hair and a slender arm were visible.

Thalion led him to the table, gesturing to a pile of papers and a map.

'What do you see?' he asked as Jarlath bent to study the map. It was a battle plan. He didn't have much experience with this sort of planning, but he stood up straight and swallowed.

'You know what they will face.' Thalion was frowning at the map as Jarlath's stomach churned, his head swimming with fire and death and blood.

'Put a shirt on,' a bossy voice said.

Laeli appeared at Thalion's side, wrapped tight in a blanket, her arms bare and that wild tangle of her hair tumbling over her shoulders like a cloak.

Thalion pulled her close and kissed her. 'Or I could take the rest of my clothes off.'

Laeli rolled her eyes, gesturing at the map, saying there were more important things to deal with, although her face was soft when she looked at him. 'Withdraw your men. Leave a skeleton force here. Don't wait for their response.'

Thalion raised his eyebrows. 'And leave my country open?'

'How far would they get? And they'll agree to your terms,' she said with a light shrug. 'They'd be crazy not to and, if I've learnt one thing about humans while in your world, it's that self-preservation is important to you. You need to show them you're serious about honouring your own agreement.'

Thalion's expression hardened. 'I am.'

'I know that, but they don't. As far as they're concerned, you're your father's son and can't be trusted. I could smell it on them while we were there. They said the right things to keep you happy, but they don't trust you.' Her voice softened at the end.

'Alright,' Thalion agreed quietly; Jarlath glanced at him in surprise. 'I'll get half of them to move back, as a gesture of good faith. I'm not sending them home until I'm certain this is over. Regardless of what their message says, the man they send can take that bit of information back with them.'

Laeli nodded and Thalion pulled a shirt on and left.

The level of trust in their relationship ate away at Jarlath's core. It wasn't that he never trusted Ash – he thought he knew better, thought his experiences in life made him the authority. His face burnt with shame because she was right – he didn't know how to help her, so he left. Self-preservation, Laeli called it.

The first thing he'd do when he found Ash was apologise for being such an arrogant arse.

He studied Laeli's face as covertly as he could. 'Are you alright?'

'I don't know,' she answered quietly, moving away from him to perch on the edge of the bed, holding her blanket tight with one hand. She glanced at the tent flap. 'I need to go back. To Sitra,' she added softly. 'But I can't, not yet.'

'He won't let you?'

Her face was fierce. 'He can't stop me.' Her expression relaxed swiftly, a smile playing on her lips. 'But yes, because of Thalion. I won't leave him, not now. He needs me, and …'

'And you love him,' Jarlath finished.

Laeli was very still. 'What is love but longing for the other half of who you are? I lied to myself about it for a long time, but I won't lie anymore. I know it doesn't make sense – it doesn't make sense to me sometimes either – but then love doesn't make sense, does it? It's never the way we think it is going to be. Thalion isn't perfect, but he doesn't try to be, and

I love that about him. I love that he's fierce and loyal and dependable. He's a good man, Jarlath.'

'But when you can't be with the person you love?' Jarlath asked quietly.

'You'll find her again.'

Thalion swept back in, a gust of cold wind following him. 'It's done. They'll be moved back by dark.'

Jarlath didn't have time to think about what it meant, how this act might change things. He was ordered out so Laeli could dress. He lingered in the winter sun, not knowing what else to do with himself. Owen joined him, nodding at three people coming towards them.

'The messenger is here.'

Jarlath glanced up to see Finn being escorted across the camp by two armed men. His brother looked so small, so young and nervous, that Jarlath wanted to take his place.

Finn was marched past him. The guards paused for a moment, then the tent flap was pushed aside, and they went in. Jarlath and Owen hurried in after them. Finn ignored them, holding out his hand, the folded piece of paper contained within his palm about to change their worlds, again. He swallowed as Thalion approached him but held his hand steady.

Thalion glanced at Jarlath, who nodded at the unasked question.

He kept his eyes on Finn as Thalion unfolded the note, reading it quickly, before passing it into Laeli's outstretched hand. She was seated at the table, and instead of her Witch's uniform and her weapons, she was wearing a simple dress of black wool, her hair a waterfall of rich brown, her eyes and skin glowing, lips plump and red. Finn stared at her, his mouth hanging open, expression vacant, and Jarlath wanted to shake him. He cast a nervous glance at the Chieftain, but Thalion's face was calm. He was probably used to having men fall over themselves around his wife.

Wife. Jarlath could still hardly believe that, either.

'Well,' Laeli said, placing the note on the table. 'Thank you, Jarlath. Because you had the courage to do what you did, no one else must die — not here, anyway.'

'It wasn't that courageous,' Jarlath mumbled.

'It was,' Thalion affirmed. He turned to Finn. 'You get to go home, soldier.'

Finn opened his mouth then closed it again. He settled on a nod instead.

Jarlath released the breath he didn't realise he was holding. 'Can I …'

Thalion waved him away. Jarlath grabbed his brother by the arm and steered him from the tent, out into the whirling wind and fierce sunshine.

'Get off,' Finn snapped, pulling his arm free.

'Why are you angry?' Jarlath asked. 'You've had your life handed back to you, Finn. You don't have to go to war, or die, or watch those you care about die. You get to go home!'

'They said you deserted. Why would you do that? And now you're here, in the Estilleon camp, sitting at the feet of Thalion Liulfur and doing his bidding,' Finn retorted scathingly. His eyes returned to Chieftain's tent and that glazed expression crossed his face again. Jarlath glanced over his shoulder as Laeli crossed in front of the open flap.

'Put your tongue back in your head before her husband cuts it off.'

'They're actually married? I thought that was a rumour.' Finn sounded disappointed.

'Yes, they're married, rather enthusiastically I might add,' Jarlath mumbled.

As they watched, Thalion put an arm around Laeli's slim waist, pulling her into him and swinging her around, her hair shifting like a living thing. It looked like they were dancing, their faces as happy as Jarlath had ever seen them. Owen's rumbling laugh echoed through the air.

Finn scraped his boot along the ground, digging at the snow. 'What happens now? Are you coming home with me?'

'Finn, I can't,' Jarlath said softly. 'I need to find Ash. I don't know where she is, but she's alive somewhere and I have to find her, and Thalion is my best chance of doing that.'

'It's true then? She's the fire caster from Tyllcarric?'

'Yes.'

Finn sighed. 'Well,' he said, a grin slowly spreading across his face. 'You've spent half your life following her around, what's a little longer?'

'What would you know? You were just a snotty-nosed brat.'

'I have eyes, and those eyes saw where your eyes were most of the time.'

'Shut up.' Jarlath punched his brother in the arm. 'Don't tell Mum and Dad where I am – they'll worry – but tell them I'm alive and I'm okay.'

Finn nodded. 'In case it helps,' he called as Jarlath turned to walk away. 'She was watching you most of the time as well.'

Jarlath didn't try and hide his smile because, for him, Ash was always the silver lining in any cloud that would darken his days. She was the light he needed to see, and he'd crawl over broken glass on his hands and knees to find that light again.

CHAPTER THIRTY-SEVEN

Ash woke from darkness to chaos.

Head spinning, she scrambled from bed and dressed, hurrying into the halls, following the sounds of pain and wretched terror. The Academy was filled with moans and the faces she saw were blank with disbelief. She raced down the halls, slipping through the press of bodies. People lined the walls, eyes dark with fear and confusion. Some clutched their arms, others cradled their hands or heads, and all were singed and coated in soot. The unmistakable scent of smoke and burning lingered in the air. She noticed dark eyes glaring at her, and some whispering behind their hands. Stomach tight, she hurried past them, looking for Senan, or Nerida.

Ash caught the arm of a Healer, the front of her white dress smeared with black. 'What's going on?'

The Healer's eyes were wide. 'A fire storm in the street not far from here,' the girl answered, her round face pinched.

'What?' Ash whispered. She dropped the woman's arm.

The Healer nodded. 'The Watch … I don't know for sure, but people are saying they have fire magic. Did you know the air mages were assigned to the Watch?'

Ash swallowed. 'But … the Queen? Surely she …'

The Healer gave Ash a strange look. 'She's dead. The High Mage announced it yesterday; didn't you hear? And now …' She shook her head and hurried away, her white dress vanishing into the groaning crowd. Ash leant against the wall, numb. People rushed past her, but she didn't see them.

The Queen … dead.

Ash pushed herself off the wall and rushed down the hall, her head spinning, stomach churning.

Gedeon had her magic!

Inside the dining room, the tables were being used as beds and each one had a body sprawled or sitting on it. Healers and students alike busied themselves about the room, ferrying bowls, herbs, salves, and tonics from one table to the next. Ash moved between the tables and hands reached for her – hands covered in burnt skin.

She felt sick. This was her fault. Her magic had caused this.

'Ash!'

Radella approached, the older woman's face tight. 'You shouldn't be here,' she said in a low voice. She took hold of Ash's arm and went to lead her from the room, but Ash shook herself free.

'What's happened, Radella?'

The White Woman rubbed at weary eyes. 'The High Mage has learnt how to use the Bloodstones. You need air magic to do it, which is why he took the mages.' Her expression grew fierce. 'Those mages wouldn't have had a choice. It wouldn't surprise me if he had that ghastly Spirit Rake of his coerce them into using their magic this way.'

'All these people …'

'Yes. Those bullies of the Watch are enjoying themselves,' Radella spat.

'I want to help,' Ash said firmly, gesturing to the wounded.

Radella stared into her face for a long moment, before she nodded. 'Alright. Nerida is over there, near the window. Stay with her.'

'The High Mage has control of the city, doesn't he?'

Radella's face hardened. 'Gedeon has crossed a line I didn't believe he was capable of crossing. To use magic like that, stolen magic, against innocent people!' She grasped Ash's hands. 'You have to be careful. You and Senan. He is looking for you. You must be ready to leave at a moment's notice. It was a blessing from the Mother that the Watch didn't see either of you when they came for the mages.'

Bile rose in Ash's throat. Across the room, she spied Gem, her hair tucked off her face, wearing a simple dress of grey linen. As she watched, Gem rushed away with a bowl, a black smear tarnishing the porcelain of her cheek. There was no sign of Yasper.

Nerida was tending a woman with severe burns to her hands and forearms. Her face was creased in concentration as she smoothed ointment on the woman's damaged skin. The woman was either sleeping or fainted, but her face was tight with pain.

Ash approached on leaden feet. 'What can I do?' she asked.

Nerida stared at her for a long moment. 'Bandage her hands and arms, to the elbow.'

The wounded kept coming, a tide of them, all day and into the night. Ash caught snatches of words as she rushed around: the dead lay where they had fallen. The Watch were beating people in the streets. Buildings were on fire. The Queen was dead.

Exhausted, Ash left the dining room, stumbling down the hall to find Senan and Radella in the White Woman's office, their faces drawn, eyes shadowed. Senan glanced up as Ash eased the door open. He handed her a piece of paper, torn around the edges.

'One of Yasper's halfkin spies dropped this off,' he said.

Ash stared at the poster – at her face, Senan's, the words that spelt their doom.

'We have to leave,' she whispered. 'We should have gone straight away, Senan.'

'I know,' he said in a low voice, his mouth turned down. 'I made a mistake. I'm sorry, Ash, for putting you in danger. Gather what you need. We'll go tomorrow, before dark.'

Ash was sent to bed. On the walk back to her room, she saw Yasper speaking with a halfkin girl, who whispered something in his ear before slinking away to be swallowed by the night. Yasper's shoulders slumped. Ash wiped her hands on the front of her dress, the taste of dread thick on her tongue as she approached him.

'They found Biel.' Yasper's voice was flat.

Something in his tone had Ash's heart racing and her stomach churning. 'Where?'

'Nailed to the front door of *The Solstice House*.'

The blood drained from Ash's face. 'Yasper … I'm sorry. This is my fault!'

He shook his head. 'You didn't kill him.'

'But if I didn't write that letter …' she swallowed, her eyes burning.

Yasper shifted his gaze to her face, his eyes furious. 'They'll have found another reason to kill him. That's what men like Gedeon do – they break the world and it's up to people like you and me to put it back together. *You* will make things right again.'

Numb, Ash sought her bed, waking the next morning to trudge to the dining room, continuing her work, following Nerida's orders. By midday, the stream of people crawling through the front doors slowed and, exhausted again, Ash ate, washed her face, and fell back into her bed, not bothering to change her clothes, wanting a quick nap before they left.

She was shaken awake by Nerida. 'You have to get up.'

'What's going on?'

'The Watch are coming. Someone must have told them you're here,' she added, disgust colouring her tone. She picked up Ash's bag, snatching the blanket from the bed and shoving it in along with some clothing as Ash scrambled out of bed and found her boots.

The sound of splintering wood echoed from down the hall. Ash jumped back as Oden materialised in front of her. The shadow-dog nodded at the door. Ash nodded, wrapping a coat around her shoulders.

'Let's go.'

They followed Oden through the halls, Ash trusting the dog to lead them to Senan and safety. Nerida didn't ask questions, creeping along at Ash's heels. Senan was waiting down the end of the hallway, engulfed by shadows. Yasper and Gem waited with him; Gem's face was pale but her expression remained calm. Senan swept his eyes over Ash's face and reached for the door.

Ash turned to Nerida. Dread was coiling in her stomach, her throat tight. 'Come with us,' she said, grasping Nerida's hands.

Her friend shook her head.

'Nerida, you'll be killed if you stay here.'

The raised voices of the Watch screamed down the dark hall, their footsteps echoing loudly. They were going room to room – people shouted in fear.

'I can't have your death on my shoulders,' Ash whispered. 'Please, Nerida.'

'But … my patients …' Nerida's lip trembled.

'Radella will protect them,' Senan said quietly. 'Gedeon knows you're friends with Ash. You'll be in danger if you stay here.'

Nerida nodded sadly. Senan placed his hands on the door behind him; the lock slid free with an audible click, and they hurried out into the chill of the evening, the Mage-Witch locking the door behind them. He led them across the Academy grounds, keeping close to the walls. Ash could hear the Watch as they continued to comb through the Academy. It wouldn't be long until they discovered their quarry missing. She prayed to the Mother that Radella would be okay.

Senan pushed open the side gate to the Academy grounds. They kept to the back streets and alleys, moving as quietly and quickly as possible through the shadows with Senan their guide, making Ash wonder how often he had crept around the streets of Tyllcarric undetected. A haze of smoke had settled over the city, bleeding through the streets, crawling along roads coated in ash and rubbish. The air was perfumed with death and dust and fear.

Senan paused. He had stopped them near one of the smaller market squares, the open space large and daunting in the darkness, the fire pit in its centre dormant, no Marshal in his orange shirt guarding it. Ash knew that beyond that square, hidden from view, was the main gates of the city.

'Ready?' the Mage-Witch asked, waiting until each of them had nodded. As one, they stepped from the sheltered dark and hurried across the square, into the next street, and a world laid to waste.

There were bodies fallen and piles of rubble still burning. Shopfronts were smashed, broken windows and doors gaping like eyes, watching as they passed. A line of people stretched towards the city gates. Trying to escape, Ash realised. Some were carrying bags and sacks of their belongings; others had nothing at all. Children were screaming. Behind them, a great plume of smoke dangled over the city.

'Where will we go?' she whispered to Senan.

'The Delta,' he said. Oden slunk alongside him, his lip curled back from his teeth, growling low in his throat. Senan turned to her. 'I know you don't want to, Ash, but you're going to have to protect us. I'll get us out. You keep us alive.'

She shook her head furiously, thinking of that black fire and its deadly power.

'Yes,' Senan said firmly, 'you have to.'

Yasper, Gem, and Nerida had drawn ahead, a pistol in each of Yasper's hands. 'If we're going, we need to go now!' Yasper called as they approached the crowd gathered near the main gates.

From around the corner came the men of the Watch, a blank-faced mage with them, a Bloodstone glimmering on a chain around her neck – Ash could see it winking at her. She could feel her trapped magic shrieking and bouncing around in its cage. Her stomach twisted.

People screamed at the sight of the Watch and the street erupted into madness. Bodies fell to be trampled against the stones by panicked feet as people rushed for the gate. The guards were quickly overpowered by desperate men and women. The heavy gates were drawn open and people spilled out onto the road, dragging carts and crying children with them. A horse whinnied and bolted through the crowd, panic in the whites of its eyes as it knocked two men to the ground.

Nerida grabbed Ash's hand, pulling her along. Yasper kept his guns ready, and Ash felt Senan's magic stir. She swallowed, blood burning, adrenalin pouring through her as they drew closer to the gates, swept along at the back of the jostling crowd. Somewhere in the back of her mind was Jarlath, telling her once that guns, while deadly, were rarely accurate, which was why the army still used swords and daggers. Ash glanced again at Yasper, at the steely expression he wore, and she knew, if he missed, if Jarlath was correct, it would be up to her to protect them.

Gem stopped suddenly. 'I can't, Yas. My friends are here!'

Cursing, he grabbed her arm. 'Gem, you'll be killed.'

'I can't leave them. The girls in the cathouse … they need me!' she cried, as people rushed past them, faces tight with fear. No one spared them a glance.

Yasper stared at her for a long time as, around them, the Watch beat people with their batons and the screaming grew louder. He leant forward and pressed his mouth to Gem's, kissing her hard. She smiled through her tears, touching his cheek.

'I'll see you soon, okay?'

She turned and vanished into the writhing crowd.

Through the press of bodies, Ash kept her eyes on the black-shirted men. One, with shining blonde hair, was dreadfully familiar. Her stomach flopped as Mal turned his head, arm paused mid-air. He let go of the man he was holding and smiled.

Ash froze as that murderer's smile deepened. In slow motion, Mal pulled the pistol from his holster, aimed it at her, and fired. For a moment, the wheel paused, and Ash could see that bullet inching through the air towards her. Senan gave a shout; his hand lifted as Ash's did.

Air and fire met, folding together seamlessly in a rippling blanket of red and orange. Ash gaped, meeting Senan's eyes as the Mage-Witch wrapped that blanket of magic around her, encasing her in a protective cocoon of swirling fire. Through the flames she could see Mal, see the anger on his face. He shouted, and the Watch began to advance on them, weapons drawn, the air mage with them following along, slack-faced and compliant. Ash's magic swelled and the Bloodstone around the mage's neck glimmered and called to her.

'You need to do your thing, darling,' Yasper called. She knew what he left unsaid – he was one against many, one weapon against ten others. She might be protected, but her friends were not.

They would die if she did nothing.

Ash bowed her head and expelled a breath. She had to face what she was. She could no longer run from it. She had to be fire and smoke and darkness. She had to become destruction and heat and sparks. With this act, she knew she would never be the same.

What will you give, daughter of fire?

Ash called on her magic again. It simmered to the surface and she let it ease over her skin, twisting and dancing, her power filled with deadly calm. She yielded completely to the raw magic that hummed in her veins, that lived in her bones and her heart. It was part of her and, with her next breath, she tasted smoke. Ash closed her eyes and thought of the Rift, of that great chasm of timeless magic. She willed it into herself and, even with the distance, it came, flooding her with heat, a glorious rush of fuel.

Senan's magic dissolved and Ash let the fire free.

She drew her hands together and shaped the fire into a ball, sending it flying – it raced across the street, the flames twisting and flickering and hungry. It engulfed the Watch and the air mage – they ran screaming, helplessly trying to extinguish the flames that licked at their bodies but one by one, those consumed fell, smoking and burning as the fire feasted on their flesh.

The magic in the Bloodstone broke free, flowing towards Ash in a thin stream. She held out her arms, unable to help smiling as her lost fire returned to her body. The people running for the gate screamed in terror and fled from her as she blasted the Watch with fire again.

Deep inside, the black fire sizzled. It begged to be set free. Ash lifted her hands again; she could hear it calling to her. Through the smoke and the flames, she saw a face she knew.

Darian. Senan spotted the Spirit Rake at the same time; the Mage-Witch's lips curled back in a snarl as he lifted his hands. Below them, the stones shook as Oden howled and Senan's magic rose into the air. Ash hesitated, her magic poised and ready as Senan shaped the air – he pulled it back and flung it forward like a wave; Ash let her fire flow in its wake. Their combined magic raced towards the Spirit Rake, his hands moving through the air. Ash watched incredulously as the air in front of Darian's body began to spin, a vortex of power.

She tugged on Senan's arm as her fire slammed into that vortex, caught up in the spinning arms of air, spiralling faster and faster with the movement of Darian's hands.

'We have to go, Senan!'

Nerida was crying; Yasper took her hand and pulled her close to him, moving towards the gate, his pistol trained on Darian. He fired – in slow motion, Ash watched that bullet race towards Darian.

It collided with the spinning air and flame and vanished.

The Spirit Rake stepped closer, that vortex of fire and air moving closer with him. Ash slashed her hands through the air – all she had to do was imagine it, and a wall of flames spread between Darian and her friends.

'Let's go,' Yasper ordered, face pale.

They ran for the gate, the Spirit Rake watching them through the fire with dead eyes, the wall of flame raging with a life of its own, smouldering bodies littering the ground at his feet.

CHAPTER THIRTY-EIGHT

The Great Hall was to be the face of their celebrations that night. Thalion and Laeli were being joined for dinner by Frode, Owen, and Angus, who'd returned from the border with them. A surprised Jarlath had been asked to come as well.

Thalion was half-dressed, fresh from a bath, his hair still wet and dripping onto his shoulders.

'You need a haircut,' Laeli said, weaving both hands through his hair, calling on her fire magic. When she was done, he touched his head and smiled at her, slipping into the shirt she handed him. He sat on the edge of the bed to put his boots on. His expression was calm, relaxed.

'I've never asked you – what happened to your mother? You don't talk about her.'

Thalion glanced at her, one boot on, the other dangling from his hand, the softness slipping from his face. He shoved his other boot on and sighed lightly. 'I was fourteen when she died. It was a particularly tough winter that year – and the one before that – the snow didn't leave us, even through summer. The crops had failed and there wasn't much game around. People were starving. We were rationing food across the country and my mother, being who she was, ate little, wanting others to be fed.' He paused, fingers plucking at the furs that covered the bed. 'She died of the wasting sickness. She had a fever for days, no appetite, and she coughed day and night. There wasn't anything my father, or anyone, could do for her. Once she started coughing blood, we knew that the end was coming.'

Thalion looked towards the window, to the world outside, where the wind whistled across the landscape and the sky was heavy with clouds. 'She's buried out there, in the graveyard behind the castle. My father dug her grave himself. The earth was as hard as rock, but he dug until his hands were bleeding. Something in him broke that day. He was never the same.'

His voice was steady, never stumbling over the words he spoke, but Laeli could see the tremble that gripped his fingers where they rested on his thighs. She could smell his sorrow, his pain.

'Thalion, I'm sorry,' she whispered. Sickness was foreign to her; starvation and hardship were things she had never experienced. She had never watched someone she loved waste away and not be able to help them. The temperament of this country – its volatility and uncertainty, its wild weather, and the cards the Morrigan threw these people, this world capable of carrying a person to their death … she sat beside her husband, laying her head on his shoulder, wanting nothing more than to protect him, to hold back the wind and the snow with her bare hands.

'My father was always a hard man, Laeli, quick with his temper and his hand, but when she was alive … he smiled more.' Thalion rested his head on hers. 'I can understand why he is the way he is. I couldn't before but I can now,' he continued. 'I'm not excusing him – he made his choices – but I know that if I lost you … I wouldn't be the same either.'

In her mind, Laeli saw Hadrian digging that grave; she saw herself digging Thalion's. She studied her hands, the smooth skin of her palms, imagining that skin shredded and bleeding and smeared with dirt. Thalion was trying to hide it from her – the truth of the future laid out before them, his acknowledgement, his acceptance of it. He'd made his peace with it, but for her, knowing she'd outlast him ... she swallowed tightly, pulling away so she could look at him.

'But it will be me that has to lose you.'

'When this is over, we will live, Laeli. Just live.' Thalion's voice was soft. 'Whether I have five years or forty left on this earth, I'll still be me until the end, and I'll still love you, even after I'm gone.'

It was the first time he'd said those words, although she'd known it, had felt it, since he came to her in Sitra, and had known it for certain the night she married him. 'Thalion, I ...'

He held her eyes, waiting, waiting for her to say it, but she couldn't. The words were right there but she couldn't say them; they carried such meaning, such weight, such *fear*, that she swallowed them away.

Laeli didn't miss the hurt, the disappointment, that sliced through his eyes before she flung her arms around his neck and buried her burning face against his skin. He was stiff beneath her touch, but he still returned her embrace, saying nothing.

She hoped he knew how important he was, how she wouldn't be able to breathe without him. She kissed his cheek gently, and they put the unspoken things aside and went downstairs to dinner.

The feasting and drinking lasted long into the night, the men getting drunker with each passing moment. They also got louder, their conversation punctuated with laughter. It made Laeli smile to hear it, to see the relief on their faces. Though each side was leaving a small force at the border, the war was over before it truly began. She had let Thalion go alone to his second meeting with the commanders of the Queen's Army, both sides agreeing to put their weapons down but maintain the pretence of war. The High Mage had to believe Estilleon still posed enough of a threat to keep Hadrian and Kiarda happy. Laeli had no doubt that once Gedeon found out the soldiers had pulled back, he would be in contact with Hadrian. Gristel and Leod had agreed to continue the lie, and Thalion had no choice but to trust them to keep their word.

But that, she decided, taking in the tranquil lines of her husband's face, was a problem for another day. There were also things Thalion needed to deal with closer to home. Whitemouth was now under his control; the only places still digging their heels in were Emrelfel and Amberwick, who continued to ignore all communication from the castle. Two messengers had been intercepted leaving Amberwick while they were away. It would have to be dealt with soon. But not now.

As two more jugs of mead were brought in and placed on the table, Laeli smothered her yawn. She stood, her eyelids heavy, head foggy. Thalion caught her hand; his warmth wrapped around her.

'Where are you going?'

'Bed.'

He shook his head, pulling her into his lap as she leant to kiss his forehead, folding his arms around her. He dropped his head into the curve of her neck.

'He won't be much use to you tonight, Laeli,' Owen laughed.

'Speak for yourself,' Thalion growled, then, when she made to get up, 'Stay, please.' It was a whisper, his mouth moving against her skin.

She nodded, and made herself comfortable, resting her cheek on his head, her arm around his shoulders. She'd been worried about how Thalion's men would view her, but the time they spent at the border, where Owen sought her opinion on things, and the smiles she'd been given tonight made her realise she'd worried about nothing. Thalion had been right – they needed time but, now, they respected her and accepted her for who she was. Her title meant nothing. It was what she did here that was important to them.

Across the table, Jarlath was smiling to himself and Angus had given up on his mug, drinking straight from the jug. He set the jug aside and lifted a small, stringed instrument from beneath the table. He strummed his fingers gently over the strings – the sound was haunting, the notes bending and slurring with the surprisingly deft movement of his hands. That sound reached inside Laeli's chest, wrapped around her heart and squeezed. The others fell silent, nothing but the mournful voice of the instrument seeping through the room to linger languidly in the corners.

Owen began to slap his hand on the table, slow and thundering, a pulse to match the beating of the human heart. Laeli let herself slip away, her eyes drawn to the flames flickering from the candles along the middle of the long table as Angus began to sing, his voice rich and melodic, plaintive and wistful at the same time. It was a song about the wild beauty of their land, of their home. Soon, Owen and Frode joined him, then Thalion, their voices weaving around each other like ribbons. Jarlath's face was closed and Laeli knew he was thinking of his own home.

In her mind, she saw the great forest of Eshlune, the trees thick with leaves, the sunlight slanting through them to kiss the ground, colourful birds flitting through the branches. She saw grass so green it glowed, a carpet of blue and white flowers, a sky so blue the weight of it hurt, and she heard the tinkle of water over rocks and smelt the richness of the earth. She was conscious of time trickling away; the solstice was close and, after, green life would rise from its slumber to cover the land.

From deep within, Laeli saw the Rift, as clearly as if she floated above it. She saw the smoke rising from the great chasm, could smell its sulphuric bitterness, and, within the darkness of that pit, she saw something move.

As she pushed the Rift from her mind and tucked herself closer to Thalion, Laeli's vision shifted again. This time, she saw the blanket of white that covered the land around her. She felt the wind touch her cheeks and run its fingers through her hair. Here, in this icy wild, the snows would melt and Estilleon would rest under a blanket of green, the sun bathing the country in warmth and light.

With her heart beating in time to the music, Laeli dozed in Thalion's arms until the songs ended and the talking began again. She half listened to the chatter about hunting and killing things, the weather, politics, and what they hoped the future would hold. Laeli smiled to hear each man – these tough, hard men – express nothing more than a desire for a quiet life.

The conversation then turned to women – Owen took great delight in tormenting Jarlath about Ash.

'When you do find that girl of yours,' Owen said loudly, slinging a giant arm around Jarlath's shoulders. He gestured across the table with his mug of mead to where Laeli was still perched in Thalion's lap, one of his hands on her thigh, the other wrapped around his drink, his cheek resting against her throat. 'That's what you need to do. Don't let her go.'

Jarlath blinked drunkenly. 'I've seen more kissing in the past week than I've ever needed to see.'

Thalion's voice was smug. 'A word of advice, Jarlath: in my recent experience, the best place to put your mouth is her—'

'Thalion!' Laeli hissed, slapping the side of his head.

He gave her a wounded look, then smirked. 'You know I like it when you're rough with me.'

'I've seen more flirting in the past week than I've ever needed to see as well,' Jarlath mumbled with a shake of his head, his comment rewarded with laughter.

'Hope you've been taking notes,' Thalion quipped.

Laeli scowled. 'You're very sure of your charm, aren't you?'

Thalion pinched her leg. 'Just imparting my wisdom, sweetheart.'

She wound her fingers through his hair, tugging his head back, ignoring his little yelp of pain. 'I'm going to bed, *sweetheart*, and remember – I can hear your imparted wisdom from up there.' She kept her voice even and loud, able to be heard by everyone, then kissed her husband hard enough to bruise his lips, pressing herself against him. His hands fisted in her hair as he kissed her back, just as fierce. A jolt of heat shot through her and her belly tightened. She couldn't help it – she whimpered, feeling him grin against her lips.

Someone cleared their throat. Cheeks hot, Laeli pulled back, not looking away from Thalion's face. His eyes were nearly black with want and it still amazed her how much she could affect him, how he sighed when she touched him.

How she fell to pieces when he touched her.

He let her up, eyes shining, lips swollen and curled into a knowing smile. Without looking at anyone, Laeli quickly left the room, heart pounding, breathing shallow. She'd made it to the top of the stairs when she heard Thalion push his chair back. His footsteps echoed on the stones; she waited, one hand on the door to their room, her body still tingling, a sigh escaping her as he spun her around and pressed her against the wall, pinning her with the length of his body.

'You can't kiss me like that and then leave,' he murmured, his lips finding her throat.

Laeli groaned and tipped her head back, her fingers bunched in his shirt. Thalion kissed his way up her neck and along the curve of her jaw, every press of his lips a burn, a spark of light and heat that burrowed beneath her skin. 'Do you remember the first time you kissed me? In that cave?' she breathed.

'If I remember correctly, it was you that kissed me.'

She rolled her hips against him, chuckling when he made a little noise in the back of his throat. She wanted to hear it again; her fingers slipped beneath his belt, hunting for the searing heat of his flesh - he groaned, making her smile. 'But you wanted to kiss me.'

'I wanted to do much more than that.' His hand skimmed the outside of her breast, his touch teasing and light; she bit her lip as he gripped her hips, pushing himself closer. Her stomach tightened at the feeling of him, and she was transported back to the library in Sitra, her legs hooked around his middle as he turned her to liquid and left her writhing on that table.

'Show me,' she whispered.

Thalion kissed her cheeks, the tip of her nose, making her giggle, then he kissed her until she couldn't breathe, until her head was spinning with the smell and taste of him. She pulled his lower lip into her mouth, ripping another groan from his throat; it became a growl, low and primal, as she undid his belt. She couldn't get enough of him lately. Winding her arms around his neck, her hands gripping his hair, she kissed him again, long and deep, wanting to crawl inside his skin.

In the back of her mind, she remembered they were in the stairwell outside their room, with his men waiting downstairs and a large and comfortable bed on the other side of the door, but neither of them moved. Her blood was boiling, her breathing thick, an inferno raging beneath her skin as his hands found their way under her skirt.

Laeli's words to Jarlath in the war camp barrelled their way inside her mind.

What is love but longing for the other half of who you are?

Thalion was the other half of her.

She'd kill for him, protect him until her dying breath, and do anything to make sure he was safe. She wanted to make him smile, hear his laughter, wake up in the morning to his face and listen to him try to convince her to stay in bed a little longer. She wanted to bicker with him about useless things and watch his eyes sparkle because he loved doing that as well.

But he was braver than she was.

Thalion had crossed mountains and stepped into another world to find her. If he could have that much courage, then so could she.

Her heart thundered so wildly, so fiercely, she thought he must hear it as he gave her a wicked grin, then dropped to his knees on the cold stone. The first stroke of his tongue against the core of her left her body boneless and it was only his hands that kept her from sliding down the wall. When she was gasping and squirming and trembling, her fingers buried in his hair, he stopped, hoisting her up, her legs folding around his middle, the strength of his arms holding her steady as he slid inside her.

The last of her inner defences came tumbling down, shaken utterly from their foundations. They fell until there was nothing left, nothing to stop the words that swam around her mouth, begging to be let out.

She couldn't breathe, couldn't hold it back any longer.

'I love you.'

Thalion stilled, fingers dug deep into her thighs as he slowly pulled back to look at her with wide eyes. His mouth opened then closed. He stared at her, as if trying to work out he'd heard correctly. She repeated the words in a whisper, a mere breath, and then he was moving slowly, torturously slowly, his eyes never leaving hers, not even when his body shuddered, and his knees threatened to buckle and Laeli's magic had wrapped them both in smoke and sparks as her heart swelled and exploded.

'I don't know how I could love you anymore than I already do, but I know that when I wake up tomorrow, I will. How is that even possible?' Thalion whispered, the muscles in Laeli's legs trembling as his voice did. He let her down gently. 'I thought …' He swallowed audibly. 'I thought you married me because I wanted it. I didn't think you …'

He still didn't think he was worthy of her, of being loved.

'I married you because I love you, Thalion Liulfur,' Laeli said softly, laying her hand on his cheek; his eyes fluttered closed, then open again, that blue sky blazing in the darkness. 'And I love you because you're brave and fierce, and generous and kind. I love you because you're determined to fight for what is right and because you let me see your vulnerabilities, and your fears. I love you because you treat me as your equal, and that is more important than you know.'

'I am completely yours,' he said earnestly, thumbs stroking her cheeks, his touch reigniting the flame that burnt in her belly. Again, a little voice urged. Again.

She kissed him gently and pushed the wanting away.

'I have to share you with your country, though,' Laeli said with a little sigh; it was very quiet downstairs. She swallowed, hoping to the Gods none of them possessed hearing like hers. 'Which means, right now, Chieftain, you need to go and get drunk with your men. They need you as well.'

Thalion shook his head, then sighed as someone called up the stairs that they were out of mead and, if their Chieftain was too busy, would he mind at least telling them where they could find more? Owen's voice dripped with cheek, and Laeli's face burnt, but Thalion's grin was smug. Although it was the last thing she wanted to do, she made him go, then hurried inside their room, stripping off her clothes and diving into bed, pulling the covers up over her head. She giggled, then bit her lip, feeling like a fool.

As she lay there, Laeli's heart was racing, but she felt light, unburdened, free of the fear that she had held on to for so long. She was still awake, still grinning, her face hurting, hours later when Thalion stumbled in, falling over himself as he tried to take his boots off. She thought about getting up and helping him, but it was fun to watch him curse and struggle with his shoes and then his clothes. Eventually, he fell into bed; she rolled over and put her arms around him.

Utterly content, Laeli stroked his hair until he fell into the deep sleep of intoxication, snoring against her throat. She felt like she'd just closed her eyes when someone was pounding on the door to their room. She gave Thalion a shove and received a snore in response. Rolling her eyes, she untangled herself from his arms and slid into the cold air. The knocking continued as she pulled on her clothes, grabbing the dagger from underneath her side of the bed, her fire magic dancing beneath her fingertips. Outside, lightning streaked across the sky, the thunder that followed rattling the castle. The air was chilled with rain.

Eric stood in the darkness outside their door, his expression apologetic.

'Sorry, but Thalion needs to come down to the Hall.'

She narrowed her eyes. 'At this hour?'

He nodded and left. Laeli had no idea what time it was. Her eyes were gritty and her head fuzzy. She closed the door and turned to the task of waking Thalion, who did not appreciate being poked and prodded, rolling over and shoving his head under the pillow and grumbling at her. With a sigh, Laeli threw the pillow away and flipped him onto his back roughly.

'It's hardly a fair fight when you're stronger than me,' he grumbled.

'Something's happening downstairs,' she said.

His eyes opened properly, and he sat up, swaying on his feet as he stood. He was still drunk. She forced his arms and legs into his clothes, ignoring his protests, then led him down the stairs, a ball of flame resting in her palm to light their path. Eric was waiting by the doors to the Great Hall and Laeli's stomach clenched in anticipation.

'You've got a visitor,' the young man said quietly.

Thalion frowned. 'In the middle of the night?'

'She rode through the storm to get here.'

She? Leaving Thalion to clear his head, Laeli stepped into the Hall, stopping in surprise.

Nara was standing by the fire, her wet hair plastered around her cheeks and neck, her clothes dripping water all over the floor. Her face collapsed in relief when she saw Laeli, that relief switching quickly to despair.

'He's dead!'

'Who's dead?'

Nara's eyes were wild. 'My brother! She killed him.' She began to pace, her wet clothes trailing over the rug, her boots sloshing. Thalion came in, the shadows under his eyes halfway down his face, but Nara kept talking frantically. 'Since I returned, Freda has been more agitated than usual. She didn't want to think about anything you said, Thalion. Her loyalty to your father outweighs her common sense.' She paused, glancing at them warily. 'I'm not saying I completely support what you're doing, but I can see the merit in most of it.'

Thalion sat by the fire and put his head in his hands.

Nara raised her eyebrows. 'What's wrong with him?'

'He's drunk.' Laeli motioned Nara to the other chair. She asked Eric to rouse Healy and have blankets and dry clothes brought to the Hall. 'Start from the beginning.'

Nara rubbed at her face. When she returned to Emrelfel with Thalion's plans, Freda had pretended to consider them. The idea of autonomy was a strong drawcard but, in the end, Freda's loyalty to Hadrian was stronger. She gathered her most loyal warriors and began to plan her own act of rebellion. Her intention was to send someone to the castle under the pretence of allegiance, as well as sending men into Reyshorn, Fairhorn, and The Hollows. Freda's plan was to hold the traitor Chief's or their Seconds under house arrest, and have the false Chieftain locked up to await the return of his father.

When Nara protested, arguing that surely there was a better way to convince people to stay true to Hadrian's rule, Freda screeched at her, called her a traitor who'd been infected with fae sorcery, and, while Nara was proclaiming her innocence, her loyalty, her faithfulness, Freda's man, Valen, had driven his sword into Kellan's belly.

In the shock and horror that followed, Nara placed her forehead on the ground at Freda's feet, and pledged her loyalty yet again, her voice wavering, her brother's blood leaking from his body.

But Freda had underestimated the bond between siblings; Nara had bided her time, smiling and sitting at Freda's table until she could sneak away.

She knew the names of Freda's men sent to each village. She knew the names of the messengers Freda was preparing to send over the mountains and into Eshlune, and now Thalion knew them as well.

'You should know also,' Nara said, eyes glittering, wrapped up tight in the blanket Healy had brought in for her. 'That Amberwick supports Freda.'

Thalion sighed deeply, rubbing at his face.

'We knew this was a possibility,' Laeli reminded him.

He nodded, his face drawn and tired, and she knew what he was thinking – one step forward, another step back. The victory at the Pass faded away as the storm ravaged the world outside. 'Alright. We're going to have to let Freda's men into the villages – that way, she won't suspect you, Nara. I'll let them know who to expect. I'll put men out on the road once this blasted weather passes and intercept her letter to my father.'

'And Freda?' Nara demanded.

'What would you have me do?'

'I want her dead,' Nara snarled. 'I want her to suffer for what she did to Kellan.'

Thalion nodded. Beside him, Laeli was frowning. 'Is that the way to solve this?'

'You didn't hear her! She's lost her mind,' Nara said, her voice rising. 'If she isn't dealt with, who will she kill next? She's got half the village terrified and the other half caught up in her ideas of revenge.' She turned to Thalion. 'It's your head she wants. She plans to hand you over to your father wrapped up in a neat bow. She thinks she will be rewarded for it, that she will replace Brenna as your father's favoured Chief. If you won't do anything to stop her, Thalion, I'll kill her myself.'

Laeli chewed her lip.

'You have a brother, don't you?' Nara turned to her; Laeli nodded. 'Would you kill for him? Would you do whatever you could to avenge him?'

'I would, yes,' Laeli whispered.

Thalion sighed again. 'I can't go near Emrelfel, obviously,' he said with a shake of his head. 'But I might have an idea.' He stared into the flames. When he glanced up, it was Laeli he spoke to. 'Would she work for me, do you think? Fox?'

'Fox?' Laeli said in surprise. 'You'd have to be willing to offer her something impressive for her services.'

'What does she want?'

'Her freedom,' Laeli said softly.

Nara was frowning as it sank in. 'You're going to send a half-breed after Freda? You're as mad as she is.' She laughed bitterly, her hair steaming with the heat from the fire.

'Did you hear what happened to Caden?' Laeli asked quietly.

'I heard you butchered him,' Nara replied, holding Laeli's gaze while Laeli shook her head. She wondered how far that rumour had spread.

It could be damaging to Thalion's cause if the people thought she was a cold-blooded killer.

Thalion sat back. 'One of the half-breed girls in Caden's house recently arrived from Tyllcarric as a slave. Her former job was as an assassin. She knows what she's doing. She's the person you need.'

Slowly, Nara nodded; the fire crackled in the background. 'But I'm going back with her. I want to wash my face in that crazy bitch's blood.'

CHAPTER THIRTY-NINE

It took three days to reach the Delta. The ferry crossing was too dangerous, so after they had waded through the small creek that snaked past the city, they entered the shade of the trees by nightfall. As the darkness grew around them, the trees seemed to be breathing. The air pulsed, a hum floating beneath the chittering of bats and the mournful hooting of owls. Ash and Nerida spent an uncomfortable night curled on the ground, sharing the one blanket they had managed to bring with them. The air was chilled, but they'd all agreed they couldn't risk a fire.

Between them, Senan and Yasper took turns at sitting watch, Senan's hands at the ready, Yasper's pistols loaded. The night dragged on, all of them twitching at noises in the undergrowth, certain the Watch, or Gedeon – or the Spirit Rake – was about to come charging through the trees. By the time dawn broke and a thin, hazy light stretched through the forest, they were all groggy and hungry. They didn't stop to eat, packing up their small camp, Senan's earth magic rising at his call to disguise any trace of their passing. He walked behind them, scattering leaves to cover their tracks, Yasper a steadying presence at the front.

After spending another nervous night under the trees, they turned due north. To the east was the farming village of Ashlar, surrounded by apple trees, the scent of overripe fruit that didn't make the last harvest filling the air; from the trees they watched black-shirted men ride along the road at a gallop, plumes of dust rising to float through the air. There was a blank-faced air mage travelling with them, a Bloodstone containing Ash's stolen magic winking from his neck. When Senan could sense no human mind other than their own, they made their way to the Sparkling Waters and followed the river until nightfall, camping on its bank. Ash was terrified out in the open, and didn't sleep that night, sitting first with Yasper and then Senan.

Senan was exhausted, and Yasper's face looked like he imagined his did – pale and pinched, eyes underlined in dark shadows.

Nerida had barely spoken since they'd fled the city. Now, as morning broke and the sun kissed the surface of the river, and with Tyllcarric far behind them, she let out a dramatic sigh.

'By the Gods, I'm a criminal and a fugitive!'

Yasper grinned broadly at her. 'You say that like it's a bad thing.' He grew serious briefly. 'You're alive, at least, Nerida. What a mess! I wonder if I'll ever see my beloved business again, ever hear the melody of coins falling from pockets to cover my tables. Oh, how I miss that sound! Do they gamble in the Delta, do you think?'

Something Senan appreciated about Yasper was his capacity to take a serious situation and spin some humour into it, even when he had been damaged by it as much as everyone else. The ability to still smile and laugh amid this terror was a magic all of its own, one they would need in time ahead. He also appreciated that Yasper was a thinker, quick on his feet and quick with his pistol. Senan had the terrible feeling they would need that skill as well in the end.

Yasper hadn't mentioned Biel's death, but it was obvious how much it had hurt to lose his friend in such a horrific way. Senan found Yasper's commitment to the halfkin cause interesting as well – answers to the gentle questions had revealed a man who saw the pain of others and who was prepared to do whatever he could to help ease that pain. Yasper had met Biel in the prison camp in Garlathe, and it was through Biel that he became more involved and more aware of the situation facing the halfkin. Yasper had seen the darker hue of the world, had waded through it, lived all those things that most people usually turned their faces from. He understood inequality; he understood why this fight was so important.

The blond man had not mentioned Gem either; Senan didn't need his air magic to be able to sense how worried Yasper was about her.

There was so much going on, so many factors that needed thinking about. Senan was by no means giving up. He needed time to sort his head out. In the Delta, at least, they would be safe. They could let their guard down and think about their next move strategically, instead of making things up as they went along, like he'd been doing for too long now. This mess they found themselves in was his fault. Ash had refused to accept his apologies, saying she had followed him of her own free will, but he knew that if anyone else lost their life, he would carry that on his shoulders until his dying breath.

They travelled east, the tinkling melody of the river soothing, Yasper and Nerida's chatter rising and falling above the sounds of the water. Senan could sense Ash's magic close to the surface; she was holding it tight beneath her skin, ready to let it out at a moment's notice. He tried not to think about the men she'd killed in the city, their charred corpses lying face-down on the stones. She'd done it because he'd asked her to and now the ghosts of those dead men would haunt her as much as him, but he knew it was Darian's face she saw in her nightmares, because he saw the Spirit Rake as well.

'How does he do it?' Ash asked Senan, walking alongside him, leaving Nerida with Yasper. 'Darian. His magic isn't normal, is it?'

Senan shook his head. 'No.'

'Is he an Anomaly, like you?'

'I'm not sure. There is more than air magic inside him, I think. Regardless of what he is or isn't, he's Gedeon's pet, and that makes him dangerous, Ash. More dangerous than any secondary power he might possess,' Senan replied quietly. That Gedeon had let the man live was testament enough of his desire for power. Twenty years ago, Gedeon was ready to watch Senan hang, ready to snuff out his life because of what he represented.

Senan had long suspected it was fear that drove Gedeon to report him to the then High Mage. Gedeon had been his friend, once, but he had been more than that – he'd been Senan's mentor, the older man taking the boy from the village under his wing and helping him hone his magic from something wild to something tempered and controlled. Senan had never had his eye on the top – he was content to return to his village and help the people there, where life revolved around the seasons of growth. Gedeon, he knew, had aspirations that soared higher than most students at the Academy, and it hadn't come as a surprise that he aimed for High Mage.

He had shown he was talented enough, that he had the charisma needed for the job, the leadership skills, but Senan's air magic had, at the end, detected more than a simple ambition. In Gedeon, he had sensed a strong desire for power but, thinking about it now, there was no way Senan could have predicted what his former mentor would become. Gedeon had a choice twenty years ago – turn Senan in, or keep his secret, help him understand what it meant. Gedeon had chosen his ambition, electing to see a man hanged rather than offer him help.

With Gedeon's wish for power fulfilled, Senan dreaded to think what the future would hold if he did nothing. Gedeon's alliance with Kiarda was the most worrying. Senan could understand what drove her all those years ago. As an earth mage, he was directly connected to the soil, the trees, and the plants that owed their existence to the rich earth that coated the land. Although Rhodiri had done what he'd promised he would and convinced the Mage Council and the then Queen that protection and conservation of the environment, rather than its blatant destruction, was required. True to their word, people had not taken more than they needed, though Senan still felt his magic twinge when men walked into the forest with their saws and axes.

Would ruling over man be enough for Gedeon, or would he want to extend his power over the earth as well, that which Kiarda sought vengeance over?

Hadrian, Senan had decided, was simply caught in the middle, a pawn in this potential battle for the land that he could see coming. Hadrian's ambitions were small compared to Gedeon and Kiarda. Senan had no doubt Thalion's assumptions about his father were correct – Hadrian would want control over Merawuld. Kiarda and Gedeon, he imagined, would not wish to hand that over so quickly, to either the Estilleon Chieftain or each other.

As they continued walking and the air grew thick with humidity, Senan's thoughts drifted to Fox. He'd not allowed himself to think of her much since the last time he saw her, but the knowledge she was in Estilleon and possibly alive burnt like a beacon inside him. He had no idea if he was ever going to see her again and, as the sun began to sink behind them, he vowed that once this was over he would find her. Beyond that, he wasn't sure and didn't want to allow himself the luxury of hope.

The sun was at its peak. The river had been moving more slowly the closer they got to the Delta, the water thick with sediment, sluggish as it followed the ancient path cut through the landscape. Now, as it neared the sea, the Sparkling Waters broke apart, spilling into a series of shallow channels. The build-up of silt over years of movement had created islands and, beyond those shifting masses of land, just visible through the haze hung over this subaqueous world, were the houses of the Delta rising beyond the stretch of wetlands.

Nerida gave a shout, pointing at the village that hovered above the water on stilts. The ground became boggy underfoot as they approached, water bleeding through the soil to pool around their shoes. Further out, past the shallows where the river and the ocean came to meet, small boats bobbed on the water. Children splashed not far from the first of the huts, watched over by parents sitting on the wooden jetty, scaling fish or untangling nets.

They waited on the shoreline, Yasper shielding his eyes with his hand, the two girls clustered close together like the slender trees that lined the riverbank further west. Mangroves spread intricate legs into the clear water, small fish darting between the roots.

'It's beautiful,' Nerida sighed.

'It is, but how do we get out there?' Yasper wondered.

'I've a friend, Mika. I'll let him know we're here,' Senan answered. He clicked his fingers and Oden materialised at his side, the shadow-dog pawing at the water delicately. With a thought, the dog vanished again, reappearing on the jetty. The people gathered there stopped what they were doing; one jumped up at the sight of Oden, bending low to pat the dog's head before leading the dog into the village.

Eventually, an unmanned boat made its way across the water, bumping gently against the sand. Yasper gaped at it, then shrugged his shoulders and climbed aboard, offering a hand to Ash and Nerida in turn. When the girls were settled, Senan climbed in and the boat moved away from the shore, ferrying them across water as clear as a crystal and through swathes of water lilies to where a tall man waited for them at the end of a long jetty.

'Mika,' Senan said, standing as the boat pulled up next to a wooden ladder. 'Thank you.' He introduced them all. The others were staring at Mika in undisclosed awe – his blue-green skin shimmered where the sun kissed it. He was loose of limb, with hair the colour of moonlight on the sand. Mika's eyes were the yellow of a fish, enabling him, like all people of the Delta, to see as clearly underwater as they did on land.

Senan had not visited the Delta in many years and Mika, like the fae of Sitra, had remained unchanged by the passage of time. The people of the Delta held no fear over what Senan was, his dual power meaning nothing in a world shaped by the shifting of the tides. The people of the

Delta believed the ocean was the source of all life, and they worshipped Nehalennia, the Goddess of the Sea, whose job it was to ferry the souls of the dead to the next world while their bodies were returned to the water. Nehalennia watched over the boats of fishermen but could grow angry and create fierce tempests if people took more than they needed from the ocean. The Delta was also inhabited by faeries – selkies, undines, and waterhorses – Senan would have to make sure to mention them to the others.

Mika showed them to two huts they could stay in, leading them over the wooden platforms that moved with the water, creating the illusion of being on board a ship. The village was centred around a large square space – a meeting and market ground, packed with baskets of fish and green leafy plants plucked from the ocean bed – with long stretches of jetties running from it in four directions. Each jetty split several times, leading to huts with verandas reaching over the water. Small boats were moored at each hut. The buildings themselves were simple, timber constructions, usually consisting of three rooms – one for eating, and two for sleeping, with families of up to five sharing the small space. The Delta people spent most of their time on or in the water, retiring to their huts to share a meal and sleep.

The huts Mika gifted them had been vacant for some time. Layers of dust coated the surfaces of the small, crudely constructed tables and chairs, and spider webs were flung across the corners of the rooms. There were gaps in the walls, allowing the warmth of the sea breeze to sneak inside, and windows on each wall, letting sun and light in. Mika left them to settle in. Nerida immediately set about dusting each surface, a fierce expression on her face. She and Ash would share one hut, while Senan and Yasper would bunk down in the other.

'Well,' Yasper said simply, leaning his arms on the railing of the veranda and gazing out at the sea. 'If I hadn't seen the world go to shit with my own eyes, I'd have never believed it.'

Senan couldn't agree more.

'How long are we going to stay here?' the blond man asked.

'Until we work out what to do,' Senan answered.

Yasper glanced over his shoulder towards the girls' hut. They could hear Nerida's voice, her prattling filling the gaps she left for Ash, who didn't speak more than a murmur. 'And them?'

'I don't know. I've got a feeling the city isn't where Ash needs to be,' Senan said quietly. He turned his gaze to the northwest, to the forests of Eshlune and the Rift.

CHAPTER FORTY

Thalion eyed the waif of a girl incredulously. *This* was the High Mage's assassin? She was clinging to her brother, eyes wide in a pale face that shone with determination, her skinny body wrapped up in layers of clothing. The half-breed siblings stood on the other side of the long table, the door open behind them, the fire crackling and dancing in the hearth. Laeli spoke softly to the girl, words too low for Thalion to hear, then took her seat beside him.

They had discussed this at length with Frode and Owen and then Nara, who had been harder to convince. Thalion glanced at the dark-haired woman standing by the fire. Freda had made a mistake and now, her Second was standing in Thalion's Hall with her own notions of revenge bubbling away.

Fox was watching him with a carefully veiled expression, those eyes sliding beneath his skin, trying to see inside him. He decided to get straight to the point. 'Will you work for me?'

'Doing what?' Her gaze shifted to Nara then back again, her nostrils flaring, as if scenting the air, reading what was flowing through the spaces between them.

'I hear you're skilled with a blade,' Thalion said evenly, watching the half-breed closely. What she'd done to Caden made his stomach turn.

Fox lifted her skinny shoulders in a shrug. 'It depends.'

'On?'

'On whom you want killed.'

Her eyes never moved from his face yet skittered around the room at the same time, scanning and taking note of everything. Thalion's fingers stroked the hilt of the sword at his hip, an action to let her know who held power in this room. Her amber eyes followed his movement, her expression accusatory.

Laeli leant forward. 'You want your freedom, Fox, I know that. But it isn't time for that, not yet. You are, however, free here, in Estilleon,' she said softly.

Fox's upper lip curled. 'Who is in charge here exactly? You'—she regarded Thalion suspiciously—'or the fae Princess?'

Elan lent over and whispered something in his sister's ear. Her expression didn't falter, as if she was carved by stone. Thalion couldn't blame her. What she'd endured … he should have moved on Whitemouth sooner. The fault was his, and he was determined to rectify it.

He tapped his fingers lightly on the table. 'I will give you your freedom if you work for me.'

She was quiet for a long time, her expression finally shifting as she considered what was being offered. Her eyes narrowed; he couldn't blame her for her suspicion either. 'If I kill for you, I'll be free? To leave here and go where I wish?'

'Yes.'

'And my brother?'

Thalion glanced at the boy, standing close to his sister, his arm around her back protectively. He took in their faces, both thin and pale, those identical eyes staring him down. 'Yes, Elan as well.'

Elan smiled for the second time since Thalion had known him.

Fox's face remained unchanged. 'You swear? My freedom in exchange for whoever you want dead?'

'I swear,' Thalion replied softly.

'I can trust you to keep your word?' the assassin pressed. She didn't take her eyes from his face, ignoring her brother when Elan whispered in her ear. Beside him, Laeli made a noise of protest but Thalion only nodded, hoping Fox could see the truth in his face. Words were not enough for her; he understood that.

'Alright,' Fox said eventually.

Nara approached the table and addressed the half-breed. 'I want you to make Freda suffer.'

'That isn't what I do,' Fox said firmly, her head held high. Proud, despite her circumstances.

'But you're an assassin,' Nara countered.

The stony expression returned. 'That may be so, but I'm not a torturer. Caden was an exception.'

Nara opened her mouth but something in Fox's face made her close it again.

'I need weapons,' Fox said, turning back to Thalion.

'Whatever you need, you can have,' he replied, and she almost smiled at him, pulling her lips back in time. 'Can I trust you? You won't run the moment you leave the castle?'

Elan spoke, his voice as soft as the wind. 'I'll stay here. That way, she has to come back.' He flashed his sister a grin. She leant close to him, her voice low and furious, but he shook his head, gesturing to Thalion and Laeli, taking his sister's hands and squeezing them. 'I'll stay,' Elan said again.

Thalion nodded, satisfied. 'In the meantime, Fox, Nara will tell you all you need to know about Emrelfel and Freda, and I'll talk to you before you leave. Tomorrow morning. Once this is done … I will speak with you about Amberwick.'

Fox nodded again, and she and her brother followed Nara out, the woman already talking. Thalion wondered, as he watched them leave, had he done the right thing.

'Well,' he murmured, 'she's …'

'Broken and completely unable to trust us; none of them can,' Laeli said sadly. He knew she was thinking of those two children, thin and starved and filthy. When they'd arrived, Fox had marched into the outer bailey and into her brother's arms and Thalion hadn't seen her until now. If Fox hadn't turned Caden into dog food, Thalion would have gone and done it himself, regardless of the danger.

'You want her to get into Amberwick?' Laeli asked.

'Perhaps. I know it isn't how we wanted things to end up, but I don't know what else to do about it. Gustav is with my father – not that he'd listen to me anyway – and Freda has gotten her claws in Daan. With Nara on side, Amberwick is the only place left with loyalty to my father.'

Laeli was frowning. 'It's not ideal, but you're right. What other choice is there?'

Thalion reached over to squeeze her hand.

She'd been emotional and unsettled recently, falling into deep silences, where she stared at the wall, as if she could look right through it to somewhere else. The news from the Queen's commanders about what was happening in Eshlune had shaken her. He knew how worried she was, for her father and her brother, for her home and her people, and he knew how hard she was trying not to let him see it again.

Thalion brought her hand to his lips, staring into those green eyes that captivated him every time he looked at her. She got up and settled in his lap, her arms sliding around his neck. He kissed her deeply, with total abandon, his blood singing like it did whenever he touched her. His hand moved under her skirt, seeking the smooth silk of her thigh, the scent of her filling his head.

He could feel the racing of her heart, her breath thick as she tilted her head back so he could kiss his way down her throat, fingers inching up her thigh. He could taste her – water, smoke and earth, the magic under her skin. He knew that now, understood it more the longer she spent by his side, and he'd never tire of it, never tire of her.

And she loved him. He'd hardly believed it when the words had left those perfect lips. Was still waiting to realise it was some wonderful, half-drunk dream.

Something pinched in his chest. Loving him wouldn't be enough, he knew that, and was silently preparing himself for it. But for now, he simply held her as close as he could, breathing in the smell of her, savouring the taste of her flesh and the way she felt in his arms.

Someone cleared their throat.

Jarlath was standing in the doorway, one foot in the room, the other planted in the hall outside, like he was preparing to run. Dressed in thick woollen pants, heavy boots and furs, with his chestnut hair ruffled by the wind and his cheeks red with cold, he could have been any young Estilleon man. Thalion was surprised Jarlath had returned with them after his commanders agreed to put their weapons down. Knowing Finn was safe was enough for Jarlath for the moment, Thalion reasoned. The fate of the fire caster was what drove him now and Thalion wasn't sure how much longer they could keep the young man here. He watched Jarlath's face, reading the language of his body, the muscles coiled tight and the hands constantly curling and uncurling.

Frustrated. He was frustrated. Thalion let a grin crawl across his face.

'If you need to release some tension, Jarlath, there's plenty of girls here – what?' Thalion laughed as Laeli slapped him. 'There is.'

'If you're not careful, you'll have to go find one of them to warm your bed.'

'Hardly. You can't keep your hands off me,' he murmured.

The door snapped closed. If Thalion thought back on the sequence of events that led him to this moment – the things that felt out of his control, that he did to please others, ignoring his own sense of right and wrong – the path was a long and winding one, filled with holes and traps, some of which he'd fallen into, many of which he'd managed to avoid.

He couldn't shake the feeling everything was fated, and his reward: her.

It didn't matter if it was to be short-lived. He'd take it, for now.

CHAPTER FORTY-ONE

Fox usually worked alone. Having Nara making so much noise with her grumbling … she shook her head. Fox thought of what she'd learnt of the woman she was going to kill. Freda. Emrelfel's Chief for twenty years. A triumph in itself, Fox thought, considering what she'd come to understand of this country in her time here. Power was something to grasp when it was offered and not something people let go of easily. Freda won her right to be Chief by being smarter than everyone around her, using her sharp wit and head for politics and economics to earn her place at the Chieftain's table. She was, by all accounts, shrewd and canny, with a capacity for cruelty, as Nara had personally discovered.

Freda's charm was why Fox was here in the first place, on the road as the sun was sinking with flurries of snow blowing around her. She was dressed warmly in thick pants and layers of shirts, as well as a cloak of fur, possibly the nicest thing she had ever worn – it reminded her of the animal it had come from and, in her mind, she could see the grey wolf sauntering over the landscape, leaving footprints in the snow as it hunted and killed.

Before they left Wilderun and the castle, Fox had sat in the Great Hall as Thalion and Nara argued between themselves about the best way to deal with the issue of Freda. Fox had thought it was straightforward

329

– she would kill Freda, and Nara would run the village. There had been more going on under the surface than either Thalion or Nara let on – it was obvious to Fox that neither trusted the other. It had been obvious to Laeli as well. The fae Princess had sat beside her husband, brows drawn together as the conversation went around and around, Thalion and Nara trying to drown each other in useless words.

In the end, it had been Fox who, with a sigh, had thrown all the cards on the table.

'You don't trust each other.'

Nara's face tightened. 'It's not that I don't trust Thalion…'

Fox leant forward. 'You don't. I can see it, I can smell it, and if you don't trust the Chieftain, how can I trust you, when I'm acting on his behalf?'

Thalion had stopped the smile creeping over his face in time.

'The opinions of a half-breed mean nothing to me,' Nara said with a toss of her head.

'The opinions of your assassin need to mean something to you,' Laeli said coolly. It was the first time she'd spoken through the whole meeting. Fox had been watching her closely as well, noting the way her eyes seemed to glisten for no reason. The smell of her continually shifted so that Fox's senses were confused. 'If you want her to work for you, you need to listen to her.'

'Why? She's being hired to do a job.'

Fox showed her teeth. 'I'm not working for you though, am I?'

Thalion tapped long fingers on the tabletop. 'You want an assurance, Nara? That once Freda is dead, I won't interfere with Emrelfel?'

'Yes.'

'Then I won't, as we discussed at the meeting. But,' he added as Nara's eyes widened. 'If I leave the village to you, those people to you, you swear you will do right by them? You won't challenge my authority when it's given?'

'Of course.'

He leant forward, eyes burning. 'I have your allegiance?'

Nara held his gaze for a long moment. 'You do … Chieftain.'

Thalion sat back. 'Thank you. You will be free to make your own decisions. Once everything is settled, you will return here, as will the others, and we will draw up our new rules for the country, to be decided on together.'

Nara nodded. When Thalion and Laeli left the Hall, the woman was staring thoughtfully at the hands clasped in her lap.

A gust of wind smacked Fox in the face, and she glared at the sky, kicking her horse forward to draw level with Nara. She wasn't a brilliant rider, not having much need for a horse in Tyllcarric, but the animal her brother had chosen for her was gentle and sensed her inexperience. Fox glanced at Nara again, studying the tight lines of the woman's face, her heavy brows and proud tilt of her head. She was beautiful in a cold sort of way, her hair as dark as a raven's wing, eyes like burning coals.

'What will you tell her?'

Nara tossed her head. 'I'll tell her I needed time to think.'

'She'll know you went to—'

'She'll know what I tell her.'

Fox already knew what that was. Why she'd agreed to pretend to be a slave when she'd thrown off the title was beyond her, but the promise of freedom was strong. Uncertainty squirmed in her belly. She didn't believe the Chieftain would betray her – she could smell his sincerity, his desire for this to all be over – but experience warned her she shouldn't trust so easily.

Nara nudged her horse into a trot and Fox followed suit. The wind shrieked across the land, battering them with ice as the walls of Emrelfel came into view. There were armed men on the tops of those walls. Fox could smell them, as she could smell the horses and the earth churned to mud beneath their sharp hooves, the wind and the snow and the warmth from the fires that burnt in hearths throughout that village.

The gates were bolted shut with a thick iron chain. Nara stopped, lifting her chin to address the man pointing an arrow at her chest. 'Don't be stupid, Tel. Open up and let me in.'

He narrowed his eyes. 'Where have you been?'

Nara gestured to Fox. 'I've brought the Chief a gift, in return for her forgiveness at my indiscretion. I overreacted.'

Tel eyed both women doubtfully, his dark eyes combing their faces, that arrow still notched and pointed at Nara's chest. They waited and, eventually, as the snow began falling harder, the gates of the village swung wide for them. Nara rode in first, Fox following close behind.

Miserable, was her first thought. It was cold and dark in the streets, no paving or stones beneath the horse's hooves, only hard earth and snow, the village not as big or obviously favoured as Whitemouth. Nara led the way past shopfronts closed for the day and a blacksmith's forge, heat and metal lingering on the air. Into the heart of the village they went, Nara stopping outside what Fox presumed was a tavern from the odour of ale and mead.

'Freda will be in here, where she is most evenings,' Nara said, swinging down from her horse. 'I'll let her see you and then take you to her home.'

Fox slid down from her horse's back, brushing the snow from her shoulders and hair as Nara pushed open the door to the tavern. The first thing she took note of when they went inside was how many windows there were, then how many men and women were gathered around tables and by the hearth. She patted her hips as inconspicuously as she could. Concealed under her clothes, sitting close to her skin, were the blades the Chieftain had gifted her. Fox appreciated their lightweight and decorative handles, the way they felt in her hand. It was like welcoming back old friends.

The Chief was sitting amongst a party of several men and two women at a long table nearest the roaring fire. The atmosphere in the room shifted as Nara approached, Fox trailing her. She worked at settling her face into a compliant expression while she studied Freda from beneath her lashes. The Chief was at least fifty, with a faintly lined face and dark red hair that had begun fading. There were noticeable streaks of grey woven through the red strands and she wore her hair piled high on her head, an elaborate bundle of braids snaking from her brow.

Nara bowed her head and launched into her tale – she overreacted, she understood, she should never have left, she was angry, but she was loyal to her Chief and her village. When Nara mentioned Fox, Freda swept her blue-grey eyes over Fox's face and body. The Chief wasn't a beautiful woman in any sense, but power and confidence radiated from her.

'She doesn't look strong enough to lift a bucket,' she snapped, her voice lower than Fox had been expecting.

'You'll find her a hard worker, won't she?' Nara turned to Fox, who nodded, not trusting her voice, and wanting to maintain the pretence of slight idiocy, as had been arranged. She was not to challenge the Chief – Freda must deem her trustworthy from the start.

'What's wrong with her?' Freda barked, continuing to peer at Fox down a nose that appeared too large for her face. Her proud mouth didn't look like it smiled much, despite the lines that bracketed it.

'She's … simple, you could say,' Nara said. 'But she's yours. A gift, Freda.'

'She's come from Wilderun.' Freda motioned at the clothes Fox wore, the wolf brooch that pinned her furs. Her pale skin darkened with rage, a muscle twitching in her strong jaw. 'Even his servants carry the badge stolen from his father.' She leant forward, her eyes nailing Nara to the floor. 'I should kill you for your treachery.'

Fox could smell the tension and could see the bead of sweat that gathered on the back of Nara's neck.

Freda's lips were a thin line. 'Did you tell him everything then?'

'Would I have returned if I did?' Nara challenged. Before she could say anymore, Freda nodded, and a big man rose from the table and slapped Nara's face, hard. Fox jumped, the sound slicing through the air as she remembered a different hand smashing into her face. She reached up to touch her cheek, her flesh stinging in memory.

'Get out,' Freda said, her tone bored. 'If I discover you betrayed me, Nara, you will join your brother. Take the girl to my house and don't be there when I get back.'

Nara turned without a word; Fox scurried after her, glad to be out of the suffocating heat of the tavern. Nara didn't speak as they mounted their horses and rode away.

Freda's house was grander than Caden's but not as fancy as Brenna's. Fox was shown the kitchen and where the laundry was done, hoping she wouldn't be there long enough to have to worry about either. She was to share a room with three other halfkin girls. This time, she didn't bother to learn their names. She would never see them again after Freda was dead.

She didn't see Nara for two days and was beginning to think she'd been a fool to trust anyone, a scowl taking place on her face, growing stronger and more painful as time went on. Nara found her late one afternoon. A feast had been planned in Freda's home – a celebration for the men about to move out into the villages as part of Freda's plan.

'You'll do it after dinner,' Nara said in a hurried whisper, pulling Fox into a room away from the eyes and ears of the other girls.

Fox nodded. 'The rest of the men? Those attending the feast?'

'Will be drugged.'

'Do you want them dead?'

'What did Thalion order you to do?'

'He didn't order me to do anything. This is my choice,' Fox snapped. 'But he asked me to help you, so I'll help you. If you want them all dead, then consider it done.'

Nara gave her a measured stare. 'Kill them all. If I'm going to rule this village, I need people loyal to me, not Freda.'

That night, Fox helped serve the meal, and when she went back to collect the plates, she found a room full of people with their heads in their food. How Nara had done it, she didn't know. Poisons and drugs were not in her arsenal. Fox considered it cheating.

Nara was sitting at the long table, her expression cool, watching Freda like a cat about to pounce on a mouse. Freda, Fox quickly noted, was bound to her chair, but was awake and glaring daggers as sharp as the ones hidden under Fox's clothes.

'You bitch. You usurper, coward, traitor,' Freda snapped at Nara, who simply smiled. 'What did that two-faced wolf pup promise you?'

'You shouldn't have killed my brother, Freda,' Nara responded. She twirled a butter knife around between her fingers, like Fox twirled her blades. 'And as to what he promised me – once you're dead, Emrelfel is mine.' Nara pushed back her chair and stood.

Freda saw Fox. 'Girl, go and get help!'

Slowly, Fox reached up and untied the apron from her neck. She tossed it away and ran her hands over her hips. Freda followed the movement, unable to avoid noticing the blades tucked there, the scabbard decorated with the symbols of the Chieftain. The daggers hissed their intent as Fox withdrew them.

She made her way around the table. Methodically, she lifted head after head, running that blade over throat after throat, Freda screeching at her to stop, Nara smiling in grim satisfaction. When Fox reached the last man, closest to Freda, Nara stopped her.

'This man killed my brother,' she said softly. Fox understood. She stepped back, gave Nara the space she needed, watching impassively as Nara lifted the man's head and removed his eyes with the blade of the butter knife she still carried, before pulling a dagger from the scabbard at her hip and opening his throat. As his blood spilled across the table, she kept cutting, hacking until her arms were slick to the elbow and she had removed his head.

Nara held the head aloft, staring into the eyeless sockets, before carrying it over to place it on the plate directly in front of Freda.

'He was your family, wasn't he?' Nara asked. 'Nephew, I believe.'

'I'll skin you alive,' Freda hissed.

'May the Allfather curse you in the next life, Freda.'

Fox took that as her cue. She approached the woman from behind, gripping her hair, forcing her head down over the blade held against her throat. Fox hesitated a moment, long enough to hear Freda's whispered threats that soon shifted to begging. Fox hated begging. She drew in a sharp breath and pulled the blade across Freda's throat in a single, swift sweep. Blood spurted, hot and wet, spilling down Freda's front, staining her blue gown and lap. The Chief jerked once, twice, then went still.

Fox wiped the blade and her hands on a napkin from the table.

Nara was watching her, taking in her calm, inspecting the neat carnage around the room, her eyes falling on Fox's hands, those small childlike hands that ended the lives of ten people. 'Why did you do this?'

Fox twirled the blade between her fingers. 'The High Mage of Merawuld sent me here to die because I refused to kill a terrified girl. Doing this will earn me my freedom – and the first thing I'm going to do is hunt him down. I want to open his body with my blades and sift through the remains of him, to see if he has a heart that beats.'

'And after?'

'I don't know.' Fox paused, studying the other woman with the same level of curiosity Nara had given her. 'Why didn't you kill them all yourself?'

'If I did, the people in this village would never follow me. Now, the problem is Thalion's, not mine.'

'You're going to betray him?' Fox asked bluntly. Her fingers tightened on her weapon.

Nara shook her head. 'I have more honour than that, even if you don't believe it.' She held up her hands, inspecting them, turning them over, taking in the blood smeared across her skin. 'I couldn't do this alone. I've never killed a man before,' she admitted in a quiet voice. Fox caught the hint of a tremble.

'You get used to it,' she answered softly. 'In a way.'

Nara hesitated, then lifted her chin. 'You would be welcome here, in Emrelfel. As payment for what you've done for me.'

Fox shook her head. 'I've got what I wanted.'

Nara nodded in understanding. 'Happy hunting, Fox.'

Fox started, recalling another voice, in another world and another time. She gave Nara a nod and left her standing in that room of death, her forearms slick with blood. As she rode from the village, she wondered what would become of Nara and the people of Emrelfel.

The sun was shining as it crested the horizon, its brilliance painful. Once the village was a speck in the distance, Fox began laughing and found she could not stop until tears were streaming down her face and she was certain her horse thought she was mad. Wind pulled at her face, her tears drying instantly as she headed out onto the plain.

She slept the night by the side of the road, tucked under a thicket of stunted trees, shivering despite the layers of fur and blankets she was wrapped in and, in the morning, the world was coated in fresh snow. Fox pulled herself onto her horse and set out again, her belly rumbling.

She rode for hours, the sun sinking fast and the wind never-ending. As Wilderun and the castle came into sight, Fox paused, pulling on the horse's reins. A dark shape lay to the side of the road, half buried in fresh snow. She dismounted; holding firm to her horse, she approached the shape hesitantly.

It was a wolf.

Its great body was defeated in death, the fur lush, the eyes staring blindly at the grey sky. She bent to touch it, running her fingers over that sleek fur, as soft as those she wore. The beast appeared to have died a natural death. There were no wounds left behind by human weapons. Fox inspected the wolf for a long time, feeling a kinship, a connection, to this animal who had run wild and free, who had not been captured or broken by man.

She turned her face to the sky as fresh snow began to fall. She was not broken, not anymore, and she never would be again. Fox rode the remainder of the journey at a walk, enjoying being alone, with her thoughts and the wind for company.

It was dark when she arrived at the castle and the Chieftain and his wife were in the Great Hall. Dinner had been served and Fox's stomach rumbled as the aroma of roasted meat and freshly baked bread hit her senses. One of Thalion's dogs uncurled itself from in front of the fire and came to butt its head on Fox's hand. Maybe it smelt the wolf, its wild cousin. She giggled girlishly as its pink tongue darted out and licked her fingers, wondering whether these dogs wished to run free, or if they were content with their life.

'He likes you,' Thalion said. He watched Fox watching the food. 'Hungry?'

'Starving,' she answered.

He indicated the table. 'Then sit.'

She did, filled with sudden nerves at the simple invitation. There wasn't a plate for her – Thalion gave her his, getting up and leaving the room, returning with another plate held between his large hands, Healy following him, scolding him for being in the kitchens.

'I've been in there loads of times,' Thalion argued as he sat down.

'You weren't the Chieftain then. You scared the girls, sauntering in unannounced like that. Meara broke a plate.' Healy put her hands on her hips.

He laughed. 'I see being Chieftain hasn't stopped you getting cross at me.'

'I'll be getting cross at you until the day the Allfather calls you home, Thalion Liulfur,' Healy said, but she was smiling as she left the room, her head held high. Fox watched the exchange with interest. It had been Healy who truly convinced her Thalion could be trusted, Healy who told her he was gentle and calm, a compassionate man who wanted what was right. She had seen it herself – seen how hard he'd tried when his wife had returned from Whitemouth with not one, but three, miserable halfkin girls and two starved children. Even though she'd ignored him, Fox had been able to scent how furious he was, how conflicted, and how sorry, even if none of them let him voice it that day.

Fox pushed it out of her mind; she didn't want to look back anymore, only forwards, to what was to come. Once her plate was piled high, she told the Chieftain it was done, and they ate without further mention of Freda or Emrelfel. When her plate was practically licked clean, Fox stood, prepared to go to bed and sleep deeply, as she often did after a kill, the adrenaline finally wearing away. Thalion's voice stopped her at the door.

'I promised you your freedom, Fox, so you have it,' he said softly.

She sucked in a breath. 'What about the other village?'

'That's my problem. You are free to leave if you wish. I gave my word.'

'A lot of people have promised me things before,' she said quietly.

'I'm sorry that we didn't get you away from Caden earlier,' the Chieftain said.

Fox swallowed. 'I'm not,' she said; Laeli frowned, but her husband kept those brilliant blue eyes on Fox's face. 'I remember something my mother used to always say. When something terrible would happen, she'd say, "sometimes the bad things in our lives put us directly on the path to the best things",' Fox said. 'I have to believe that what I went through in Caden's house happened for a reason. That it was the final step on my path to being free. It has helped me realise what is important to me, and what I am truly prepared to fight for – the people I'm prepared to fight for,' she added.

'Fate enjoys tormenting us sometimes,' Thalion said. 'But we cannot truly know what is planned until it happens. Be safe, Fox.'

'Thank you.' The words were out of her mouth before she could stop them. Fox couldn't remember the last time she had thanked anyone. She possessed an uncanny ability to push people away, her senses too ready to sift through faces and thoughts, searching for the negative in people, the ulterior motives, and base desires. Rarely did she give herself leave to see a glint of goodness, of genuine affection and sincerity.

Laeli smiled at her. Fox might not have trusted the Princess in the beginning, but now, she did. She was the most striking person Fox had ever seen, so bright and shining in such a cold, dark world. And her husband, he glowed from the inside out with promise and hope. They were genuine, so much so that she thought one day, maybe, she might return to Estilleon, to see what this place could be like when offered a different future.

As she left the Hall, Fox looked back. Laeli had her head resting against Thalion's upper arm, her hand on his chest, his fingers curled around hers, his face serene in the candlelight. Fox wondered if he knew about the baby in his wife's belly, about that tiny piece of them both growing there. She understood what it was now – that shifting smell of newness, that promise of life, like an unfolding flower in the first flush of spring.

The way the Chieftain looked at his Princess, as if her smile was the one thing that would make all the darkness disappear; that was something else Fox realised she wanted.

Love.

CHAPTER FORTY-TWO

'I've seen that look before.'

Yasper lowered himself to the edge of the jetty next to Ash, long legs dangling towards the water while she sat cross-legged, her hands clasped in her lap. It was nearing dark, the sun slipping away, the water around them painted in gold, red, and orange hues.

'What look?' she asked softly. It was so quiet in the Delta at night, nothing but the rhythmic sound of the waves gently pushing against the piers and the hulls of boats. Ash had taken to sitting here most evenings, watching the sun set, bearing witness to the end of the light and the fall of darkness. She didn't know why she did it, only that, somehow, after all she had seen and experienced, it felt fitting. That if she made herself watch the light be swallowed by the rising darkness, she would be able to face whatever it was that was coming for her, for all of them.

Yasper didn't look at her when he spoke, his eyes on the sun as it slipped towards the mountains. 'In the prison camp, I saw faces like yours all the time – faces stamped with the look of defeat.'

Ash hesitated, then, softly, 'Do I look like that?' She had made the conscious decision not to allow herself to be defeated, but if Yasper could see it on her face, she mustn't be trying hard enough. She had barely been able to convince herself of it, so why would anyone else, especially someone as observant as Yasper, be fooled?

'Sometimes. Like now, when I know you're thinking of how hard it is to keep going,' Yasper answered. His voice was gentle, as if he knew how hard she'd tried, and was still trying. All she could see when she closed her eyes to sleep was the fire, *her* fire, feasting on the flesh of the Watch as they lay on the hard stone. All she could see was that air mage, expression blank, even in death.

Ash swallowed tightly. She squeezed her fists, fingernails biting into her palms, the sharp burst of pain bringing her back to the present moment. A breeze blew in from the ocean, sending her hair dancing around her cheeks. She pushed it away. 'It is hard.'

'That doesn't mean you give up.'

'I'm not giving up,' she shot back hotly; her magic surged in response to her emotion, and she took a deep breath, trying to calm it. 'At least, I'm trying not to. I told Senan I wanted to fight, and I do, it's just … I don't know how.'

Yasper was quiet for a long moment and as the sun finally slipped beneath the horizon and the world was cast in darkness, he sighed. 'You can't wait for him to show up, Ash.'

Her heart started thundering; she dug her nails into her skin again. 'I'm not.'

He went on as if she hadn't spoken. 'In the end, it has to be you who makes the decision to act. No one else can decide for you.'

'What if I don't know what the right decision is?' It was a shamed whisper. From the moment this began, on Mabon in a city square turned black by her fire, Ash hadn't known what to do next, but she felt she should know. Everything she'd learnt, everything she'd been taught … it wasn't enough. She wasn't enough.

'Who ever knows what the right decision is?' Yasper said with a shrug. 'All I can say is this – when it comes down to it, and you leave to do whatever it is you're going to do, it has to be your decision, or else you won't be able to do it; whatever it is,' he added with a small smile.

'What makes you so sure I'm going to leave?'

'I'm no expert on magic, or on anything, really. I've made it through life by being smart, by using my wits and my charm'—he threw her a wink—'to survive. But you're different. You've got this incredible power inside you and yes, it scares the fuck out of me if I'm being honest, but, Ash, you can't let it scare you. I know you didn't want to hurt those people but sometimes, you have to, in order to save the things you care about.'

She stared into the water, not knowing what to say.

'Jarlath knows this,' Yasper said softly, and she glanced at him in surprise, her cheeks reddening as Yasper grabbed his shirt by the collar and slipped free of it. He turned so she could see the criss-crossing of scars on the pale skin of his back like some horrible decoration. She swallowed, recalling the silvery lines that marked Jarlath's flesh. 'I got mine by being dumb, by shooting my mouth off and thinking I could charm my way out of the shit I'd buried myself in. Jarlath got his defending someone's life, standing up for someone who couldn't, in that moment, stand up for herself.'

Ash licked dry lips. 'What did he do?'

She listened as Yasper explained about Gem, how she was about to be beaten and no doubt something much worse when Jarlath swooped in and saved her.

'We weren't friends then, but I made myself stand and watch as they tied him to a post and whipped him, because this man had the balls to do what he did, and I respected that. I envied it, in fact. Everyone thinks they're the hero, right, but when it came to it that night, he was the only one brave enough to actually do something about it, regardless of what it cost him.'

Ash was very still and quiet. Jarlath had not told her and she hadn't asked, too afraid to know the answer – and ready to blame herself for it.

Yasper pulled his shirt back on, giving her a serious look. 'But you can't wait for him to be the hero this time, Ash. You might have to do it yourself.'

'I'm scared,' she whispered.

'I know, so am I.'

He squeezed her arm and left her to the water and the silence of the night. She stayed on the jetty until the moon was high, splashing her silvery light over the world. Ash heard again that voice of power in her head and, this time, felt something deep inside her stir as the raw energy of those words, spoken by a goddess, flowed through her:

What will you give?

Jarlath's face flashed into her mind, slamming through her in a medley of images and memories that left her gasping. Then it was Nerida, Laeli, Mahelivar, Senan, Yasper, her parents … was that the price she would have to pay? Her friends and family? If she gave herself to the power that writhed beneath her skin, would she become something else, someone else?

She thought of Biel, of his bravery, because he had been brave. The manner of his death only made him more so.

That's what men like Gedeon do – they break the world and it's up to people like you and me to put it back together. You will make things right again.

Ash closed her eyes. She would.

She still didn't know how she would do it, but she would.

Ash let her magic out, let it flow from her, seeking and probing, hoping that somehow, an answer would make itself clear. She swallowed, trusting in her magic, trusting in what the Mother had given her, trusting in her gift, because it was a gift.

She would make herself worthy of it.

Her magic licked the surface of the water, painting it red and golden, before it raced across the landscape, moving steadily north-west, leading her through the forests of Eshlune, to the smoking, burning chasm of the Rift.

CHAPTER FORTY-THREE

The wind dragged claws across the landscape. Estilleon was so bitterly cold and thick with snow Jarlath thought they'd all freeze before they found Thalion's path through the mountains. They spent one night in Fairhorn, guests of the Chief, and one night shivering violently, the cold ripping into the tent and burrowing beneath their blankets with them. The three-day journey to the Peaks was filled with silences so thick and deep Jarlath thought he could drown in them. Fox and Elan spoke little; they communicated without words. Their closeness made Jarlath think of Finn. One day, when this was all over with, he'd return to Brenveil, hopefully with Ash in tow, to see his family.

Thalion's little-used path was a winding track through the mountains. He'd told them to follow the spirals, and it was Elan who found the first one, a swirling, unbroken line etched into the rock with neat precision. The spaces between the towering limestone and granite were so tight, at times Jarlath feared the horses wouldn't make it, but Fox's keen senses picked the best places for the animals to lay their feet. They followed the carvings dutifully, the path leading through rock that looked like it had been sliced apart with a sharpened sword. As they left Estilleon behind and began the descent, Jarlath could smell softness in the air – grass and running water, leaves and the rich earth of Merawuld.

Home.

They passed the swamps, mist curling from the water to snake into the air before vanishing, the village clustered on its bed of reeds a mirage in the soupy air. As night was falling, Jarlath pulled his horse up beside the nearest trees. Fox and Elan survived without rest, or food, or water, drawing on that fae strength lurking in their bodies, but he needed to sleep, and the horses needed a break.

Fox scowled at the trees. 'That is the Forest of Wights. No one stops here and we shouldn't either. We should keep going.'

Around them, the trees grew tall, their trunks twisted and gnarled, branches stretching into a sky painted with the growing darkness. The forest stared back at him, but Jarlath dismounted, ignoring the twist in his belly as invisible eyes tracked his movements. In the weak moonlight he could see faces carved into the tree trunks, put there by human hands or something else. A shiver crawled down his spine, and he tried not to think about the fact those faces looked like they were in pain.

'Here will do,' he declared.

'You're insane,' Fox hissed.

'I need to sleep,' Jarlath replied wearily. 'Stay awake all night if you wish but I'm going to get some rest.'

Fox mumbled under her breath, but she helped Elan with the tent while Jarlath checked their food – salted meat, bread, some vegetables – noticing their water supplies were running low already. He unwrapped a hunk of bread and meat with a grimace. What he wouldn't give for an apple, or a pie with apples in it, or anything other than pork and whatever else this was Healy had packed for them. Elan wouldn't let them light a fire, his eyes darting nervously into the trees, his shoulders twitching at every sound. The two halfkin sat close together in the darkness of the tent, eating little.

'Well,' Jarlath said quietly, 'this isn't so—'

An unearthly wailing filled the air, lifting the hair on the back of Jarlath's neck.

'I told you we shouldn't have stopped here,' Fox said in a low voice.

Jarlath swallowed as the wails became a moan that rippled through the air. 'If we stay in here, we'll be fine,' he said with more assurance than he felt.

'If you say so, oh expert on faeries,' Fox muttered scathingly.

Grumbling, Jarlath slid into his bedroll, tucking the blankets tightly around him. It might be warmer during the day this side of the border, but the temperature dropped fiercely at night and his muscles were pulled tight with cold.

He'd not been asleep long before Elan was shaking him awake. His eyes were large and dark, the amber swallowed by the blackness around them.

'There's something out there,' he whispered. Jarlath sat up, scrambling for his weapon. Fox was crouched near the door of the tent, a blade in both hands.

'What is it?' Jarlath asked quietly, throwing back the bedclothes and creeping to her side. Outside, there was nothing but silence, and the deep black of night. His bowels clenched painfully.

'Death,' the halfkin assassin said simply, not taking her eyes from the shred of night that pushed its way through the tent flap.

Jarlath swallowed nervously. That unearthly wailing sliced through the air again. Footsteps raced past the tent, a high-pitched giggling following them. The tent shook violently as Jarlath's stomach flopped and his dinner threatened to rise. Silence fell but no one relaxed. Jarlath thought about the Dark Grey Man and the Red Cap and shuddered.

Something screamed in the darkness; the hair rose on Jarlath's forearms, his skin puckering painfully, all his bravado turning to liquid and sliding from his body with the sweat that gathered in his armpits and on the back of his neck.

Fox glared at him, her eyes flaring in the dark. She didn't say another word, slinking back to her bedroll, sitting close to her brother, those blades held at the ready. An hour passed – nothing. Jarlath's bladder was burning. He picked up his dagger and moved to the opening of the tent. Fox and Elan didn't utter a sound, but he could feel their eyes as he eased out into the night, scooting as far from the tent as he dared to relieve himself. The moon had vanished behind a thick layer of cloud.

Once he was done, Jarlath walked backwards to the tent, keeping his eyes firmly on the forest, on those trees that seemed to pulse with an ancient and otherworldly presence. Dawn was still hours away, leaving them with no choice but to wait out the darkness.

As he neared the safety of the tent, he turned, stumbling back in shock.

Standing by the flap was Orin, exactly as Jarlath had seen him last, a grin on his face and wild excitement in his eyes, his army uniform pristine, his weapons hanging from belt and shoulder.

'Orin?'

Orin said nothing, walking towards the trees, stopping to glance at Jarlath over his shoulder. Swallowing, Jarlath took a step towards him.

'Orin, where have you been?'

Orin didn't reply. He stepped between the trees, hidden from sight. Jarlath started running before he could think better of it. Orin was here. He was alive. He was ... the forest closed around him, deep and suffocating, the darkness falling like a shroud. Orin was leaning against the trunk of a tree, his eyes on Jarlath's face. The carved face in the tree trunk beside Orin's head looked like it was screaming and, as Jarlath watched, the wooden mouth opened further. He swallowed and made to step forward, but a hand closed around his arm. He jolted violently, but the grip remained firm.

'Whatever you think you see, it's not real,' Fox whispered. His arm burned where her fingers pressed against his skin.

'My friend ...'

'Isn't there,' she said, her voice softer than he expected. 'Come on, Jarlath.'

It was the first time she'd spoken his name since they left the castle.

'How do you know?' he asked painfully, his voice close to breaking. He could feel the tears gathering in his eyes, but he didn't care if she saw.

'Wight's will trick you, often with the things you desire most in the world, and lead you to your death. It is in their nature to torment humans.' Fox's voice remained soft. There was no reproach, no accusation. Just sympathy. 'Come,' she said again.

Jarlath took a shuddering breath and nodded. The thing that was Orin glared at them; its eyes flashed red, then it vanished. Jarlath's stomach fell into his shoes. That wooden face, he noticed, had closed its mouth. Fox tugged on his arm once more, leading him back to the tent. He couldn't sleep, staring at the canopy until the sun had risen, face burning in shame, his tongue coated with fear and regret and loneliness.

They packed up in silence and set out with haunted expressions and shadows under their eyes. Jarlath cast a glance over his shoulder at the Forest of Wights with a shiver. When he turned forward again, he found Fox looking at him, her expression wary, as if she expected him to throw himself into the trees. He simply nodded his gratitude, unable to speak, and she inclined her head in understanding, turning away from him.

They followed the river, the water sparkling in the sun, for some time and, as they neared the ferry, Fox's head swung to the east.

'We need to go to the Delta,' she said urgently.

'I'm going to Sitra,' Jarlath reminded her. The longer he spent from Ash the larger the ball of anxiety in his stomach grew.

Fox shook her head. 'The Delta.'

'Fox …'

She wheeled to face him. Her eyes were wild in her narrow face. 'She's there, your fire caster,' the halfkin stated simply. 'And Senan.' Her voice softened, her whole posture relaxing for the briefest moment.

'How do you know?'

'It's what I do,' she said stiffly. 'Find people.'

'What you did,' Elan corrected gently. He reached across and touched his sister's arm.

'Are you sure?' Jarlath asked frantically. If he wasted time in the Delta…

Fox nodded. 'Trust me. I know her scent. I can smell the magic on her, even from here.'

They passed the ferry; the eyes of the ferry master followed them long after they had continued east, staying near the riverbank. On the other side of that river was Eshlune and the smoking innards of the Rift. Jarlath peered over his shoulder, his gaze drawn north-west. From here, there was nothing but a dense thicket of trees and green grass, but he knew, within those trees, everything had changed.

As they headed steadily towards the sea, the air became thicker, heavy with moisture as winter and its chill was left behind. The sky was a clear and shocking blue, so bright after all that time under the frost-bitten sky of Estilleon Jarlath had to lift his hand and shield his eyes. The sun cut across his skin, sweat beginning to trickle down his spine and along the sides of his face. He paused, pulling off his jacket, letting the sun kiss the colour of winter away.

They slept under the stars that night, the air sticky with humidity, insects tormenting them relentlessly. Jarlath's skin itched the closer they drew to the Delta. He went over the last time he'd seen Ash, trying desperately to find the right words, the ones that would help her forgive him, help her see how sorry he was.

When the sun had risen over the ocean, they set out again. The halfkin siblings rode ahead of him, sticking close together as usual. Jarlath could only imagine what Fox had been subjected to in that village. Laeli's face when she returned from her rescue mission spoke volumes, as did the haunted eyes and nervous tension of the other halfkin who had returned with them. It was those children who stalked Jarlath's dreams, so thin and wretched he couldn't stop his heart twisting painfully when he saw them. Their faces held such terror, their eyes tight with the unspeakable things they had witnessed.

When Thalion had laid his eyes on those children, one of them bundled in his wife's arms, he didn't know what to do, where to offer comfort. Fox had stalked past, going straight to her brother, and the other two halfkin girls were terrified of him, no matter how much Laeli tried to tell them they were safe. The whole episode dripped with such tension, such emotion, Thalion had left Healy and his wife to manage it, storming through the castle in a mood as dark and foul as Jarlath had ever seen.

After they returned from the Pass, Jarlath had watched as Thalion sat on the top step to the castle with a whetstone and sharpened his sword, the halfkin boy peering at him from the safety of the bottom of the steps. By the second day, the boy had drawn closer and by the third, Thalion gave him a dagger, the child flashing a smile and racing off with his new toy. Chuffed, Thalion had gone inside to be confronted by an exasperated Laeli, who reprimanded him for giving a child a weapon. That led to them bickering about what you should and shouldn't offer children to play with, which ended when Laeli was pinned between the wall and her husband, a smile on her face as he kissed her concerns, and her insults, away.

That was the sort of love Jarlath hoped to have with Ash – fierce and passionate, confident, but with none of the drama Thalion and Laeli could cultivate from nothing. They were both hot-headed and rude, with biting mouths, but Jarlath had seen with his own eyes how attuned they were to each other, how focused and attentive and caring they were. That was what he wanted – that connection.

He found Fox and Elan in the stables, who told him they were leaving the following day. When it was safe, Jarlath prepared his words and found a tousled Thalion sitting by the fire in the Great Hall, to have the Chieftain tell him with no fuss he was welcome to leave with the halfkin if he wished. Grateful, Jarlath hadn't known what to say, only able to mumble his thanks, wondering about this man he was just getting to know. Underneath the gruff exterior was a gentleness that drew people in, when Thalion let people see it, that was, and Jarlath had seen it many times, that mask slipping more and more.

If there was one thing Thalion had taught him in the time he was in Estilleon, it was not to let an opportunity pass by – Jarlath needed to stop thinking and act. Ash's face flashed into his mind, his blood warming with more than the hot sun beating down.

He was pulled out of his dreaming by Fox, who shouted and pointed ahead.

The ground became boggy under foot, the mixture of sand and mud churning beneath the horse's hooves. Coming across the water was a boat with one man perched inside. Jarlath tensed, kicking his horse forward until he was level with the halfkin.

'What do you think?' he murmured.

Fox narrowed her eyes. 'He's not armed, that I can see.' She patted her leg, where Jarlath knew she had a blade stashed. Her expression was closed, her face perfectly composed as the boat approached them, the only sound the gentle rubbing of the waves against the shore; the boat stopped several metres out, the water a natural barrier between them and its occupant, a tall, slender man. He stood at the prow, his body balanced perfectly as the boat bobbed beneath him. His skin shone in the sunlight – muted blues and greens shot through with a coppery tone, his silvery hair shimmering.

Jarlath had never seen a Delta man before. Dressed in flowing clothes the colour of sand, the man's unusual yellow eyes surveyed them with interest, but his face remained still.

'State your business,' he said, folding his arms, his tone stern.

Jarlath swallowed. 'We're looking for someone; two someone's,' he corrected, wincing under Fox's glare. The halfkin swung herself from her horse, her feet sinking into the muddy sand.

'Where's Senan?' she demanded, marching to the edge of the water. 'You can't tell me he isn't here because I can smell him.'

The Delta man's eyes swept over them again, reading their faces, their postures, the exhaustion painted in heavy lines over their bodies. 'You've travelled a long way,' he stated. His voice was like the water – shifting and fluid, a soft lapping sound.

'From Estilleon,' Elan answered. 'We were slaves but no more.'

The Delta man's strange yellow eyes widened. Without him touching anything, the boat slowly moved forward, cutting a graceful path through the water until it bumped gently against the sand.

'You'll have to leave the horses,' he said simply. Fox nodded as Elan and Jarlath dismounted, Elan's face tight. He stroked the nose of his horse as Jarlath removed the saddle and bridle from his. Elan and Fox did the same, the boy whispering to the animals the whole time. Eventually, he turned from them and smiled, his face opening like a book.

'They won't go far,' he said with certainty. 'I can call them back when we need them.'

They loaded their tack and supplies into the boat, which was dangerously crowded with an additional three bodies. Once they were settled, the Delta man turned the boat around with a flick of his wrist and they were gliding across water so clear Jarlath could see the sandy bottom below, the silver fish darting underneath the boat, the rocks and shells littering the bottom of the river. Once past the shallows, the hue of the water changed to aquamarine, burnished gold rising to tickle the surface of the bubbling waves left in their wake.

Jarlath studied the Delta man as covertly as he could as they came nearer to the rectangular structures raised on piles, the water flowing smoothly beneath them. Not faery, but not human either, the people of the Delta usually kept to themselves. They traded occasionally with the passing merchants, but everything they needed they sourced from the sea or the eastern side of the forest of Eshlune.

Up ahead, the strange and otherworldly settlement of the Delta grew more visible. Beyond the main cluster of buildings were others, scattered throughout the face of the water, small boats moored at each one. They passed through swathes of water lilies and hibiscus, wort and water hyacinth, the air thick and syrupy. Fish, oysters, and crabs inhabited this murky, shifting world. Long-legged birds waded through the water, ducking slender heads to snatch small fish into long beaks, and ducks floated casually nearby, the passage of the boat through the water no hindrance to them.

Where the wetlands met the sea, a long wooden jetty rose from the water, leading like a sun-kissed road to the first cluster of buildings.

'I'm Mika,' the Delta man said, the boat pulling up alongside the jetty. 'I'm the leader of this community. You can stay as long as you need, provided you follow our rules. Firstly, no weapons,' he said, eyeing Fox, who scowled and handed over her blades, one at a time. 'Secondly, no violence of any kind. It is not tolerated. And thirdly, while you are here you must respect the sea and what she provides, or you will be sent to Nehalennia to join her ship of ghosts ferried to the next world.'

'Thank you,' Jarlath said.

'You need to be aware of the faeries that inhabit this place – the selkies and the undine are of no danger to you, but steer clear of waterhorses. Most want to play, but some are fixed on drowning you,' Mika said simply. Jarlath swallowed. He'd had enough of faeries to last a lifetime after their night near the Forest of Wights.

The boat rocked as they climbed out one by one, Elan, Jarlath and Mika carrying the tack. Fox darted impatiently along the jetty. At the end of that stretch of water-smoothed timber, she veered right. They followed, Jarlath's heart beginning to race.

Ash was here. He could feel it

Fox led them deep into the floating village, past the timber houses and onto a large square space surrounded by more buildings and wooden foot bridges leading away in all directions. She paused a moment, her face alive, the gentle sea breeze teasing her hair. Jarlath set the tack down gently, glancing at Elan, who was watching his sister intently. Fox started moving again, taking the northern road, her feet making no noise on the timber.

At the far end of that bridge were two huts, a boat moored close by, bobbing gently. The door of one hut eased open and Senan stepped into the bright sunshine as Fox stopped abruptly, then raced forward.

Jarlath watched in astonishment as the halfkin, the High Mage's personal assassin, threw her arms around the dishevelled Mage-Witch and buried her face in his neck, her shoulder's shaking. Senan stumbled back a step and then his face collapsed in undisguised relief; his hands stroked her hair, ran over her arms, her shoulders, her back, as if checking for injuries, checking she was really there. He pulled back to search her eyes, before taking her face between his hands and kissing her on the mouth as she laughed and cried and kissed him back fiercely.

From within the shadows of the second hut, a voice Jarlath knew in his dreams called his name.

CHAPTER FORTY-FOUR

Her eyes were different. Jarlath could see it immediately. Something had happened, something that had changed her, moved her further from the village girl he knew.

But he didn't care about that. He cared about her.

He'd found her, she was alive – they were both alive – and this moment was the one he'd been anticipating the whole time he was surrounded by ice and snow and darkness. He swallowed as she approached him, stepping around Senan and Fox, who were still clinging to one another. She didn't spare Elan a glance, her eyes, so filled with sadness and pain, locked on his.

The words he'd prepared fell away.

'I'm sorry,' he whispered, his throat thick. Her face twisted and he thought she'd turn and walk away from him, but she flung herself at him, punching him square in the nose. 'Gods, Ash!'

He clutched his face as she planted one hand on her hip. The other poked him hard in the chest.

'How could you?' she seethed. Her eyes flashed with sparks. 'Of all the things, Jarlath! Of all the shitty things anyone has ever done to me—'

He wrapped his arms around her, pulling her into his chest, feeling the warmth and slight weight of her against him. She fought him, the strength and power in that small body surprising, before she let out a ragged breath and flopped against him. Laughter cut through the air – Jarlath glanced up to see Yasper, blonde hair shining in the sun, leaning against the wall of one of the huts.

'Yas?'

His friend smiled. 'You and I will talk later,' he said, nodding at Ash.

With her head tucked under his chin and the sun bouncing off the water, Jarlath was content to stay exactly where he was, but as Yasper strode past them and clapped him on the back, she pulled away, lifting her eyes to search his face.

'Are you …'

'I'm fine, Ash. Totally fine.'

Ash listened as he recounted everything he'd seen and done since he rode from Sitra.

'And you?' He was afraid of the answer, her face becoming so grave his heart started thundering painfully. She took his hand and led him into the hut. Inside, two beds were tucked against the walls, a smattering of woven blankets the colour of rocks covering them. There was a small table and two chairs, a stove for cooking, and some utensils and bowls. The walls were bare, the ceiling low, two windows opening to the watery world outside. Sunlight slanted through them, catching on the smooth timber floor.

'I've been staying with Nerida, my friend from the Academy. Yasper and Senan are in the hut next door. Things in Tyllcarric are bad, Jarlath,' Ash said softly. Jarlath sank onto one of the beds, drawing her down next to him.

'Tell me.'

She did. By the time she was finished, he was ready to find his horse, or walk back to the city – swim if he must – and peel the skin from Gedeon's bones. He told her as much and she raised her eyebrows at his vicious tone.

He shrugged. 'Some quality time with the Chieftain of Estilleon …'

'Is Laeli okay?'

Jarlath burst out laughing. 'I'd be more worried about Thalion to be honest. She's scary ... they're both scary, which makes them perfect for one another, Ash. I pity whatever or whoever is stupid enough to try and get between them.'

This time, Ash smiled. She leant her head against his shoulder, and he slipped his arm around her, pulling her closer.

No more wasted opportunities. No more hiding what he felt. The idea of her had kept him going, even though he thought it would never be more than a glorious dream.

This was the moment they should have had all those years ago, on Beltane night, if he hadn't been so scared. He could see it in her eyes, the memory of that night, of what should have been.

What had occurred between them in Sitra before he left didn't count anymore. That moment had been one borne of desperation and jealousy, of fear and indecision. Jarlath slipped his finger beneath Ash's chin, trailing it along the length of her jaw. She kept her eyes open; although her eyelids fluttered, she continued to look at him, right until the moment he lowered his head and kissed her.

Everything disappeared. Nothing was more important than the feeling of her lips, of her arms as they snaked around his neck, or her body as she pressed herself as close to him as she could.

He should go out, find Senan and Yasper, talk, plan, but he didn't. Ash's arms were wrapped around his neck, her chest against his, the soft curve of her moulded to his body. They lay side by side on the narrow bed, her head resting on his arm, her fingers under his shirt, stroking his skin with a tenderness he wasn't sure he deserved. He wanted the wheel to stop turning for a moment, so he could catch his breath. He wanted it to be only them, the soft breaking of the water around them and the thumping, syncopated melody of her heart in his ears.

No one came searching for them and soon night drifted across the Delta. Jarlath slept, waking some hours later. Ash was propped on her elbow, watching him sleep.

'You know you talk in your sleep,' she said, her voice no more than a breath of air in the world.

'And what did I say?'

'Gibberish, mostly, but something about how sorry you were.'

He shifted his position until he was mirroring hers. 'I am sorry.'

Her eyes flashed in the darkness, moonlight slinking through the curtainless window to paint silver lines on her skin. 'Show me,' she said boldly.

'What?'

'Show me how sorry you are.'

His breath hitched as it sank in. 'Ash …'

'I should hate you for leaving me, but I don't. Not at all,' she whispered. 'I tried to, but I couldn't.' Before he could stop her, she sat up and pulled her shirt over her head. He tried not to stare as she sat there with her hands clasped in her lap, her breathing short and rapid with nerves. A slice of hair fell over her shoulder, creeping across her breast. Fingers trembling, he reached out and moved it away, brushing her flesh. She jumped; a blush spread across her chest, visible in the moonlight.

Her breathing deepened as he closed a palm over one breast, marvelling at how soft and sensitive her flesh was – she gasped, then laughed softly, that laugh turning into a moan as he swiped his thumb over her nipple.

This was what he had survived for. This moment.

'You're beautiful,' he said, throat thick, his body on fire. His hand burnt where it touched her, and he couldn't get enough air into his lungs.

'They're just breasts, Jarlath.'

He caught the wicked glint in her eye. 'Well, if they're 'just breasts' then maybe I should st—'

'I didn't say that.'

She grinned at him, a feral grin that had him grinning in return. There she was. The girl he knew, full of bravado and fire. He shifted so he could close his mouth over her nipple, and she gasped, turning to liquid in his hands. Her fingers trailed down his body until she reached the waistband of his pants.

It was clear to both of them how much he wanted this, but her?

'Ash …'

'It's now or maybe never, isn't it?' she said matter-of-factly. 'We don't know what is going to happen to us and I want you. Right at this moment, I want you, Jarlath, nothing more. You don't have to promise me anything. I don't want to be scared anymore.' She climbed off the bed. His heartbeat thundering and threatening to drown him, his blood roaring in his ears, Jarlath didn't look away from her as she wriggled out of the rest of her clothes and stood, completely naked, before him.

He shuffled to the edge of the bed, swinging his legs over, planting his feet firmly on the floor, trying desperately to anchor himself to something. Below them, the tide was coming in – Jarlath heard the rush and suck of water as it swirled and danced around the stilts of their hut. Keeping his breathing steady, he placed a hand on each of her hips, his fingers tracing the sharpness of her bones, splaying across her lower belly as she sucked in a breath. He ran his hands over her thighs, that supple muscle flexing beneath his fingers, up over the curve of her, his touch as light as air.

He glanced up at her; her eyes were dark, cheeks flushed, her breathing heavy. 'I love you, Ash Griffyn. I always have. For years. I've always known it was you.'

'Why didn't you say?'

'Because I was scared.'

'I didn't think you feared anything,' she whispered.

'I was terrified that you wouldn't want me in that way, that I wasn't enough, and I nearly wasn't, was I? I am so sorry for leaving you when you needed me.'

She leant down and kissed him gently, then harder, until she groaned and sank her teeth into his lip. 'Jarlath, for the love of everything … take your clothes off before I burn them from your body.'

'I thought you might want to tear them off with your teeth,' he murmured. Gods, he'd spent too much time with Thalion.

Her answering laugh was a warning, so he did what he was told.

She didn't try to keep her eyes on his face, exploring his skin with featherlight touches, the tips of her fingers tracing the lines of his body. Every nerve in his body shuddered and exploded into flame as she touched him, so painfully gently, so hesitant. She bit her lip as she explored his body, her inexperience such exquisite torture as she worked out where and how hard to press her fingers against different parts of him.

When she wrapped her hand around him, so gently, her skin so warm and smooth, his knees buckled. Pulling her to him, he kissed her hard; she dug her nails into the flesh of his arse and ground her hips against him, her breathing shallow, her eyes dark with want. Jarlath cupped her face and kissed her deeply. She pushed herself against him again. While he saw stars, she broke away from him and pushed him back onto the bed.

Ash swept her gaze over him and he could see the nerves stamped on her face. Jarlath reached for her hand and gently eased her down beside him. He didn't want to do anything to hurt her ever again. He lay her on her back and kissed his way down her body, pausing to give each breast the attention it deserved, then the sweeping curve of her waist and hips, over her belly, his hands cupping her arse to lift her off the bed.

She squirmed, her hips shifting, his name dropping from her lips.

He didn't realise she could make such sounds as he brushed his mouth against the silky, sensitive skin of her inner thighs. When he buried his face in her, she gasped and arched her back, her fingers delving into his hair, a stream of wordless noise rushing from her throat.

His head was spinning, his brain washed away with the tide. He kissed his way back up her body, over her chest, licked the sweat from her neck. Her thighs fell either side of his and as he reached between their bodies, he paused, looking into her eyes.

'It might hurt,' he warned.

'I know,' she whispered back, then kissed him, as he slowly slid inside her. Her sharp gasp quickly became a low moan as he moved again, and soon, nothing mattered anymore, save the woman in his arms and the way she melted beneath him.

CHAPTER FORTY-FIVE

Mahelivar closed his eyes and let his mind soar. The net was still there, air magic threaded through the space above and around him. He nudged it, searching for that weak spot he'd discovered several nights ago. This particular Witch binding his magic to this room was tiring; the others were stronger, and when they were working their spells, he had no hope of pushing through. He knew each one through the different feel of their magic – the colours and tones he could sense, the textures. Tonight's Witch, for example, her magic was a pale silver, like rain clouds, and soft, like cotton. The most powerful of Kiarda's guards had magic that glowed red, and that burnt when he brushed it. Air and latent fire magic. A dangerous combination, one he wasn't willing to test.

He slid his mind over the silver net, searching and probing, and there it was, a thin place in the woven, cottony threads of magic. He pushed on it gently, felt it buckle, and pulled his mind back. Mahelivar coiled his power tight, then released it in a burst of energy, his magic shaped and sharpened like a weapon.

It slammed through that net and, with a gasp, he was free. His power surged and soared, and he sent it beyond the walls of the palace, beyond the forest, locked on to the familiar shape and feel of his sister's thoughts. He could feel Kiarda's Air Witch chasing him, her scrambled magic trying desperately to pull him back. He paused, throwing a solid wall of trees behind him, branches twisting and curling together, holding the Witch out.

Kiarda had underestimated him, as he often underestimated himself.

He fled over the mountains, across land dressed in blinding snow, and was stretched to his limits when he found Laeli, her hair spread across the pillow like ribbons of the night sky. Her eyes were closed, but she was wide awake, smiling contentedly, Thalion's face buried against her neck. Mahelivar skimmed the outside of his sister's thoughts – a burst of fire and death, ecstasy and heartache, blood and snow, shadows, and within those shadows, a blinding light wrapped around her mind. Curious, he followed the thread of light.

And pulled back in shock.

Thalion's mind was wrapped around Laeli's as surely as his arms were wrapped around her body. Mahelivar had never seen anything like it and, as Thalion started speaking, he lingered to listen. Eavesdropping, Laeli would call it.

'You can't come with me to Amberwick,' Thalion told her.

'And why not?'

'Because I'm a fucking mess when you're around, Laeli.'

She laughed. 'You're a mess anyway.'

'Cruel and beautiful woman.'

'You love it,' Laeli breathed.

He murmured his agreement, then, 'I love you.'

Laeli's face became softer than Mahelivar had ever seen it. 'I love you, too.'

Mahelivar's stretched magic was spinning and he reeled it in, pulling himself back to his sister. Laeli had been so damaged and broken by Solen that Mahelivar didn't think she'd ever trust anyone with her heart again. He had to respect Thalion for that, he decided, because whatever else he was, he was obviously worthy of his sister's love. Mahelivar might have had his doubts about the human, but he couldn't ignore the power of that bond between them.

Feeling the strain of the distance and afraid he was about to see something he couldn't unsee, Mahelivar quickly nudged Laeli's mind, gently at first, and when she didn't respond, harder. She hissed and shoved Thalion off her, sitting up, the blankets bunched around her chest, the peacefulness vanished from her face like smoke caught on the breeze.

'What in the Gods, Laeli,' Thalion whined, reaching for her, but she shushed him and slapped his hands away. He shoved his head under the pillow, complaining loudly.

'Mahelivar?' Laeli whispered, her eyes flitting around the room, her cheeks flushed. 'If you've come to say hi, I don't appreciate your timing. Show yourself or go away.'

He grinned, then concentrated, allowing his ghostly form to materialise. Laeli smiled warmly when she saw him, her face crumpling in relief to see him unhurt and whole. He sat on the end of the bed, smoothing his fingers over the soft wool of the blankets.

'Hi,' he whispered, and she rolled her eyes.

He explained Kiarda's net; Laeli's eyes widened.

'Mahelivar, that's impressive.'

He heard the surprise and gave her the mental equivalent of a punch in the arm, making her smile.

'How's Father?'

'As best as he can be, considering we're locked in his rooms and under heavy guard.'

'I'll leave tomorrow,' she declared.

'No!' His mind bunted against hers forcefully; she glowered. 'Sorry,' he said gently. 'It's too dangerous at the moment. I know I said I wanted you here by the solstice, but you need to stay there, where you're safe, Laeli. Kiarda has the tools of the Cailleach, her hammer and staff,' he added quickly.

Laeli's face paled. 'What? How?'

Thalion pulled his head free. 'What's going on?' His frown was deep as Laeli explained what was happening in Sitra.

'But why would the Bone Mother give Kiarda her magic?'

'I don't know,' Laeli mumbled.

'Ask about my father,' Thalion said, sitting up and pushing his hair from his face. His eyes skittered around the room, coming to rest on nothing but air and darkness. Mahelivar took a deep breath and pushed his magic into Thalion's head, allowing the human to see him perched on the end of the bed like a cat. Thalion sucked in a breath in shock but managed to keep his composure.

'The Chieftain is here,' Mahelivar replied.

'Does he know what's happening in Estilleon?' Thalion asked, his blue eyes dark with worry.

Mahelivar shook his head. 'Not that I'm aware of, but I'm not privy to any important information, remember. Although, I'm sure if he knew, you'd know. He doesn't strike me as the sort of man to just let you steal his crown.' He paused, watching Thalion's face darken. 'How's the revolution progressing, anyway?'

Laeli quickly explained what they'd accomplished. 'Even Solen would have to admit Thalion's done a good job,' Laeli added wryly, giving Thalion a warm smile. That smile faded quickly. 'How is Solen?'

'He managed to get away, Magus as well, and quite a few of the Fire Witches and the guard. They're in the forest but so are Kiarda's soldiers. There's been a few deaths, but I don't know who,' Mahelivar explained quickly. Thalion told him about the treaty between Estilleon and Merawuld. That would explain the whispering Mahelivar had heard about the Queen's Army picking off Hadrian's and Kiarda's men but leaving the remnants of the fae guard alone.

'Can you escape?' Laeli asked, eyes glittering.

'Maybe, but I won't leave Father here alone and defenceless.'

Laeli nodded, then gasped, her eyes flying to Mahelivar's head. Alarmed, he reached up to touch his hair. 'I thought ...' She shook her head. 'What do we do, Mahelivar? About Kiarda? Now that she has the Cailleach's magic ...' Her voice was soft and small, but Mahelivar could feel the furious pace of her thoughts.

'I don't know. I don't know how to fight that.'

The connection was weakening. Mahelivar swallowed, holding tight to his sister, to Thalion as well, as the doors to his father's rooms flew open and people poured inside.

'What is it?' Laeli asked urgently, sensing his fear.

'Kiarda ...'

Something hit him in the head; his mind snapped back to Sitra so fast it hurt, and he vomited, his eyes streaming and his nose dripping with blood as he fell into momentary darkness. When he opened his eyes, he was lying face-first on the floor, the stone smeared with his blood and the remains of his dinner.

'What did you do?' Kiarda stood over him. Her voice was calm but her face was tight with fury. 'My Air Witch is dead, Mahelivar. What did you do?'

Shaking, Mahelivar sat up. His head ached. Three Witches and three armed guards stood behind his aunt and behind them, through the open door, a body lay on the ground. Mahelivar swallowed.

'Kiarda.' Rhodiri's face was pale, but he lifted himself from the bed, rolling over and sitting up. 'Stop this, please.'

She shook her head, pointing at Mahelivar. 'He killed one of my Witches. I assume he forced his way through the net, and I want to know how he did it.' She narrowed her eyes at her brother. 'Did you help him?'

Rhodiri laughed bitterly. Mahelivar scrambled to his feet, ignoring the man waving a spear in his direction. He crossed to his father's side, staring at his aunt and those with her in blatant defiance.

Kiarda gave him an interested look. 'You contacted your sister, didn't you?' She stepped closer; snow swirled from her skin. 'Where is she?'

Mahelivar remained silent. A mind probed around his own and he clamped down on it, shaping his magic into sharpened claws; one of the

Air Witch screamed and clutched at her head. Feeling sick, Mahelivar pushed harder – a ribbon of blood unfolded from the woman's nose. She stared at him, dark eyes wide, then collapsed into a faint.

Kiarda struck him across the face. Mahelivar's mind reached for hers, those claws scrabbling helplessly against the wall of ice shielding her mind. She laughed; two of the guards took hold of Mahelivar's arms and pinned them behind his back.

'You're not strong enough, sweet boy,' Kiarda purred, patting his cheek, then unleashed her mind on his. He fought it, fought desperately to keep her out, making his mind as jagged as the tops of the mountains, as smooth as the ice sheets in the north, letting the images in his head jumble until they would make no sense to anyone except him. He pulled up memories of his sister, from years ago, and threw them to the front of his thoughts, feeling Kiarda's magic grab hold of them and toss them aside quickly.

Then it was childhood memories.

Trees and more trees. His father, sitting on the throne. His mother. Her smile. The touch of her hand on his cheek. Sunshine and rich earth. Fire.

Kiarda withdrew her magic, her expression dark. No triumph littered her face and Mahelivar's heart thundered. He'd kept her out. She'd gotten nothing from him.

He could barely believe it.

'Increase the net,' she demanded of her Air Witches. They nodded, one bending to lift his unconscious companion from the floor and carry her from the room. The door was snapped closed and locked again.

Rhodiri glanced at his son in concern.

Mahelivar swallowed. 'She didn't get in.'

His father nodded in relief. 'You saw Laeli? Mahelivar, that's …'

'Foolish, I know but I needed to see she was alright and she's perfectly fine.'

'Thalion?' Rhodiri spoke directly to Mahelivar's mind.

'Alive.' Mahelivar shook his head. 'He's fallen in love with her.'

Rhodiri snickered, the first time he'd laughed since Kiarda stormed into their home. 'Well, he's braver than I thought he was.' He paused. 'Is she happy?'

'She loves him.'

'Well.' Rhodiri's face was soft. He settled back against the pillows, his eyes on the ceiling. 'Protect her, Mahelivar, with your dying breath if you must. Protect your sister like I should have protected mine – both of them.'

CHAPTER FORTY-SIX

Kiarda paced the throne room, the staff of the Cailleach clutched tight, its thrumming power giving her comfort, as it had most days since she began the march on her brother's kingdom, her warriors and Witches at her back.

It was clearer now than it had ever been that her nephew, that snivelling, weak-minded boy she'd last encountered one hundred and thirty years ago, was more powerful than she imagined. He'd done it alone, she knew that, broke through that net with his own power. Rhodiri was in no state to help him do anything, but still she'd asked, unwilling to admit that Mahelivar was possibly strong enough to challenge her right to rule. He kept her out of his mind, even with the magic the Cailleach's tools gave her. She also didn't want to admit how easy it had seemed for him – what she'd felt of his power had been more than she'd anticipated, and she wondered if he knew just how strong he was, how much he could accomplish.

Perhaps she had gone about this the wrong way, but it was too late for any change in plans now. He would never trust her.

The solstice was fast approaching. Kiarda chewed her lip, stalking the length of the room and back again, circling the throne but not sitting in it, her brows pulled tight. She had come so far, sacrificed so much.

There was no way she was going to give up, despite this new challenge her nephew had unknowingly presented her with. She would find a way to ensure the throne was hers and, once it was, she would round up those rogue Fire Witches and learn the secrets of the Rift.

The door opened and Kiarda scowled, expecting to see Hadrian come to whine at her again, but it was Birka, her face creased in concern as she took in Kiarda's pacing.

'What is it?' No one else would dare ask such a blunt question.

'Mahelivar,' Kiarda mumbled. She let Birka into her head; the only one she trusted enough to allow that sort of invasion of her thoughts. Her friend withdrew her magic and her frown deepened.

'You wish for him to die?'

'I don't know.'

'The Cailleach …'

Kiarda stopped pacing to sit on the throne. Snow fluttered from the ceiling and drifted around them, settling on the arms of the throne, and resting in Birka's dark hair. 'If I am the only one of the blood-line left alive …'

'Laeli?'

'Somewhere close if her brother was able to reach her. Double the search efforts. I want the whole forest turned inside out. Search the Forest of Wights as well. I want her found by the solstice,' Kiarda ordered.

'And if she has gone further? Into the human lands?'

'Find her!'

Birka nodded and left. Not long after the door had closed, the room grew icy, a wind rippling through the air so fiercely Kiarda had to shield her eyes with her hand. When the wind died, she prised her eyes open a crack.

The Cailleach was sitting on the empty throne beside her, the one that Kiarda knew was reserved for her missing niece.

'You have not forgotten our bargain I hope?' The Goddess said by way of greeting.

'I have not. How could I?'

'Your daughter is still over the mountains,' the Cailleach pointed out.

'She will be here, as promised,' Kiarda bit out. She could feel the staff in her hands, its power coalescing beneath her fingers, straining to reach the Goddess beside her.

The Cailleach knew this and cackled, showing her red-stained teeth and ghastly face as she lifted her veil. Her squat legs did not reach the floor, dangling childlike from the carved timber throne. She sat back, running her withered hands over the arms of the chair, a smile on her face.

'It has been many years since I sat here,' she commented.

Kiarda said nothing, turning away and willing the Goddess to be gone. She had hoped in vain that the Cailleach would have forgotten their deal, but she knew it had been a fool's hope. The Mother of All would never let her forget, and if Eira was not here by the solstice as promised, the Cailleach would never allow Kiarda to rule.

When she glanced at the throne beside her, the Crone had vanished, nothing but a pile of snow left in her wake. Kiarda glared at it, wanting to scream.

Eira was the one thing that she held truly dear, the one thing that mattered. Everything she did, everything she had done, had ultimately been for her daughter and now, the hag would take her away for the dark months of every year. It would not happen, Kiarda decided fiercely. She would find a way out of that bargain as surely as she would find a way to trick the Earth into choosing her to rule Eshlune.

She needed to speak to Eira. Needed to see with her own eyes that her daughter was safely tucked away in Estilleon. That she was surviving in the human land and with the man she had made no effort to conceal her disgust of. Eira had not wanted to stay behind when Kiarda and Hadrian had left for Whitemouth, before Kiarda travelled on alone to Veshlir to rally her troops. But Eira had done her duty to her mother, and her Queen.

Kiarda stroked the staff in her lap, its power humming through her, and went in search of Birka. She would need her friend's magic if she was going to contact her daughter.

Birka was in the courtyard, deep in conversation with one of Hadrian's Chiefs and one of Kiarda's men, the leader of her armed forces, second only to Birka. They bowed when they saw Kiarda crossing the snow-covered lawns towards them.

'The forests between here and Veshlir will be searched again, my Queen,' her man, Ilyian, said, his pale face composed. 'The humans will search both sides of the Rift and the base of the Peaks for her.'

'The humans will need a Witch with them,' Kiarda announced. 'My niece is not likely to come along quietly.'

'You think my men can't handle a little girl?' The Chief demanded. Brenna, that was his name, Kiarda recalled. A brute of a man, with a broad chest and a swaggering arrogance that she could almost taste in the air around him. He was old, too old to be here, she reasoned, and his age made him think he knew better, made him think he understood his enemy. In the human world, perhaps that age and experience counted for something, but not in her world.

'It is no child you hunt, but Rhodiri's daughter. She is a powerful Witch who has mastered three elements but favours one – fire. She is, by all accounts, dangerous. A trained warrior. But if it means I can relieve myself from seeing your face again, lead the hunt yourself, Brenna of Whitemouth, and let's see if you return to tell me I'm right,' Kiarda said smoothly.

Birka's lips curled in amusement as the Chief repressed a snarl. Kiarda didn't care. They'd all be dead soon, anyway. 'Take a Witch with you,' was all she said, before turning away, the human dismissed. As he stalked off into the snow, Kiarda could hear him grumbling under his horrid breath. Ilyian left to gather the Witches, leaving Kiarda and Birka to survey the snowy courtyard.

'You truly believe she is out there?' Birka asked.

Kiarda closed her eyes, letting her mind fly, beyond the palace grounds, beyond the city, into a forest that dripped with white. She pushed through trees, their trunks slick with snow, moving towards the Rift, to that pit of fire, to the last place Faleria had been. Sighing, she opened her eyes and pulled her mind back. 'She's out there.'

Birka only nodded and did not question Kiarda's certainty.

'I am sorry I snapped before,' Kiarda told her friend, voice low. Birka dipped her head in acknowledgement; no more words or explanation were needed beyond that. 'These humans are giving me a headache even the Mother could not dissolve. I have need of your magic. I need to reach my daughter.'

'Of course. We will scry for her in the flames.'

Kiarda followed Birka back inside, to the Hall where they had been holding war council. There was no sign of the Estilleon Chieftain and Kiarda was glad. She didn't need Hadrian hovering over her shoulder asking useless questions about a boy Kiarda cared nothing for.

Birka cleared a space on the table, then lifted one of the metal braziers from the marble columns that lined the walls. Kiarda waited while Birka slipped outside and, soon, a young man brought a bundle of sticks and twigs collected from the forest. They were coated in snow, but that wouldn't matter. Kiarda's fire magic would be enough to light the flame. Birka's air magic would open the scrying portal and reach across the mountains. Even though Kiarda's magic was strong, she could not hold open the portal and light the flame at the same time.

When she was ready, Kiarda called on her fire magic. It was weak, nowhere near as strong as her water or air magic. She poured her energy into the haphazard collection of sticks. For a moment, she didn't think it had worked, but smoke curled from the wood and the flame was brought to life. Once it was dancing high, Birka's magic flooded the room.

Kiarda focused her energy on the flame, feeling it suck her deep inside its fiery glow. She closed her eyes and when she opened them, it was to see the Great Hall at Wilderun, the room shrouded in darkness. She cast her eyes about, finding Hadrian's son sitting at the table, his posture relaxed. He was reading. A single candle burnt on the table, casting him in a halo of golden light.

'Hello, son-in-law.'

Thalion dropped the book and jumped up, his face paler than usual, like he'd seen a ghost. Kiarda laughed in delight. He approached the fire hesitantly, one hand on his hip, where his sword would normally be resting. His brow folded into a frown, and he swallowed, dropping to one knee to stare into the flames.

'Kiarda?'

'Where is my daughter?' she demanded.

'She's … I'll get her.'

'You do that. And hurry.'

Thalion left the room, returning a few minutes later with Eira, who knelt by the hearth.

'My daughter,' Kiarda said with a smile. Eira's features were distorted through the flame, but she returned her mother's smile. 'Before I speak of Sitra, Hadrian is keen to know how things are there, and you know how we must keep our allies happy.' She could sense the boy in the background, listening although he pretended not to be. He had returned to the table and his book but was not reading it. It didn't matter.

'Things are as the Chieftain ordered them to be,' Eira said simply. 'The men have been sent to the border and, from all reports, are prepared for battle. You can let the Chieftain know his army will be ready to move into Merawuld within the week.'

'Good,' Kiarda said. 'And are you … happy?'

Eira wrinkled her nose. 'As happy as I can be, considering. Although, I'm sick of this place, mother.' She lowered her voice, bending closer to the flame. 'When can I join you?'

'I will need you here by the solstice,' Kiarda answered, her heart pinching enough to be painful, but she kept her expression composed, her face smooth of her emotion. 'When the Cailleach comes to give me the crown, I want you here to witness it.'

'Of course,' Eira said, eyes shining. 'I wouldn't miss it.'

Kiarda thought she detected a hint of something sharp in her daughter's tone, but maybe it was the distance and the flame. Scrying like this was not something she or Eira were used to. They had never been apart for more than a few nights before, her daughter's presence always a comfort in the great castle in Vellir. Birka's face was creased in concentration. As powerful as she was, maintaining contact like this was obviously draining her.

'How long will it take you to be ready to leave?'

'The weather is horrendous but as soon as it clears, I will leave.'

'And your husband? Will he be coming with you?' Kiarda glanced over her daughter's shoulder to where Thalion still sat. His head lifted at her words.

Eira made a face. 'Does he have to?'

Kiarda laughed. 'No, my darling. That is up to you. I am sure his father would rather he stay there and do his job.'

'The King and his children?' Eira asked.

'My brother is not long for this world. Laeli … is still missing, and Mahelivar …'

Eira was watching her carefully.

'He is to die.'

'When?'

'On the solstice.' Kiarda felt Birka's surprise; and she was surprised herself. She hadn't made her decision until this moment. Seeing her daughter's face, remembering how close she was to victory, and how easily it could still be snatched from her … with Mahelivar gone, the only thing standing in her way was a rogue princess who couldn't hide forever.

Eira's face wavered; the connection was fading.

'I will see you on the solstice,' Kiarda promised before the flame faded and Eira was gone.

'I'm sorry,' Birka panted, her face drenched in sweat. 'I could not hold it any longer.'

Kiarda sat back; her fire had gone out, the wood blackened and still smoking. 'Something feels wrong,' she muttered.

'How so?' Birka wiped her face on her sleeve.

'It was Eira, but it didn't feel like Eira.'

'She is a long way away,' Birka said softly, touching Kiarda's arm reassuringly. 'And things are sometimes distorted during scrying, especially over such distance. Eira is a married woman now, remember Kiarda. As much as she didn't want this marriage, perhaps she has come to care for him, like the Chieftain says? Perhaps she has changed.'

'Perhaps,' Kiarda mumbled.

Birka was quiet. 'He is to die then?'

'Yes. Make the arrangements.'

'The Cailleach—'

'Won't be able to stop me,' Kiarda growled. 'By the time she gets here, it will be too late.'

CHAPTER FORTY-SEVEN

The Cailleach came riding right up to the castle steps while Laeli watched from the window, the snow swirling on the shifting wind. The Goddess paused, gazing up to catch Laeli's eye as she slipped from the grey wolf's back and laid a bundle on the bottom step. With a deep hunger clawing at her belly, Laeli raced out into the wild weather, but the Goddess was gone, nothing more than a flurry of snow on the chilled breeze. Left behind, wrapped in a soft white shawl, was a wolf cub, black as the depths of night, with eyes as blue as the summer sky. Laeli scooped it into her arms and held it to her breast.

Silvery light cut through the window. It was early morning, the sky dressed in clouds. Thalion's arm was a warm weight around Laeli's middle, his steady breath coating her neck. She closed her eyes again, smiling lazily as she pressed herself closer to him. He didn't stir – well and truly asleep, then.

Around them, the castle was slowly coming to life – in the kitchen, Laeli could hear Healy and her staff of halfkin, including the girl, Faren, stoking the cooking fires and beginning the breakfast preparations. Down the hall, Jarlath's bed lay empty. She wondered where he was now, where Fox and Elan were. If they had found Ash, and Senan. If they were indeed marching off to war.

As she should be. She grasped her husband's hand tightly.

Beneath them, the guards changed shifts, Eric's heavy footfall echoing down the hall and up the stairs as he sought his bed.

The sounds of the morning came to Laeli like pieces of a fractured mirror, one that she slowly and carefully put together, as if committing them to the deepest part of her memory. She could even hear the snores and snorts of Thalion's mongrel dogs, lazing before the fire in the Great Hall. Supposedly, they were hunting dogs. She'd never seen them hunt anything other than warmth and their master's generous hands.

The last snatches of the dream still lingered as Laeli opened her eyes again. It was the same dream as the night before, and the night before that. She'd ignored it. After their last encounter, she was hoping to avoid whatever message the Goddess was sending her, but she couldn't ignore it any longer. Untangling herself from Thalion, she slid the blankets back and climbed from the bed, relieved when he didn't wake. Naked, she padded to the window as weak sunlight crept over the snow, the night giving way to light.

On the horizon, something moved. Laeli opened her fae senses, her sight racing across the endless white plain to see an old woman with frost-bitten hair riding a grey wolf, its massive paws churning the snow as they glided across the landscape. They stopped, snow rising into the air as those great paws anchored themselves to the ground. The woman's head turned, her veil covering her face.

Laeli felt the ancient power that sang beneath the earth and whistled across the snow moving through her body. The Cailleach nodded once in acknowledgement, in knowing, then she and the wolf moved off.

Slivers of chilled air reached through the window to lick at Laeli's flesh. Shivering, she snatched a blanket from the bed to wrap around her shoulders, where she worked the length of her hair into a braid. Thalion was snoring softly. Laeli crawled back onto the bed, cocooned in the blanket. Her hands ached to touch him but touching him would wake him and, at that moment, all she wanted was to watch him sleep.

She tipped her head to one side, studying him, as she had done countless times before. His face was pushed against the pillow, mouth partly open. The bedding had slipped down, resting above his hips, exposing the sweeping muscle of his back, the battle scars long faded to silvery-pink against the paleness of his skin. His hair was tussled, so dark compared to the rest of his body, his eyelashes midnight crescents brushing his cheek.

He was more than simply familiar to her now – he was everything, from her first breath in the morning to the last thought in her head at night. She never imagined she could love somebody so much, so deeply that her heart beat in time with his and every breath was a breath shared. She was in danger of losing herself completely but each day the wheel inched closer to the solstice and each day was a further reminder that she needed to be elsewhere, regardless of what her brother said.

Regardless of the man whose bed – whose life – she was sharing, for she had bound herself to her family, to her home and her people, long before Thalion had even existed.

Yet, the idea of leaving him, of leaving this place that had become her home as well, was enough to tear her guts out. She smiled sadly, reaching out to trail the tip of her finger down the side of her husband's face, feeling the comforting heat of his skin, the hard line of his cheekbone, and the short, sharp shadow of hair that grew through his flesh with a magic of its own. She traced the curve of his shoulder, down his arm over the sculpted muscle and achingly supple skin.

He was awake and was enjoying her petting him.

'You need to shave,' she told him bossily.

She forgot how quickly Thalion could move; he snatched her hand from his face and had her pinned on her back before she could blink. His eyes were brilliant and shining in the morning light, so blue they may have been carved from pieces of the sky.

'I might grow a beard,' he announced, voice soft from sleep. 'What do you think?'

'I think not.' Laeli burst into laughter as he rubbed his stubbly face against her neck, then sobered quickly, her chest tight. She would miss moments like this – carefree moments where they weren't worrying about rebellions or wars or politics, where the world outside their room faded to nothing. She swallowed and Thalion pulled back, sensing the shift in her mood. His eyes roamed her face, his fingers brushing her cheek, so tender she wanted to cry and forget everything except how she felt when he touched her.

'I saw her, the Cailleach; the Bone Mother,' Laeli said quietly, her eyes drawn towards the window, to that spot on the snow where the Goddess had appeared to her. 'She's been in my dreams every night.'

Giving Thalion a gentle shove, she climbed from the bed again, the stones chilly under her feet, the blanket trailing her like a furry cape as she paced. 'The solstice is in a week. The wheel is turning. They're running out of time.'

Thalion sat up and reached a hand towards her, but Laeli shook her head, continuing to pace. There were sparks on her skin and with her next breath the water in the basin froze over, the ice cracking and melding to itself. Her earth magic tingled, begging to be let out.

'Mahelivar needs me, and as Kiarda has requested her daughter's presence by the solstice, I'll be able to walk right in there.'

'And then? When she realises you're not Eira? What will you do then, Laeli? How will you fight the magic of a Goddess?'

Laeli's heart skipped a beat. 'I don't know.' Snow billowed through the window, swirling around her. Thalion was frowning. She swallowed the taste of dread, going to sit by him, to take his large hands in her smaller ones as the snow swirled around them. 'I can't do anything for my father, but my brother … I won't let her kill him.'

Thalion's eyes darkened; a rolling storm rushing over the sky. 'I'm coming with you.'

'No,' she said firmly. He opened his mouth, but she cut across him. 'What about Estilleon? What about everything you've worked for? You can't throw that aside now. You need to stay here.'

'It means nothing if you're not here.'

She put her head in her hands, biting her lip. 'Thalion ... please.'

'You're my wife. I'm not letting you go alone,' he said fiercely.

Laeli shook her head, ripping her hands away from her face. She took a deep breath and turned away as she spoke the next words, the words that would break her, break him, but she needed him to stay alive. This time, she couldn't promise him that he wouldn't die.

'It wasn't real. This whole thing ... you and me. I've done what I said I'd do. I've kept you alive and helped you hold the country and end a war, and now, I'm going home.' She risked a glance at his face, her heart hurting, and forced her voice to be steady. 'None of it was real, Thalion.'

'I don't believe you.'

Of all the stubborn men in the world, she'd found the most stubborn of all.

'You can believe whatever you like, but it's the truth.'

'You're a dreadful liar.' He took her gently by the shoulders and turned her around to face him, his expression untroubled. 'Fine. Look me in the eyes and tell me you don't love me, tell me you feel nothing for me at all, and I'll let you go. I'll do as you ask. I won't follow you. You have my word, Laeli.'

She took a deep breath and held it, letting it out slowly, trying desperately to be as calm and composed as he was, to pull her emotions together, to be as water flowing over rocks. She lifted her head and stared into his eyes. He stared back.

In her mind, she recalled every time he had ever looked at her, a kaleidoscope of moments, from the first time in the forest in the singing rain, to when he was standing before her naked body with the fireflies dancing around them, to their wedding, where she thought she would burst with sheer happiness, and every moment since then. Every shared slice of time and every press of his lips on hers, every touch of his hand and every bit of the strength he had given her barrelled its way inside her head almost painfully.

The lie sat on her tongue, heavy and bitter, refusing to come to life again.

Laeli cursed explosively, returning to the window, pulling the blanket tight around her body. She heard Thalion's feet padding across the stones, his stride casual, calm, and could feel his confidence, his complete assurance in *them* as he slipped his arms around her. His chest pressed into her back, his body warm and strong; her pillar, her landmark, there for her to navigate by.

'You love me,' he said smugly, kissing the side of her head.

'You're insufferable,' she whispered. 'And human.'

'You're not unbreakable, either.'

'I know, but …'

Thalion put his mouth near her ear, his breath tickling her skin. 'We'll face it. Together.'

Laeli sighed and nodded. His hands came to rest below her belly button, his fingers stroking her through the blanket, his lips brushing the nape of her neck.

Warmth flowed through her, settling beneath his hands, a tingling sensation in her belly.

The wolf cub, dark furred, like her hair.

Like Thalion's. And the eyes …

How could she have missed it? She'd bled … hadn't she? She swallowed, mouth dry, her heart pounding so fiercely, so loudly, she thought it would burst from her chest. Laeli covered Thalion's hands with her own as the truth roared to life like it had a mind of its own.

And it did, a tiny mind, resting peacefully in the dark, watery cavern of her body.

Thalion was bathing while Laeli sat by the fire, a lazy smile on her face. She couldn't stop touching her belly, wondering if the life in there knew she loved it already. She would do anything to protect it. She would kill and fight until she had nothing left. She glanced across the room to the screen that shielded the bathing tub, her hand still stroking her belly.

What a father he'd make, but she didn't have the courage to tell him, not yet. Not until this was over, and they could breathe freely.

Now that she was returning to Sitra – that *they* were returning – it left her drained. The mental energy needed to plan for this, to try and cover every tiny thing that could go wrong – no matter how hard she thought, how hard Thalion thought and schemed, that warriors' intellect seeing things that she didn't, it all ended the same way – in death.

Hers, maybe.

She stroked her stomach again, guilt draping itself over her like a cloak.

Laeli prayed to the Mother they'd be there in time. If Mahelivar was already dead … she'd know, she reasoned. She'd know it, as surely as she'd know if her father no longer drew breath. She could feel both of them, their hearts beating alongside hers.

They were alive. For now.

Frode had arrived earlier that day, and he and Thalion had been locked away for most of it. Laeli had lingered outside the door, eavesdropping, her stomach churning as she listened to her husband calmly make contingency plans in the event of his death.

It wasn't right.

If he died, for her, Laeli would carry that on her shoulders for the rest of her long life; but nothing she said would convince him to stay behind. Part of her was glad he would be beside her, but the other part was terrified for him, for the both of them, and for the furiously beating heart in her belly.

Exhaustion had been nipping at her heels for what felt like years – in reality, it had been a scant few months, but so much she could never have prepared for had happened in that time. What she truly wanted was to be able to relax and simply live. To get through this next hit, the next knock to her life, and be able to let her guard down completely. To love and be loved in return, nothing more arduous than that. She drew lazy little circles on her belly.

Thalion called out to her, so she stood and stretched, yawning as she poked her head around, finding him lying back for all the world like nothing out of the ordinary was about to happen, his expression relaxed and calm.

'Is the water cold?'

He shook his head. 'Come here.'

'What?' she moved closer to the tub. He held out a dripping hand; she took it, weaving her fingers through his and he tugged her closer.

'You should get in here with me.'

'Thalion, that tub isn't big enough for the both of us.'

He gave her a cheeky smile. 'You could always sit in my lap.'

Laeli rolled her eyes, and his expression became serious.

'I want to hold you,' he whispered, and she nodded, her throat thick. He didn't take his eyes off her as she shed her clothes and climbed into the tub, resting against him, back to chest, her head tucked under his chin, their legs tangled together. The water rose dangerously near the top of the tub. Her hair floated around them as his hand closed over her tender breast.

'I thought you said you wanted to hold me?'

'I didn't say which parts of you,' he replied innocently, pinching her sensitive nipple between his thumb and forefinger, a bolt of heat shooting between her legs. His other hand travelled down her body, brushing against her belly, lower, and she sucked in a breath.

'Thalion …'

'You're beautiful,' he whispered, his voice low, rough. 'So beautiful, Laeli. I can't believe you're here, sometimes.' He pressed against the sensitive bundle of nerves between her legs; her thighs shifted apart, and her breathing quickened. 'I can't believe you love me.'

She wanted him to keep touching her but he folded his arms around her instead, his head resting against hers. Laeli's heart was thundering, her muscles tight, her breathing short and sharp. Heat coiled through every part of her and the words were right there.

But if she told him, he'd find some way to get himself killed trying to protect her.

Slowly, she pulled away, turning to face him, sliding her legs either side of his torso; his fingers gripped her knees and he tugged her closer, until she was sitting in his lap with her legs wrapped around him. His smile was wistful, almost sad.

'I love you,' he told her, resting his forehead against hers; her arms wound around his neck. 'Whatever happens, I love you.'

'Do you want children?' Laeli blurted, her voice a mere whisper in the candle kissed dark. Thalion's eyebrows rose; nerves skittered along her spine.

'I don't know.'

She watched his face carefully, watched the emotion flash through his eyes. 'But you must have thought about it?'

'I have, yes, but,' he paused, sighing lightly. 'I've always been terrified I'd be a dreadful father, like mine is. It's why I've never married before now. No wife meant no children.'

'You wouldn't be a dreadful father, Thalion. Do you have any children?'

'If you're asking has a woman ever shown up at the castle door with a baby on her hip claiming it's mine, then no, I don't have any children anywhere that I know of,' he answered, his eyes tearing a hole through her. 'Do you want children, Laeli?'

'I never did, not even with …'

'Solen,' Thalion finished. He traced little circles on her knee, his touch excruciatingly gentle. 'What happened?'

Laeli sifted through her mind for the right words, while he waited patiently, trusting her to tell him as much or as little as she would. 'When you've got all the time in the world to spend with somebody, you tend to take it for granted. It wasn't all his fault. We both said and did the wrong thing, many times. In the end, Solen's ambition got in the way of who he was. In the end, I accused him of using me to get what he wanted – his position, his favour with my father – and I left him. I should forgive him but I can't. It's my revenge for his cruelty, for his disregard for me, and for never taking me seriously. If Solen had his way, I'd have never left the palace and have been nothing more than a trophy,' Laeli said softly. 'You're the first man I've loved since him. I haven't let anybody this close to me in forty years, Thalion.' She touched his cheek. 'But I would have waited another forty years. For you.'

He was quiet for a moment; candlelight caught on the surface of the bath water and reflected off the lines of his face, painting his skin golden and warm. 'How long were you and he …?'

'Twenty years.'

'Twenty *years*?'

'I'd give you that ten times over if I could,' she whispered fiercely. She watched Thalion's throat move as he swallowed; his chest paused as his breath hitched and he was very quiet and still. She could hear his heart, the steady rhythm that was burnt onto the inside of her.

'You didn't answer my question,' he said eventually. 'Do you want children?'

She took his face between her hands. 'When this is all over, I will gladly have your children, Thalion. As many as you want.'

He kissed her, and she knew she would never tire of being close to him, of loving him, her blood singing his name, no matter how much time they had left together.

CHAPTER FORTY-EIGHT

'She's late.'

'She'll be here.' The Cailleach patted the wolf at her side. The Allfather grumbled under his breath. They waited, the wind pulling at their hair and clothes. Not long until the solstice and the turning of the wheel. Spring would come again, regardless of what did or did not happen here.

From the top of the mountain, they could see all, could peer through the veil and watch the pieces fall and shift. Estilleon, Eshlune and Merawuld – what a lovely game board. The Cailleach had never spread herself over so much at once and the Morrigan, well, the Goddess of Fate was in her element. Sometimes the Cailleach thought the feathered woman tossed her cards around wherever and whenever she liked but no, the Morrigan had plans, as they all had plans.

A black bird came screeching across the world, landing on a boulder and transforming into a woman with feathers caught in her hair. 'I can hear your moaning from Eshlune, Allfather,' she said lightly, examining fingernails stained red with blood.

The Allfather waved his spear at her. 'Your feathers would make a nice cloak, Witch.'

The Morrigan laughed. 'What's the matter, old man? You've still got pieces on the board.'

'You leave him alone,' the Allfather warned. 'He's mine.'

'Is he?' The Morrigan asked slyly. 'I think he belongs to another.'

The Cailleach smiled. 'Yes, and you didn't have anything to do with that, did you?'

'I merely pulled some strings, that's all. What people do with what they are given is up to them. If the young Chieftain and the Princess saw fit to tie themselves together, what am I to do about it? Now, they're tied together for life, aren't they?' The Morrigan turned her face west to where the castle rose from the earth like a great monolith. They all remembered when that castle was built, watching from this very place all those hundreds of years ago.

The Allfather turned to the Cailleach. 'What of your Witch of creation and destruction? Your fire caster?'

'She continues on her path,' the Cailleach said simply, lifting a withered claw to point at the Morrigan. 'This one has seen to throw the girl favourable cards at least.'

The Morrigan smiled. 'As if my cards can stand against yours, Mother. You have them all dancing to your tune, regardless of what the Father and I wish to see.'

The Cailleach cackled. It was true, but it didn't hurt to let them think they had some control over this round of the game.

'But,' the Morrigan continued, 'nothing is set in stone.' From within her cloak, she withdrew a bundle of cards, tossing them into the air, where they spun slow enough for them all the see the faces branded on each rectangular piece: the High Mage and the Spirit Rake, the young Chieftain and the old, the fae Princess and the Prince, the Queen of the Ice, the fire caster, the soldier and the assassin, the Mage-Witch and the convict.

An interesting assortment indeed.

The Goddess of Fate clapped her hands and the cards vanished.

'So,' the Cailleach said softly. 'Where to now?'

'Merawuld for me,' the Morrigan said, rising and stretching her sinuous body luxuriously. Feathers grew on her arms, but she waited for the others to declare themselves.

'Allfather?' The Cailleach inclined her head.

The God of War smiled. 'I think it's time I visited Eshlune.'

The Cailleach nodded.

'And you, Mother?'

'I think I shall stay here,' the Cailleach said simply. 'So I can keep an eye on all things.'

'So you can interfere, you mean,' the Allfather snarled. She waved him away as the Morrigan took flight, the black bird following the course of the river before veering to the southeast, towards the city of men. The Cailleach shuffled to a boulder. This would make a nice resting place. She eased her body down, the grey wolf curling at her feet.

With a bow and a wink from his one eye, the Allfather vanished, off to play amongst the trees of Eshlune.

The Cailleach stretched. Her empty hands twitched. It didn't matter. She would soon fill them again.

The solstice was close.

CHAPTER FORTY-NINE

Snow drifted lightly around them like a fine mist; the trees at the northern end of the Rift held firm to their leaves and the grass was thick under the horse's hooves, but that awful stench of sulphur still saturated the air. Weak sunlight filtered through the trees, the dappled light making for perfect camouflage. Laeli pulled her horse up abruptly, the animal snorting in protest. Thalion's muscles tightened as she held up her hand. His fingers dropped to caress the hilt of his sword as a body uncurled from the shadows, arrow notched and ready.

Thalion groaned.

'We've been here before, human.' The captain of the fae guard was looking worse for wear; a bruise coloured his cheekbone and a claw-like scratch ran the length of his neck. 'Get off the horse.'

'Don't be ridiculous, Solen,' Laeli snapped.

His eyes narrowed, then widened as she threw off the glamour. 'By the Mother, Laeli,' he hissed, lowering the weapon and darting towards them. He touched her knee, gazing up at her in undisclosed relief and, Thalion realised with a twist of his gut, love. He chuckled; Solen scowled. 'Still got your pet, I see,' he muttered.

'Where's Magus?' Laeli asked sharply.

'Not far. There's a group of us.'

'How many?' Thalion asked.

'Forty. Fae guard and Fire Witches. We've done what we can but we're sorely outnumbered. Avivers and Levalun are lost to us.' Solen shook his head.

The fae soldier still had his hand on Laeli's knee. Thalion wondered how angry she'd be with him if he cut Solen's hand off. He wanted to give the captain of the fae guard the thrashing of his very long life. He suspected Solen knew what he'd lost, but he could still be annoyed with him.

Solen was frowning. 'What are you planning? You can't just ride in there.'

'That's exactly what we're going to do,' Thalion declared.

Laeli threw him a terse look then addressed Solen. 'I want you to move closer to Sitra. We're going to need you, Solen, you and Magus and everyone who can still fight. Thalion has men inside the walls as well.'

Solen eyed Thalion doubtfully, but he nodded. 'What about the fire caster?'

Laeli shook her head. They had no idea where she was at this moment, blind to everything that had been happening outside of Estilleon and the small bits they knew from Mahelivar's night-time visit, and Hadrian and Kiarda's letters.

'Alright,' Solen agreed in a quiet voice. 'But, Laeli, we have no idea what's going on inside Sitra. There's a net of magic wrapped around the city. I can't get through – my magic is all but useless.'

Laeli explained what Mahelivar had managed to do. Thalion listened closely, trying to understand, but he couldn't hold the threads of this magical world together – it was as if Laeli and Solen were speaking another language as they discussed whether they'd be able to maintain contact once Laeli had slipped under this net. Thalion swallowed; it was another reminder of how different his wife was to him, how extraordinary her life was. He'd tried not to let it bother him, but the closer they drew to her home, the more obvious it was.

'What about your earth magic?' she asked Solen.

The captain's face folded into a frown as he held out his hand, palm down, towards the ground. A tiny shoot of green pushed through the snow, then vanished again as he sighed.

Laeli's expression was hard. 'If we can free Mahelivar—'

'You're as strong as your brother, you know,' Solen cut in. He held her eyes for a long moment until Laeli nodded, just once, as if this was an old argument.

'But I can't do it alone,' she said softly. 'We get him out and we'll have a chance against Kiarda. The solstice is upon us.'

Thalion knew what she left unsaid – come that final turn of the wheel, at the end of her father's life, either Laeli or her brother would be blessed with an extraordinary power.

'The Rift?' Laeli asked Solen.

'Delphine says the Lasair aren't the same as they were before. She says it's as if they're waiting for something. None of them have gotten out, that we're aware of. Maybe they're weak? Maybe they need to feed? I know they *are* fire, but doesn't all fire need a fuel source? Kiarda has allowed the Fire Witches to continue their job, a bargain made with the King, I believe. That bargain did not extend to the guard though – we've been fighting both Kiarda and Hadrian's soldiers on both sides of the Rift. The Merawuld army hasn't come near us, but they have engaged the enemy,' Solen added in disbelief.

Laeli indicated Thalion. 'You can thank him for that.'

Solen didn't, keeping his attention on Laeli. 'Laeli ...'

Thalion's horse shifted beneath him as an icy breeze skittered across the landscape. The trees were nearly all bare, a few stubborn leaves clinging tight to life. 'How many guards around the city?' he asked impatiently. He had no idea about magic, but he could work out the most effective way to end someone's life.

Solen ran a hand over his messy hair. 'About fifty, spread out around the perimeter. Your father's men mainly. Kiarda is keeping her own warriors inside the walls, when they're not out here hunting us, that is.'

Thalion nodded. 'Give me four hours. I need to get my allies out of there, then kill those remaining.'

'Are you sure?' Laeli asked. 'They're your people, Thalion.'

'They're my father's people,' he answered, but his stomach dropped.

'How will I know?' Solen asked him.

'I'll tell them not to engage.' Thalion hoped he could find Ulfe or Niall in time. He gave Solen a tight look. 'Can I trust you on this?'

'You can.'

They left Solen behind; when Thalion glanced back, the man had melted into the shadows. Laeli glamoured herself again and for the next hour silence was their only companion. The great forest of Eshlune was eerie in its stillness, life suspended and held within the winter landscape – no birds sang from the magnificent trees, no small feet thumped through the undergrowth. The only sounds were the steady beat of the horses' hooves as the animals cut a path through layers of snow.

Thalion glanced at Laeli, wondering what she was thinking, what she was feeling, to see her home so changed. Her face was utterly focused on what they were going to do – fight the power of a Goddess.

Most probably die trying.

He drew his horse closer to hers, so that he could reach out a hand and close his fingers around the curve of her knee. The warmth of her was a blazing fire in the frosty air. 'Are you alright?'

She nodded, then nudged her horse forward, drawing ahead of him. He let her go, let her have this moment in the hollow, white-clad silence alone.

Visible through the trees was the great city of Sitra. Thalion tensed as Laeli did, before they pushed on. There would be no more talk between them now. He noted the stiffness in her spine; her fists clenched and unclenched, and he knew she was thinking of her swords, bundled carefully in the pack tied to his saddle.

As they drew closer to the city, the gates in view, the statues of the Mother of All coated in snow, something moved in the corner of Thalion's eye, something ancient and of the landscape itself. He felt something stir in the pit of his stomach, and something shifted deep in his blood, a primal surge that swept through him, its power a potent, living thing.

A man in a fur cloak walked beneath the trees, a spear held tight in one hand.

Thalion pulled his horse up hard, heart hammering.

Here? Surely not.

Sensing something wasn't right, Laeli twisted sharply in the saddle, her unasked question burning in her eyes.

Thalion blinked, scanning the forest. There was nothing but trees dripping with white surrounding them; on the breeze, he heard a chuckle and his insides clenched. 'I thought … it doesn't matter. Let's go.'

They guided the horses through the ice-encrusted forest, straight up to the gates of Sitra, snow falling thickly around them, the path behind them lost in the blinding whiteness. The men on watch, two fae with shining blonde hair, carrying pike staffs and short swords, let them through, bowing to Laeli as they passed. She inclined her head but didn't stop, nudging her horse in the ribs and pushing the animal into the main square at a trot, the mare keeping her feet on the icy ground. The streets were deserted, the once bright and lively shop fronts and market stalls shut up tight. The city was unnervingly quiet; the horses' hooves echoed off the stones as snow tumbled down all around them, coating their hair and catching in the manes of the horses.

Thalion kept his hand on his sword, the other holding the reins lightly. As they neared the palace, the snow lay thick, piled up along the edges of the cobbled street and resting casually on the windowpanes like artfully placed decorations. The trees were cloaked in white, the gardens buried beneath a foot of snowfall. A fae in thick furs took their horses. Laeli headed for the stairs urgently, Thalion hurrying to keep up with her. Over his shoulder he carried the pack filled with Laeli's weapons and her Witch's uniform. He caught her arm gently; he could feel the panic beneath her skin. His hand slid down to catch her fingers and he gave them a squeeze, struggling to release her hand, struggling against the urge to bundle her into his chest and fight this fight for her.

'Easy,' he managed to whisper.

She took a steady breath, pulling the frosty air into her lungs, then walked gracefully up the sweeping stone steps, her head held high, chin lifted proudly. Thalion's heart was thunder in his chest as the men on guard duty, Estilleon men, nodded to them both and pushed open the heavy wooden doors.

The expansive hallway was much the same as it was the last time Thalion was there, except it was freezing inside, the gold threads on the marble walls glinting behind a layer of ice, the potted plants shrivelled. The generous windows showcased a winter scene this time, but Laeli didn't pause, marching towards the throne room. She veered left, ducking into a small room tucked off the hall, Thalion following her.

'Quick,' she whispered, and he passed over the pack. She stripped off the furs and woollen gown, slipping into her fitted green, sliding her swords into the scabbard against her back with a sigh of relief. She tucked two daggers into her belt, strapped one to her thigh and slipped another into her boot. He helped her drape the thick white cloak over herself, helped her arrange it to hide what lay beneath, his fingers trembling the whole time.

She noticed, catching his hand, and planting a kiss to his palm.

'It'll be alright,' she said, her voice soft, and he wanted so badly to believe her.

Before they stepped out into the unknown, he pushed her against the wall and kissed her deeply, feeling her features shimmer so she could kiss him back in her own face, with the lips he could taste in his sleep. He ran his hands over her body, feeling the shape of her, though he had it memorised, hoping to the Gods this wouldn't be the last time he touched her. She'd shattered him completely. His heart had been torn from his body and shoved back in. She held a piece of it inside her, a piece he'd gladly given and would continue to give until he'd breathed his last.

'You're my world,' he said, running his thumbs over her cheeks. 'Don't you dare die.'

'I love you,' Laeli whispered back fiercely as the green of her eyes faded to pale blue, the blush that stained her cheeks vanished and her hair lightened.

She took a deep breath, then squared her shoulders and led the way to the throne room.

Niall and one of his men were guarding the door. Niall's eyes widened when he saw them, a muscle quivering in the line of his jaw. He lowered his voice, addressing Thalion. 'Your father and the Witch are in there, along with at least ten others, all heavily armed. Brenna is with them.' He glanced at Laeli. 'The Royal Suite. Alive.'

She nodded her thanks, and Niall reached for the door.

'Get your men and Ulfe's and get out of here. The fae guard will attack the perimeter in the next two hours – don't engage them or they'll kill you,' Thalion whispered as the door swung open. Laeli marched in before he could say anymore and he had no choice but to follow her down the carpet that was littered with snow and frost, past the men and women lined along the walls, heading straight for Kiarda, who reclined in Rhodiri's throne like she'd sat there all her life. Hadrian stood by her side, his hair dusted with the snow falling from nowhere. Thalion could feel Brenna's eyes on his back, and he kept his hand on his sword as his father addressed him.

'What are you doing here?'

Kiarda was watching Laeli through narrowed eyes. Thalion's heart sped up.

'Thalion! What's going on? What's this we hear about the Pass?'

Word had reached his father at last. The confusion on Hadrian's face was not something Thalion was used to seeing. He was a good son. He did what he was told, when he was told. He grovelled and shoved his own thoughts aside because his Chieftain, his father, didn't share his opinions.

He'd spent his life trying to please a man who was impossible to please. Whatever there was between them was irreversibly broken.

'Frode has the castle. Arne and Freda are dead. All those you left behind to make sure I continued to do your bidding have pledged their allegiance to me, including Cuyler,' Thalion said smoothly. He kept his tone low and measured; the voice of a man people now listened to. 'The war at the Pass is over and a treaty has been drafted. I don't know how that will upset your plans, but I'm assuming it won't make it so easy to march your army, my army now, through Merawuld and into Tyllcarric.'

Hadrian gaped at him; from the corner of his eye, Thalion saw Brenna scowl and slip from the room as his father regained his words.

'Your girl was meant to keep him in line,' Hadrian snarled at Kiarda, whose face was frozen in silent anger. 'And now the brat tells me he's taken over my country? What happened? Why couldn't you do what you were asked?' Hadrian whirled to face Laeli, his expression one of contorted rage.

The tumbling snow paused as Kiarda leant forward. 'That's not my daughter.'

'What do you mean?' Hadrian gestured wildly in Laeli's direction.

Kiarda laughed, a terrible, hollow sound that echoed around the room and throbbed with undeniable power. 'Hello, Laeli. How lovely it is to see you after all this time. I've wasted a lot of manpower and hours combing the forest, trying to find where you were hiding. This,' she said to Hadrian, 'is the missing Princess. Your son has something else he's been keeping from you, it seems.'

Thalion tensed as Laeli let her glamour fall, the magic shimmering from her skin. Hadrian fell back in shock as Kiarda's lips curled into a poisonous smile.

'You can't save your brother, though it's admirable that you're about to try.'

Laeli threw off her cloak and drew her swords; Thalion slowly drew his own weapon, shifting his weight to the balls of his feet, his legs bunching up.

Kiarda's face was a mask of barely contained anger. 'Where's Eira?'

'What is remembered, lives.' Laeli's voice was low, a hint of sympathy mingled with her defiance and as Kiarda's face twisted, Thalion inched closer to his wife. The air pulsed with anticipation. It flowed through him, digging into his muscles, into his blood as he released a steady breath and tightened his grip on the hilt of his sword.

Kiarda ran her fingers along the staff, her eyes never leaving Laeli's face, her expression frozen, caught somewhere between rage and grief. She blinked furiously, then motioned to the men standing against the wall.

'Entertain me,' she demanded. 'Isn't that what your Stadium is for?' she asked Hadrian, who ignored her. His eyes were on Thalion, his expression calm but instantly assessing; the one he had always worn before each match Thalion had ever competed in. Laeli shifted into a crouch beside him; flames ignited along her blades as Thalion tore his gaze from his father, not missing the flash of emotion that passed across Hadrian's face.

Even as he faced his own opponents, cutting them down, Thalion watched his wife, the way her arms moved, the way she spun and sliced and how those swords never stopped moving. The way her face, her beautiful face, was set in hard lines, her green eyes blazing. Men died screaming, melting in Laeli's fire, the stench of roasted skin crawling through the room. They became puddles on the floor as those swords twirled and danced with inhuman speed. Another man, one Thalion recognised from the Stadium, came towards him warily. But this was not the Stadium, and Thalion split him open before he could speak, turning to face a fae woman who wielded a spear with a barbed end. She shoved it at him, but he stepped aside and rammed his foot into her stomach; Laeli's blades slashed and the fae's head tumbled from her shoulders.

Thalion wiped his face with the back of his arm, the wetness of blood smearing his skin.

It had taken them less than ten minutes. The floor of the throne room was littered with bodies, the carpet soaked with blood and gore. The fae warriors decapitated head rested near the toe of Thalion's boot, white, soulless eyes staring at the ceiling, yet he paid it no heed, did not pause to think of the woman it had belonged to.

Laeli turned the fierceness of her gaze on Hadrian, who was staring at her in undisguised wonder. 'And you. What sort of animal allows women and children to be kept as slaves? What sort of man treats his own son with such contempt? You have no power anymore, Hadrian Liulfur.' Her expression was as cold as the ice that lined the walls. 'You should get on your knees and beg Thalion's forgiveness before I cut your head from your body.'

Hadrian took a stumbling step back. 'All that time …' he murmured, looking at Thalion in astonishment.

'Enough!' Kiarda stood; an unearthly wind ripped through the room, battering them with tiny pieces of stinging ice. Blood gleamed on their skin like tiny jewels. Kiarda stepped down from the dais, staff lifted in Laeli's direction, her face as ferocious and dangerous as a winter squall. Blue flames were left where she walked, crystals of ice growing from them, their tips sharp enough to slice through flesh.

'You will die screaming, daughter of my brother. You will die with your veins filled with ice, your heart slowly freezing until it can beat no more. Your fire magic is nothing against the power I wield!' The end of the staff began to glow with bright blue light.

Laeli's fire ignited, and a shield of flame spread around them, brighter and stronger than the one Thalion had seen her conjure that day outside Whitemouth. The air was sucked dry as the ice began to melt, the floor soggy with blood and water. The flame grew hotter and larger.

Kiarda screamed, a horrible sound, filled with agony and despair.

'Wait!' Hadrian hurried down the steps from the dais. 'Stop!'

Kiarda ignored him; he wrapped his fingers around her arm.

Through the wall of flame, Thalion watched in disjointed horror as she turned the staff on his father.

A blast of blue light roared from the end, an ear-splitting crack tearing through the room. Hadrian sailed through the air, slamming into the wall beneath the frozen vines with a sickening thud.

The wall of flame quivered.

Laeli was shouting something, but Thalion couldn't take his eyes off his father's unmoving body. He took a step forward, his ears full of raging white noise; Laeli's fingers slid beneath his belt. She tugged, but his body was frozen, the chill in the air sinking inside his bones. He could barely feel the heat from her fire anymore. He took another step forward; through the flames, he saw Kiarda and lunged towards her.

Suddenly, he was being dragged from the hall, away from that wall of fire. He fought every step, but Laeli was too strong and too fast and in moments, she hurled him out a side door into the garden, propelling him across the snow and into the forest, pushing him roughly between the trees, shoving with that unnatural strength until he was pinned between her arms and the unyielding steadiness of a tree trunk.

Thalion struggled fiercely, but Laeli held him firm, that determination he loved burning in her eyes.

'Let go!'

'No. You'll be killed!'

He tried to shove her off; she slammed him against the tree, so hard the snow on the branches quivered and fell around them while he snarled at her.

'Please.' Laeli's voice broke. 'My father … my brother … I can't lose you as well. I'm sorry, I'm so sorry for what she did, but I need your help. I have to save Mahelivar. Please.'

He stared into her eyes for a long moment, then shook his head.

'Thalion, if I leave you here, they'll find you. I won't be able to protect you.'

'Then don't protect me!' He barely heard himself speak the words. His head was filled with that white noise again, burning and tunnelling into his brain. His anger was omnipotent; it flowed through him, filling every space inside his body. His skin itched, his sword arm tingling, his will unwavering.

'Thalion!'

'Let. Go!'

Laeli's breath hitched. 'As you wish,' she said quietly, releasing her grip and moving away from him, giving him the space he craved. The space to make his next decision. He held her eyes as she slowly took another step back, then another, each step ripping him to pieces.

He would follow her to the very edge of the earth, but not this time.

When he didn't move, her face collapsed. 'I love you,' she mouthed, then turned and darted across the white lawn so quickly he lost sight of her in moments.

CHAPTER FIFTY

Something had changed.

Mahelivar could feel the wheel turning, slowly, as if the hand that guided it was taking her time. Deep in his bones, in his blood, at the core of his magic, at the very centre of who he was, he could feel the Cailleach. She approached, those ancient feet making their way steadily towards him, that primal power in her veins charged like lightning, the beating of her heart as strong and fierce as thunder, never-ending and everlasting.

But there was something else …

While his blood beat in time with the Mother, his heart pulsed to a different beat, one that he had felt since the moment she took her first breath: bound together as children not only of the earth and the rich soil of Eshlune, but as children of their father's blood. Their family had been chosen since the beginning of time itself to be the bridge between worlds, to carry the weight of their people, to guide and protect and nurture.

His sister was in the palace, in a burst of fire and death and sorrow.

Mahelivar scrambled from the chair he was resting in. He cast a look at his father, at a King at the end of his time. Rhodiri slept like one dead, but his chest still rose and fell, a steady rhythm that matched the breathing of the earth. Mahelivar could feel his father's magic as it shifted with the slow turning of the wheel. He knew Laeli would feel it as well.

He hurried to the door of the suite, the ice beneath his feet crunching. Pressing his ear against the cold timber, Mahelivar listened to the murmur of voices on the other side, and sent out his magic, immediately encountering a wall of ice and snow. The net.

Kiarda may have him trapped, caged like a beast, but Laeli had come.

He glanced again at his father – his gaze lingered there. Rhodiri's face was serene in his almost-ending, but there was a fierceness still evident in the line of his jaw and Mahelivar could have sworn his father's fists clenched and unclenched, that the veins on the back of his hands flared with green life.

He could have sworn those eyes, so like his, so like Laeli's, opened for a moment.

Protect your sister, Mahelivar.

Mahelivar readied his magic, felt it race through him in anticipation. He had done it once; he could do it again, but this time, he needed to give everything he had.

Into his air magic he wove the power of the earth: the strength of the trees and the life-giving essence of the soil. He thought of buds unfolding, of shoots of green surging towards the sun. Of fleshy fungi and grasses that swayed in the breeze, of the mists that shrouded the canopy and the rain that dripped from the sky. He thought of the stag, the King of the Forest, of the birds and animals that lived and died with the turning of the wheel. He thought of the never-ending dance of the earth and everything that existed, fed and watered and borne of the Mother.

And, deep within, a tiny flame smouldered. Mahelivar drew it to the surface, that spark of heat, and let it fill him, let it burn and blaze as his sister would burn and blaze, a powerful light in the deepest dark.

Taking a deep breath, Mahelivar let it out, let all that he was flow through him, let the very heart of himself push against that net woven tightly around the suite. That net that, from the moment it had existed, symbolised everything he believed he was – uncertain, weak, indecisive.

Unworthy.

In his pocket, lay the Morrigan's feather.

As his fingertips brushed it, he felt fate spark within.

He smiled, triumph surging through him as, with his sister's mind planted firmly in his, Mahelivar ripped the fabric of Kiarda's net to pieces.

CHAPTER FIFTY-ONE

Thalion closed his eyes and rested his head against the tree. Inside the palace, Kiarda screamed again and the world trembled with the force of her pain, her sorrow, and a century of rage. The snow fell harder, the wind throwing handfuls of white at the world. He drew a breath that tasted of pain and despair.

He saw Kiarda turn the staff on his father again and heard the horrible crunch of bone as Hadrian smashed into the wall. Thalion's stomach heaved, and he swallowed the taste of blood.

'You fucking fool,' he chastised himself, dropping to the ground to sit with his head in his hands. Something exploded inside the palace, and he stood and pushed further into the trees. He needed time to work out what to do next. He barrelled through the forest, colliding with a body. Arms pushed him back as he drew his weapon, swinging from one face to the next. He recognised them. Brenna's men.

Snow swirled, veiling the world in thick white; the only sound was singing metal as swords were drawn. The men spread out, until they circled him, wolves on their prey.

Only Thalion was no one's prey. Not now and not ever.

Brenna stepped into view. The old man was smiling, his silver hair flowing over his shoulders. 'Thalion,' he said. 'Put the weapon down, boy.'

Such was the command in Brenna's tone, so scrambled were his thoughts, so broken and bruised was his heart, that Thalion lowered his sword an inch; the first man rushed him, and he snapped like a bow string, giving himself over completely to the roaring, fiery anger that surged through his body.

Only when Thalion's leg was opened, the blood freezing before it touched the ground, and his ears rang with the melody of steel on steel, did Brenna draw his weapon, the sound of the sword sliding free of the scabbard echoing ominously through the cold air. Three bodies lay spread at the Chief's feet.

At that moment, someone stepped from the trees.

The captain of the fae guard took in the bodies and the crimson stain kissing the snow, the blood staining Thalion's face and neck. Swiftly, he notched an arrow, his golden eyes swinging between Thalion and Brenna.

Thalion pointed his sword at him. 'You need to stay back, Solen, unless you want to be sent to your Gods because, the Allfather help me, I'll kill you if you come any closer.'

Solen didn't leave. He nodded, and waited beneath the trees, his face impassive, that arrow at the ready. Thalion wasn't sure whose chest he would aim for if it came to it, but he couldn't worry about the fae soldier right now. He counted his breaths – ten, in and out, his body steadying with each pull of frozen air into burning lungs.

Not taking his eyes from Brenna's face, Thalion drove the point of his sword into the ground, then stripped off his thick furs, followed by the heavy woollen shirt, tossing both in a heap on the snow. He inhaled, exhaled, and removed the last shirt, until he was bare chested in the freezing air. His skin puckered; every scar he'd earnt burnt with memory.

'What the fuck are you doing?' Brenna barked.

'The Stadium is a place of honour,' Thalion said. He plucked the sword from the ground and drew a line in the snow with the tip of the blade, then stepped back, blood thundering. Brenna's skill with the sword was a gods-given gift, a trail of corpses scattering through the Chief's life, victory after victory stamped with his name. Thalion only rolled his shoulders, kept his breathing steady.

Brenna bared his teeth. 'You traitorous bastard, Thalion. I should take your head.'

Thalion ignored the threat, the promise of bloodshed from a warrior who was much more than he was. 'This isn't the Stadium, and you are not a man of honour, Brenna. You're a coward, and a brute, who's spent years hiding behind my father, kissing his feet, and doing nothing while he plotted to turn the world inside out.'

Brenna laughed. 'You've lost your mind, boy!'

'Don't call me boy.'

All the humour vanished from Brenna's face as Thalion let his weight rest in his legs, the muscles in his calves pulling tight, his shoulders loosening, his body fluid like the ice after the summer melts. The pain of his wound settled inside him, mingling with the vicious, primal rage contained there, straining to be let out again. Brenna swung his sword, the blade piercing the air with an audible hiss as something moved beneath the trees behind him.

This time, Thalion knew what he saw. The God of War and Strength stood behind Brenna, spear in one hand, his cloak brushing the ground. His one eye surveyed them. The Allfather inclined his head and gave Thalion a smile.

'Have it your way,' the Chief of Whitemouth sighed, and stepped forward.

CHAPTER FIFTY-TWO

In the Delta, the full moon was silhouetted against the sea, the waves licked with silver. From the deck, Ash watched the water, pouring her thoughts, and her fears, into its inky depths. Tomorrow, she would leave here, leave the still peacefulness of a world that existed outside of the one she had run from. The temptation to stay here, to give herself over to the ebb and flow of the tide as the people of the Delta had, was strong, but as the stars drew light across the sky, she understood she couldn't stay.

Kiarda and Gedeon would come here if she did nothing.

She'd finally embraced what she was. Now it was time to be *who* she was.

Ash had tried not to think too much about what had happened as they escaped Tyllcarric, but whenever she closed her eyes, she could still see them – the angry red flesh bleeding through the charred black, the ashes of the dead coating the ground. She could smell them, and their screams echoed in her nightmares.

She slipped back inside the hut and crawled into bed, into Jarlath's arms, seeking the peace and security of him. She slept, waking before him, the gentle light of the dawn sneaking in through the window. Ash had never been so close to another person physically. Jarlath's chest pressed into her back, his arm draped over her body. She could feel the heat of his breath tickling the back of her neck, and the wiry muscle of his bicep under her cheek, the skin on the underside of his arm softer than she imagined it would be. The callouses on his fingers had weakened in the time he'd been in Estilleon – callouses he'd earnt from swinging a sword for years.

After what he'd told her, she didn't think he'd ever pick up a weapon again. He'd tried to hide it from her, forgetting that his eyes could speak on their own – the wounds he carried weren't visible on his body. Neither were hers, she realised, but if there was one person who understood that, it was Jarlath.

Seeing him again, whole, and alive, she couldn't understand how she'd never truly noticed it before, in all the time they'd ever spent together – the way he smiled at her, the light that shone behind his eyes when he glanced her way, how his gaze would linger on her face longer than was necessary. How could she have missed it? There had been moments when she'd thought there might be more between them, but they'd been so fleeting she was convinced she'd imagined them. Now, it was like she'd overlooked a hidden jewel, a masterpiece that was created for her.

Jarlath may not be flawless, but he was still somehow perfect.

She rolled over to face him, continuing her scrutiny – the freckles that were scattered across his nose like stars across the sky, the curve of his cheeks and the shadow that dusted the strong line of his jaw. His hair was longer than she'd ever seen it, wild and curly and windblown. She reached up and ran her fingers through it, pushing it away from his face. His eyes opened and she blushed to be caught staring at him.

'What?' he asked her, a lazy smile on his face.

'I love you,' she blurted.

He was quiet, so quiet, she thought she'd made a mistake.

'When I was trapped in the darkness, and when I thought I was going to die, it was your face I saw, Ash,' Jarlath said softly. 'I nearly did give up, but someone made me see that I had a choice in what I did next.' He took a deep, steady breath. 'I love you, and I'm never leaving you again.'

She studied his face, the lines on it that weren't there before. 'Jarlath—'

'We've both had to do things we didn't want to,' he said softly. She glanced at him, heart thundering. He smiled tightly.

'We have,' she agreed. 'It pulls at me, what I did.' She'd told him everything. 'Perhaps I shouldn't have done it. Perhaps I should have found another way.'

'Then you'd all be dead,' Jarlath affirmed quietly. His arms tightened around her. 'And I'd be dead if I didn't do what I had to do.' He paused. 'They kept me alive, Ash. Laeli, and Thalion. They kept me alive so I could be here, with you, in this moment. What happens now will be up to you.'

She frowned. 'What do you mean?'

He rolled onto his back, drawing her into his side. 'Yasper and Nerida are going back to the city,' Jarlath announced, his fingers stroking the skin on her arm. 'Senan and the halfkin are going with them.'

There had been a meeting last night, but Ash had been so tired she'd excused herself and went to bed. She wasn't made for planning wars, or what to do in them. That was better left to others, people like Jarlath, with his army training, and Yasper, who could read people and intentions better than she could. People like Fox, and even Senan.

'What will we do?' Jarlath murmured. It was her decision, she realised. Completely and utterly hers. He was giving her that and she knew, without having to ask, that whatever she decided, he would follow her.

She ran her fingers over his chest, watching his skin tighten and pucker at her touch, wondering at it, at how she could elicit such a response from his body. She traced the scar across his abdomen; he was thinner than before he left, the tan shed from his skin, along with the lightness in his eyes.

'Ash?'

'The Rift.' She closed her eyes. It called her, like it had been calling her always, and since that day when she'd hung her head over the edge, the fire of the Rift had been in her blood, singing and surging and pulling at her. She'd learnt to shove it away, store that terrifying longing in a deep, dark part of her mind. The magic of the Rift had driven her to unleash the power of her fire on the High Mage, and the Watch.

Ash shivered.

Yet her fire was more than destruction and death. It was creation as well. She could feel that in the deepest part of herself and wondered how, and when, she would be given the chance to truly test her magic, and herself. Part of her was excited at the idea of seeing what she was capable of. Another part was terrified.

'I have to go in there,' Ash said quietly. She'd known it for a while, and here, so close to the edge of the Rift, the longing, that invisible force that dragged her eyes to the west when she let her guard down, was impossible to ignore.

The arms holding her tightened. She could hear the furious pounding of his heart. 'Okay,' Jarlath said eventually.

Ash lifted her head from his chest in surprise. She'd expected at least some opposition, but he only smiled.

'As if I can stop you.'

'I just want it to be over,' she whispered. 'Kiarda, Gedeon – everything. I don't want anyone else to die for this, for me,' she added pointedly.

She could tell he understood.

She could also tell he'd ignore that wish, even if it was her last.

What would happen in the Rift, she didn't know. She had no idea what she would find down there.

Answers.

Questions.

Fire. Always fire. In response to her thoughts, her magic whispered beneath her skin.

But she knew, felt it, a steady beat against the walls of her magic, that the fire would lead her to Eshlune. To Sitra, and Kiarda.

Beyond that, she had no idea.

'I'm afraid,' Ash admitted.

'So am I,' Jarlath said quietly. 'I wish I was braver. That I'd had the courage to tell you how I felt years ago. That I'd had the courage to – I don't know.'

Ash shifted so she could see his face. 'Maybe courage isn't what either of us believed it to be,' she said, sliding her arm around him so she could trace the scars on his back. Jarlath swallowed, then quirked a smile.

'You sound like Thalion.'

She raised her brows. 'I do?'

He nodded, and then his face changed – it became soft, tender, as he reached up and traced the curve of her cheek with the tip of his finger, then trailed it along the length of her jaw, towards her mouth. 'But I don't want to talk about Thalion right now.'

Her heart began thundering. 'What do you want to talk about?'

Jarlath traced her top lip, then her bottom, with his finger. 'I'm not sure I want to talk at all, if I'm being honest.' His eyes grew dark, and he smiled slowly. 'What I'd like is for you to kiss me, Ash.'

Heat surged in her cheeks, her belly swooping low, warming as it flopped. Ash swallowed, and kissed him gently, then harder, desire rising in her body like a great beast at her command, like the fire in her veins did. Jarlath's breathing quickened as she kissed her way down his chest, over the smooth planes of his abdomen, her fingers running over the sharp line of his hips, the muscle pulled tight over bone and under flesh.

He went to roll them over, but she stopped him, her hand firm in the middle of his chest, his heart fluttering under her fingers. Weak daylight poured through the window in the hut, golden fingers stroking the wooden floor, specks of dust caught in the sunbeam. The remains of their dinner sat on the small table, their clothes littered across the ground like crumbs as the glowing breath of the sun crested the horizon and painted the world reborn. The Delta was silent except for the gentle slap of the waves against the stilts of the huts.

Was this normal? Ash wondered. The need that churned in her belly? The unbelievable hunger that she couldn't shake?

She kissed him again, shifting her body over his, her knees braced against his hips, the bedclothes unbearably soft and rough against her flesh at the same time. Her body sang and thrummed as her nerves threatened to drown her, but one look at his face had those nerves vaporised. Jarlath's eyes trailed over her flesh, his gaze searing and scorching with a magic of its own, devouring and ripping through to the raw inside of her. He ran his fingertips lightly over her stomach, up over her breasts, her throat, until he reached her lips. Where he touched her, it was like stars dancing over her flesh and exploding through her veins.

Would her reaction to his touch ever change? To the way he looked at her, she wondered, or was it part of what it meant to love someone? To give someone everything you were, to let yourself be consumed completely?

Ash knew she couldn't give him everything, not yet, not until this was over and they had the freedom to simply be. They deserved it, she thought fiercely. In her mind, she saw the scars on his back, those silvery-pink lines. She heard the way his voice cracked around the edges when he spoke of what he'd seen on the battlefield and what he'd done in the Stadium. She could see the truth of how it had changed him in his eyes and she was determined that they'd get through whatever happened next and be happy.

But, for now, all she wanted was to love him, to savour this moment with him.

'I love you,' he told her, as she took him inside her body with a gasp, shivers shooting along the length of her spine as she rolled her hips. He let her have control, let her set the pace, let her experiment, and learn, until the pressure building inside exploded, waves of heat and light rippling through her, her fire clamouring to be let out. Panting, she pushed her magic away, the hand of her mind closing around it until it simmered and was still.

Ash slept, Jarlath curled into her, his arm around her, and when she woke the sun was high and the ocean sparkled like a blanket of jewels.

She slipped from the bed, pulling on her clothes and going to stand on the deck.

Four days until the solstice. Her blood sang. Mahelivar had been right. Her magic felt different – stronger, more potent – drawn to the surface by something bigger than she was.

Jarlath joined her, his face rumpled, his hair tousled. He slipped an arm around her, and she smiled at how natural it was, how easy.

In the distance, a boat bobbed on the water, and the world was calm, renewed, but the shadow that hung over it was growing darker each moment they spent here.

'I need to leave today.'

'I'm coming with you. I might not be able to follow you into the Rift, Ash, but I'm coming to Sitra,' he said, kissing the side of her head.

'Is she there, do you think? Laeli?'

He nodded.

'Do you think she's alive?' Ash asked, dreading his answer.

'Yes. Thalion would kill everyone in that place before he let them touch her,' Jarlath said with certainty. 'And she'd do the same.' He made a face and Ash smiled.

'I think it's sweet.'

'It's sickening,' he laughed, pulling a hand through his hair.

'Mahelivar?' she asked quietly.

'I don't know.'

Across the water, they spied Nerida closing the door to the hut she'd been staying in since Jarlath arrived. She glanced up and waved and, even from a distance, Ash could see her smirk. She wondered bleakly whether she would see Nerida, or any of them, again.

'She'll be safe with Yasper and Senan,' Jarlath declared.

Ash wasn't so sure. None of them knew what sort of face Tyllcarric was going to present to them. She suspected things had gone from bad to worse since they left, and her friends were going to be walking to their doom. Gedeon still had the Bloodstones and her stolen magic. Ash cringed thinking about it, that some part of her was in his hands. She could hear her lost magic crying out to her – it was like a piece of her was missing.

She shook her head. There was nothing she could do about it. Jarlath's arm tightened around her. White birds hovered above the ocean, drifting on the warm currents. The smell of seawater and the oily scent of brine was all around them.

'Senan wants to kill Gedeon,' Ash said, peering over the edge of the balcony. Below her, the water was clear as crystal; small fish darted through the shallows and water weeds danced with the current.

'You think he will?' Jarlath asked.

'If Fox doesn't get to him first.'

The halfkin assassin was terrifying. For such a small thing, Fox sure packed a lot of animosity, her face twisting into a snarl whenever one of them mentioned Gedeon's name. Her hatred of him outweighed Senan's, and they equally hated Darian, although, in Senan, Ash sensed a bitter disappointment for what Gedeon had become. She didn't think the Mage-Witch had the capacity to hate, not truly.

Ash glanced across the water to the broad sweep of the ocean. Sometimes, in her dreams, Darian was dead. But sometimes, he stood over her body, staring at her with those fathomless grey eyes.

By noon, Ash and Jarlath climbed into a boat, Mika at the helm. As the Delta man waved his hands and the boat began to move through the water, the knot of anxiety in Ash's belly grew larger, as did her anticipation of what she would find at the bottom of the Rift. Mika left them at the edge of that great spread of water, his eyes serious, the sunlight sliding over the blue tinge to his hair, painting him like the water – golden and sparkling.

CHAPTER FIFTY-THREE

Laeli crept down the wide hallway that led to her father's rooms. She had no idea where her husband was, or if she was ever going to see him again. Her hand fluttered to her lower belly briefly, to that tiny life that clung to her. If she'd had the courage to tell him - she shook her head. She didn't think it would have made a difference, not now, not after what Kiarda had done.

Seeing her aunt sitting on her father's throne had conjured a fury like nothing Laeli had felt before. The fire in her veins had burnt brighter and more powerful than ever, startling her with its strength.

And Thalion ... something in him was broken, she knew that. She'd felt it, his rage, his powerlessness, and had felt a part of herself break with him as his father's body had shattered.

Laeli swallowed, forcing herself to focus as she approached the next junction in the labyrinthine halls of her home. Voices eased around the corner, so she flattened herself against the wall, wishing for the hundredth time she possessed a shred of air magic. She could turn those people around in a matter of moments. She could make them fall on their own swords if she wished, but she needed to find another way through them.

Bending, she placed a palm on the floor, sending her mind out, searching for the water beneath the palace. It was there, far underground, too far to reach, but she could use the ice that coated the walls instead. The only green life she could sense was withered and weak, trapped in this unnatural winter, but the fire in her veins surged with power, more than it ever had before as the wheel turned another notch.

It would have to be fire, then. After what she'd done in the throne room, the death she had delivered … Laeli made a silent vow to herself – when this was over, she would toss her swords into the belly of the Rift because a world of violence, of destruction and pain and blood, was not the world she wanted. Until Thalion had crashed into her life, she'd never realised how much she truly needed the world to be a good place.

Laeli's lower lip trembled, and she choked on a sob, pressing her back into the wall, her magic faltering as despair gripped her tight.

She needed Thalion. She needed his sword arm, his confidence, his strength, the determination he had to fight for what was right. He'd been by her side every moment since this all began and now he was gone, that steadying presence – gone. She glanced back the way she had come, as if by some miracle he would appear, but he wasn't coming. She felt it as surely as she could feel her father's life slipping away and her heart fractured down the centre.

The Cailleach was near, she could feel that as well, could see the Goddess behind her eyes, a superimposed image over the world, shrouded in snow and wrapped in wind, that primal power surging with each step she took, each second the wheel turned closer to the solstice.

Laeli peeked around the corner, quickly pulling her head back. Six of Hadrian's men and three of Kiarda's warriors awaited her. She took a wobbly breath, closing her eyes as she forced her breathing to steady.

Nine people. Nine more lives.

When she opened her eyes, the Morrigan was standing before her, her raven's wing hair tumbling over her shoulders, her feathered cloak brushing the ground. The Goddess of Fate reached out a long-fingered hand, resting her palm over Laeli's heart. Heat shot through her – her racing heartbeat slowed and her nerves, trembling long before she'd stepped into that throne room, solidified as she was filled with shining clarity and the brightness of courage.

There was no space anymore for fear. If she did nothing, Kiarda would win, and she would lose everyone she loved.

The Morrigan smiled and vanished into a pile of black feathers, as a mind Laeli knew slammed into her own, leaving her gasping and clutching at the wall.

Mahelivar. She didn't have time to think about how he had broken through Kiarda's net again. Her palms tingled as she reached out her magic, seeking that web of power that shrouded the Royal Suite. Nothing. The net was gone, as if it never existed.

She took a deep breath, then let it out slowly.

Her brother was alive. That was all that mattered.

And she was not going to let him wait any longer.

The wheel paused as Laeli stepped around the corner. Her feet moved on their own, featherlight and soundless. Those nine people stopped their chatter when they saw her. She didn't miss the disbelief that crossed their faces. One man, a human, even started laughing, but she smiled.

The human body was mostly water, after all.

Laeli flung her hand out towards him. His laughter died as she clenched her fist and ripped the liquid from his veins and organs, the air filled with a bright red mist. Before he hit the ground, she hurled a dagger at the next man – it flew down the hall, embedding itself with a thud between his eyes. As the others reached for their weapons, the ice tore from the walls, her water magic flinging those shards towards them. The men covered their faces with a shout. Laeli pulled her swords free, set them ablaze, and ran.

She targeted the fae first. She would not give the Witches time to use their magic.

Using the wall as a springboard, Laeli drove her blade through the throat of the nearest fae. He fell in a tangle of white fur and blood as she unleashed on the others, her blades slashing as she spun and wove through them, cutting a path closer to the Royal Suite. She could see the golden threads that ran from the sun engraved in the middle of the doors as her father's heartbeat drummed in her ears.

Her hair was gripped in a strong hand and she was yanked backwards, scalp screaming and eyes watering. Twisting sharply, Laeli drove her sword into a man's gut, hearing his gurgling breath in her ear as he went limp. The next blow was to her face, so hard she saw stars, but she ducked an oncoming punch, calling on her fire magic – balls of burning light shot from her palm, engulfing one of the fae. He screamed horribly, slapping at his face with his hands. Laeli cut him down, staring at those remaining, her body burning as the magic in her veins blazed.

Flaming swords held out beside her, Laeli slipped into a crouch, ready to throw herself at those remaining, when a mind brushed against hers.

Magus.

Her mentor came at them from the other end of the hall, arrows ripping the air apart, fire flaming from their tips. Two fell beneath them. Magus gave her a nod then turned to face the men approaching from the opposite direction. Laeli caught a glimpse of Solen before she swung her swords again, taking another man down as the captain of the fae guard ripped through two others. More joined the fighting at the end of the hall – Magus and Solen ran, drawing them away; the sound of screaming echoed down the halls and the horrible smell of burning flesh followed it.

Laeli kept her breathing steady as she found herself facing a fae woman armed with a long spear of ash wood. The spear was topped with a gruesome, barbed blade, and in her other hand the woman held a double-edged battle-axe, sharpened so fine Laeli could hear the sound the blade made as it sliced the air. The fae woman was tall, a scar running proudly down one cheek, the muscles in her bare arms well-sculpted and covered in swirling, black tattoos.

She smiled slowly and Laeli realised who she was looking at.

Birka. Her aunt's most devout supporter. The first to join with Kiarda over a century ago, the killer of her own people. She was a ferocious warrior, highly skilled, and lethal. Laeli swallowed as the first real spark of fear shot along her spine. She had no desire to taste the end of Birka's spear or the biting mouth of her axe, but Birka was standing between her and her family.

'I haven't seen you since you were a tiny thing.' Birka's voice was low and prickly. 'It will be a shame to kill you – you remind me of Faleria. She was fierce and determined – I can see her in your eyes.'

'Don't say her name,' Laeli hissed. She adjusted her grip on her blood-slicked swords.

Birka laughed lightly, her head tipped to the side, the braids of her dark hair tumbling over her shoulder, her eyes cold. 'Kiarda can be forgiving if you're willing to make amends for Eira's death.'

'Let me see my father and brother, Birka,' Laeli said firmly. She would not beg. Not to Birka, or anyone, because the last person she had pleaded with …

'I'm afraid I can't do that, sweet girl,' Birka replied. She attacked with her magic first – Laeli threw up a mental wall of flame that had the Air Witch quickly withdrawing, looking at her in surprise.

'You think I've spent over one hundred years with my brother and not learnt any tricks?' Laeli said.

Birka made a noise of consent, her lips curled into a smile, and then struck, that spear reaching across the space between them. Laeli bent backwards as the razor-sharp tip swung past her face, her muscles fluid beneath her skin. Before she righted herself, Birka was on her, the axe swinging, curling towards Laeli's body. Muscle-memory her guide, Laeli let herself move, let herself be back in the training yard at Wilderun. She watched Birka as she'd watched Thalion, trying to read the other woman's movements in her face, but Birka was Kiarda's best for a reason.

There was nothing, no tells, no slight shifting of her eyes.

Laeli countered Birka's next attack, arms aching with the force of the blows, and the sudden weight of both swords. The floor was slick, blood and water smeared across the white marble, the air saturated with the smell of death. There was no more magic from Birka; she was a blur of strong arms, the axe glinting, the spear whirling with expert precision through the air. Laeli darted left, under that spear, and drove her sword into Birka's thigh. Without pause, Birka's elbow connected with Laeli's head, the force of the blow knocking her to the ground.

She rolled as the axe crashed into the floor, splitting the stone, jumped to her feet and lashed out with both swords – but all she sliced through was air. Birka was already gone, already striking again, and again, rattling Laeli's bones. Taking a step back, Laeli adjusted her grip.

She wanted it to be over.

She wanted to see her family. There was nothing but a door separating them. Birka wasn't smiling anymore. Her expression was lethal, nothing but the promise of death in her eyes.

Laeli clenched her jaw and flames licked the blades of her swords, brighter and stronger than before as she poured her all into her magic. Birka attacked, driving Laeli back, back, her feet slipping, her grip beginning to falter. Birka lunged with a fierce cry and the spear slid between Laeli's swords to punch into her flesh.

The pain was like lightning, snapping through every part of her, burning and ripping and tearing. Birka yanked the spear free, readying herself for another hit. Laeli gasped, her swords falling from her hands, her flames extinguished. She fell to her knees, blood dripping, mingling with the gore carpeting the floor. Her vision swam as Birka lifted the spear, the gaping wound between her breast and collarbone screaming.

You're not unbreakable.

'Don't kill her. Not yet.'

Laeli blinked, the edge of the world fading to black as Kiarda knelt before her, taking her chin in her hands, and staring into her face. With the other hand, she stroked Laeli's cheek.

'Let's give her what she wants,' Kiarda said softly. Laeli started as blue flames licked her aunt's knuckles. They were warm, like fire, but damp, leaving droplets of water on her skin as they brushed her cheek. Laeli recoiled; she could smell the wrongness of it, this twisted magic, this thing that should not be, and tried to pull her face away. Kiarda held her firmly.

'The net—' Birka began.

Kiarda's smug expression shifted.

'He beat you,' Laeli whispered.

'You really think it matters now?' Kiarda asked.

'It matters. It matters because she won't choose you, and you know it.' Laeli paused, studying Kiarda's face, the ice-pale eyes and sharp cheekbones, the shape of her jaw, features that she shared with her daughter: the face Laeli had been wearing for months. The words escaped of their own free will. 'We tried to talk to her; Thalion tried but she wouldn't listen and—'

Kiarda struck her forcefully across the face, then stood, nodding at Birka while Laeli spat a mouthful of blood onto the ground. Hands grabbed Laeli roughly. She screamed as those fingers pressed into her wound. Sweat ran down her face but she was freezing, her teeth beginning to chatter, her cheek burning.

Birka placed her hands on the door to Rhodiri's rooms; the magical locks shifted and clicked, and the door swung open. Laeli didn't fight as they dragged her into the room, flinging her onto the ground. Before she fainted, Kiarda addressed her.

'You have until the solstice.'

CHAPTER FIFTY-FOUR

They journeyed west for two days across a landscape that was relatively flat. The days were mild but the further they travelled from the Delta, the cooler the air became, the nights bitter. They didn't risk a fire, so they slept curled around one another, Ash's head tucked beneath Jarlath's chin, cocooned in their blankets, trying to keep out the chill.

On the third day, Jarlath led them north, and the gradient of the land changed. They hiked uphill for half a day, panting and perspiring by the time they reached the top of the rise. Ash's blood sang, her fire dancing and twisting beneath her skin.

Below them, stretching as far west as they could see, was the Rift. They had arrived at the southern end of that great rip in the earth. The smoke pouring gently from the ground was quickly dashed away by the wind fanning in from the ocean.

Ash led the way down the other side of the rise, approaching the Rift with her magic surging beneath her skin. They skirted the tip, mindful of the jagged edge. The ground around the edge of the Rift was barren; Ash bent to touch it, finding it warm beneath her fingers.

Jarlath adjusted their packs; he carried one over each shoulder, and a length of rope dangled from his belt, along with two daggers. He'd left the sword he'd carried from Estilleon behind, a gift for Fox, who curled her lip but managed a thank you. Ash had decided she liked her, despite the way her heart thudded whenever Fox was around; she was a straight-talker, and she was tough, a heavy contrast to the softer-spoken Mage-Witch, although Ash had seen Senan's darker side. Still, she was happy for him. He smiled a lot more now Fox was back, alive and whole. She was still healing from whatever she had gone through, Ash could see that, and Senan kept her close, her brother, Elan, who spoke little, sticking to her other side.

Ash turned her attention to the Rift. 'Something's not right,' she whispered.

'What do you mean?'

She shook her head, standing and brushing her hand over her pant leg. 'It feels wrong. Weaker. It's different to when I was here with Laeli.'

Jarlath shrugged. 'Maybe it's different at this end?'

Ash wasn't sure that was it, but she simply nodded, and they continued. The trees began to thicken the further west they travelled, following the zig-zagging curve of the Rift. They both found themselves glancing to the north-west, where Sitra lay surrounded by trees. They had no idea what to expect beyond the green, leafy life that stretched before them and no idea how far Kiarda's soldiers might have travelled from the city. Jarlath jumped at every sound and shadow, his hand constantly on the dagger at his hip.

If anyone appeared to challenge them, Ash had already decided she would blast them into nothing, for her, and Jarlath, and everyone they had left behind.

The smoke from the Rift increased and Ash felt a loving tug on her magic.

She stopped.

'Here.'

Jarlath didn't question her. He dropped the packs on the ground and uncoiled the rope they had carried with them. Ash turned to him, soaking up the sight of him, as he was now, because she had no idea what was going to happen to her once she entered the Rift.

'Did you want to rest first?' he asked her gently.

'I don't think it makes much difference,' she replied. They both glanced up at the sky. The sun was moving closer to the horizon – night was creeping up swiftly. 'Will you be alright up here?'

'It's you I'm worried about.'

'I don't know how I know, Jarlath, but I will be fine. I need to go in there.' As she spoke, the fire that lived beneath her skin pulsed and twitched. She put her arms around Jarlath's neck and kissed him for a long time; when she broke away, his smile was shaky. He let out a broken breath, then got to work, tying one end of the rope around his waist, the other around hers, her flesh tingling where his fingers touched her.

'I'll lower you down, okay? I'll leave the rope so I can pull you out when …'

Neither of them finished the sentence.

Ash bit her lip, leaning to peer over the edge of that smoking hole in the earth. 'Jarlath, I don't know if I will be me when I come out,' she whispered. Fear gripped her, fear of that deadly power inside. Even though it was part of her, and she had managed some degree of control over it, she knew this would be different. In there, where Faleria had unleashed her magic, she felt everything would change.

'You will still be you, Ash, no matter what happens. And I'll be here. I love you for what you are, for who you've been, and for who you will be. Remember that.'

She nodded. 'I mightn't be able to think properly.' She gripped his hands. 'I need you to guide me. If I hear your voice, I'll listen, I know I will. And if I don't, then you need to run. No heroics – promise me.'

'I promise.'

She tightened her grip on his hands and made her voice as firm as it could be. 'Jarlath, I mean it. Don't you dare.'

'I won't,' he said softly, but she wasn't sure she believed him.

Ash glanced up at the sky. Time was getting away from her – the wheel was turning. She took a deep breath and began her descent into darkness, eyes on Jarlath until she lost sight of him through the smoke.

CHAPTER FIFTY-FIVE

Warm hands were on her face, Mahelivar's voice in her ears. Laeli smelt burning flesh; it took a moment for her to realise it was her flesh as her brother cauterised her wound, his long fingers pressing down on her.

'I'm sorry,' he whispered, holding her steady as she thrashed around, her head smashing into his thighs, his hair falling to tickle her face. 'You're alive, Laeli. Breathe, just breathe.'

Darkness closed over her head again as he used his magic to put her to sleep.

When she woke, she was covered with a blanket, a pillow under her head, another blanket beneath her. She sat up, mouth dry, the pain causing her head to spin. Mahelivar pressed a drink into her hands, helping her lift the cup to her dry lips. She drank deeply, then tossed the cup aside and threw her arms around him, hissing as her wounded shoulder shrieked in objection.

'Father?' she rasped.

Her brother gently removed her arms and indicated the grand bed, where Laeli could see Rhodiri's body. 'He's somewhere else. He hasn't spoken in days. The closer it gets to the solstice the further he is from us.'

Laeli let her brother help her to her feet and lead her across the room so she could sit on the edge of their father's bed. Crystals of ice clung to the trimming of the bedspread and dangled from the headboard like jewels. It was bitterly cold in the Royal Suite, but her father's face was warm, his skin soft and smooth beneath her fingers.

Rhodiri lay like one sleeping, his lips curled into a slight smile, like the one he wore when she did something that pleased him. Would he be pleased now? she wondered. She'd been reckless, she knew it, and now, now … Laeli swallowed, fingers fluttering briefly over her lower belly. As she stroked her father's forehead, she wondered what he was dreaming about, if he still dreamed. She kissed his cheek, then stood, her wound burning, moving to the window to peer out at the snow-covered garden and bare trees.

Her heart ached, the weight of everything she had been through closing over her head. A wave of dizziness slammed into her and she swayed on her feet, Mahelivar catching her before she fell, sweeping her into his arms like she was a child. He carried her to one of the armchairs, depositing her gently and draping a blanket over her. Laeli was too tired and bruised to object. She studied his face through eyes that refused to stay focused. She just wanted to sleep.

Mahelivar ran a hand over his hair, nodding at her wound. 'Does it hurt much?'

'What do you think?'

He smiled at her, a beautiful smile. She'd never told him how beautiful his smile was. It was like their mother's – he was like her: selfless and giving, kind. Mahelivar touched her cheek, where she knew a bruise had already formed.

'My magic is different,' he said softly. 'Stronger.'

She nodded. 'Mine as well. It must be the solstice, but you know as I do, just before that final turn of the wheel, we'll both be powerless, until…'

He swallowed. 'I know.'

'So, we need to get out now, while we can. While that net of hers is gone and before she has time to come up with some other plan.' Laeli made to stand, but Mahelivar put his hand on her shoulder and pushed her gently back down.

'You're amazing. I can't believe you're here.'

'Mahelivar—'

He shook his head firmly. 'You're hurt, Laeli. You're lucky to be alive, you're lucky—' he paused, as if realising something was missing. 'Where's Thalion?'

Laeli's throat constricted and, unable to hide it from the one person who knew her better than anyone, she burst into tears.

'I'm sorry,' her brother murmured, gripping her hand tightly. He smoothed the tangled mass of her hair from her forehead, his fingers warm and gentle.

She sniffed, wiping her nose on her sleeve. 'He isn't dead,' she whispered, her voice breaking. 'I can feel him. But he's a stubborn, stubborn fool who's about to get himself killed and I don't know how I'm going to live without him.'

Mahelivar perched on the arm of the chair and slipped his arm around her. She let his air magic inside her, soothing and calming her, and she let him see what she hadn't realised she longed for until it happened, that which would let her keep some part of her husband long after he had gone.

'Does he know?' Mahelivar's voice was soft.

Laeli shook her head. She buried her face against her brother's chest and sobbed.

'Mahelivar, her magic is wrong. It's wrong. How did she do it? How did the Mother allow it?' Laeli paused. 'What are we going to do?'

Her brother was quiet for a moment, then, softly, 'We'll live, that's what.' His face became harder than Laeli had ever seen it. 'I won't let her kill you.'

Laeli could only nod. She slept again, her head on Mahelivar's thigh, until the sounds of fighting echoed through the hall outside their prison. She sat up, rubbing at her face, forcing the grip of sleep from her body. Swords clashed and then, a ringing silence, followed by a muffled thump, then another.

They waited, eyes pinned to the door as the locks shifted and a crack of the outside world snuck in. Laeli tensed. She should get up, fight, but her heart was bruised, and her body defeated, and she was tired of it all.

Someone was hurled inside, landing in a heap on the floor.

Laeli blinked. She knew that body, that hair that she'd wound her fingers through, those hands that had held her. As Birka shut the door, Laeli scrambled from Mahelivar's arms, crawling on hands and knees, mindless of the wound that pulsed and burnt, mindless of the ache that clawed its way through her muscles.

Thalion was alive, a nasty gash across his thigh that was weeping blood and his nose was probably broken again, but he managed to smile at her as she flung herself at him, his smile shifting to a wince as she landed across his chest.

'I should break you into a million pieces, you head-strong, reckless man,' she whispered fiercely, pressing her mouth to his, tasting the salt and rust of the blood on his lips as he kissed her back.

'Your father ...'

'Not yet.' Laeli's lip quivered but she took a deep breath, pushing the flood of tears aside and sitting back on her heels, her eyes on her husband's face, drinking him in, not caring where they were, only that he was there, and they were both still living.

'I'm so sorry, Thalion,' she whispered, reaching out to run her fingers over his face gently, pushing the hair off his forehead, touching his cheeks and lips. He caught her hand, pressed her fingers to his trembling mouth, before he sighed deeply, his expression shifting as he noticed her wounds.

He sat up, carefully moving aside the torn fabric of her shirt. His face tightened at the sight of the damaged flesh, and the swollen and bruised jaw.

'Who?'

'I'm okay, Thalion.'

His face darkened further; from the other side of the room, Mahelivar sighed. 'She took on the guards. I don't know how many,' he added.

'Nine,' Laeli whispered, then, to her husband, who was staring at her with a mixture of awe and anger, 'Where have you been?'

'Settling a score,' Thalion answered, then gently cupped her bruised and damaged face in his hands and rested his forehead against hers as, around them, the world continued to fall apart and the wheel turned.

CHAPTER FIFTY-SIX

It was dark in the belly of the Rift.

Shadows swathed the sides of the great cavern, light penetrating from above, running down the middle of that charred earth like a golden river. Ash untied Jarlath's rope from her middle, leaving it dangling. She walked slowly, her feet making no noise, the air thick with smoke and sulphur. She could hear nothing, all sound from the world above sucked away into the darkness. There were no rocks or trees or anything down here. Nothing but craggy walls and the ground, which throbbed with a steady, warm beat that sank into her blood.

Her heartbeat echoed through the shadows, her pulse racing, the magic under her skin bubbling and sizzling, pleading with her to release it.

Ash took a deep breath, pulling sweet smoke into her lungs, and let her fire out.

It raged from her skin, curling and coiling around her body, a shroud of flame and burning. Something touched her mind, a gentle brush, inquisitive and soft, like a cat around her ankles.

'Hello?' Ash called, her voice echoing and disjointed. Her fire flamed brighter as a small bundle of orange materialised from the shadows.

The Lasair was small, much smaller than she imagined, no bigger than the fox it had been crafted after. It moved hesitantly, its body shimmering, golden eyes filled with sparks, smoke coiling from its magnificent tail.

Ash felt no fear as it came close, only a loving tug deep inside, a yearning for something she didn't understand. She lowered herself to one knee on that silken earth and held out her hand. The flaming beast hesitated; its fire flickered to a dull orange as it assessed her. It's sentient, Ash realised. The revelation made her smile – she wondered did anyone else know. Did Laeli? Did any of the fae Fire Witches? Ash swallowed, allowing bright flame to lick at her open palm.

'It's okay,' she told the creature. The Lasair tipped its head to the side, before it leapt forward and closed the gap between them, rubbing against her outstretched hand.

Ash's fire flamed brighter and more powerful than ever. In response to her touch, the Lasair glowed. She giggled as it rubbed against her, cavorting playfully, bounding and jumping around her.

She laughed again. How was this the thing that everyone was terrified of?

The Lasair skipped away, peaking over its glowing shoulder, waiting for her. She could hear its voice in her mind, soft and warm, childlike and wise at the same time. It wanted her to follow, so she did, walking deeper into the shadows, no fear in her heart, letting the fire guide her as around her, the walls of the Rift took shape.

Blasted with constant heat, the walls glittered and shone like red jewels. Like the Bloodstones Gedeon had used to steal her magic. She reached out a flaming hand, trailing her fingers along the wall – it was like glass, smooth and silky beneath her skin, and it pulsed with magic, leaving her tingling, pulling a gasp from her throat as that magic flowed into her.

They kept walking, Ash and the blazing fox, the Lasair staying close to her side, her hand dropping to touch its glowing head. Her magic sang and danced in her veins, and it was calm and steady. Waiting.

The fox halted suddenly, then bounded forward to be swallowed by the shadows.

'Don't go!' Ash called, and then sucked in a breath.

She felt them before she saw them, the song her magic sang growing louder as slowly, they came, emerging from the fiery darkness to greet her: deer with magnificent antlers wrapped in fire; horses who tossed flaming manes and stamped, spark-shod, on the earth; large cats, wolves and dogs, their eyes blazing; smaller creatures – squirrels and rodents, rabbits, and weasels; and birds that soared on glowing wings.

Ash held out her arm – a falcon landed, fiery talons gripping her flesh gently. It inclined its blazing head in acknowledgement of what she was.

The Lasair swarmed around her, a writhing mass of flame and energy. She could feel their excitement, their relief, their desire, their whole being, as if it was hers. They were pure fire and magic, instinct and appetite, destruction, and creation.

Her magic thrummed, its song shifting.

Ash glanced up; the creatures of the Rift glanced up also. Blue sky smudged with smoke and the faint light of the winter sun peered down on them.

'Well,' she mused aloud, 'now what?'

As if they could understand her, the flaming birds soared upwards, and she was filled with a desire to fly as well. Her power burst through her, glorious and menacing and beautiful; her feet left the ground, her arms spread, wings of flaming feathers rising from her glowing skin.

What will you give, daughter of fire?

Me, she thought – this time with clarity, with purpose, because she finally understood.

Ash closed her eyes and opened her mind, letting the last of her barriers disintegrate beneath the flames. The magic poured through her, filling every space inside her as she was reborn, forged anew. She was a vessel, a conduit for that power. It tore and raced through her; all that she had been and all that she wanted to be vanished and all that was left was the fire in her veins, her blood, her bones, muscle, her heart.

She was an alchemist now, a creator, destroyer, transformer.

She paused, hovering high above the ground. The edge of the Rift was in sight, so close, yet she didn't want to leave. Beneath her, bright in the darkness, the Lasair waited, their faces turned to her, their glowing eyes on hers.

The fire that was Ash thought it heard a voice calling. It thought it saw a face, peering down as she floated, paused in her hesitation, her desires pulled in different directions.

The fire was darkness and power. It was all-encompassing, slowly consuming her. It rippled through her body, from her body, and it shaped and bent her, and she was the conductor and the composer of the song it sang.

Fire can be a weapon, but it can also be a light in the darkness.

Above her, the world had been ripped apart; those she cared about, ripped apart.

Ash swallowed the burning air – it filled her lungs, as sweet as the finest kiss of oxygen.

The voice called again, and, in that voice, she could hear love. She could hear peace.

The Fire Caster lifted her face to the sky, the Lasair streaming behind her as she left the darkness of the Rift behind and rose into the light.

CHAPTER FIFTY-SEVEN

Yasper thought the plan was solid.

'This is a terrible plan,' Fox growled. She pointed to the crude map of the city Yasper had drawn with the help of some of his halfkin friends. If anyone knew the city back to front and inside out, it was the halfkin.

Yasper raised his eyebrows. 'What's wrong with it?'

Nerida, and some of the halfkin, looked at Fox warily.

'If you think the Watch are going to leave the outside of the *Mages' Keep* unguarded, you're an idiot,' she said, sitting back and folding her arms. Yasper's eyebrows lifted further, and he shot Senan a look.

The Mage-Witch shrugged. 'She might have a point.'

'You might be biased,' the blond man retorted, before sighing and rubbing at the back of his neck. 'Alright, so who has a better plan?'

Senan, Fox, Elan, and Yasper, as well as Nerida and Gem and about ten halfkin, were in the cellar of one of the beer houses, abandoned in the chaos the city had become. It was growing dark in their hide-out, the one window at street level barely letting in enough light to see by. Their bellies were as empty as their hands – Yasper's supply of bullets was dangerously low, and no one except Fox carried any weapons of any sort.

Fox had been mumbling beneath her breath about it constantly, her fingers stroking the hilt of her blades as she did so.

She thought they were unprepared, and she was probably right.

While they were away, Gedeon and the Watch had tightened their hold on the city. The streets had been swept clean of pickpockets and prostitutes; the prison was full to bursting. Gem had been hiding out in the dark corners of alleys. She was thin and pale and grubby, but her eyes still shone with determination.

The Watch had gutted buildings across the city. For the first time in living memory, the fire pits had been left unguarded and had gone out, the Marshals gone to ground or fled with those who managed to get out. The road leading to Tyllcarric had been virtually deserted, but they had seen evidence of the city's refugees as they drew closer – Fox had pointed out the areas where people had stopped and camped, and they found random things scattered along the roadsides and beneath the trees: shoes and books, articles of clothing, food that had been trampled and was now a meal fit for ants and worms.

As the city had come into view, Senan had put a lock on his magic. Gedeon would sense him immediately, he figured, and before he allowed that to happen, they needed time – to rest, to gather who and what they could to aid them, and to plan.

Since the moment Gedeon had removed those Bloodstones from their box and stolen Ash's magic, Senan knew it would be this way. He knew, as surely as he knew the sweet kiss of the forest and the rich smell of the earth beneath his feet, that he would need to get close to Gedeon. He knew it would be his former mentor's blood on his hands.

And he felt sick because of it.

The one thing, the one light in this darkness, was that Ash would not be the one to end it, would not have to take another man's life. Part of Senan still hoped it wouldn't come to that, but the last time he'd looked into Gedeon's eyes, there hadn't been much of the man he'd once known shining there, only a lust for power that had driven the High Mage to do such terrible things.

Senan wasn't walking into this to be a hero. He wasn't one for heroic actions – he'd spent the better part of his life hiding from the world and there was nothing heroic in that – but his dual magic gave him an edge over other mages: he was unpredictable, hard to plan against. Magic like his was dangerous; he understood it – had always understood it, regardless of how wrong it was to fear what was different.

It had been that knowledge that had driven him to find Ash, to school her as best he could, not only in magic, but doing what he could to keep the fear of herself at bay, to allow her the time to come to accept what she was, and to embrace what she had been given. He didn't know if he'd succeeded in that, but as she'd left the Delta, Jarlath in tow, the eyes that had met his across the water were steady. He could sense the fire inside her; it had been growing more powerful the longer they'd dwelt within range of the Rift.

He didn't imagine he'd see her again, that he'd see any of them again once this was over. He thought of his home buried in the trees with a pang of regret and longing – perhaps, when he was gone, someone would find it, someone like him, who would love it as he did, and use it not to hide from the world, but to give themselves over to the earth, to live closely with the Mother.

Fox touched his knee and leant forward again, fingertip tracing the outline of the Keep on the crudely drawn map. 'There is more than one way in,' she said, methodically tapping the map. 'Here, here and here.' She glanced up, those shrewd amber eyes glowing as she surveyed them one by one. 'The front door, obviously, the back entrance which leads to the palace, and a little-known side door that the most trusted of Gedeon's friends know about.'

'Your entrance, I take it?' Yasper asked.

Fox snorted and sat back. 'Don't be stupid. I wasn't a trusted friend, but I was good at listening and watching. There are all sorts of things that go on in this city if you know where to look and who to follow.'

Gem rubbed at her tired face. 'Since you've been gone, Yas, most of the cathouses, beer halls and gaming houses have been boarded up or burnt out. Drinking, gambling, and flesh are not big sellers in Gedeon's brave new world.'

Yasper nodded, as if this was to be expected. 'Alright. We target the areas where the Watch have been most active, which are around the market squares and on most of the main streets.'

'The Watch still has an air mage with each unit, I assume?' Senan asked.

'They do,' Gem said slowly, 'but they've also decided to arm themselves with some of the nastiest dogs I've ever seen. Apparently, they brought them in from Garlathe, from the prison camps. The guards have been using them to keep the prisoners in line. Most people are not fond of dying underground for Gedeon's darn Bloodstones.'

'Can you speak dog, Elan? I remember you used to have all the alley mutts following you around,' Fox said to her brother, who shrugged skinny shoulders. It had been Elan who had found them their horses for the journey back to the city from the Delta, the animals trotting out of the forest at his silent call.

'These are no alley mutts,' Gem said seriously. 'They're huge, like wolves, and they're vicious. I've seen them tear a man's flesh to pieces in seconds.' She shuddered.

Fox only shrugged as her brother rubbed at his face with grubby hands. Elan's pointed face folded into a frown. 'I can try but if they've been trained to kill, it might not work.'

'What about the men of the Watch?' Senan asked. Oden growled at the mention of the Watch, the shadow-dog more attuned to Senan's emotions than he ever had been before. He let the dog bunt against his side, a comforting gesture for them both.

'Leave them to us,' Yasper grinned. 'It won't be difficult to find enough people who have a bone to pick with the Watch. There's enough thieves and criminals and hookers who the Watch have ticked off over the years. They'll be happy to take a shot at them.'

'And the mages?' Senan asked quietly.

Yasper held up his pistol. 'Bullets kill them like they do everyone else.'

Senan frowned. 'It isn't their fault though. They're being coerced.'

Gem sighed. 'Senan, I can understand how you feel, but there might not be any choice. Ash isn't here to control that fire, and I don't want to burn to death.'

They all froze as footsteps marched past the window; Senan glimpsed polished black boots and between them, the bare feet of what he thought was a child. His stomach rolled, his resolve strengthening. He could do this.

Gem had told them that during those first few days, people wandered the city in a daze, their expressions blank, like they couldn't make decisions or act for themselves. Mass coercion, Senan had realised. Air magic, wielded by someone whose powers had been honed to manipulate: Darian.

But it hadn't lasted, and as people came back to themselves, more and more packed up what little they owned and left the city. There had been many deaths – Senan had seen the bodies himself, strung up in the main square next to the effigy of the Corn Mother, their flesh blackened and peeling like overripe fruit, the stench of decay woven through the air. So desecrated were the corpses, he hadn't been able to tell if they were male or female, young or old.

Earlier that day, Senan, Fox, and Elan had left the horses not far from the city and had slipped through the main gates under the cover of darkness, Fox's blades slashing the throats of the guards, Yasper's bullets ready to rip through whoever might intercept them. The streets had been eerie in the darkness, no lanterns lit, no sign of life anywhere, save Watchmen stationed at each corner.

With air mages roaming about, their faces blank, Senan couldn't risk undoing the binds he'd placed on his magic the closer they came to Tyllcarric, so it had been up to Fox to clear them a path through the streets in silence. She'd slit six throats that night, Yasper and Elan helping her pull the bodies out of sight and tuck them into corners where no one would think to look.

A halfkin, slick as shadows, had appeared from nowhere and told Yasper to follow him. The boy had led them to the cellar they now hid in. Nerida had wanted to go to the Academy straight away, but Senan had convinced her to wait. He was also worried about Radella and the students they left behind. When he voiced his concerns, the halfkin girl told him all fully-fledged mages and the White Woman were being held at the Keep, in the cells below the building. The other students had either managed to get out of the city or were locked down in the Academy.

'How will we draw Gedeon out?' Yasper asked eventually. They were all looking at the Keep on the map. Even on paper, the place was dark and oppressive. Silence fell.

Senan squared his shoulders. Before he'd spoken a single word, Fox glared.

'Forget it.'

'I'm the one thing he is likely to leave that building for,' he said gently.

She shook her head, eyes shining. 'No.'

'Yes.' He stroked the back of her hand, and she did not pull away from him. 'You have to let him catch me, Fox. I have to get inside the Keep.'

'And then what?' she argued, her voice rising. 'You're not a killer, Senan.'

He swallowed. She hadn't been in *The Solstice House* that night. He still felt sick thinking about it. He had never used his magic in that way before – he'd never harmed another living creature in his whole life. It felt wrong to use life-giving earth magic to take it away, but everything about this situation was wrong. There would be time later to atone for what he'd done, the Mother willing, but, for now, he needed to get into the Keep. He needed to find Gedeon. If he could talk with him, maybe, maybe he could change things.

Yasper stood up and stretched, his hands on his lower back. 'Whatever you're going to do, be ready to do it by midnight tomorrow night. We will give you a clear path to the Keep. What you do from then on is up to you two.' He paused, a half-grin on his face. 'The Anomaly and the assassin. It has a nice ring to it. Maybe someone will write a song about you two one day.'

Fox growled, making him laugh.

'Just make sure someone kills the bastard,' Nerida hissed, her usually pleasant voice low and deadly. She had sat apart from the planning, her arms pulled around her, eyes wide, her blonde hair glowing in the darkness. Now, those eyes flashed with fire. 'For Ash. And for everyone he's hurt. And rescue Radella and the mages.'

They spent the rest of the day and the night in the cellar, sleeping wherever they could find comfort, Fox curled in Senan's arms, his back pressed against the cold wall. Oden slept on his other side. Before dawn, one of the halfkin crept out, returning an hour later with food and water snatched from the Mother knew where. They shared their meagre supplies and waited out the day. Outside, they could hear the occasional shout, but it seemed the city was as tired and beaten as Senan felt.

Gedeon was winning. What Senan didn't understand was what the High Mage hoped to gain from all of this. Surely, he was smart enough to realise that his three-way alliance wasn't going to hold.

Senan closed his eyes.

Of course. It was never supposed to. He wondered which of his allies Gedeon planned to double-cross first. Was he simply going to play one off the other and let them kill each other, or did he have a more sinister objective? Senan thought about the Bloodstones and shivered. Gedeon could not get his hands on Ash again.

As night enclosed the city once more, Yasper ripped the top off one of the crates packed against the wall, withdrawing a bottle of whiskey. He pulled the cork with his teeth.

'Well,' he said, 'I can't promise we're going to win this battle, but I'll be happy dying knowing I fought.' He lifted the bottle to his lips and took a long gulp, passing it to Gem. By the time the bottle made it back to Yasper, it was empty. Senan took a moment to look at each person in turn before they stepped out into the bleakness that was waiting for them. They didn't wish each other luck – they all needed more than that.

Yasper's plan was to hit the prison first – he was confident those locked up would be willing to fight with their bare hands if necessary. His halfkin friends had been busy sneaking around in the darkness, ferrying messages from Yasper to others across the city. From the prison, Yasper's rebel army would move through the streets, taking out the Watch wherever they could, starting with those stationed nearest the Keep.

Nerida was going to go back to the Academy. As they prepared to leave, Yasper pressed a pistol into her hand and gave her a fast lesson on how to use it when she couldn't be convinced otherwise. The girl tucked the weapon into her belt, squared her shoulders, and was gone.

Elan gave his sister a sharp hug.

'We just found each other,' he whispered, and Senan felt a stab of guilt.

Fox's expression was fierce. 'Don't die, then.'

He smiled and followed Yasper and the others.

Senan settled in to wait, Fox sitting by his side. The shadow-dog lay his head in her lap, but she had no idea Oden was there.

'You don't have to do this, Fox.'

'You don't understand,' she said quietly. 'I've dreamt of it, Senan, so clear and real it was like it had already happened, and then I'd wake up and still be in that shit hole of a house. The night Laeli pressed those blades into my hands I became me again. I've killed for my freedom. This time, I'll kill for me, and for you, for us, because we owe him the taste of death. This will be the last thing I have to do before I am completely free. Only … once it's done, I don't know how to be free. I don't know how to own myself.'

'You'll live, Fox,' Senan replied softly; she let him run his fingers down her cheek. 'Just live, one day at a time.'

CHAPTER FIFTY-EIGHT

Laeli woke with a start, removing the comforting weight of Thalion's arm from her middle and sitting up, rubbing at her face. They'd been sleeping on the floor, wrapped in blankets that didn't keep out the chill. She was desperately thirsty and touched her belly gently, praying that the tiny being growing there was alright. She'd been dreaming of the Rift, of the Lasair, and of Faleria's magic. She dreamt of a bird of fire that swept over the landscape. She dreamt of music, of the song of destruction and creation.

She dreamt of power.

The solstice was upon them, the heartbeat of the Earth a steady thrum.

Mahelivar was sitting on the other side of the room. He didn't speak; he didn't have to. They both felt it deep inside, in the very core of their bodies, in their blood and bone, that which they would one day be returned to. She who gave them their existence, their magic, the essence of who and what they were. She who made them custodians of the earth they walked upon.

She who turned the wheel.

Mahelivar's green eyes glowed in the darkness.

Outside, the full moon cast her light over a world painted white. The trees bowed under the weight of snow, crystals of ice dripping from their bare branches. In the forest, armed men patrolled and, outside the wide window, four fae stood with their backs to the room.

Mahelivar climbed to his feet and moved to their father's side as Thalion woke with a grumble. Laeli shushed him, pulling away from his warmth to join her brother.

'Give us light,' Mahelivar murmured, and Laeli sent two balls of simmering flame into the air. They floated above them, casting their fiery glow over the room like twin suns. Together, Laeli and Mahelivar lifted Rhodiri's body, lying him gently on the floor. He barely weighed anything at all, so insubstantial he had become, nothing remaining of the vessel that had held his power except a shell.

Thalion was watching curiously, but he remained silent. Somewhere in the back of Laeli's mind was the knowledge that no human had ever witnessed what he was about to witness.

Once their father was settled, the siblings sank to their knees and took their places on either side of his body, opposite each other.

The heartbeat of the earth stilled for a moment, and the balance of everything paused and waited, and then, in slow motion, the wheel turned that final notch.

That heartbeat stopped as Rhodiri's eyes flew open, and he reached for his children. Laeli gripped his hand tightly, her brother doing the same. She kissed her father's wrist; his skin was as warm as the summer sun over the gardens. She blinked away the tears as he smiled at them. The balls of floating fire coated his skin golden, the light catching in his eyes and hair.

'What is remembered, lives,' he said softly.

'What is remembered, lives,' they echoed.

His eyes fell closed again, shutters over a forest of memory and life. They placed his hands in the middle of his chest, folded over one another, and sat back. His breathing gradually slowed until his chest was still.

Mindless of the ice and the snow, the Earth came to collect, the Mother reaching out to embrace her child. Grass erupted from the floor around Rhodiri's body, pushing up through the stone with ease. Vines crept from all corners of the room, shooting across the cold floor, and coating the ceiling and the walls as the room became a tomb of life. Thalion sucked in an astonished breath as flowers exploded from the grass, but Laeli didn't acknowledge it, didn't turn from her father.

With unnatural speed, the green life covered Rhodiri's body, enveloping him with gentle purpose. As her father's face was entombed, Laeli gasped and reached for her brother's hand as light, white and hot, speared through her.

Her hair lifted from her scalp and her skin tingled as the power of the earth flowed through her veins, a river of undeniable magnitude. It sang and burnt and swam through her body, carving a path through the landscape of her, as if she were a conduit for something beyond her earthly form. She became something ancient and primal and of the trees and the water and the rich soil beneath the grass. Her mind shuddered with the weight of it, and then soared, free of everything that held it.

It ripped down hallways, past people and out of the palace, away into the forest, brushing against the trunks of trees and the bodies of animals tucked away from the cold. She floated over the Rift, that great wound in the earth silent, as if sleeping, no flames flickering in its depths but somewhere, beneath the trees, was fire. And it was moving, but Laeli did not pause. Stretching and seeking, her mind grazed the border that separated Eshlune from the human world, and she went further, over rocks and hard earth. She brushed the snowy peaks of the mountains and paused.

There was something else, holding tightly to her, something that bound her, that held her where she belonged as she turned to the west, to a land coated in snow and kissed with wind.

She retreated, following that glowing link, that tether, reeling her mind back, her consciousness shrinking as she shoved the power away, propelled it out of her and towards her brother, feeling that glorious potential flow from her body and into their linked hands. The white heat and light faded, and she was herself again, panting and sweating and blinking back tears of loss and relief in the cold air.

Laeli lifted her eyes as the heart of the earth began to beat once more.

There, on Mahelivar's head, showing through his hair, were the buds of antlers, so small they were almost hidden. She gasped, extending her hand to touch them at the same time he did.

Their eyes met.

'You could have kept it,' he said.

'I told you already, I don't want it, Mahelivar. This is your path. The Morrigan chose it for you,' she said firmly.

'The Cailleach meant it for you.'

Laeli shook her head. 'I have a different path.' For the second time in recent days, she willingly let her brother inside her mind. His eyes widened, then narrowed. He leant sideways, peering around Laeli to Thalion.

'You married my sister?'

'Sorry you missed it. I'll marry her again, if you like.'

Mahelivar gave a bark of laughter. The door was flung open, making them all jump. Kiarda stepped into the room. A flurry of snow blew in with her and Laeli's blood turned to ice. Kiarda's gaze fell to the grass and the flowers, so green and alive against the white floor.

'He's gone then.'

'Yes,' Mahelivar said, climbing to his feet. Laeli stood slowly; with her eyes on Kiarda, she held out her hand and Thalion closed his fingers around hers. She wanted to throw herself in front of him, shield him with her body. He was completely vulnerable, so human in that moment that she wished she'd pushed him harder and forced him to stay away.

But if this was to be her end, she was glad he was with her.

Kiarda looked from Laeli to Mahelivar. Her eyes lingered on Mahelivar's head.

'You both die.'

People rushed into the room; weapons raised. Laeli flexed her fingers, but Kiarda lifted the staff of the Cailleach, and they were frozen where they stood. She wanted to scream. She wanted to fight, but Kiarda's magic, the Cailleach's magic, was too strong, and Mahelivar – he could not yet use what she had given him, not until the Goddess allowed it.

Mahelivar was dragged from the room, Laeli ripped from Thalion's grip; she heard one of the men offer to kill the human. She struggled against the hands that held her, reaching inside for her magic but it wouldn't come, her flame flickering and dying. Her wounded shoulder screamed as loudly as her voice.

'Don't kill him yet,' Kiarda said, her voice fading as Laeli was pulled further away. 'He might be useful later. Leave him here and …'

Silence, only their feet scuffling on the floor, their heavy breathing, Laeli's tears that she hadn't realised she was shedding.

The doors to the throne room were thrown open and brother and sister tossed inside.

CHAPTER FIFTY-NINE

Where she walked, the forest burnt.

Jarlath glanced behind him. The night couldn't hide the destruction she left behind; moonlight caressed the blackened trunks and scorched earth gently. The smell of burning was all around them, the heat searing. Jarlath held his hand in front of his face, following at a distance. Ash was lit up like a torch ahead of him, the Lasair following in her wake. Flames trailed her like a cape, the ground sizzling beneath her feet.

She didn't slow as the grass gave way to a white blanket of powdery snow. It melted as she ploughed through it, and the ground ran with water. Jarlath watched as that water converged on the trees around it and, though he could hardly believe it, the grass grew before his eyes, the blackened trees shedding their damaged bark like skin. Leaves began to bud along the branches and on the ground, flowers and fungi exploded from the earth.

What had Laeli told them?

Fire destroys, but it also creates.

Mouth hanging open, Jarlath gaped at Ash, in complete awe of her. He didn't fear it any longer, what she was, what she could do, what she would do. He simply loved her, all of her. Up ahead, she paused, her hair moving in an invisible wind, her body bright and golden inside the cage of fire she'd made around herself. She tipped her head to the side, waiting, the Lasair turning to watch him as well.

'Keep going, Ash. We're nearly there.'

Her eyes slid to his, bathed in gold and rimmed with fire – with the promise of death and destruction, with creation and life.

A man stepped from the trees on the path ahead of them. Another man joined him, then another and another, until there were at least twenty armed men standing before them. Some were wearing furs and others were fae, with flowing hair and pale skin. Jarlath drew the dagger at his hip but before he could make a move, before any of them could make a move, the Lasair streamed forward.

Ash lifted her arms and unleashed white-hot flame, the fire racing from her body, threads of gold weaving between the Lasair, rushing forward to burn and incinerate and reduce the world to nothing. Jarlath gulped, his mind hurling backwards to a battlefield of fire and death and burning bodies as he closed his eyes and waited for the screaming.

But there was only silence.

He cracked open his eyes and peered through the trees.

There was nothing left of Kiarda and Hadrian's men. Nothing but piles of ash that, as he watched, were snatched by the breeze and tossed to the night sky.

He swallowed. No fear.

Not of her.

'Keep going,' he managed, and Ash continued walking, one foot in front of the other. It was like she'd told him – she trusted him to guide her, she needed him to guide her, because the fire had a mind of its own. She'd told him what had happened to the High Mage, unable to look at him as she spoke, afraid of his judgement, but he'd given none, not anymore.

The walls of Sitra came into view, shining white in the glowing moonlight. Men ran screaming from the gates, their weapons tossed aside. They became ashes on the ground, obliterated as if they'd never existed. Ash passed through the gates, Jarlath following her, the smaller creatures from the Rift frolicking around her body, rubbing themselves against her joyfully, while the large cats and wolves stalked in her wake, the deer and horses following on their heels.

Inside the city, the once beautiful, lush gardens and lawns were withered and frozen. Snow floated through the air, although the sky was clear of clouds. It was bitterly cold, colder than Estilleon, and Jarlath shivered, drawing closer to Ash and the Lasair, drawn to the heat they radiated. The snow melted and life sprang from the earth. Anyone they met was destroyed. Where the bodies fell, their ashes bled into the melted snow; flowers pushed their heads from the ground.

Once they reached the courtyard, the palace was in sight. Jarlath stayed as close to Ash and the Lasair as the scorching heat would allow. His eyes burnt and his skin felt paper-thin, ready to split. He saw a flickering shadow beneath one of the great trees, its branches bare. He paused, sucking in an astonished breath as the shadow became solid, and a hunched old woman stood beneath the tree. She reached up to remove her veil, her withered face twisted with age, skin-tinged blue with the cold, her eyes glowing red in the fiery light.

Jarlath swallowed as an enormous grey wolf, as big as a small horse, appeared by her side, the memory of another wolf still stamped firmly on his brain. Neither woman nor wolf moved; they simply watched, two sets of eyes trailing Ash and the Lasair. He glanced ahead; the smooth walls of the palace were close.

When he looked over his shoulder towards that skeletal tree, both the woman and the wolf were gone.

CHAPTER SIXTY

Kiarda's guards, one human and one fae, enjoyed tormenting their prisoner as much as his father's did. The fae held a vicious looking spear with a barbed end, perfect for tearing flesh. He traced the line of Thalion's throat with the sharp tip, his grey eyes menacing.

'She'll be dead soon,' he said.

'Then so will you,' Thalion promised.

The fae laughed, withdrawing the spear and sticking his face close to Thalion's. 'And what are you going to do about it, human?'

Thalion slammed his head into the fae's face. Howling like an animal, the man stumbled sideways as Thalion flung his head back, connecting with soft tissue and a hard cheekbone. He heard something crack and his vision danced with black spots. The man holding him yelped and released his grip; Thalion freed his arms as his captor slid to the floor, moaning in pain.

The fae held his shattered face with one hand while the other lifted the spear. Thalion twisted away from it, smashing his fist into that already broken face. The spear and its owner fell to the ground. Thalion knelt, one knee in the fae's chest, and hit. That face exploded but he kept on hitting until his knuckles were torn and the pulpy mass of the fae's head soaked the floor and was splattered across Thalion's cheeks.

He'd never killed a man with his bare hands before. He sat back and examined his blood-smeared knuckles – misshapen from numerous breaks, his fingers strong, capable of holding a sword for hours. His hands were the hands that would build the future of his country. They were the hands that held his wife's body, her face, her heart, that which gave him strength.

Thalion sucked in a ragged breath.

These are the hands that will hold your children.

He was not dying tonight.

He staggered to his feet, turning to the other man, who was moaning and clutching his cheek. Slowly, the man's eyes moved about the room and fell on what was left of his companion's face. He swallowed, pushing himself to his knees and preparing to stand, but Thalion's fist connected with the side of his face, and he fell back against the wall, unconscious.

Wiping his bloody hands on his legs, Thalion bent to collect the fallen spear. He weighed it in his hands, spun it around. Lighter than what he was used to, but it would do. He pulled daggers from belts, tucking them into his own, and stepped outside. The guards were gone.

The hallways were deserted, which made him uneasy. Where were his father's men? Kiarda's? She'd brought hundreds with her and yet, there was no one here, human or fae. He paused at the end of the hallway, listening as voices floated through the space beyond the walls.

Gripping the spear tight, he stepped around the corner. The men froze, noting his clothes, trying to decide if he was friend or foe. While they were puzzling it out, he slashed one throat with the razor-sharp end of the spear and shoved a dagger in the chest of the other, before continuing towards the throne room, his mind locked on his wife, willing her to be alive.

He thought about what he'd witnessed. She'd explained what would happen to her father before they left Estilleon and, if he was understanding correctly, Laeli had given the power she received to her brother. She'd chosen not to accept it, to let that power go.

She would have been a Queen.

'Gods, Laeli,' he whispered. His mind was spinning.

At the end of the next hallway was the throne room. The door opened; Thalion threw himself around the corner, pressing against the wall as two men walked away from the room, heading in the opposite direction. There had to be another way in, and he still didn't know what he was going to do once he got in there. His body was exhausted; he was running on adrenaline, and pain. Cursing under his breath, he backed away, retracing his steps until he found a door that led outside.

He stepped out into the early morning light and gazed across the city; there was nothing green here anymore. The sight of so much snow and ice shouldn't bother him, but it did.

His head shot up; smoke and burning.

Laeli.

Thalion raced towards the smoke, killing two men on his way. They were running away from something, their faces twisted in fear and, in the distance, he could hear panicked shouts. As he rounded the corner of the palace, Thalion skidded to a halt, his stomach plummeting.

The main courtyard was filled with flames, twisted into the shape of animals. He had seen a creature like that before and had seen what it could do. There was no way he could fight such power. Around him, bodies lay face-down, still smoking, their flesh bubbling.

'They're kind of impressive, aren't they? Terrifying, but impressive,' said a voice at his elbow. Thalion swung around to find Jarlath, leaning casually against a wall. The man at his feet was dead, a dagger sticking from his throat.

Jarlath grinned. 'I don't think I've ever seen you frightened before,' he said simply. 'It's a nice change. Makes me feel better to know you're as human as the rest of us.' His calm was bewildering, until Thalion realised who, or what, was standing in the middle of that pack of flaming creatures and death.

The Fire Caster.

She was floating a foot from the ground, her body held aloft by the flames that raged around her.

'Come on.' Jarlath stepped past him, turning back swiftly. 'Wait, where's Laeli?'

Thalion growled. 'The Witch has her. Her brother as well. I'm not sure where she's taken them, but I would guess they're in the throne room. The King is dead. I was working out how to rescue them.'

Jarlath gestured to the girl, Ash, and her horde of unnatural animals. In a daze, Thalion watched as Jarlath approached the Lasair, keeping his distance as the heat of their flaming bodies blasted them, the air sucked dry. Sparks drifted from the ball of fire that was Ash. She didn't move, as if she was waiting for something.

'Ash,' Jarlath called; she turned her head as he motioned towards the palace and without a word, without a single gesture to show she understood, she turned towards that grand building of white stone and marble. As they neared, Thalion kept one eye on Ash and the other on their surroundings, although he couldn't imagine anyone would be stupid enough to come near them. He hurried to catch Jarlath's arm.

'Let me go in first. If Laeli …' he stopped, unable to say it, afraid that if he said it out loud, it would be real. He swallowed, forced it away.

Jarlath nodded in understanding, calling out to Ash again.

Thalion took a wide berth around the burning girl and the Lasair, staying as far away from that magical fire as he possibly could. Ash let him past, her golden eyes following his every step, the hair on the back of his neck standing to attention, soldiers commanded by his quickly withering nerves, as he realised those creatures of fire were watching him also.

Back inside, he hurried down the hall and rounded a corner, coming face-to-face with a bleeding Solen. The fae was clutching his side; blood dribbled from between his fingers and his breathing was harsh. Two men lay behind him, an arrow and a dagger protruding from their chests. Further down the hall were more bodies.

'Where is she?' Solen managed. Those golden eyes were dull.

Thalion motioned towards the throne room. With a painful grimace, the captain of the fae guard drew his sword. Thalion's muscles bunched but, instead of swinging the sword at him, Solen flipped it in his hands and held it out, hilt first.

Keeping his eyes on Solen's face, Thalion reached out to take the sword from the fae's bloodied fingers. He curled his hand around the grip, nodding his thanks, his throat thick. Solen sank to the floor, his back against the wall. Blood was running freely down his side.

'You need to get out of here,' Thalion said roughly. He pointed back the way he had come. 'The Fire Caster is on her way and unless you're fireproof ...'

Solen's golden eyes widened, and he struggled to his feet; Thalion gripped his upper arm and hauled him the last bit up, then turned towards the throne room as the captain of the fae guard stumbled off in the other direction.

The man on guard duty was easily killed. His body hadn't hit the floor before Thalion pushed open the doors, running through two men who didn't have a chance to draw their weapons. The third man, a fae, was faster but, by the time he was dead, his chest was opened so deep Thalion could watch his heart beat its last.

With the sword and spear dripping, he turned towards the dais as a blast of icy air wrapped around his body.

CHAPTER SIXTY-ONE

As the wheel turned to midnight, magic thrumming through the earth, Senan and Fox climbed out of the cellar and into the streets. They'd heard fighting, but the sound had been muted by the heavy stone ceiling above them. Now, the city was brimming with it. They cast a quick glance at each other, Fox pulling her blades free, spinning them between her fingers. Her eyes were hard, shining with the promise of death to any who got in their way.

They hurried through the streets, Fox leading the way. The lanterns were extinguished, but a haze hung over the city; not far from them, the remains of a building pulsed smoke into the sky. They passed dead Watchmen lying face-down on the stones. An air mage in white robes, a flower of blood blooming from her chest, lay beside them. Senan swallowed and looked away.

In the street approaching the main square, as promised, Yasper led a large group of men and women: street brawlers and drunks, thieves and gamblers, cathouse whores and halfkin. The scum of the city – risen, their rage palpable. Senan could feel it threaded through the air. He watched as a woman in a red dress clubbed a black-shirted man with what looked like a table leg. Blood splattered her face, but she ignored it. The dogs of the Watch turned on their masters as Elan worked whatever fae magic he had in his veins. Fox laughed wickedly at the look on the Watchmen's faces as their dogs snarled and snapped at their legs.

The air was alive with gunfire and shouting, with screams of victory and the scent of death, the streets coated with blood and running feet. Fox took hold of Senan's arm and steered him into the shadows. In the next street, they found more Watchmen, dead and dying. Fox cut the throats of anyone they discovered still breathing. Her face was set, her fingers steady on the knives, her grip tightening the closer they came to the Keep.

The main square was devoid of life; only the dead inhabited this space now. Above them, the Mages' Keep loomed like a beast out of the darkness, the spires of the palace poking above it desperately. Fox growled but hid herself when Senan told her to, and he waited as the sounds of fighting grew dimmer.

Taking a deep breath, Senan released his magic, letting it call Gedeon to him. His air magic rose into the night and flew towards the Keep and his fingers curled as grass poked through the stones.

From out of the shadows, the Spirit Rake came, hands raised. There were four Watchmen with him, including the blonde-haired Mal, smiling with wicked glee. One side of his face was burnt, and the disfigurement only served to accentuate his cruelty. Thankfully, there was no air mage, no fire for Senan to have to contend with. Darian's magic slammed into his head, and he let it, falling to his knees as Oden howled, and then vanished.

Senan allowed Darian into the deepest part of his mind, where he quickly ensnared him with a net of magic. It was subtle and delicate, and Senan's power slid alongside Darian's, the other man having no idea of what he'd done. A trick; he silently thanked the fae Witch who had tutored him all those years ago.

The Spirit Rake smiled. 'The Anomaly. Gedeon has been expecting you.'

'I'm sure he has,' Senan managed. His knees were trembling. At a nod from Darian, the Watchmen rushed forward and grabbed his arms, and Senan let them march him away.

The Keep was as silent as the grave, dark and empty and suffocating in its quietness. He was led up flights of steps, one after the other, his feet heavy, his brow littered with sweat as he kept as light a hold as he could manage on Darian's power. Behind him, moving swiftly through the dark, he could sense Fox, as silent as the shadows she darted through.

He was taken to Gedeon's office this time.

The High Mage was sitting calmly behind his desk as if he'd just finished some paperwork. The Watch dragged Senan in and shoved him into a chair, where he was quickly bound with ropes of air. Gedeon's magic.

'Thank you, Mal,' Gedeon said smoothly. 'You can go.'

The men left, closing the door behind them, Mal sparing Senan a knowing smile.

A sigh. 'You've made a grave mistake coming here tonight.'

Gedeon's face was a hideous thing to behold. The damage done by Ash's magic would never be undone. The High Mage reached up to stroke the leathery skin on his cheek.

'I think it looks good on me, don't you? We all earn our scars, Senan.'

'Gedeon, think about what you are doing,' Senan began, but found the words stuck in his throat. The High Mage shook his head regretfully.

'That's the difference between you and me, my friend. All I've done these past twenty years is think. And think and think, so much that I grew tired of it, and decided it was time to act.' He paused, stroking the broken skin on his face once more. 'If only you could think as well, dream as I do. We could still be allies, Senan. There is still a place for you at my side. With your power, with mine, we could rule Aileryan.'

Senan shook his head, letting his eyes speak for him, letting Gedeon see that no matter what he was offered, he would never ally himself with such terror and pain, with such bloodshed and ambition.

Gedeon sighed sadly.

The door opened. The High Mage's expression didn't change as Fox stepped inside, dragging Mal with her. Her blade was pressed against his throat, the young man's eyes wide. Her other hand sent a knife flying across the room. It embedded itself deep in Darian's shoulder. The Spirit Rake was taken by surprise. He hissed, falling back against the wall, and released his grip on Senan's mind.

Fox launched a second blade in Gedeon's direction. Her aim was true, and it would have burrowed between his eyes had he not held up a hand. The knife paused in mid-air and slowly spun around. Senan heard Fox swallow.

'My dear,' Gedeon said with a smile. 'I see Estilleon wasn't able to break you.' He stood up and came around to the other side of the table, the knife following him obediently. 'You've still not learnt any manners. Please, come in.'

She pushed her knife closer to Mal's pale flesh. 'I'll kill him.'

Gedeon shrugged. 'No doubt you will. It will be a waste, though. He reminds me of you, did you know that? The same tenacity, same ferociousness.' He sighed. 'Go ahead then, if it will make you feel better, Fox.'

Senan saw the look of shock on Mal's face. He was expendable, like everyone. The young man struggled then, realising his master wasn't going to fight for his life. Fox calmly slit his throat and he tumbled to the floor, the scent of his blood ripping through the air.

Gedeon flicked his hand. Fox's knife flew, coming to a halt in front of her face. She lifted her chin, eyes burning, that promise of death never faltering. The knife moved back, allowing her to step further into the room, until she was standing beside Senan. He cast a quick glance at Darian. The Spirit Rake had his hand held to his wounded shoulder, a deep scowl on his face.

Senan clamped down on the piece of Darian's magic caught in his net; he imagined claws, blades like the ones Fox carried, a club like that wielded by the whore in the street. He imagined bullets and arrows, spears of sharpened wood and his power obeyed, twisting itself into all the shapes of violence Senan could think of. Darian screamed and went limp, falling into a faint as Senan's power ground down, pushing into his head forcefully.

'Well, well,' Gedeon murmured. 'I can see this will be harder than I anticipated.'

CHAPTER SIXTY-TWO

A smug Kiarda was sprawled on the throne again, Rhodiri's crown on her head. Laeli and Mahelivar were standing either side of her, a wall of shimmering blue surrounding them, each one guarded by two fae, whose faces were tight in concentration. Laeli's eyes widened, and she shook her head a fraction as Thalion walked the length of that room until he was standing before her, that icy wind still curled around his body. A single tear rolled down Laeli's cheek, freezing at the curve of her jaw.

'The conquering hero,' Kiarda purred. 'She can watch you die. The last thing your princess will hear will be your screams. The last thing she'll see will be your blood painted across the floor. Or maybe,' she continued, 'I'll kill her first and you can watch her die.'

'Or maybe,' Thalion retorted, 'I'll open you up and rip your heart from your chest and show it to you while it beats its last.'

Kiarda laughed in delight.

Laeli struggled. Crystals of ice littered the ground at her feet; the more she struggled, the more they grew, until they inched up her legs. The Witch guarding her was starting to sweat.

'Tell me,' Kiarda said in a low voice. 'Which one of you killed my daughter?'

'I did,' Thalion answered.

Kiarda's face twisted into a snarl. She motioned urgently and a fae woman with a spear in one hand and a battle-axe in the other stepped into Thalion's line of sight. She was tall, almost as tall as he was, with dark hair that hung in braids down her back. She gave him a knowing smile, the sort of smile shared between warriors before a fight. Thalion recognised her from outside the Royal Suite – she'd not engaged him then, standing back and watching as he fought his way through until he could fight no more.

He was tired, and wanted this to be over with, so they could all get on with their lives. He rolled his shoulders, then his wrists, ignoring the ache there, letting the sword swing wide and settle in front of him, the spear held level with his hips.

She was by far the most challenging opponent he'd faced in a long time. He avoided the tip of her spear, and the axe. Her foot smashed into his stomach and put him on his back, forcing him to roll as the axe crashed into the ground, narrowly missing his head.

He couldn't get close to her; she dodged everything he threw at her, every twist of both arms, both weapons. She was confident, the smile never leaving her face. He was just another human, another easy target, and he had the overwhelming impression she was playing with him as she snapped her spear against his wrist. His bones screamed. The sword dropped to the ground.

She smiled again, and tossed her axe away, spinning the spear expertly, before she attacked again. He slipped beneath her arm, managing to drive his fist into her jaw, then deliver a sharp jab to her face. Her head snapped back and, taking advantage of her surprise, he hooked his foot behind hers and brought her down, throwing his weight on her and closing a hand around her throat. Her fist slammed into his jaw so hard his teeth rattled, and she threw him off with ease.

They staggered to their feet. Blood ran down her face from her shattered nose. She hefted the spear again. That cat-like smile was gone – her expression was deadly, her eyes ripping him to pieces.

She gave him no rest, no quarter, no moment in which to gather himself.

His muscles were liquid, his feet heavy, his movements sloppy.

At his limit, Thalion decided to take a hit; as she thrust the spear at him, he clenched his teeth, and let it pierce his side, just below the ribs. The pain was white hot and sharper than any knife. He pulled a ragged, determined breath between his teeth. The fae woman's eyes widened but, before she had a chance to do any more than rip that spear free, Thalion grabbed her by the shirt front, pulled a dagger from his belt and drove it into her neck.

He twisted the blade, pushed it higher, until it was wedged to the hilt below her chin. He watched the light leave her eyes, watched so he would remember her face. As the fae warrior fell to the floor, Kiarda screamed and screamed, the room shaking with her rage and grief.

Thalion stumbled back as Kiarda stood.

He made himself smile at his wife. If this was to be the last time she saw him, he didn't want it to be on his knees begging for his life. He wanted to tell her not to cry, but his vision swam, and his wounds were screaming.

He needed ten minutes, only ten, to take a breath.

Kiarda stepped down from the dais, the Bone Mother's staff lifted.

Thalion kept his eyes on Laeli's, on that brilliant green that was now as much home to him as a snow-covered landscape.

The atmosphere in the room suddenly shifted; Laeli's face froze. She closed her eyes, her back arching, arms spread wide. The air was sucked towards her, pausing, swirling around her body before she burst into flame, the ice at her feet vaporised. Thalion flung himself to the side, shielding his face with his arm. The Witch beside Laeli screamed as she was engulfed in fire.

Kiarda pointed the staff in Laeli's direction as the building shook violently. Vines and plants burst through the walls and the floor, pushing aside fallen stone and rubble, reaching across the room. Thalion watched in amazement as Mahelivar's chest thickened and spread, the buds of the antlers on his head growing until they stretched proudly above him. He lifted his arms and the Witches guarding him slumped to the ground.

'No,' Kiarda was saying, shaking her head.

A gush of fire entered the throne room as Ash and the creations of the Rift flowed inside. The beasts scurried and leapt playfully around her. One broke away from the pack and headed towards Laeli. She held out her hand; the monster flowed against her, butting its fiery head against her palm, twisting around her legs. She laughed, spinning around, the Lasair dancing with her, ashes left in their wake.

The glowing beast paused, turning its flaming head to look at Thalion. It took a step towards him, and he backed up until he was pressed against the wall, willing it to go away.

'Laeli!' he shouted as it inched closer, its golden eyes on his face. She darted across the room, the flames pulling into her skin, and stood between Thalion and the Lasair. The Lasair looked at her a moment, before returning to the pack of writhing fiery beings gathered around the Fire Caster.

Their mistress.

The girl turned towards Kiarda, who was paler than the snow.

'What is this?' Kiarda whispered.

'This is the Fire Caster,' Mahelivar said simply. 'Faleria's magic belongs to her, now. It's over, Kiarda.'

'No. It isn't over until the Cailleach makes her choice,' she snapped.

Laeli gestured to her brother, to those magnificent antlers. 'The Cailleach made her choice. You should get on your knees and bow to the King.'

Kiarda started laughing. She brought the staff around in front of her and slammed it on the ground. Ice spread out towards them. Mahelivar's hands lifted and the magic that erupted from his palms thickened into branches that reached across the room to coil themselves around Kiarda's body. She snarled but held firm to the staff as Laeli enclosed her brother in a shield of flames. Mahelivar stood calmly within that fiery sphere;

he closed his fists and the branches around Kiarda's body tightened. She gasped as the ice coating the walls began to melt, water sliding down the stone to pool on the floor.

Laeli backed up, until she was pressed against Thalion's chest, one hand extended towards her brother, holding that shield of flame in place. He could feel the room pulsing with magic – hers, Mahelivar's, Kiarda's, and the Fire Caster's. He glanced at Ash – the girl was incandescent with light and flame. The air swelled and breathed with her power.

'You need to get out of here,' Laeli told him.

'No. I'm not leaving you again.'

'Please,' she whispered. Sparks danced from her skin, smoke coiling from her hair as Ash moved closer to the dais. 'Get Jarlath and get out of here. Thalion, I'm begging you. You'll die, both of you. If she can't control it …'

'What about you?'

'I'll see you again, I promise.' Her voice broke.

She reached back and found his hand; her skin was hot. Thalion swallowed heat and ash and burning. He hesitated, decided to risk it, and kissed her before he ran across the room, one hand clutching his side, boots sloshing on the drenched carpet, his feet scattering flowers and the fresh shoots of grass.

'Run, Jarlath. Now.'

Jarlath hesitated, casting a look at Ash, then nodded.

At that moment, Kiarda exploded. The branches shredded and shards of ice and splinters of wood screamed through the air, as lethal as any weapon Thalion had ever seen. They embedded in the marble walls, so hard they split the stone. The building groaned in protest. Thalion ducked as the shards and splinters went shooting over his head; one sliced the skin on the back of his calf. Cursing, he scrambled for the door, but Jarlath wasn't with him.

He was crumpled on the floor, and slick, hot blood inched from his body.

CHAPTER SIXTY-THREE

Through the curtain of flame, the arrow of ice sailed through the air. In slow motion, where time stood still, that arrow found its mark. The fire faltered, confused, the screaming deep inside the vessel that bound it deafening. It waited as that broken body was lifted from the ground and swept away.

Let me go! The fire demanded, and this time, Ash listened.

She screamed and the world exploded with the force of her anger and the searing heat of her grief. The roof of the building lifted and was flung away; the walls shattered, stone and marble scattering across the sodden floor and the courtyard as the city shook with the strength of her anguish.

The creatures of fire, of magic and creation and destruction, rushed to embrace her. As she took their heat and power into herself, the fire blazed and roared through her blood; she shaped and moulded it until it was a cage that bound the ice, that melted it, transforming it into a river that dipped into cracks and crevasses left behind by the destruction.

There was fire and there was darkness. The darkness sang a siren's song, called to her with loving whispers. At her command, the flames raced through the air, wrapping themselves around the false Queen. Ash bent and shaped them with her will and her cage of flame began to shrink, encasing the cowering woman within the fiery womb of creation.

The urge to destroy was as potent as the finest poison. It filled her veins with its heat. Her fingers flexed; the flames shivered and became as black as death. The ground beneath her feet blazed.

The earth cracked.

'Ash!'

She turned to face the fae Prince, the King now, those glorious antlers rising from his head, the God of the forest on Earth. Something inside her remembered – a memory that was not hers, coming from a time long before she existed, when the earth was forged and given life by the Mother. She bowed her head.

'Don't kill her.'

Why not? The fire asked, but it paused, listening.

It was the Princess who spoke, she who understood the language of the flame, who had given much of her life to its protection. 'She needs to live to see justice delivered – but not by us.' The Princess gestured and Ash turned her head.

Where the building was no more, across a courtyard littered with stone and bodies, a hunched figure was approaching.

CHAPTER SIXTY-FOUR

The Cailleach picked her way through the rubble, over bodies and stone and the remains of ice. Green shoots poked through the ground; she stomped on them. *Not yet little ones*, she thought with a smile, *but soon.*

The Allfather was waiting for her.

Crouched at his feet were two men, one mortally wounded. The Cailleach bent to examine the wounded one. The soldier. And the other one – the young Chieftain, smeared with blood that was not his. He'd bathed in it this night, but no more. His fight here was over. The Cailleach glanced at the soldier again. Curse the Morrigan for making her job more complicated.

The hag stood, her old bones creaking, and addressed the Allfather.

'Well?'

The God of War and Strength gave a shrug. 'It's your choice, Mother.'

'Very well.' She waved her claw-like hand. The Chieftain fell back in shock as the Goddess materialised before him and lifted her veil.

'What …'

The Allfather tapped his spear on the ground and made himself known.

The man swallowed and gestured to the wounded one, whose life was quickly slipping away. He didn't bother with reverence or worship. He simply accepted what he saw, asking no questions, demanding nothing, except one thing: 'Can you save him?'

The Cailleach eyed the young Chieftain with interest. She was the Mother of mountains, the Creator of the rivers and the forests, the valleys and the storms that lashed the world. She was the Protector of wolves and deer, the Goddess of All. She was power and destruction. She was life and death itself. 'You could ask for a great many things, Chieftain of my Snow, but you ask for the life of another. Why?'

His eyes, blue as her most dazzling summer sky, shifted from her terrible face to the ruined palace. 'Though it is your hand that turns the wheel, not even you can give me what I want, Bone Mother.'

She shook her head, understanding. 'No, I cannot give you that, but your lives will run together for many years, for neither of you will die today.' She dusted her hands on her ragged skirts, the skulls jangling together. Her fingers twitched; her tools were close. 'Bring him.'

Inside the shell of the building, they found the Morrigan sitting on the throne, shuffling through her deck of cards, her dark eyes scanning the faces of those gathered within the rubble: the Princess, her skin still smoking; the King of the Forest, fresh and reforged; the Fire Caster; and the Queen of the Ice, cowering beneath the flames. Anyone else who had stood within this space was gone.

Two pairs of identical green eyes found the Goddess's face. They bowed, as they should, neither moving as the wounded man was laid gently on the ground. The Cailleach nodded, giving her leave; the Princess tore across the room, falling to her knees. She put her head in her hands as the young Chieftain gathered her against his chest while she wept.

The Crone eyed the Morrigan, who gave her a knowing smile, holding up two cards, which she swiftly tied together with red thread. She tossed them into the air and they vanished, fates decided and dealt, never to change.

The Cailleach then turned her attention to the King, beckoning him to approach. She could feel the eyes of all in the room swing in their direction as she addressed him.

'You seek to rule?'

'If it is what you deem right,' he answered. The Earth had chosen his sister, and she had chosen him, but he knew who controlled the earth, who could undo the choice with a thought.

The Goddess smiled. 'Will you allow me to see for myself?'

He nodded, closing his eyes, inclining his head towards her. The Cailleach lifted her hands, catching sight of her withered skin as she placed her fingers on his temples. Inside his mind she flew, for she could see along the threads of time. She saw life, and rebirth. Choice and acceptance. Peace. A future shaped and crafted by his hands because he recognised that power meant strength, but it was the strength he would give to others that would see the world grow and change.

His eyes opened and in the swirling green there were stars and the turning of the wheel.

Releasing him, the Cailleach took a step back, stretching her hands wide, calling on the magic in the earth below her. When she could feel it brimming under her skin like water, she drew her hands together sharply and from the space between them, a staff of elder and blackthorn grew from the ground, stretching until it reached her shrivelled breast. Around the length of the staff, she wove trees and leaves, and the creatures of the forest. She wove stars and the moon and the sun. She wove the wheel of existence and the passing of time.

The Crone clicked her fingers and the crown rose from the false Queen's head and floated across the room, all eyes watching it as it fell into her outstretched palm. She stared at it a moment, remembering when she had made it, remembering what she had bound to it as she ran her fingers over it: creation and destruction, death and rebirth — that never-ending cycle that she had called into being with her own hands.

As the Cailleach raised her eyes, it was the Princess she sought, the Princess who could have been Queen. There was no regret on her face as she watched her brother, only pride. Yet, the hag still had to be certain.

It could have been yours.

A slight shake of the Princess' head, her eyes flickering to the human man who still held her close. Two bodies, three heartbeats. The Cailleach could hear the furious beating beneath the Princess' fingers, could feel the strength and power contained within. She understood, for she was also a Mother who loved her children.

Come. She beckoned the Princess, who rose to her feet, for even she who had refused what she had been offered could not refuse the Goddess this request. The Crone passed the Princess the crown; as her long, slim fingers closed over it, the Princess smiled, and it was a peaceful smile.

No words needed to be spoken, for they all knew what the next step was in this ancient dance, this ritual as old as the earth itself. The Princess, eyes shining, lifted the crown of the fae and placed it on her brother's head, where it came to rest between those splendid antlers.

'Now,' the Cailleach told the new King of the Forest, 'you shall rule.'

He swallowed and his eyes flashed orange, the eyes of the great stag, the King of all beasts. As his hand closed around the staff, a rush of warm air and the charged crash of summer thunder split the sky. Waves of golden light rippled over his face.

The Cailleach bowed. On her throne, the Morrigan tossed away another card.

There was a soft thudding sound. A heart, beating its last. The Goddess turned towards the wounded man, the young soldier, his face as pale as death, his skin pulled back so that she could see the glorious outline of the bones below his flesh.

The Allfather stood close by, his cloak of fur brushing the ground, his hair as white as the snows that coated the land he ruled over. His one eye, as amber and bright as that of the wolf, sparkled. 'I will claim him if you don't.'

'You would?'

'He has courage, and strength.'

The Cailleach considered this. 'Yet he is not for you.' She glanced at the Morrigan. The Goddess of Fate held two cards now – the soldier and the Fire Caster. The Morrigan flicked the cards and the Cailleach snatched them from the air. Fate had decided not to intervene this time – the choice was hers, and the Earth's. She studied the face of each card, turning them over in her hands, considering. She turned away from the soldier, holding out the cards for the King, who took them carefully.

'A life for a life,' the Cailleach said. 'Creation and destruction, death and rebirth.'

The King nodded. 'A life for a life.' He stepped to the side, and the Cailleach turned to the woman in the ball of flames, her skin untouched by the fire's kiss, her eyes closed, her forehead touching the ground. She lifted her head and glanced up at the Goddess through the flames.

With a thought, the fire was gone, but the Queen of the Ice did not rise from the ground.

'You disobeyed me.'

The Ice Queen's eyes were desperate now. 'You said …'

'I said I would choose,' the Cailleach replied sharply. 'But you couldn't wait, Kiarda of Veshlir. To the ice I should banish you for your belligerence, but who is to say you won't try this again? Your need for vengeance has driven you to do terrible things. I had hoped you would use my powers to accomplish something great here but, instead, you fell victim to the same human trait you fought against all those years ago: greed. Your greed is your failing. That is why you will never rule.'

Kiarda put her head on the floor and wept. 'My daughter.'

'Yes, your daughter who you agreed to give to me for your own selfish reasons.' The Cailleach paused. 'Your daughter who you ultimately sent to her death. You will see her again. What is remembered, lives.'

'You're going to spare me?'

'I'm going to let you live, but this time, my mercy shall not be as merciful as your brother's was.' The Cailleach straightened. She stretched her arms; the staff and hammer flew across the room and leapt into her hands. Her fingers closed around them, and a jolt went through her at the kiss of their power.

'What will happen to me?' Kiarda asked.

The Crone closed her eyes. 'You will be one with the wind and the ice. Every winter, for one hundred years, when the wind blows from the north, that wind shall be you. You shall never look at anything green again, for your eyes will see only snow. That is my mercy.'

The Morrigan tossed the card wearing the Ice Queen's face into the air.

As it vanished, so too did Kiarda of Veshlir, the wind that she became sucked inside the Cailleach's staff until the Goddess saw fit to unleash it on the world.

The Cailleach turned to the Fire Caster. The girl still smouldered, her magic threaded through the air, singing the song of destruction and creation. The Crone waved her hand, and the flames were gone. The girl fell to her knees, pulling gulps of air into her lungs. She looked around wildly, eyes unfocused. Her gaze fell on the wounded soldier; the Allfather's charge cradled his head as he would a child, those large hands that had dealt so much death as tender as a sigh.

The Fire Caster scrambled across the floor, mindless of the sharpness of the broken stone. Tears flowed freely down her pale cheeks, and she showed no pain as her knees and palms were sliced by the debris. She put her face on the soldier's chest and wept.

With a snap of her fingers, the cards of the soldier and the Fire Caster returned to the Morrigan's hand. The heartbeat had slowed further. The Cailleach considered him carefully. His skull would make a grand edition to her belt; she could hear the song it would sing already. But it was not his time. She shook herself, lowering her staff to touch the soldier's foot. His body glowed briefly; the Fire Caster, who wept still, held him tightly.

The Cailleach closed her eyes and, when she opened them again, she was standing in the courtyard, the ruined palace behind her, charred bodies on the ground. The Morrigan walked amongst them, tossing her cards, frowning to herself, a flock of ravens gathering around her skirts, preparing to carry the souls of the dead to the next place as the earth claimed their bodies.

The Allfather stood with the Cailleach, white hair shifting in an invisible breeze. The wheel was turning.

'Where to, Mother?'

'There are still cards on the table,' the Morrigan called.

'I hate cities,' the Allfather grumbled as he vanished. The Morrigan took flight, leaving the Cailleach to make her own way across the landscape she had crafted all those aeons ago. She hefted the staff and hammer and walked into the trees where the grey wolf lay in wait.

A tiny shoot of green poked through the snow and soot.

She left it there.

CHAPTER SIXTY-FIVE

Fox couldn't move. She was pinned to the floor, her knees screaming, Gedeon's magic holding her there. The more she struggled, the harder that invisible hand on her head became. She felt as if she were being pushed through the stones. Her knees cracked and she bit back a sob.

Gedeon chuckled. 'You thought you could defeat me?' he cooed. That knife, her knife, appeared in front of her face again, hovering like a deadly insect. Fox swallowed. She would not beg for her life, not from him.

He knew this though; he knew her. He had always known which buttons to push, how to manipulate her. He didn't need his magic for that, Fox realised suddenly. She had let him, had let herself be manipulated and used because she thought that was all she was worth. He had taken a scared girl and turned her into his personal weapon. And she let him. He had used her anger at the world to twist and bend her.

But Gedeon knew that, too.

With a lazy smile, he flicked his hand and the knife floated away, coming to rest by Senan's throat.

'No!' Fox shouted. She clenched her fists, feeling the High Mage's magic bearing down on her. Her head was yanked sideways, so she was staring into Senan's face, that knife dangerously close to his skin.

'You can watch while I cut him to pieces,' Gedeon mused. 'But,' he said, 'you're the expert, Fox. Tell me where I should start. Here?' The knife moved to Senan's wrist, first one, then the other. 'Or here?' It hovered near his heart. 'Maybe I should take an eye? An eye for an eye, isn't that the saying?' Gedeon asked, indicating his twisted face.

'You're insane,' Fox whispered.

'Insane? No. I'm a visionary, my dear. This world will rise from the ashes, and it will be *my* world,' Gedeon said, his good eye sparkling. 'I am growing impatient. Where shall I start, Fox?'

Senan's eyes locked on hers. His face was calm but, beneath it, she knew his mind was working. Her gaze fell on the bonds of air wrapped around his wrists and ankles. They flickered.

Darian stirred, sitting up and rubbing at his head.

'Back with us,' Gedeon said. 'I warned you about the Anomaly.'

The Spirit Rake snarled and lifted his hands, his face contorted with anger.

At that moment, Senan broke free of Gedeon's magic; an ear-splitting crack echoed around the room, bouncing off the stone walls to settle inside Fox's head. His hands went to work immediately, slamming Darian into the wall. There was a sickening crunch as the Spirit Rake's head hit the stones.

Gedeon lifted his hand and from behind the desk flew his staff, the staff of the High Mage. Fox had never seen it in all her time working for Gedeon, but she knew it possessed powerful magic and would obey no one but the High Mage.

Senan was lifted from his feet and slammed into the ground. Fox tried to reach for him, alarmed at the blood she could see seeping from his head onto the stones. He groaned, conscious, but barely. Gedeon released her, for his own amusement no doubt. She was out of knives anyway, powerless and helpless.

This was not how her dreams went.

Fox crawled to where Senan lay and lifted his head into her lap. Her hands came away wet and smeared with his blood. 'You're a monster!' she shouted at Gedeon.

'Thank you,' the High Mage said with a chuckle. He waved the staff in Darian's direction. The dark-haired man opened his eyes and sat up. Clutching his head, his face tight with pain, the Spirit Rake turned his gaze on them.

'Get away from us!' Fox yelled as his mental fingers stroked her mind. She steeled herself – he was not getting in there, not this time. Never again would she be rendered useless by him. She was *not* broken. She was not a bird to be trapped in a net; she was not an animal to be ensnared by the hands of men. She thought of the dead wolf by the roadside. She thought of the strength in its body, the strength of its will. She thought of survival and freedom.

With a great shove, she pushed Darian aside.

His eyes widened. 'What the ...'

She glanced around the room, looking for a way out, for any path of escape, but there was nothing except her spinning head and Senan's ragged heartbeat, his blood in her lap.

Behind the High Mage, three figures materialised. Fox knew them, although she'd never seen them before. She sucked in a breath, but Gedeon gave no indication he knew the Cailleach, the God of War, and the Morrigan stood behind him. The Goddess of Fate flickered in and out of focus, shifting across the room in the blink of an eye to kneel in front of Fox. She swallowed as the Morrigan took her chin between strong fingers and stared into her eyes. The Goddess nodded once, then vanished.

Fox looked up, into the damaged face and milky white eye of the High Mage.

'You stupid girl,' Gedeon snarled, stepping towards them. All the amusement had fled his face. He was going to kill them. Fox turned pleading eyes on the space behind him, where the God of War and the Mother stood, watching her.

'Help me,' she whispered.

The Cailleach appeared by Fox's side. The stones beneath them started trembling. Senan's hands curled, his breathing laboured. A tiny shoot of green slipped up through the stones to curl around Fox's wrist. The Goddess lay her withered hand on Fox's fingers and suddenly, the plant breathed with her; Fox could feel it, its life force, slipping inside her, alongside her, a great wave rushing through her body. She could hear birds and feel sunshine on her skin, could smell the forest and hear water trickling over mossy rocks. Inside herself, she felt a shuddering, as if something was begging to be let out. The veins along the back of her hands were shot through with green.

'What's happening to me?' she cried.

'Let it come, and use it,' the Cailleach commanded, and disappeared.

Fox's head was spinning, her blood churning with that invisible force that writhed and fought the confines of her skin. She could feel the magic in her blood and the marrow of her bones. It was in the very core of her, in that space she kept only for herself.

Gedeon waved one hand through the air as the other lifted the staff. A wave of water appeared from nowhere, rising into the air. With hand and staff, he shaped it into a sphere and, slowly, it made its way across the room, its centre folding back like a great mouth, ready to swallow them whole.

Fox frowned. Gedeon had tried to drown her in this very room once before, filling her lungs with water.

'You're an Anomaly,' she whispered. Senan's eyes opened a crack.

Gedeon laughed, a crazed sound, and her blood sang in response.

Green energy shot through Fox's veins, as if the forest itself was inside her. She could smell the forest floor, the rich damp of leaves and soil.

She could smell life – it was at her call.

From the corner of her eye, Darian moved. No. Fox lifted her arm. She willed that green life forward into the light and it came, pushing through the cracks in the stone, growing at an unnatural rate, a tidal wave of green. Vines reached for her, embraced her as Darian extended his hands and the God of War smiled at her. Fox let go.

Those vines thickened and grew, flying across the stones.

With her mind she shaped them. *They* were her weapons now.

Darian screamed as one of those vines wrapped around his neck; thorns grew at Fox's whispered command and sliced through his skin as the vines tightened. He slapped them uselessly, eyes wide with fear. The vine rose and forced its way between his lips, ramming its way down his throat. Darian's eyes bulged; they found her face and Fox flexed her fingers as the vine erupted from his chest in a bubble of blood and bone and green life.

Gedeon's deformed face twisted with rage and fear.

'How is this possible?' he hissed. Darian was a mess of blood and pulp on the stones.

Fox eased Senan's head from her lap and climbed to her feet. Very calmly, without taking her eyes from Gedeon, she extended her hand towards Senan: the magic of the earth flowed from her fingertips, reaching out to stroke his face and his eyes opened. Fox took his hand and lifted him up as if he weighed nothing at all. The Mage-Witch took a deep, steady breath as Gedeon stepped towards them. Senan gripped her hand. His magic flew through her, mingling with her own, feeding each other. Gedeon lifted the staff as Fox fed Senan the magic the Mother had given her; his fingers beckoned and the staff, the staff of the High Mage, flew to Senan's outstretched hand.

Gedeon snarled. Water rose from the stones again; Fox felt the magic in her falter as that water crept towards them. Senan gripped her tighter, pulled her close, and swung the staff above his head, twirling it around and around. The wind pushed the flood of water back across the floor towards Gedeon. It pulled at their hair and clothes with snarling fingers. The force of it pushed the High Mage back as papers and books flew through the air; the furniture shuddered and the great desk ripped from its place to slide across the stones, pinning him against the wall.

'Senan,' he pleaded, his face twisted and broken, his hair torn from his scalp with the force of that wind. 'You can stand by my side. We can rule this land together!'

Senan shook his head; the wind died, but Gedeon remained trapped.

Fox knew what she had to do. The thorny vines trailed her as she approached him.

'Please,' he whispered.

'I don't think city life suits you, Gedeon,' she whispered back. A vine crept up his side; it stroked his cheek lovingly. His eyes, one wide and panicked, the other broken and ruined, stared at Fox desperately.

'Please,' he said again.

She hated to hear people beg.

Fox smiled and her power purred. She watched as slowly, so slowly, that vine grew and split and travelled across Gedeon's face, seeking and probing. He screamed as the vines pushed their way with deliberate slowness into his eyes, his nose, his ears and, finally, his mouth. That mouth that had, for years, given her orders. That had broken her and tried to kill her. That had sent her to torment and pain. Fox watched as that green life, her green life, filled him entirely, his blood trickling down his ruined body, the vines encasing him, wrapping him tight until there was nothing left of Gedeon except a green cocoon.

Fox fell to her knees, the staff clattering to the ground as Senan raced across the room to kneel before her, his eyes searching her face. She was exhausted, her mind drained, her limbs weak. She had no explanation for what had happened.

Whore. Assassin. Slave.

She was none of those things any longer.

She was free.

CHAPTER SIXTY-SIX

In her old bed, with her head pressed against Thalion's arm, Laeli was reminded of the first morning they'd woken tangled together and naked. She'd slept with her head on his chest then, his arms folded around her. He'd been sleeping when she'd woken, so she'd kissed his skin, then sank her teeth into him, making him gasp and flip them over, pinning her to the mattress.

'I'm dead, aren't I?' Thalion had asked, those beautiful eyes scanning her face.

Laeli chuckled. 'You're not dead, Thalion.'

'Then I'm dreaming.'

She rolled her eyes and wound her arms around his neck. 'I thought we established last night that you were not dreaming.'

His gaze moved around the room almost cautiously as he took in the grand bed, the floor to ceiling windows and lush rugs. 'I spent the night in your bed?' It was a question.

Laeli smiled. 'Well, you spent half of it in the forest with me but, yes, the rest of it in my bed; or my room at least.'

Thalion chuckled, removing a leaf from her hair. He turned it over, holding it gently between strong fingers, examining it with interest, before his expression turned wicked. He kissed her, hard, and she wrapped her legs around his hips. 'Since my memory seems a little hazy, perhaps you can remind me exactly what we did last night,' he'd murmured against her lips, making her laugh and kiss him until neither of them could breathe.

Now, Laeli wondered if she'd ever see such lightness from him again, or if he would always be shadowed by what had happened. It had been two days since the solstice, but it felt like two years. The sun had risen and set but they had barely registered the passing of time. They'd slept, and woken, and slept again. Laeli sighed and pressed her lips to Thalion's shoulder. He was awake, staring blankly at the ceiling. He managed a mumbled good morning, kissing her forehead gently, before he pulled away from her and climbed from the bed.

She watched him dress; his movements were stiff, and he tried to hide his wince as he pulled on his shirt. Birka's spear had left a gaping hole, in both of them. She'd had terrible nightmares after falling to sleep, Thalion's body curled around hers. In her dreams, Birka killed him in front of her eyes, Laeli helpless and unable to look away.

Thalion didn't glance back at her as he left the room. She let him go, let him take the space he needed. It was more than what had happened to his father, she knew that, but she didn't have the words that would help him process what he had gone through, because she didn't have them for herself.

Laeli rolled over and burrowed into the blankets, not wanting to come out for a long time, but her brain was already flying, refusing to let her rest. Kiarda was gone. The Cailleach had come, and her brother was King, as he should be. She thought briefly of the power she had let go, of how it had felt as it surged through her. She didn't regret it and knew she never would. That sort of power was not what she had ever desired.

Her fingers stroked her lower belly.

Ash's face floated into her thoughts. In a room down the hall, the Fire Caster slept like the dead, Jarlath close by her side, his own healing just beginning.

With a sigh, Laeli threw back the covers and found clean clothes. The air was chilled; not like it had been, but the cold lingered beneath the gentle warmth of the winter sun that poured through the windows. The halls of the palace were silent as she moved through them; the few people she passed nodded to her, but no one tried to talk to her and she was grateful. She had no words for them, either.

She found Thalion sitting on the edge of the ruined fountain in the courtyard. Leaning against a broken wall, she just watched him, hoping he'd talk when he was ready. She was content enough in that moment to know he was alive and whole. They had the rest of their lives to deal with what had happened here. And they would, slowly.

Leaving Thalion to his thoughts, she made her way into the city. The gruesome task of collecting the dead and wounded had begun, and the funeral pyres were being built. The Morrigan's ravens were picking through the dead, as was their job, but Laeli found she couldn't look at them, couldn't watch them set to their work. The bodies of the dead fae had either been returned to the earth or the process was partially complete. It was rare for the Mother to have to work so hard but their bodies would be fuel for the life that would spring from the soil when the wheel turned towards spring.

The main market square and the shop fronts were intact, as were the residences. The palace had borne the brunt of everything. Not only was the throne room destroyed, but the council room was gone, and the dining hall was missing half a wall. Everything was scorched and blackened, the stones charred and coated in ash. Grass pushed through them, stretching for the sun as Mahelivar's power spread further, reaching into the forest to coax the earth back to its peaceful winter slumber, ready for the steady burst of growth come the turning of the wheel. Mahelivar would rebuild this world, and it would be a better place for his temperance and his strength of will, his kindness and his courage.

People moved through the peach-hued light, ferrying bodies and clearing debris. There was no rush, but Laeli knew her brother wanted a sense of normalcy back as soon as possible. Her brother, the King. She smiled, gladder than ever of her choice.

He was where he belonged.

The wounded were being taken inside the palace, where a makeshift hospital had been set up in what remained of the large dining room. Laeli had avoided that room, not wanting to acknowledge the true cost of what Kiarda had done, not yet. She had seen Solen yesterday – alive but wounded, stuck in bed – which he absolutely hated.

When she returned his sword to him, cleaned and polished, Solen had held it for a long time, the silence deep, until he eventually lifted his eyes to hers. 'He would have gone in there armed with his bare hands, Laeli. For you. You deserve to be happy.'

But being happy in the middle of all this death was hard.

Magus was waiting for her at the edge of the courtyard. She embraced him tightly, wanting to cry her eyes out, but she held it in. Those of the fae guard not wounded and healthy enough were heading north to Avivers and Levalun with a team of Witches. There were two other cities to bring out of the wintry darkness and into the light.

Laeli walked with her mentor to the edge of the forest. Magus was nursing a slight limp but nothing she said would make a difference, so she stayed silent. Smoke still curled from the trunks of the trees, dancing into the sky. No birds sang, and the undergrowth was still and unnaturally quiet. After Magus and his team had left, Laeli returned to the palace, walking her usual path through the avenue of trees that led to the sweeping lawn and the garden she loved so much; the garden where she had sat with Thalion in the warm sunshine and listened to the words that would change her life. Only now, the trees were bare and snow clung stubbornly to the ground.

The side door to the palace was ajar and half hanging off its hinges, as if someone had pushed their way outside in a great hurry. As she came closer, Laeli noticed a large shape, bundled against the wall. She sucked in a breath. It was a body. Male, and human, by the smell. The heartbeat was dangerously slow and weak.

She hurried over and knelt by his side, touching his shoulder, gently rolling him over.

Words of comfort died on her lips.

Hadrian.

He coughed once; blood trickled from the corner of his mouth. How was he still alive? She bit her lip, realising he'd lay where she found him for days, slowly dying. In the chaos, no one had thought to look for him. Thalion believed he was dead.

Recognition lit Hadrian's blue eyes. 'Are you going to kill me, Witch?' he whispered, face twisted with pain.

She shook her head.

'Why not?'

Laeli couldn't answer.

'Thalion?'

'Alive,' she managed, then, 'I'm going to get help.' She jumped up and vanished inside before he could speak, returning with two of the men Mahelivar had tasked with helping collect the wounded. 'Take him inside,' she ordered softly.

They paused. 'But …'

'Do it,' Laeli snapped, turning away so they couldn't see her tears, tears they wouldn't understand and she didn't have the words to explain. She dashed a hand over her face, and went looking for her husband, her senses locked on to his scent and the heartbeat she would know in her sleep. He was still sitting near the fountain, staring vacantly at nothing.

'Thalion,' she murmured, resting a hand on his shoulder. He grabbed her fingers and twisted to look at her, his eyes tired and haunted. She wondered if he'd slept at all. He made to pull her close and it was all she wanted, to curl against his chest and stay there, let someone else deal with this terrible aftermath, but she shook her head. 'Your father – he's alive.'

Thalion scrambled to his feet and she took his hand and led him inside. Hadrian was lying on a cot on the floor, one body amongst a sea of others. Healers and Air Witches moved about, careful and vigilant in their work, murmuring to each other in low voices. They had already decided they couldn't help Hadrian – his ankle was marked with a white silk ribbon. The wounded were mainly human, a few of the fae guard amongst them.

Releasing Laeli's hand, Thalion approached his father, his steps hesitant, his shoulders curled in on themselves. He stopped, turning to look at her. His face was shattered, his eyes ancient, filled with the weight of a thousand worlds.

'I can't do this alone.'

He mouthed the words, but she heard them anyway.

Hadrian's eyes, so like his son's, flickered over Laeli's face as she approached and wrapped her fingers around Thalion's. He looked between the two of them, assessing and weighing up all he had seen. He was running out of time – Laeli could hear his heart, its weak, irregular rhythm.

'You need to kill me, boy,' Hadrian wheezed eventually.

'I can't.'

'You can. The Allfather knows I deserve it.' A pause, then a hacking cough. 'Brenna?'

'Dead,' Thalion said quietly.

Hadrian nodded, understanding. 'I guess he deserved it, too, didn't he?'

Thalion closed his eyes a moment and when he opened them, a lifetime of longing was etched through the dazzling blue. 'Why was I never enough for you? I did everything you ever asked of me, even when I didn't agree with it, or want to do it.'

'Perhaps that was why. You never fought me, not in earnest,' his father said. He coughed again, blood bubbling from his lips. 'The truth is, you remind me of her. Your mother. There were seven before you, Thalion, all tiny, wrinkled red things that never drew breath and … and every time I look at you, I see her face, her smile, and I remember that I failed her.'

'How did you fail her? She was ill.'

'You mother needed help. I could have ridden through the storm that night for her – I should have ridden through the storm for her – to get help from that healer in Reyshorn, but I didn't.'

'Why?' It was a whisper, hesitant, as if Thalion dreaded the answer.

Hadrian closed his eyes and didn't speak for a long moment. When he did, his voice was low, rough and choked. 'Because she begged me not to go. She begged me to stay away from that foul night, for you, so you wouldn't be alone when she was gone.'

Thalion put his hand over his face.

'You sat by her bedside for days, even when you were sick yourself. I was scared, but she wasn't. Your mother was the bravest person I ever met. She saved my life that night. If I'd gone out, I'd most likely have died by the roadside,' Hadrian whispered. 'But I still should have tried.'

Thalion's shoulders shook. His grip on Laeli's hand became painfully tight.

Laeli swallowed and knelt by the dying man, looking into the face she had imagined carving away with her blades, the flesh she imagined melted and the eyes she'd wanted to pluck from his skull. She didn't smile, or cry. She looked at him, and he at her, his expression calm.

'It was you, wasn't it, after he returned before Samhain.' Hadrian said. 'Why didn't you kill me? I saw you in that throne room. I'd have been dead before I realised what was coming for me.'

Thalion's eyes were glassy, his mouth a tight line.

'Your son wanted your death to hold some honour, because he's an honourable man and, because I love him, I respected that,' Laeli replied.

'You love him?'

'Is that so hard to believe?'

Hadrian fell silent again; around them, the healers continued their work, their soft voices floating on the air. 'It isn't,' he said eventually.

He reached a death-pale hand towards his son, who gripped it tight. 'I punished you. For twenty years, I punished you. I was wrong.' Hadrian coughed. 'I failed you, Thalion. Now, you can do what you've wanted to for a long time.'

Thalion shook his head.

'You will see him again, Thalion. What is remembered, lives.' Laeli's voice broke, for her husband and for this moment. Hadrian, despite what and who he was, had been a fool to trust in Kiarda.

Thalion pulled his dagger from his belt. He stared at it, then flipped it in his hand, holding it out for her, hilt first. 'I can't, Laeli.'

'I won't do it for you.'

'You said—'

'I know, but after, every time you look at me it will be a reminder of this moment, and I don't want that to be between us for the rest of our lives together,' she said quietly, pushing the dagger back towards him.

He took a deep, shaky breath, and nodded. With his hand in hers, Laeli sat beside him, and they waited. The hours crawled by and, as Hadrian's eyes closed for the last time, Thalion slipped his hands free and climbed to his feet to stumble outside, leaving her sitting vigil over the dead.

CHAPTER SIXTY-SEVEN

The funeral pyres were built on the flat land outside the city walls. It was the easiest way. Digging graves would have taken too long, even with Earth magic, so the debris from the broken city – the timbers from businesses and carts and broken furniture, was carried out and piled up. It took three days for the bodies to be gathered up and laid to rest after being claimed by loved ones; the fires burnt for days, a new pyre being lit every hour or so.

Senan's heart sank as Yasper walked towards him, a body cradled in his arms, blonde hair and porcelain skin glowing in the sunlight.

Gem.

Yasper lay her gently on an unlit pyre, smoothing her hair back from her face, before stepping away. Senan had no words of comfort for him. No one did. Peoples' faces were stamped with shock and disbelief, with loss and grief, but not with anger. He hadn't known what he would face after walking from the Keep with Fox, Radella and the rescued mages behind them.

'You might be surprised at their resilience,' Radella had said when he'd expressed concern. 'I think people are smarter than what Gedeon ever believed – why else would he have to coerce them? Hopefully, they will see the evil behind the man, not the magic.'

She was right. While there were grumblings about magic being at fault, most people were glad it was over, that life would be able to return to normal. What that normal was, though, nobody knew. With the Mage Council and the Queen dead, leadership of the city had fallen to the mages from the Academy, and Radella, whose calm manner soothed the fears and tempers of many.

It would take months to undo the damage Gedeon and the Watch had inflicted on the city. The remaining Watchmen had been rounded up and were being held at the prison. Some had fled the city, but they had no power anymore and posed no danger to anyone.

When the smoke from the pyres was choking the sky, Senan returned to Gedeon's office. The bodies were gone, the blood cleaned away, but nothing could erase what he had seen and experienced in that room. As he was bending to collect papers from the floor, Fox appeared in the doorway, her expression carefully composed. She came in, her footfall as light and soundless as a cat, and helped. They worked in silence, stacking the papers in a pile then moving the heavy desk back into position. Fox went to the window and stared out.

She hadn't spoken of what she'd done, and Senan had seen no evidence of the extraordinary power she'd displayed. He wanted to ask her but didn't. Fox turned to watch him arrange the papers on the desk.

'What will happen now?' Her voice was soft and husky.

He shrugged. 'I don't know.' He joined her at the window. From up here, they could see the main square; Radella was directing a group of students. The healers were out in the streets, attending to those unable to make it to the Academy. Senan watched a water mage use her magic to wash the black soot from the stones. 'How's Yasper?'

Fox shrugged. 'Still smiling. Everyone seems to think he's fine, but I know different. He has the same look in his eyes that I saw in mine, in Estilleon, while I was in Caden's house. He will be fine though. He's tough.'

'I think we're all tougher than we thought,' Senan mused. He turned back to the desk, leaving Fox to the view, wondering what would happen to them now this was all over. He rubbed at this face. Oden materialised beside him, and Senan's heart swelled. The shadow-dog had been absent while he was recovering his strength and he'd had a horrible feeling that he'd lost the black beast, but Oden had been at his bedside a few mornings after Gedeon's death, like he had on the first morning Senan had seen him. The dog nudged his nose at a wooden box on the floor.

Curious, Senan lifted it to the desk and flicked it open, pulling out a stack of paper – documents, lists, letters, and maps. He spread them over the desk, frowning.

'Fox, look at these.'

She stood beside him, her face screwed up as she looked at the papers and he remembered suddenly she couldn't read very well. 'Gedeon's plans,' she said, her voice soft and sad. 'I recognise his handwriting. What do they say?'

He told her and her sadness switched to anger. What he felt was bitter disappointment. The terror and harm Gedeon used his power and influence to create was the beginning of a wider plan that would have seen the forests destroyed and the earth stripped bare, polluted, and degraded. He found it difficult to believe a mage, someone with powers like his, could even consider doing something so against everything they had been taught to believe. Gedeon thought to play God, to bend the wheel and break it, reshaping it to suit his desires. There was a terrible irony in the High Mage's death – had the Earth known what he planned for it? Had the Cailleach known?

Fox had told him what she'd seen in this room – Senan had a memory cloaked in shadow of the Goddess crouching on the stones but had thought it a dream. What pierced his heart the hardest was the knowledge that Gedeon was like him – an Anomaly. They could have helped one another, all those years ago.

Senan bundled up the papers and tucked them under one arm. With the staff of the High Mage in the other hand, he carried the papers from the room, Fox following. They left the gloomy, empty Keep and entered the main square. The fire pit had been relit and the flames were purring over the coals again. Senan approached the pit, forcing away the screams and the visions of people burning. The staff in his hand thrummed with power. He took a deep breath, and dropped Gedeon's paperwork into the flames, watching until the orange and yellow tongues had devoured it.

It was a fitting end to such ideas, Senan decided, at the same time thinking it was time fire was given back to the people.

Radella seemed to agree. The White Woman had come to stand by his side, watching the papers burn. She didn't ask questions and when the last piece of parchment had been eaten, she turned to him with a smile.

'We need to teach people not to be afraid of fire,' she said quietly. 'I don't know if Ash is the last Fire Caster we're likely to see, but no one needs to fear the flame anymore. It will take time, though – there are a lot of bewildered and injured people in this city and by now every village will have heard what happened. I'm grateful you were able to stop him before he spread his terror.'

Senan nodded, his thoughts shifting to the red-haired young woman with the power of a Goddess, of creation and destruction, in her veins. He wondered when he'd see her again. He sighed softly. 'I had been holding on to useless hope though, Radella.'

'How so?'

'I'd hoped I could get through to him, but it was too late. Gedeon had made his choices.'

'And he's had to suffer the consequences of them,' Fox put in. 'I saw with my own eyes that power over others doesn't have to mean brutality. It can be gentle and peaceful, in the end.'

'What's next then?' Radella asked.

'Why are you asking me?' Senan said blankly.

Fox laughed and nodded at the staff of the High Mage, still clutched in Senan's hand.

Senan shook his head. 'No.'

Radella smiled. 'Gedeon was right in one thing – it's time for change, but not the sort he had in mind.' She put her hands on her hips and glanced around, her shrewd gaze sweeping over the square, and, it seemed, the whole city. 'There is a lot to do here. I'm sure if we looked in the store houses, we would find more than enough food and produce to see us through winter. That should be the priority.'

After she left, Senan and Fox sat beneath a tree on the edge of the square. There was a chill in the air; the wheel had turned and the days were short and brushed with cold. In his forest, the earth would be sleeping, life resting until Beltane and the return of summer warmth.

'What are you going to do now?' he asked Fox.

'I'm going to go and see how Yasper is,' she told him, climbing to her feet. 'Elan says he wants to rebuild his gaming house. He'll need help.'

'So you're staying?'

She smiled and kissed his cheek. 'For now.'

He took her hand and pulled her back down, so she was sitting close to him. 'The power you unleashed in the Keep …'

'It's gone,' Fox said quietly. Senan thought he detected a tiny bit of disappointment in her tone. 'It never belonged to me,' she continued with a shrug. 'But it was nice for the time I had it. I guess I'm ordinary again.'

He laughed until his stomach hurt. 'You are by no means ordinary, Fox. You're quite the opposite.' He kissed her, feeling free and light, the magic in his blood singing when she kissed him back.

'Senan,' she began, her voice soft. 'I don't know what to do now.'

'What do you mean?'

She indicated their linked hands. 'We're so different. I live in the moment. I spend my life always on the edge. I don't know how to be still. There's a darkness in me that frightens me. I enjoyed killing them,

Senan. I don't know how to be different when my life has been one bad experience after another.'

He took a deep breath. 'When I first met you, all those years ago, it was like I'd been waiting for something to happen, something that would change things, and then you were there, bleeding in that grove and you needed me.' He paused, cupping her cheek. 'You're the perfect combination of chaos and peace, Fox. You make me feel alive. I know there's a darkness in you, because it's in all of us, but it isn't all you are.'

She squeezed his hand and nodded.

As he walked back to the Academy where they had been staying, Fox's hand gripped tightly in his, Senan decided he would stay to see things right. He thought of the forest, of his hut hidden in the trees, and had an overwhelming desire to be back there, where he could hear the birds and feel the energy of the trees. He glanced at Fox to find her looking at him, a smile on her face, her amber eyes glowing. Waiting for them were Elan and Yasper. The four of them stepped inside the Academy gates.

Before they went inside the building, where Radella and some of the senior mages were waiting, Senan felt something pull at the edge of his mind. He glanced across the courtyard.

Beneath the tree he used to sit under as a young man stood the Morrigan. The Goddess of Fate held up two cards. These she bound with red thread and flicked at him. They halted near his face, hovering in the air, slowly turning. Before they vanished, he saw his face, and Fox's.

When he looked up, the Morrigan was gone.

CHAPTER SIXTY-EIGHT

Thalion was standing where the generous window in the throne room used to be, gazing out over the cracked stone and rubble that had been shifted into piles in the ruined courtyard. Where Ash had burnt the earth, new life had crawled through the soot, fed with the melted snow and ice. The blackened trunks of the trees had turned brown again, each branch covered in buds that would wait until the first breath of spring before bursting and unfolding into being.

The Rift was gone. The hole created by Faleria's magic remained, but the Lasair were gone.

Laeli took Thalion's hand. He glowed in this strange, new world, his skin marked by wounds that would heal, as hers would. She smiled, feeling oddly dazed by him, by everything he'd done, although she never wanted to see him fight as hard as he had against Birka ever again. She gently traced the place below his ribs, where his new scar would be. She'd never forget what he did to get it – what he did for her.

They were alone. Mahelivar had requested their presence but had still not arrived. The throne room was open to the air and the light, the roof gone, the walls crumbled, but the mess inside had been cleaned away. Laeli liked the room this way – the sounds and smells of the forest were invited inside. She glanced towards the dais – the throne sat proudly on the red carpet; the two smaller ones beside it once more. Her eyes lingered on her throne.

'What will you do now?' Thalion asked.

'What do you mean?'

He gave her a sad smile. 'You were right, before. You're not my property. You are free to do as you wish, Laeli. If you want to stay here, I'll understand.'

Something twisted in her stomach. 'Why are you saying this?'

He shook his head slightly. 'I watched you burst into flames. I saw things I never thought were possible, things I am still trying to understand, even though I don't think I will ever understand what happened here, not fully. *This* is your world.'

'Thalion ...'

'You could have been Queen, Laeli.'

A pang went through her as she recalled that magic, the feeling of it flowing through her. 'It wasn't what I wanted,' she said softly.

'You're amazing,' Thalion whispered. 'That word is not enough to describe you, but it's all I can think of at this moment. You're beyond anything I can offer you, beyond me and my world. It all pales in comparison. Maybe you were right – this isn't real, and I've been living in a dream since that night I first met you.'

She shook her head furiously, her heart heavy and hurting. 'No. I'm who I am now because of you. Because of what you've given me. The fact that you're standing here, after everything, willing to let me go – because of you I've been able to realise where my path lies.' She paused, taking a deep breath. 'I've spent eighty years guarding the Rift and now ... it's gone. I'm free. Only, it was never a burden. It was a choice I made, and it became part of who I was.'

'Now you can be whatever you want, walk whatever path you want,' Thalion said softly, his voice cracking.

'I am though, don't you see? The Morrigan put you and I together in that forest for a reason. She put me on my true path that night, and I've been changed beyond everything because of it. I chose you and I would choose you over and over given the chance again. Fate gave me you, and you gave me the promise of a *life*, and the Morrigan gave us both this.' Her hand dropped to her belly, her fingers trembling; something fluttered deep within, a response to her, to Thalion. 'A promise of the future.' She smiled. 'I'm pregnant.'

The colour drained from his face. 'What?'

'I'm pregnant, Thalion.' She hadn't meant to tell him, not yet, not when everything was so raw, when they were so damaged by what had happened, but maybe that was why she told him – they needed something else, something *good* to come from what they had experienced. He needed to see how important he was, how important *they* were. She couldn't lose him, not now, not after everything, not when the world was beginning to be reborn.

He stared at her for a long moment, then, the words rushed out of him. 'You should have told me before I let you go running around here, alone, doing whatever you were doing to get that!' He glared and gestured to her injury. 'Just how long have you known, Laeli?'

She rolled her eyes, hands on her hips. 'I'm pregnant, not dying, Thalion.'

His hand reached towards her, hesitated, before he rested it over her belly. 'Really?' His voice was softer than Laeli had ever heard it, soaked with such yearning, her eyes filled with tears. All she could do was nod.

He wrapped his arms around her. She clung to him, her face buried in his neck, breathing deep the smell of him as he lifted her off the ground; her legs wrapped around his middle.

Someone cleared their throat. Mahelivar and Jarlath were standing in the doorway.

'I get that you're the good guy, Thalion, but I'm not sure I'm overly comfortable with you pawing my sister,' Mahelivar said lightly.

'Well, you won't have to watch for much longer,' Laeli retorted as Thalion let her down.

'You're returning to Estilleon?'

She nodded.

Her brother folded his arms. 'What if I said no?'

Laeli held out her hand; flames licked her palm. 'What if I said piss off?'

'You can't talk to me like that anymore, Laeli. I'm the King,' Mahelivar replied, sighing when she shrugged. He turned to Thalion. 'Are you sure you're willing to put up with that mouth for the rest of your life?'

Thalion didn't miss a beat. 'I'm rather fond of that mouth, actually.'

Mahelivar groaned and put his head in his hands while Jarlath laughed until Laeli thought he'd be sick. She raced across the room to hug first her brother, then Jarlath, who hugged her back fiercely.

'How do you feel?' she asked him, pulling back to scrutinise his face. Jarlath had been sleeping since the Cailleach had returned him to them. Ash was still asleep. Laeli wasn't surprised. The amount of magic the girl had used should have left her as ruined as the room they stood in, but when she'd gone to check on Ash she was whole and unmarked, breathing the steady breath of someone in a deep, healing sleep.

Jarlath rubbed his face. 'I don't know, to be honest. I was dead, wasn't I?'

'You would have been, without the Cailleach and her magic,' Laeli answered.

He nodded. He was still coming to terms with what had happened, like they all were.

'Let's sit outside,' Mahelivar suggested. 'I'd like to feel the grass under my feet.'

He led them into the garden, stepping over the broken wall and into the warmth of the winter sun. Mahelivar eased himself down to the ground with a sigh, slipping his feet free of his boots and stretching his long legs out in front of him. Around him, the grass thickened.

'I've got to learn how to stop doing that,' he mumbled with a lazy smile.

Jarlath lay back and linked his hands behind his head, closing his eyes. Behind them, the faint sounds of voices and the moving of rubble continued. Laeli had no idea how long it would take to fix the mess Kiarda had left, here and in Avivers and Levalun. She was hoping to see Magus again before she left, but she knew she wouldn't. While Sitra would always be home, there was another place she longed to be.

Laeli snuck a look at her brother. He looked happy, confident, and relaxed – in charge. She could feel his power; it hummed through the earth below her, making her blood buzz and her heart race and she knew, as she had always known, that she'd made the right choice.

A servant came out bearing a tray of food – thick slabs of bread and cheese, fruit, and cold meats. The smell of the meat was too much. Laeli's stomach heaved, and she turned away with a groan, her hand on her belly, the queasiness she'd been feeling occasionally since she woke suddenly intensified, as if now that it was out in the open, her body wasn't going to let her forget for one moment what it was about to go through.

'Oh gods,' she moaned.

'You are looking green,' Mahelivar commented. He laughed and she managed a smile, enjoying the sound of his laughter. It proved that no matter what Kiarda had done, she hadn't managed to break him. She hadn't broken any of them, but she'd come close.

Laeli felt her brother's magic inside her head.

'This will change things,' he said softly, glancing first at her, then Thalion. 'A halfkin heir.'

'Halfkin heir,' Jarlath mumbled; he sat up, his eyes wide. 'Oh!'

'You do know where babies come from, don't you, Jarlath, because sometimes I wonder about you,' Thalion drawled.

'If anyone ever had any doubt, all they'd have to do is spend a few weeks with you two,' Jarlath shot back.

Thalion laughed, a beautiful, joyous sound tinged with a hint of smugness, a sound Laeli hadn't been sure she'd hear again mere days ago.

'Well,' he said casually, draping his arm around Laeli's shoulders. 'You're obviously very relaxed. I'm going to assume you've been fu—'

'Thalion!' Laeli hissed.

He ignored her. 'Honestly, Jarlath, sometimes you just need a good—'

Laeli clamped her hand over his mouth. He laughed again, pulling her hand away so he could lean over and kiss her. She melted, as she always did, collapsing into him and staying there, her head tucked under his chin, his fingers stroking the back of her neck, a reminder that he wasn't going anywhere in a hurry, that he was still here.

CHAPTER SIXTY-NINE

Ash woke to the sound of birds singing in the trees outside her window. Jarlath was already up. She rolled over and watched him dress.

'Do you have to?'

'We can't hide in here forever,' he replied, smiling, and she sighed. He was right.

She'd woken two days ago, startled to discover she'd been asleep for a week. Her memory of everything since she climbed down the rope into the Rift was hazy, and part of her was glad. Ash stretched her arms above her head, bringing her hands around in front of her eyes, turning them over, inspecting her flesh. The same as it always was. It fascinated her, that her skin remained untouched by the flames when they peeled the flesh from others' bodies.

She knew what she had done. She'd made Jarlath describe it to her in detail, even though he hadn't wanted to. Not because he was afraid or ashamed of her – he was trying to protect her, wanting to spare her the deaths of all those people she now carried on her shoulders.

What had chilled her blood more was how close she had come to losing him. On his chest where Kiarda's arrow of ice had pierced his body there was nothing – no mark on his skin, no scarring. Nothing to show it had even happened. But it had and she could see on his face the fear and wonder of it.

Ash sat up, rolling her shoulders. She felt light, unburdened, free. Her power thrummed beneath her skin, charged, and she let it flood through her a moment, energising her, giving her the strength she needed to get out of bed. The Lasair were seemingly gone, vanished as if they'd never existed in the first place. She felt it as surely as she felt the magic in her blood, in her bones and inside the very core of who she was. Faleria's magic was her magic now, the power of destruction and creation buzzing through her.

The flame-bird watched her from the back of a chair, its fiery eyes fixed on her face.

Jarlath said the bird appeared while she was still sleeping. It had scared the life out of him, but he'd recognised it for what it was – a Lasair. It looked like an ordinary bird, its feathers deep red, fading to orange then yellow on the tips – the colour of fire. The size of a raven, it had golden eyes and a long tail that shimmered when it moved. Ash thought it was one of the most beautiful things she'd ever seen. She could hear its heartbeat, could feel when it moved, and it in turn was attuned to her – to her emotions and her thoughts. If she thought of fire, the bird glowed with it.

Outside, the sun was shining, ribbons of golden light pouring through the forest canopy with ease. The branches of the trees were mostly bare of leaves, but the ground was covered in fresh shoots of grass, thick and lush as the first time she saw it. The shrubs were green and crisp looking, fresh with buds ready to open into a flush of colour, and the sky was a brilliant, dazzling blue.

The world was changed again, and she was changed in ways she hadn't yet come to understand. She figured they all were.

'Jarlath,' she said, her voice soft. 'What are we going to do now? I know Mahelivar said we can stay here, but I'm not sure I want to.'

Mahelivar had come to see them last night, and Ash had smiled at the sight of the antlers on his head.

'They suit you,' she'd said.

'It's thanks to you.'

She'd been able to feel his power throbbing through the room and it awed her, made her want to bow her head, but she'd barely been able to lift it from the pillow.

'Kiarda would have killed me, Laeli as well. If it wasn't for your extraordinary power, Ash, I've no doubt about it.'

Ash had blushed and fiddled with the edge of the bedspread. 'She's gone?'

'She is. Gedeon as well.' Senan had sent his shadow-hound to Sitra with the story of what had happened in Tyllcarric. Ash could barely believe it. She was sorry to hear about Gem. Yasper was taking it hard but was determined to rebuild his business, but with a new name: *The Gem of Tyllcarric*. People like Yasper amazed her – even though everything was taken away from him, Yas's determination to keep living showed her that what mattered was not what was lost, but what you did with what was left. And that, Ash decided, was what hope looked like.

'Hadrian?'

'Dead.'

'How's Thalion?'

'Grieving. Laeli says it's not so much for the loss of his father but the loss of what might have been, had Hadrian been a different sort of man,' Mahelivar had explained. Seeing she was looking tired, he bent and kissed her forehead, then left, and she'd slept again, waking with a ravenous appetite and a terrible thirst to find Laeli sitting on the edge of her bed.

A married and pregnant Laeli, who'd shrugged off Ash's excitement but couldn't hide her smile, and couldn't stop her eyes from shifting to the door and the hall outside, where Ash assumed Thalion was waiting.

Ash stretched luxuriously, smothering a yawn. Jarlath was smiling at her. She'd never tire of that smile, the way the corners of his mouth pulled up, one higher than the other. He cocked his head to one side when he smiled at her. She'd never noticed that before.

'You're the boss, so where do you want to go?'

'I don't know. I want to see everything in Aileryan, from the snow to the desert and everything in between.' Ash threw back the bedclothes with an enthusiasm she hadn't felt in a long time. Everything was fresh and new, different, and the world was theirs to explore. They had friends across the land now and would never be without a place to call home. 'We should go back to Brenveil and let them know we're alive. I want to see my parents before we go wherever we're going to go,' she said. She wondered if they knew what had happened, in Sitra or in Tyllcarric. She would decide how much to tell them when the time came.

A pile of clothes sat on the chair near the bed – a long, red dress and a warm, long-sleeved undershirt. She slipped both on as Jarlath handed her a pair of unbelievably soft leather boots. They left the room and walked the long hallway together, the flame-bird fluttering along behind them. Repairs had begun on the throne room and the dining room.

There was no sign of their friends, so they went outside into the sun. Ash watched her bird soar into the air, her heart racing at a vague memory of what it felt like to fly.

'You're up.' Mahelivar joined them on the steps. 'I was coming to get you. The happily married couple are leaving.'

Ash felt a pang of despair. She desperately wanted to talk to Laeli about what happened in the throne room. She had so many questions, questions she knew no one could answer, but she wanted to voice them. It could wait though, now that they had time.

A stillness floated over the city, but it was a peaceful quiet, the quiet of endings and new beginnings. Despite the damage, Sitra was still beautiful. They followed Mahelivar across the courtyard and into the main market square, the cobblestones blasted clean by Water Witches. The people there stopped what they were doing to bow to him.

'They're bowing to *you*,' Mahelivar told her in a whisper.

Ash was mortified. 'Tell them to stop!'

He smiled, clearly enjoying himself. 'I don't think I will. You're a hero, Ash Griffyn.'

She hurried out of the square, face burning. The flame-bird appeared, an ember floating across the sky, and she held out her arm. It landed there and burst into fire. She smiled and stroked it, rubbing her finger on its head as she got a handle on her emotions. The bird spread its wings and sucked its fire inside. Ash let it ride on her shoulder, its heartbeat echoing her own.

Thalion was waiting under the trees, in the forest outside the city gates, two horses standing behind him. Through the trees, Ash could see a small band of men in dark clothes on horseback. She swallowed, noticing a body wrapped in white cloth, resting carefully over the back of a horse. There was no sign of Laeli.

'Where's your better half?' Jarlath called cheekily, slinging an arm around Ash's waist as he and Mahelivar joined her.

'Probably plotting my murder somewhere,' Thalion answered, rubbing at his face. He sighed, the deep sigh of confusion. 'Last night, I was her God, but this morning – this baby can't be born soon enough,' he added. Jarlath laughed and Ash hit him.

Thalion stared at her, and she got the distinct impression he was frightened of her. The Chieftain of the toughest place in the land, champion of the Stadium, leader of a rebellion, and the one who, according to Jarlath, took down Kiarda's fiercest warrior, scared of her? It was so absurd she had to smother a laugh.

The bird on her shoulder shook itself, flames curling from its feathers.

Thalion took a step back. 'What is *that*?'

'It's a Lasair,' Mahelivar said; Thalion's face turned the colour of milk. Mahelivar reached up to pet the flame-bird. 'The last one.'

'You're not going to keep that are you?' Thalion asked Ash warily.

Ash laughed. 'I don't think I have much choice. It won't leave.'

Thalion mumbled something under his breath. Laeli came striding across the grass, wearing a cross expression and rubbing her belly. She glared murder at everyone, turning her scowl on her husband.

'What?' she snapped.

Thalion's lips twitched. 'Is this going to be every morning for the next eight months?'

'It could be every morning for the next eight years if you don't watch yourself.'

'Only eight?' he teased. 'Remind me again how I got so lucky?'

Laeli opened her mouth to retort but Thalion grabbed her, ignoring her hissing protests, planting kisses over her face until she started laughing and kissed him back, her arms tight around his middle.

Ash smiled at them both; her bird took flight, disappearing into the sky. They all watched it go. Laeli broke away from her husband to grab her brother in a tight embrace. She hugged Jarlath next, then Ash.

'I'm sorry I'm leaving,' she said when she pulled away. 'But Thalion needs to bury his father and we've got a country to rebuild.'

'And a family to think about,' Ash whispered. She was absolutely delighted for them.

'But you'll visit,' Laeli said. 'Both of you,' she added.

'It's about time for another Stadium,' Thalion announced. 'If you're up for it, Jarlath.'

Laeli rolled her eyes and shook her head at him.

Jarlath ran a hand through his hair. 'I think I've seen enough snow to last a lifetime.'

'Come after Imbolc then,' Thalion said. 'When the snow begins to melt, it's a different world.'

'What's it like?' Now that they were free, Ash wanted to see everything. She listened eagerly as Thalion described how in the north, when the ice melted, patterns appeared in the landscape as the grass returned – stripes and rings that stretched across the ground. He told her about the cotton grass and mosses that spread to the northern mountains, and the flowers that only lasted a few days along the coast where it was foggy, the grass a matt of green and brown; the tiny rosettes of flowers that bloomed in rock cornices and shallow beds of gravel and how inland from the coast, the heathlands rushed into life, covered in pink and purple flowers that rippled like water when the wind passed through them.

Ash couldn't help but notice how Thalion's deep voice softened when he spoke of his home. 'It sounds beautiful,' she said sincerely.

'It is. It even gets *warm*,' he added, giving Jarlath a wink.

'One last lesson,' Laeli said. A ball of flame appeared in her hand. She held it towards Ash. 'Take it from me. With your mind.'

'Don't I need air magic to do that?' Ash asked.

Laeli shook her head. 'Most would, but *you* don't.'

Everyone held their breath as Ash poured her energy and her magic, her whole being, towards that flame floating above Laeli's palm. The fire shuddered, then jumped neatly to Ash's hand. Laeli grinned at her. Ash closed her fist and the flame vanished.

She stayed beneath the trees for a long time, watching until Thalion and Laeli had been swallowed by the forest. The flame-bird returned to perch on her shoulder, rubbing its beak on her cheek.

As she walked back into the city, passing through what was left of the grand oak gates, Ash gazed up at the statues of the Mother and thought about the future. All their lives had been completely shaken up, ripped apart and rearranged, changed in ways none of them would have predicted. She was determined to embrace the uncertainty life had, to enjoy the beauty of nothing becoming something, and to allow herself to believe that anything was possible.

She didn't feel like the creator of life, or the destroyer of it.

She finally felt like herself.

CHAPTER SEVENTY

BELTANE

Dawn.

The sun lit the world, crawling over the sea in the east and slowly stretching across the land, fingers of gold seeking and probing, shaking free the last breath of cold from the land and bringing warmth and promise.

From the top of the Wolf's Head, as the light met the mountains, the Cailleach felt the sun touch her tired old skin, the shell she wore ready to rest.

The Allfather stood by her side, his muscular body draped in fur as usual, despite the warm breeze blowing over them.

Far to the east, the land of the Delta was coming to life, the fishing boats heading out onto the water, nets thrown wide to catch Nehalennia's bounty. To the south, on the other side of the singing river, the people prepared the bonfires and the maypoles. Spring was at its peak and the true warmth of summer was approaching. Beltane saw the end of the dark days as all of nature awoke and the power of life and the greening of the world was celebrated, for with new life came new beginnings.

There had been a lot of new beginnings recently.

The Cailleach sighed, shuffling her old body to the nearest stone. She was tired, the hammer and staff growing heavy in her hands.

In the land that lay before them, life had crawled back over the earth, the melting snows filling the bogs and the fens, the frost-cracks, and the lakes. All that was barren and cold had warmed and was teeming with life. The land knew peace and at the heart of that peace was a continued promise of the future, a mind growing stronger as each day passed, a will as fierce as those who would come to shape it.

The Cailleach had kept a close eye on everything since the solstice, more so than usual. The great forests of Eshlune were restored, thanks to the magic of the new King, and in the northern land of Veshlir the people who remained forged ahead, their city of ice and snow readying itself for the turn of the wheel. The Cailleach stroked the staff. The north wind would be ferocious when it blew again. She chuckled.

'You are ready,' the Allfather commented, and she nodded. It wasn't a question – it was as it should be, as it had always been.

It was nearly time. She felt her blood warm, and her bones begin to shift into stone. Soon she could close her eyes and rest until Samhain called her back.

The Cailleach turned to the growing light; the sun burnt orange and bright, and her thoughts shifted to her Fire Caster, somewhere in the wilds of the world, content with the cards the Morrigan had cast for her. The Cailleach looked up – high above, a smudge in the dazzling sky, a black bird circled.

The Crone breathed a sigh of relief and let herself go.

In the turning of the wheel was a heartbeat.

The Allfather waited and, soon, from the warmth of the air around him, she came – a woman with hair like spun flame wearing a cloak made of sunbeams. She smiled at him, the red of her lips the red of the berries that grew by the river. The beauty of a summer sky was caught in her eyes and her skin was the skin of a young woman on the cusp of motherhood.

Bridghe inclined her head. 'Father.'

He offered her his arm and, together, they made their way east.

ACKNOWLEDGMENTS

I firstly wish to acknowledge that the *Fires of Aileryan* series was conceptualised and written on the lands of the Widjabul people. I acknowledge and pay my respect to the traditional custodians, past, present and emerging, of the Bundjalung nation, and their continuous connection to the landscape and the rivers of this ancient place.

I cannot possibly thank all the people involved in bringing my dream of being a published author to life. The support I received for *Shadow of Fire*, the first book in *The Fires of Aileryan* series, was phenomenal and much more than I ever expected. Being an indie author is hard and the journey to publishing this second book has been made so much easier with the support and encouragement of wonderful people.

To my writer's group - Ciara, Fabee, Jess, Lana, Karo and Rose - thank you so much for everything - for listening to my rambles, for reading random things for me, and for helping me work things out! You are all such beautiful people and I value your friendship and your opinions more than I can say.

I want to give a shout-out to the following, for being my cheerleaders and just being amazing humans: @jpmcdonaldwrites, @the_zephi, @devoured_pages, @amazingbooksiread, @annesengstock, @c.a.farran, @the_sassy_sidekick, @leahasreading, @gonewithflynn, @lanasworlds, @thebibliophilegamer, @cafeyre, @alix_reads_and_dreams, @itsmejayse and @faithe.in.books.

To the small, independent Aussie bookstores who have stocked my book baby - thank you so much for your support and for taking a chance on an indie author.

My cover designer - just how freaking amazing is this cover? Fran, you are a goddess and I love working with you. You have brought my visions, for both covers, to life so perfectly. Thank you!

My editor. Danikka Taylor. You, my dear, are the most amazing person and I feel privileged to not only know you, but to consider you a friend. Thank you for helping make *Heart of Flame* the best it could be, and thank you for your encouragement and your belief in my work, and in me.

To Jessie at Book Blurb Magic - thank you so much for untangling my story and making my blurb shine! I truly appreciate your efforts.

To all my family and friends - I know half of you don't even read fantasy, so it means even more that you decided to support me on this journey.

And lastly, to my partner and my children. We went to a deep and watery hell on the 28th February 2022 and yet, you still found the energy and the capacity to help me realise my dream while we were clawing our way back to something normal. I love you.

ABOUT THE AUTHOR

KATE SCHUMACHER is a writer, mother and teacher. When she isn't writing, she is reading her way through an ever-growing TBR pile. Kate has wanted to be an author since she was a child, and finds time to write in the in-between moments of life.

Kate completed a Bachelor of Arts in Creative Writing and Journalism, and an Honours degree in Screenwriting, followed by a Graduate Diploma in Education.

She lives in Northern NSW, Australia, with her partner, two children and three very spoiled cats. *Heart of Flame* is the second book in *The Fires of Aileryan* series.

Follow her on Instagram and TikTok @kate.schumacher.writer or visit her website kateschumacherauthor.com